Nothing to Know

Landry Brennan

ISBN 979-8-9901538-6-8

To my dad, a high school teacher and coach who took me to my first NHL game 44 years ago. He's not here to see the memories I tucked into this queer romance novel, but I think he'd be incredibly proud.

Playlist

Playlist

- Apocalypse - Cigarettes After Sex
- Never Tear Us Apart - INXS
- Machine - Amber Run
- Mandolin Rain - Bruce Hornsby and the Range
- I Done You So Wrong - The Paper Kites
- All I Want Is You - U2
- The Night We Met - Lord Huron
- Pictures of You - The Cure
- It's Not Like You - The Paper Kites
- One More Try - George Michael
- Dark Blue (Strings Attached Version) - Jack's Mannequin
- Drive - The Cars
- Scars - James Bay
- Over the Rainbow - Eva Cassidy

CONTENT WARNING

SPOILERS BELOW!

For those who prefer to know as much as possible in advance, I do have one broad content warning to share. That said, it **does** contain plot spoilers, so please consider skipping this page if you are comfortable doing so. If you have questions, please reach out and I'll try to address any concerns you have prior to reading Jamie and Mateo's love story.

Warning: There is more than one character death in this book. With the exception of a single side character, the deaths occur when the characters are significantly older, and do not involve tragic circumstances. None of the deaths take place on-page, nor are any of them described in detail when mentioned.

Contents

PROLOGUE

(I Was There)

All of us experience millions of unremarkable moments in our lifetimes, and that night was full of them. Returning to my seat next to Sophie with two beers in my hands. Watching the players line up for the second period face-off. Turning at the sound of a baby squealing from a few rows back.

Being at the game was fun, of course. But not remarkable. Not then.

Sometimes, the moments we experience become moderately more notable in the context of whatever happens next. That night, a sip and a half of beer spilled over the back of my hand when I stood to make room for an older woman passing by. I started to fumble for my phone to get a picture of the puck drop until I remembered I had taken one at the beginning of the first period. The baby smiled at me and reminded me so much of my nephew that I almost texted my sister right then and there.

Still, I'm not sure any of those details would've mattered if the rest of the game had wrapped up like the dozen or so others I'd been to. I was familiar with the excitement of a couple of goals, the songs that make damn near everyone sing along, and the predictable complaints about a bullshit penalty somewhere between one shot attempt and another. That night was different though, and I'm glad I'd finished my beer by the time everything changed, because my stomach wasn't quite the same afterward.

And Jameson Sinclair's leg would never be the same again.

Some empathetic part of me wondered if he'd ever look back and think about how unremarkable his night had been before it became impossible to forget. Then I realized there was a good chance he'd remember almost nothing, the trauma tucked somewhere out of his reach to keep him safe from having to relive one of the worst moments of his life. There were enough people who would tell him about it someday, though I could never be one of them.

I saw him go after the puck in the corner. I saw him get checked into the boards. I saw him fall.

But I didn't see *how* he fell.

I only heard the unholy sound he made on his way down.

Plenty of others would go on to watch gruesome replays of the injury—shared in slow-motion and zoomed all the way in—but I already knew I would suffer with the memory of a moment I barely saw. And if the universe was kind enough, maybe Jameson Sinclair would live without the memory of a moment that broke his leg in four places.

All of us were on our feet while he lay on the ice, an irony not lost on me. While waiting for a stretcher to be brought to him, I had time to notice that the beer I'd spilled had landed on my sneaker and seeped through to my sock. I was grateful I'd taken that picture of the opening face-off, the last of Jameson Sinclair's stunning career. I heard someone behind me mutter *what the absolute fuck*, which sounded a lot like something one of my students would say. Hell, it might've been one of them, but I couldn't tear my eyes away from the medical staff long enough to check.

Moments.

So many of them crashing together now. Extraordinary. Outrageous. Remarkable.

Whatever else was true, or however much he'd remember, that night became the irrevocable divide between before and after for him. He'd shown up at the arena hours earlier, dressed in his gear, warmed up with his teammates, and had two assists. Then he'd been taken away amid one last standing ovation, and nothing would ever be the same.

One freak injury—one moment—and Jameson Sinclair's life changed forever.

It would be years before I understood how much that same moment changed mine.

Part One

(We Waited for Pomp and Circumstance)

Chapter One: Jamie

(I Met Him on a Friday Night)

I'm craving something greasy. Heavy. Spicy, maybe. Savory, at the very least. I want too much of whatever might make me regret giving in, and I want to smile all the way through, like nothing could hurt me.

Once upon a time, late August would've been the end of that kind of thinking. An entire staff and a locker room full of teammates in Los Angeles had expected me to be better to my body by the time September came. Rigorous training and the need to remain among the best had been reasons to demand it of myself. Rules that had relaxed through June and July usually tightened right about now, my late-summer hunger met with meals that wouldn't leave me questioning my choices in the middle of the night, a beer too many no longer washing them down.

But once upon a time hasn't mattered for about five years now, and nobody will care what I eat tonight.

I laugh a little when I look in the mirror, amused by the boredom dulling my eyes. Or it's what I tell myself I see. Once upon a time, I also used to sit comfortably on my oversized sectional in my oversized great room in my oversized house and order dinner to be delivered, but maybe more changes are coming. Harper isn't home, and I don't feel like being alone. Whether it's all that smart to drag my ass to an out-of-the-way dive bar just for human contact—and the greasy, heavy, spicy, savory meal I can get there—I tug a baseball cap over my messy hair and shrug.

There's nobody to stop me from doing this, either.

On my way out the door, I grab my wallet and keys, my phone already in my hand. When I lock up behind me, I ask myself for the first time whether I should consider moving away from a place I might not belong anymore. The imagined voices of at least a few people suggest I'm being dramatic, but sometimes it feels like I'm living a dream I woke up from a while ago. It could be the hunger talking tonight. Another hour or several might convince me to stay. The ocean air I can breathe from where I stand could make me selfish enough to cling to the high life either way.

Okay, yeah, I'm fucking dramatic. As soon as I'm inside my black luxury SUV—part of the same expired dream—I make sure the music is blasting. It'll keep me from feeling anything but the bass replacing my heartbeat.

There isn't much traffic at this time on a Friday night—mostly an absurd number of red lights familiar to me since before I owned a car—but I still park in the first available spot I find when I'm anywhere close to my destination. I'm too impatient to drive in circles looking for something better. It means I'm about four blocks away, but the injury that cost me my career has left me able to do almost anything but chase another Cup, and I reach the bar without trouble.

Slipping inside, I dodge a pack of college kids who could afford to drink elsewhere, and two old bikers who can't be bothered to try. There are a bunch of tired women pressed to tired men, and some asshole is already whining about the baseball game on tv, or the music overhead, or the food he's still waiting on, or the beer he's just finished. None of it's a shock to me. I only raise a surprised eyebrow when I see one stool available at the furthest side of the bar.

Kai couldn't have known I would stop by, but I consider the seat in front of him a gift, and I slide onto it with a smile.

He fires one back. "Been a while, hotshot. Where've you been?"

It's predictable when he doesn't stick around long enough to hear my answer. His question was made rhetorical by circumstance, the demand on him too high to allow us an actual conversation. He's been running this place since his dad dropped dead of a heart attack eight years ago. The fact that we became best friends when we were six means I'm both a top priority and the easiest person in the building for him to ignore.

I think I'd love to tell him I took a long vacation with Harper. Or that I spent some time on a former teammate's boat. Maybe something about binge-watching shows that have been off the air for a decade. I don't think I'd mention how many hours I spent in the pool, clinging to the aquatic therapy that hadn't frustrated me when everything else in my life did. As it is, Kai is busy with the bikers. Someone else nudges my shoulder too gently for a place like this.

"Sorry, I—there's nowhere to sit, but can I—I'm just trying to order something to go."

This guy hasn't been here before. No repeat customer would think it's a good place to attempt a to-go order on the weekend. Before I can respond to something he hasn't finished asking, Kai returns with a bottle of Fat Tire for me and an exhausted grin for the man crowded against my side.

"The food's worth it, but the kitchen is slammed, so you've gotta be willing to wait," Kai says. "What're you drinking?"

A flustered glance at the taps only takes a second or two. "The

Sam Adams seasonal would be great, thanks."

Kai pours a pint and is just classy enough to throw a coaster down before he leaves it on the bar. Then he nods at me. "The usual?"

"Yep."

"And you?"

"A dozen wings. Mango chipotle. And onion rings and mozz sticks, please," the guy answers. "Take as long as you need—I'm not in a hurry."

It's cute that he thinks it would matter if he were, but Kai is long gone, and I'm not interested in being a dick about it. I take a slow pull from my bottle and turn my head. As much as I'd rather not be recognized tonight, I take a chance and finally get a good look at the man wedged between my stool and another. He's angled himself toward me instead of the woman on his other side, a random choice he'd made when he'd pushed himself close to the bar. It's a choice made more comfortable after Kai addressed us as an inadvertent pair.

Taking our orders back-to-back had meant nothing to Kai, and I can't thank him for it, but I'll be grateful for a while.

He's tall, this stranger. Strong in a way I know from years of being checked into the boards by men built just like him. Maybe softer in the middle if he's not particularly athletic, but underestimating him seems foolish from where I sit. He's close to my age—a couple of years older if I had to guess—and he's pulled his dark hair into a small ponytail. When his eyes meet mine, I clock shades of kindness and wisdom that suggest he's nicer and smarter than I've ever been. I look away before he does, so he's probably braver, too.

If I'm being honest, he's attractive enough to make me want to buy him this beer and a thousand more.

If I allow myself to lie, wanting more time with him makes no sense, my past littered with reasons to walk away without buying him a goddamn thing.

"What's your usual?"

I blink up at him again, surprised he's after small talk. Silently drinking next to me would've worked out fine. "The Santa Fe burger—green chiles, pepper jack, guacamole. Fries on the side."

"There's a lot happening there," the guy muses. "I've had similar sandwiches, but I'm not sure I would've been creative enough to put all that on a burger."

"Is this where I point out that you weren't adventurous enough to look past the appetizer section?"

"Okay, that's fair, but mango chipotle is a little different, right?"

"It's one of my other favorites," I admit, tapping my bottle against the bar when I decide to keep talking. "What made you hit up a dive bar tonight?"

"Am I that out of place here?"

I scan the crowd and shrug. "Only in a good way. You look like you've got your shit together more than the rest of us."

"Are you calling me boring again?" he asks, his head tilted with the seriousness of someone who's offended. I'd reexamine my tone if his smile weren't busy giving him away.

"I thought I was paying you a compliment."

He blushes at that, or at least ducks his head as if he's trying to hide something like it. His skin is darker than mine, and combined with the shitty lighting in the bar, I'm not sure I would've been able to catch the pink in his cheeks. Honestly, the stubble covering his jaw distracts me from looking much beyond it anyway. After another second, I force myself to meet his eyes again and realize my mistake as soon as I get there. The brown is unbelievably deeper now. It's threatening to drown me if I forget to come up for air.

There are secrets there. I guess that's true of everyone, but there's a split second when I wonder how easily I'd give up all of mine for the chance to hear one of his.

"I appreciate it then," he says, quieter now. I think I'd move closer if we weren't already touching in a few different places. The buzz of the bar is loudly alive all around us. "I wasn't expecting compliments tonight. At least not from—"

"From?"

He studies me briefly and takes a sip. "From someone who doesn't know me."

"Well, sure. If you usually grab takeout without sitting down for a beer, you don't give most strangers a chance to say anything at all."

"I'm not even sitting now, and yet—"

I laugh, my head tipping backward until my entire face must be on display, my hat unable to grant me privacy when I don't look down. If this guy figures out who I am, he doesn't say. I'm grateful because I'm usually recognized most at the times I want it the least. Plenty of hockey players—or *former* hockey players in my case—can go to a bar with little trouble, and in Southern California there are enough celebrity sightings to keep gawkers busy. But the winning combination of my mouth, my looks, and my talent meant I was splashed all over the place for a while. Attention was heaped on me when I didn't know how to beg for anything else.

I still haven't learned. I drop my head again and offer a grin he may not be able to see. "No, you're not. Would you like me to give you my seat so we can talk, or is that not something you're used to either?"

"You tell me," he says with a shrug. "You seem to be the expert on all of this."

"*All of this*?" I echo, shaking my head. "If you're talking about giving compliments and how to surrender a seat I was lucky enough to snag first, no, I'm really not. I've been told I'm too arrogant and selfish for that."

"Told by whom?"

My parents, my ex, a few coaches and teammates, most rivals. The media often. Fans more than I would've liked. Never Kai or Harper, but they've always been the exception, not the rule.

"Enough people to have convinced me before I knew any better."

He frowns, then chases it with beer. "I'm not sure the majority is supposed to rule on that sort of thing."

The majority flits in and out of my life these days, so I don't argue the point. I also don't know if there's a reason to keep the conversation going after I've let that much slide. Sure, this guy is attractive. He makes me smile. He's willing, maybe, to defend me against things that could've been my fault. His eyes haunt and heal. And he's nice enough to talk to me without needing a selfie to prove we were here together.

He's nice enough that he could be an exception, too.

But something feels really good where my leg brushes his—or maybe it's the other way around—and I already know there are too many ways I might end up hurt if I don't move away from him soon. I note the warning ache in my heart and my lungs and somewhere more damning than either of those. It's a chronic thing that can't have anything to do with him when he'll disappear from my life tonight.

How could I ask for more when I don't know whether he's into men?

How could I ask for more when even the greediest gossip sites have never found proof that *I* am?

Then he leans into me a little more, and my breath hitches, embarrassing me in a way I can't explain. Kai catches my eye, and I want to reassure him I'm fine, but I'm only sitting here with a beer and a stranger. There's no reason for me to be anything else. When a couple of guys near the front door get into it with another bartender, Kai throws a lime wedge at my head and turns to deal with the chaos.

I do my best to keep staring at the blank space he's left behind.

"Are you guys friends? Or do you just come here often enough to get fruit thrown at you by the people who work here?"

"Both, actually." I shift to put a couple of inches between us and ignore the flicker of loss I pretend he might've felt. "For all the time we've spent apart over the years, Kai's been the constant. I don't remember my life without him in it. I was also hanging out here long before I could legally drink. His dad owned the bar 'til he died, and Kai and I grew up here because, most of the time, I liked it better than being at home."

"Shitty parents?" he asks.

"Single-minded parents," I amend. I can't explain more than that without getting into a past I've been trying to dodge tonight. I pick up my bottle and make a vague gesture with it. "They're fine. I'm fine. But when I was a kid, this was one of my favorite hiding places."

"Are you still hiding now?"

For a second, I think he knows, and I can't breathe *again*, but there's no recognition—only curiosity that could keep me here forever. "I can't imagine what good that would do."

"I'm glad you—"

Whatever he's glad about remains a mystery when we're interrupted by the sound of shattered glass from the other end of the bar and half a dozen shouts to go with it. I get rocked by a rush of adrenaline I hate in this context, mostly because I know how to fight, and I know I can't do it here. The feeling rolls into panic when I try to stay entirely still instead. Even with a more immediate concern in front of him, Kai hisses at me and jerks his head toward the back door.

Everything becomes a blur then, or maybe things I don't understand have made themselves clear. Once my beer bottle has fallen from my hand, I'm free to grab the man next to me and tug him away from the brewing brawl. He's clumsier than I am when it comes to running from a fight, but the questions he's asked for the past several minutes stop when he follows me without a word. There's relief in not having to explain myself as we go. The bar isn't all that big, so I lead us past the bathrooms and around a couple of corners. I shove my hip into the crash bar on the back door, but I've forgotten how easily it opens. We tumble into the alley behind the building, my grip on his forearm just enough to steady us both.

The cool air is jarring after being somewhere that had become warm without my knowledge. I pause to adjust to the dark when I let him go. My pulse is so loud in my ears, but maybe silent to the man staring at me now.

"That was—"

For the second time in as many minutes, a thought goes unfinished, and we both startle when the back door flies open again. Still thrumming and too aware of the fight happening inside, I move instinctively, quick to help us dodge trouble one more time. The force of my body colliding with his leads to a rough landing against the stucco wall. Then I turn my head in time to see three drunk women trip and fall from inside the bar. They probably followed us when we fled, and now that they're outside, they seem wholly uninterested in us. Ignoring the shaky breath at my cheek, I watch until they're coordinated enough to walk away, clinging to each other while one of them calls for a ride home.

It takes another heartbeat or two for me to realize I've got a handsome stranger pinned to a wall. My mouth is far too close to his as soon as I'm facing him again. I'm enamored, and probably needy, but neither is a problem that belongs to him.

"Shit, I—sorry—"

I start to step back, but I get lost in wide eyes that seem far from bothered by whatever liberties I've taken. I feel his fingers curl into my t-shirt and hold me there. His chest rises and falls more obviously than when we'd talked with beers in our hands, and this newfound proximity confirms he's exactly as strong as I'd guessed at a glance. Then he smiles, and if I'd planned to finish my sentence, the apology is long gone now.

"Are you on probation or something?" he whispers.

Or maybe it's not a whisper, but the entire world feels hushed, and I shiver. "Probation?"

"I—no, I don't mean—" He stops and looks too closely, but he hasn't given up on me yet. "I appreciate the swift escape you provided, but I also saw the look your friend gave you before we ran. And that was after you froze." He stops again and shrugs. "You look like you could hold your own in a bar fight if it came to that, so with him encouraging you to get out of there, and you being willing to go—I don't know. I guess I was curious whether you've been in trouble before."

"I've been in a lifetime of it, but not the way you're thinking. Kai's just had my back for a really long time."

"Why'd you have mine?"

And isn't *that* the fucking question of the night? I think I'd blow him off entirely, but he's still holding on to my shirt and he doesn't flinch when my hand finds his forearm again. I sigh and settle for a safe middle ground.

"We were in the middle of a conversation. I thought there might be more to say."

He nods. "Maybe I could even get your name this time."

It's a line. Or it sounds a lot like one. My wishful thinking makes it easy to answer him. Twenty minutes ago, I'm not sure I could've been convinced to introduce myself to anyone.

"I'm Jamie."

It's a step forward, but I have to take a step back when he finally lets me go to shake my hand. Some of his hair has fallen free from its ponytail. A couple of unreadable expressions are there and gone when he grins again.

"Hi, Jamie. I'm Mateo."

"Did you leave anything inside the bar, Mateo?"

"Other than a half-finished beer and the mango chipotle wings you love?"

"Other than that, yeah," I say.

"Just the unpaid bill."

"Kai isn't coming after you for it," I promise, brushing away his concern with the wave of my hand. "He might've closed the kitchen anyway, depending on how bad everything got."

"Is there a reason we're not going back inside to ask him?"

"Do you have somewhere else to be tonight?"

He laughs, but he's nearly as breathless now as I was before. "Other than my empty apartment and its empty refrigerator?"

"Other than that, yeah," I repeat.

"Well, I'm still hungry."

I could've guessed that much was true, but the way he's almost teasing me about it settles something in me. I only wish it settled everything. I'm not ready to invite Mateo into my car—one crowded with a couple of sticks, old practice jerseys, and lord knows what else branded with *Jameson Sinclair*—when there's a chance I can be a stranger named Jamie a little while longer. I'm also sure there are pieces of Harper's life scattered all over the leather seats. As unfair as it might be, I don't want that part of my life to complicate tonight either.

For all I know, Mateo is straight, and I have no plans to let the public know I'm not. If this is the only dinner I'll ever share with him, I don't want to talk about anyone else.

He watches me until I stop thinking so hard and make him an

offer. "You fly, I buy?"

"Sure. Are we still getting burgers and wings?"

"How do tacos sound?"

Mateo's stomach growls in the relative quiet of the alley, and we both laugh before he answers. "They sound pretty damn good."

He leads me to a modest sedan that suits him perfectly. It's neater inside than any car should be, making my decision to leave my SUV behind a great one. Once we're buckled up and the music he'd left blaring is turned down, I give him enough directions to get us close to where I want to be. If he's concerned about how far away we're going when there are a hundred taco options on any given street, he doesn't say. Mateo doesn't say much, actually. He simply coasts through an almost magical series of green lights while I daydream about other obstacles we could conquer together. After another few minutes, he reaches the freeway on-ramp, and we speed up so smoothly that I almost don't notice how fast we're going. The comfortable silence stretches on, and I become unusually certain of a couple of things.

Whatever happens between us over the next few hours will be unlike anything I've ever experienced before.

And I'll spend far too many years chasing a way to turn those hours into forever.

It's already so easy and so hard, because while I have no idea who he is or what he wants, I know I'm afraid of myself and need it all. I'd love to be charming, but I'm dragging him from a dive bar to a food truck. I'm not sure what promises can be made between an alley and a parking lot. I might have a better chance if I can figure out another hundred places for us to go, but that many safe spaces don't exist for me. I also can't guarantee he'll follow me any further, so I push away the fantasy for now and don't waste time practicing the smile I mastered years ago.

"We'll drive just past it," I tell him once we're on side streets again. "There's a small lot on the right. It'll be easier to park there than to pray for a spot on the street."

"I mentioned that I'm hungry, right?" he teases. "You're really gonna make me drive past the food just to walk back?"

"Mmmm, there might be a line for the tacos, too."

"I hope the wait's worth it."

Mateo barely takes his eyes off the road when he says it, but his tone and a glance in my direction are enough to make me whimper weakly. I can only hope he misses it entirely when he's staring straight ahead again and I stumble toward something at least as flirtatious.

"Won't the wait be better if I'm right there with you?"

His eyes dart to me again, and I'm about to insist I was joking, but then he nods up ahead. "That's it, right?"

"Yeah, and you'll see the lot next. Park anywhere in there."

He does, and we're quiet again when we walk to the taco truck. The line isn't too bad, and after Mateo has cracked a small joke about it, he studies a menu I know too well. I think this is a friendly thing we're doing, grabbing a casual dinner together on a busy street. I can't be sure when all my friends have come from a pool of 30 years of teammates, and Kai.

I don't remember the last time I was out with someone romantically. That comparison ends before it can begin.

Mateo nudges my shoulder with his. "So, what's the least boring thing I could order here?"

"Ah, the jackfruit, probably," I say, shaking myself free from the past. I grin from beneath the hat I tug a little lower. "But order whatever you want. I think you've proven plenty just by being out with me tonight."

"Because boring people don't accept invitations for an impromptu taco date from a guy whose name they didn't know half an hour ago?"

I flinch, perhaps for a couple of reasons, but then I hum in agreement. "They do not."

He doesn't respond—not really—but after a few sticky seconds and blame that always lies with me, Mateo uses a single finger to tip the bill of my hat upward. His dark eyes demand something when they lock with mine.

"Which tacos are your favorite?" he asks.

"Mahi-mahi or carne asada."

"Let's get an order of each, then."

We do exactly that, and somewhere around the time we're walking away from the truck with our food in hand, I find the certainty my voice had lost and the composure I've always faked just fine. I lead us to a side street and sit on the curb, my legs extended because now and then my body demands it. We've got our tacos and beans and rice and chips and guac, and it's easy to share everything but the straws in our own separate cups of Coke. Food gets passed back and forth with a familiarity we're bold enough to claim for the night.

Whether he knows it or not, Mateo leans a little closer after each bite or two, and I meet him halfway because I want us to share that, too.

In between bites, we don't talk about ourselves. Or we do, but not in a traditional, small-talk, getting-to-know-you sort of way. I don't know Mateo's last name or where he lives or what he does for a living. Mostly, I think I want to avoid stumbling onto a series of questions I'm not ready to answer. I already know I won't be able to refuse anything he asks of me. And even while I tell myself there's a decent chance he doesn't know who Jameson Sinclair is—hockey is still a niche sport here, no matter how much of a superstar I might've been while playing it—I'm not ready to risk the loose grip I have on anonymity.

Just for tonight—just with Mateo—I want to be nobody.

I think back to when I was 19 and won the Calder. A magazine did a dumb Q&A as part of a Rookie of the Year spread they wouldn't have bothered with if I hadn't been marketably mouthy and a very valuable shade of beautiful. Back then, I couldn't imagine that anyone cared about my breakfast habits or favorite scent or weirdest fear. I've never bothered to share them with people in the years since. But for the first time in my life, I get it. I want to know about Mateo's breakfast habits and favorite scent and weirdest fear, so I ask him.

He answers everything. And then he asks me right back.

We don't stop, and I learn about his favorite food truck and its five different kinds of macaroni and cheese. Another minute or so has him confessing that he'll always turn to creamy soups and pastas when he's in need of comfort. I tell him that ice cream is the one food I crave a little too often, happy to treat myself to a scoop or two even if I'm standing in the middle of a snowstorm. Mateo laughs at the number of impersonations I can perform on demand, and I get to hear about a grunge phase he had when he was probably too young to have it, a teenage neighbor nearby to dress him in flannel and introduce him to Pearl Jam. I mention that my favorite movie when I was little was *The Wizard of Oz*, and skate too close to a story about singing one of its songs to Harper years ago. He argues with me about the existence of ghosts and tells me about a scary slumber party when he was in middle school.

It's too easy and too comfortable, and none of it has a chance of changing my mind about wanting more time with him. Safe spaces are still a scarcity, but an idea starts in my head and drops to knock around my ribcage. I speak, mostly because I think it will hurt more if I don't.

"Do you have somewhere else to be tonight?" I ask, my eyes on the last few chips in my lap until I remember I'd rather be looking at him.

"I thought I already answered that."

"Last time I asked, you said you were hungry. What happens now that we're done eating?"

Mateo steals one of my chips. He waits until I'm watching a couple of teenagers run across the street before he steals the other two. If he'd rather sit here all night, I'm not sure I'd argue with him. Hell, I'd go buy him more chips, but before I can offer, he takes a deep breath and exhales a single word.

"No."

"No, what?"

"No, I don't have somewhere else to be," he says. "So, where do you want to go?"

Chapter Two: Mateo

(I Made a Wish on a Star)

I don't get an answer right away, nor do I need one when I think I'd drive Jamie anywhere, just to spend a little more time with him. And he's gorgeous, sure—no baseball cap was going to hide his face for long, and his t-shirt did nothing to disguise his body—but I'm almost 40, and past the point when his looks would've been enough to make me this reckless. I want to go somewhere with Jamie for the chance at another hour or two with someone special, and maybe most people do, but as often as he might've been accused of arrogance in the past, I'm not convinced he knows just how magnetic he is.

In fact, after having watched his confidence waver a couple of times, I think he may doubt it entirely.

Still quiet, we leave the curb behind to throw our trash away, then carelessly wipe our hands on our jeans before we walk toward the parking lot. I don't reassure him about how close I'd like to stay, nor do I confess that this is more spontaneous than I've been in years. It'll be fun to tell Sophie all about it, and she'll be thrilled that an entire summer spent raving about a local bar's chicken wings led me here, but that will be a Monday morning conversation. Right now, it's Friday night, and I only want to talk to the man next to me, my car visible from several steps away and my curiosity humming.

"So, how long are we going to be driving before you give me some idea of where you'd like us to end up? Do I get any vague directions, or should I guess and hope that I've read your mind?"

Jamie gives me an almost shy smile. "Any chance you've got a blanket in your car? And maybe a jacket or sweatshirt or something?"

"I—yeah, I've—" I pause next to my trunk when I figure out why he's asking. "We're not driving anywhere. We're walking to the beach."

"It's right there."

It's true. The ocean's maybe half a mile from where we stand, and I'm sure he knows I'm not lost. He's nervous though, his hand rubbing the back of his neck where I'd rather reach for him instead, and I pop my trunk to give us both a few seconds with our thoughts. His restlessness combined with his plans—the two of us on the beach is entirely different from the two of us hitting up a club—makes me even more sure of what I'd first guessed at the bar.

Jamie is queer.

My next question is whether he knows it, too.

He could simply be closeted, and I won't ask him either way, pushing my favorite Baja hoodie into his arms instead. He thanks me and pulls it over his head just as I do the same with an older hoodie I'd forgotten I owned. After taking a moment to fix my messy ponytail, I grab a blanket and a bottle of water.

"Ready when you are," I say, about to close the trunk when Jamie catches it with his hand.

"You're very ready, yeah. I thought I was gonna have to buy stuff off a random tourist on our way."

"Do you do that often?"

"No, I—it was just a—" Jamie rolls his eyes when he clocks that I'm giving him shit, and then he looks down at everything still in my trunk. "Do you do *this* often?"

"No more often than I have tacos with strangers," I deadpan. "But really, I just have young nieces and nephews with soccer and t-ball and playdates in parks and birthday parties at pools. I try to keep a bunch of things in the car so I'm prepared for fun on short notice."

"And is that what this is? Fun on short notice?"

There's so much I want to say to that—more ways I want to tease him—but there's an uncertain edge to Jamie's question, as though he needs an actual answer from me now. I study him for another few seconds, then I tuck the blanket under my arm and grab a soccer ball from the trunk, dropping it to the asphalt and the empty parking space next to my car. He's surprised and curious, and though I may be more familiar with what we're doing tonight, it's been a while since I've remembered to try. I kick the ball to him and watch him respond with ease, his hands in the front pocket of my hoodie and his hat still pulled low. The blanket and water bottle don't slow me down, and we pass the ball back and forth while I answer.

"I'm having a great time, but which part is throwing *you*? The fun, or the short notice? Because I feel like anyone who's earned a reputation for being arrogant and selfish must have some experience with both, and I don't know what I'll do if you try to tell me you're as boring as I am."

The small but visible huff of laughter I earn is enough to make me break into a stupidly fond smile, and I can't help but want him to see it. Jamie isn't really looking at me though, and the next time he sends the ball my way, I trap it beneath my foot and give him a way out.

"You don't have to answer any of that," I tell him, flicking the ball into the air and catching it with my free hand. "You're allowed to have fun without also having to talk about it."

I put the ball away a second later and close the trunk a second after that, and Jamie shakes his head. "That. *That's* what's throwing me."

"That we're not taking the soccer ball with us, or that I'm not making you talk?"

I step closer to him then, close enough that our arms brush against each other when we leave the parking lot behind and walk toward the ocean, the contact as much for my own good as it is for his. We continue down the sidewalk, passing homes that cost more than I'll make in my lifetime, and I give him the bottle. He takes a long, grateful sip and wipes water from his mouth with the back of his hand.

"That you're okay with me having fun without conditions," he finally says. "There's a period at the end of every sentence with you. We can eat tacos. We can go for a walk. We can have fun. Most people want those sentences to run on and on, and I've never been good at putting the period there myself."

"You seemed relatively sure of yourself at the bar, but this isn't actually a habit of yours, is it? Inviting someone to spend time with you."

"It's never had to be."

I nod, probably to myself. "You're the prettiest man most people have ever seen, and they'll give you a ride before you ever have to ask for one."

It's careless, a mistake even before the words have fully fallen between us, and Jamie's suddenly further away from me than I want him to be. I'm not even sure which part hurt him the most—only that something did, and I don't know how to take it all back. My next step falters, and then I stop entirely, because maybe we can return to the parking lot or the taco truck or the bar. I'm still holding the blanket close to my chest when he notices the distance between us and turns to face me from a few feet away.

"Mateo—"

"No, it's—I'm sorry."

"For calling me pretty?" he asks. "I led you halfway there, didn't I? Maybe I should've worn a better hat."

I smile and sigh, somehow simultaneously. "Or maybe I shouldn't have been looking so closely."

Jamie stares at me for a long time, and I shouldn't stare back, breathless at the sight of him in something I've worn a hundred times. He's not at all small, but my Baja hoodie is a size too big for him anyway, and while I've been happy to get peeks of him from beneath his cap all night, I'd rather see him curl further into my clothes if he has to hide at all. As it is, it's later now and predictably dark, except for the streetlights and a moon kind enough to bless me with a glimpse or two, but I'm struck again by something familiar about the man in front of me.

I'd made a probation joke earlier, but it's far more likely that he's famous for something I haven't figured out. I'm almost certain he's not a tv or movie star, and I couldn't say why except that he doesn't strike me as *that* kind of celebrity, and I've spent years with the children of plenty of them. He's beautiful enough to be a model, but I'm not sure I'd know if I'm walking shoulder to shoulder with a guy who's tried to sell me cologne during an unskippable ad, and I shrug off the idea now. He could be a singer, maybe. Or anyone in a band, I suppose.

Of course, he could be nobody but Jamie, and I could ask him exactly that.

I swallow the question because I don't think I want to know.

It almost looks like he swallows something too, but then he toys with the water bottle in his hand and cocks his head. "Do you still want to go to the beach with me?"

I clear my throat and take a step closer to ask the same question I've already answered twice. "Do you have somewhere else to be tonight?"

"Don't want to be anywhere else."

His honesty makes me ache, and I can't do anything but keep walking toward it despite the longing that will leave me hungover tomorrow. We're quiet when we reach the end of the street, but I make some sort of sound when he leads us to the left, surprised that we're not going to the main stretch of beach further to the right.

And then wholly unsurprised when I think about it again.

"Not a fan of the late-night beach crowd, huh?"

"Probably mostly teenagers doing the end-of-summer thing. Music, fire pits, cheap beer, first kisses," Jamie says.

"Other than the cheap beer, it doesn't sound like a terrible night," I joke, but he's right that we should avoid whatever is happening down there, for reasons I hadn't considered and won't thank him for now.

"It'll all get shut down anyway," he mumbles. "The beach closes soon."

With my phone in my pocket, I haven't cared what time it is, but Jamie's probably right, and it only makes me wonder how he thinks we'll get away with something after hours. We're approaching a much smaller area now, but it's subject to the same rules, and I can't imagine we'll find it empty when we make the last little turn toward it. Still, I've gone this far, and I know I want to go all the way, every typically cautious part of me left in an alley miles from here.

Or at the bar with a half-drunk Sam Adams.

I hear laughter and the faintest bits of conversation just as other people come into view—probably twenty or so sprawled on blankets or kicking at the water as waves fade into nothing—but when I look at Jamie, he seems unconcerned by their presence. Our steps get clumsy in the sand, and if the silence didn't feel so right, I'd ask for the chance to go barefoot here. We keep moving though, and after another minute, I understand—and absolutely don't.

"You wanted to bring a blanket, but we're not going to sit on it here," I say stupidly, so many rocks beneath my feet now that we've walked past everyone else.

"No, there's—I know of another spot, if you're okay with that."

"I'm okay with that."

It's an understatement, of course. A longer walk hasn't helped me figure out how to want less time with him.

Jamie nods and navigates the uneven shore as we put the rest of the world behind us. There are gorgeous houses to our left, set at least a hundred feet above us on top of a brush-covered hillside, and the Pacific Ocean to our right. I'm still trying to figure out where we're headed when Jamie brings us to what looks like a narrow path toward someone's backyard.

He must clock my hesitation, a small smile thrown my way. "We're not going that far. Nobody living up there will have any idea we're here."

"Is trespassing a regular hobby of yours, or do you save it for taco night?"

Jamie pauses, not quite looking at me and not quite focused on anything else, and then he takes a sip from the water I'd forgotten he still held. When he offers it to me, I don't think about whether I could taste him there—or whether it's something that crossed his mind either—waving it away instead. I'm impatient now, eager for the rest of the night to begin, and we're working our way up the hill when he finally responds.

"This has been here for years, but it's been a long time since I've bothered to find it in the dark," he says. "And I've never brought anyone here—not like this."

I want to ask what he means by that, but then he slows me with a whisper and leads me further. It feels like a moment that should demand he hold on to me, but when I catch his subtle struggle through a step or two, I wonder if I have it backward. Jamie conceals his effort smoothly, practiced at it for reasons I don't know and don't like, but he was right that we wouldn't have to walk far. The two of us are closer to the rocks below us than to the house above, and I forget his unsteadiness when I see a bench nestled into the hillside, out of sight of anyone who might wander through either place. I forget my unsteadiness too, looking over my shoulder at waves that don't care about us before I face Jamie again.

"The privacy here. It's so—"

He starts to reach for me, then pulls back, conflict all over his face. "It is. Yeah."

"Then it seems like the perfect place to sit with you."

When he doesn't move, and doesn't try to touch me again, I worry he may have changed his mind, probably as aware as I am that there are so many safer places we could go. Naive or desperate or eager, I claim a seat before he can lead us back down the hillside, unfolding the blanket as I blink up at him. Jamie is caught up in thoughts that may have nothing to do with me, but I want him here, and I'm not exactly sure how to tell him that. He turns slowly and watches the ocean, and I give him as much time as I can, interrupting only when the quiet hurts.

"I'm sorry you don't get to invite more people to dinner," I start, my voice low enough that I've barely disturbed the dark. "I'm sorry for all the strings attached to your fun. And I'm sorry for calling you pretty when it has nothing to do with why I'm here."

That gets his attention, the corner of Jamie's mouth curling into a near smile when he finally comes closer. He crouches next to the bench to tuck the water bottle behind one of the legs, and I frown at the way he winces before he straightens again. We both know I saw it, but he shakes his head and makes me forget all over again.

"You don't think I'm pretty?"

"That's definitely not what I said."

"I brought you here, but I don't know what happens next," Jamie admits. "This wasn't—you just wanted dinner."

Still unwilling to say too much of the wrong thing, I shrug. "What happened next all the other times you were here? What did you do the nights you sat on this bench alone?"

"I let go of everything. I shut out all the noise. I pretended my time here didn't count—that the rest of my life could leave me alone long enough for me to catch my fucking breath."

I adjust the blanket to make room for him beneath it. "Then that's what we'll do now."

Jamie doesn't accept the invitation as quickly as I wish he would, but he gets there after another few seconds, and I feel his warmth immediately. Our view of the ocean is unlike anything I've ever seen, which should be a stupid thought to have when I've lived near the coast my entire life, except that I can't remember a night when I've been treated to such an intimate show.

It's almost sacred, but I don't say so out loud.

I'm not sure how much time passes, nor do I care when I'm satisfied a sweep of the beach won't disturb our privacy or get us in trouble, but as much as I think I'm content to sit in this silence forever, I don't realize how much I've missed Jamie's voice until I hear it again.

"I don't want to mislead you. About my life. Whatever it sounds like, it's not—" He shakes his head and stares at the water. "I'm very, very fortunate, and I know that. There have been some really incredible highs, and running away from those to sit here by myself probably makes no sense. And the lows—it's not fair of me to complain."

"Not fair to whom?" I ask.

"Anyone who's had it worse."

"Was that another lesson from everyone who's told you you're arrogant and selfish?"

Jamie glances at me before he returns to something he knows. "They're not all wrong."

"Doesn't mean they're all right, either," I say, cautious when I let my leg fall against his beneath the blanket, a touch that could be explained away easily, if he notices it at all. "You know, in a lot of sports, there are timeouts, and they don't only give those to the teams who are behind. Everyone gets them. Even the winners."

It's true, what I've said, but it leaves us with another stretch of silence that my heart won't let me hate. I hope he believes me, even if I'm one voice against a lifetime of others, and while it might mean nothing, I take the fact that he hasn't moved away from me as a good sign. It's made even better when he slides his hand over his blanketed lap and lands against the edge of mine, the contact far from significant and still enough to make me wish I could have a hundred others just like it.

He taps me with his pinky, and I only have 99 more to go. "In your life, do you think you've won more or lost more?"

"Won more," I say easily. "But I don't think—you mentioned incredible highs and all the noise, but my life is a lot quieter than that. Maybe not always literally, but we're more or less back to the start, right? You're the one nobody seems to get right. I'm the one they've always figured out from the first hello."

That has him turning toward me again, his cap failing to fully hide the sharp crease between his brows when it's lit up by the moon. I want to take the hat from him entirely, but when his mouth opens and closes and opens again, I'm caught up in the sweep of his tongue and the words that follow.

"I'm not sure I've figured out a damn thing about you, and I'm scared of what'll happen if I leave this bench without trying."

"Try, then," I murmur. "I'm right here."

Even hushed, I think I must've been too loud, and Jamie's gone again when he sighs and tucks himself further into my hoodie. I'm not surprised when he carries us back a moment or two, and I'm willing to follow him there. It's become clear most people don't.

"You like your boring life, though. You don't want all the highs and lows."

"I think I learned to be afraid of the highs and lows," I admit. It's too honest, but everything about where we're sitting calls for it, and I keep going. "I'd need someone who's used to it to take my hand and tell me they won't let go."

"Would you believe them?" he asks. "Kinda seems like people let go all the time, no matter what they've said."

"I always want to believe."

"Do you have someone holding your hand now? At home, where it's quiet?"

"Nobody is holding my hand anywhere," I say. "Even here, where it's quiet."

It's an easy hint to take, maybe especially because of everything else we've said and the places our bodies still touch. Jamie's faux arrogance and very real insecurities keep him from doing anything about it, and he aims a sad laugh at an ocean that's heard it all before.

"All of this would be easier if you could go back to writing me off as pretty."

"Even when I called you pretty, I don't think I wrote you off."

"No?"

"I'd rather not make everyone else's mistake," I murmur.

Jamie takes a long, slow breath. Then he reaches up to remove his hat, and the time between each of my heartbeats disappears altogether. He bends to set it down next to the water bottle, and I only get a glimpse of his hair when he combs his fingers through it as he sits up again. The movement itself is something I'm strangely sure I've seen from him before, but I only get a second to appreciate it before he's tugging my hood over his head.

If I had the words to stop him from hiding, I'd use them. I'm still not sure whether he knows he's queer—or whether my own queerness is part of what he wants to figure out—but asking outright feels like it would send at least one of us tumbling toward the sand, and I'm not ready to move from where I am.

And while it hasn't been true for most of my time with Jamie, in this exact moment, I'm glad we're facing the sky instead of each other.

"Holy shit, did you see that?" he hisses.

"A shooting star," I breathe. "God, I haven't seen one in years. Maybe since I was a kid."

"We're supposed to make a wish."

I turn toward him with a smile. "Do yours usually come true?"

"Honestly? A lot of them have." He pauses as if he wants to say more about that, but I can almost see the moment he changes his mind and makes this about me. "If you could use your wish to be anywhere in the world right now, where would it be?"

"I mean, it's kind of hard for me to complain about the view I've got now, but if you're suggesting there are better things to want—"

"Yes, Mateo. I'm pretty sure you can want more than what you already have."

"Okay, then. I'd be on a different secluded beach. With sunshine. Hammocks—"

"Plural?"

I nudge his shoulder with mine. "I'm wanting more than I have, remember?"

"Okay," he chuckles, nudging me back. "Anything else?"

"A good book and several Mai Tais," I say. "And what about you? Where would you be?"

"Standing in front of a frozen lake."

"You won't be cold there?"

"Well, it's not Mai Tai weather, but I'd be dressed for it."

My shoulder. His. "Or you could borrow something warm from a man you've just met."

There's more I want to say. Or ask, really. A frozen lake is a hell of a wish for someone raised in Southern California, but maybe it's as simple as that. A wish for something he's never had.

Either way, I keep my mouth shut when he touches me.

His pinky hooks around mine on top of a blanket nobody in the world can see, and when I don't flinch, Jamie keeps going. It's still careful, the way he takes my hand and threads our fingers together, and I wonder whether he keeps our hands resting on my thigh because it's safer for him to be the one who will have to pull away.

I don't care. I'll give this beautiful stranger whatever he'll allow himself to take, and then I'll go home and pray for the chance to do it again.

"Do you let all the boys touch you after they buy you tacos?" he asks.

The levity feels out of place now, but I shrug. "Depends on how much I liked the tacos, I guess."

"So, you liked them tonight?"

"I've liked everything tonight."

My thumb arcs over the back of his hand in case it's the extra reassurance he needs before the next several seconds are spent staring straight ahead, the silence brought to a gentle end when Jamie takes another deep breath.

"I really don't know what I'm doing here."

"You're letting yourself get lost in something so much bigger than you and pretending your time here doesn't count."

He looks at me then. Really, really *looks* at me. "I want it to count."

"So do I."

"Mateo—"

I cut him off by pressing the fingers of my free hand to his lips, and his grip on me tightens almost imperceptibly in response. Without the benefit of more light, I can't see whether his troubled blue eyes have been overcome by black, but his mouth opens against my fingertips. It's not wide enough to suggest he has something to say, but the cockiest part of me thinks he'd let me slip them inside, even if it would be unfair to try.

"Have you done this before?" I ask.

In the next split second, I expect Jamie to close his mouth and frown or look away. Maybe let go of my hand. He could even stand and leave me all alone with the blanket and the arousal that warms my blood and kicks at my chest.

None of it happens, though.

I feel his fingers close around my wrist before he pulls my hand away from his mouth, and I barely have time to register his strength before he's kissing me, the tenderness of it matched only by how goddamn sure he is. His confidence probably answers my question, and for a long time, I don't worry about it, both of us opening for each other when something more passive isn't enough. I don't realize we're not holding hands anymore until we have fistfuls of clothes and Jamie's fingers are surprisingly light against my cheek.

He tastes vaguely of tacos and hope, and I think he could say the same about me.

When we take separate breaths again, our foreheads are pressed together, and I can feel him shake.

"Yeah, I've done this before, but it's not—" Jamie trails off and steals the softest kiss before he goes on. "All the rides other people gave me—the places we went and the things we did—it wasn't like this."

"They were men, though?"

"They were everyone."

"And they used you?"

"Hey, no, careful," he warns. "Don't believe for a second that I didn't use them, too. If this is—if you and I are doing anything here, I need you to understand how many of my lows have been my own damn fault. There are things they've been right about, and they're—perfect moments don't last, Mateo. Please don't sit here and pretend that's not true."

This time I cut him off with a kiss, deep and devastating, my tongue dragging against his when he meets me there. It feels too good to stop right away, and we don't try, desperate little sounds offered back and forth. I'm not sure how much time passes before the awkwardness of being turned sideways on a bench isn't working for me anymore, the blanket already falling off our laps. I grab it and pile it on the other side of me before I tug at Jamie, needier than I should be when nothing we've said tonight makes him any less of a stranger.

But I already know I want him to be more.

I'm not usually this careless. Not that I haven't had my share of semi-anonymous encounters lasting a matter of minutes, but those were years ago, in situations that called for it. Even before Jamie and I agreed to leave the alley behind, this was going to be something different for me, the spark between us impossible to smother against a stucco wall. There's danger now in holding too tightly to something that would need room—and plenty of time—to grow, but when I pull Jamie into my lap, he comes so willingly that I can't be embarrassed by the moan I pass from my mouth to his. He swallows it before he takes my blanket into his hands and drapes it over his shoulders, both of us shielded from the ocean breeze that's grown sharper since we first sat down.

"You're right, and I'm sorry," I say, moaning again when Jamie bumps my hoodie aside with his nose and sucks the bare skin he's uncovered. "Perfect moments don't last, but we can love them while they do."

"In a hammock?"

"Anywhere."

Jamie leans back at that, and the space between us is cold. "You barely know me, though. Once you get a closer look, you might change your mind."

He's not wrong, I suppose. And I'm not sure he means it literally, no matter how much he's used his hat and my hoodie to hide tonight, but I take the chance I've been given now and I look.

Closely.

I've given up trying to figure out whether I should recognize him, though there's some small part of me that pauses to consider the unwanted attention I'd draw at work if he's anybody the kids would know. But then he lets me push his hood away and run my fingers through his thick hair, and when I hold him there, he doesn't close his eyes. I use my other hand to trace the arc of an eyebrow, the shell of an ear, the slope of his nose, and the strong line of his jaw. Jamie's classically beautiful, but as much as I could stare at him until morning, I'm already convinced his looks are the least interesting thing about him. I press a thumb to his chin when I open his mouth for mine, not because I want to kiss this pretty boy, but because I might get to know him better if I can taste him one more time.

And then another thousand times after that.

Eventually, I stop to nuzzle at his neck. "I believe that you've played a role in a lot of your lows, but what about the highs? Are you giving yourself credit for some of those, too?"

"You think I'm gonna say no, don't you?"

"I think it would be stupid of me to assume anything about you is that simple, but I sure hope you don't say no."

"Yeah, I'll take credit for some of the highs, too," he says, his smile there and gone again. "I think I've made a decent number of my own decisions, for better or worse."

"Agency's good. It probably earned you some of the arrogant, selfish rap, too."

"Probably."

I bring him into another kiss, just because, and then look up at him. "You don't have to tell me what it is, but of all the highs in your life, is there a number one? A single high that stands out as the very best?"

"Yes," Jamie answers.

"That was fast. Do you also have a single lo—"

"Yes."

"And that was even faster," I say.

There's a pause when I think he might tell me about them, but then he cocks his head. "Why do I feel like you don't have a simple answer for either one?"

"Because I don't have a simple answer for either one. I've had a lot of wonderful days—getting my degrees or my nieces and nephews being born. And yeah, obviously shitty ones too—breakups and funerals and that sort of thing. But I couldn't pick one event. One memory."

I yawn then, an obnoxiously exaggerated thing I can't cover well enough. Jamie is quick to laugh at me and then kiss the sleepy smile that must've been left behind. It's too good, again and still, all happy and tired and honest and smitten, so we don't rush our way through it, even when every clock must be ticking. I need to go home and sleep, and Jamie has to fetch his car from wherever he left it. The beach has been closed since shortly after we arrived, and while I'm increasingly confident nobody will find us here, I'm not sure we have an actual reason to stay.

But I really, really don't want to leave.

Jamie moves closer again, his arms—and the blanket—wrapped more tightly around me than before, and I know he's clinging, too. It's silly, I think, when we can plan to have tacos next week and the week after that and the week after that. We can spend afternoons on the beach or try dinner again at the same bar, and whatever desperation we feel tonight can be something we laugh at then.

We don't pull away from each other though, our kisses close to promises we haven't made, until my attempt at a deep breath turns into another ridiculous yawn. Jamie doesn't laugh this time, but he slowly slides off my lap and back onto the bench, extending his arm to make room for me against his side.

"Don't go," he whispers. "Not yet."

I'm too big to do this, and I don't care, resting my head on his shoulder while he rearranges the blanket over us. It'll be fine for the few more minutes I'm here, my eyes closed while I rest with one last kiss pressed to the top of my head.

One last kiss.

Chapter Three: Jamie

(I Swore it Wasn't Love)

I wake him in time for the spectacular sunrise.

The sun is technically behind us, and I'm already sure the man next to me will be the most perfect thing I see all morning. Still, the slow spread of color in the sky is something worth watching. Mateo startles, confused and probably terribly stiff no matter how comfortable I'd tried to make myself while he slept against me. And then he remembers where he is, and in that moment of unbearable honesty, his entire body relaxes as his tired eyes find mine.

For the rest of my life, on the very worst of days, I'll beg myself to believe he saw something perfect, too.

"Were you worried it was a dream?" I ask.

"I never remember my dreams," Mateo says, his voice raspy and easy to lose to the sound of the waves below us. "But I remember everything about last night."

He wipes the sleep from his eyes and blinks toward the ocean without bothering to fix the messy ponytail barely resembling one now. The fog will blur his view more than the exhaustion he'll take home with him. He stares for a while anyway, and I understand the compulsion. I've been watching the horizon for a very long time.

I still barely understand my decision to bring him here, to a place I've made mine because I don't always like to share. The goal was a longer conversation, I think. I didn't expect the shooting star that dragged whispered vows across the sky. I didn't expect the need to hear them again today.

I listen carefully, just in case.

Beachfront mornings aren't new to me, so I easily drown out the chatter of the seagulls. I know they've arrived by now, but I don't care about the surfers gathering just north and south of where we sit. A few wealthy homeowners may be sipping gourmet coffee from the comfort of the backyards above us, and they're mostly uninteresting to me. Mateo and I remain secluded in a bubble that has to burst, however gently it might happen.

"I really don't know what I'm doing here," I tell him.

I'd first said it hours ago, and everything had turned out fine then. Great, even. My hopes are higher this morning, but it's been years since I've dared to look up. Mateo shifts beneath the blanket, and he lands further away. His fingers are threaded through mine before I let any of my past take me from something that feels suspiciously like a future.

"Have you done this before?"

I smile, comforted by another echo. "You asked me that last night, and then I kissed you."

"And this time?"

He rubs his thumb against the back of my hand, just like he had before, and I'm stunned that anything can feel so familiar to me already. I want to give him something back, but I think this view of the Pacific is all I've got.

"The sun is up."

"And you're not out," he murmurs. "You've done this before, but nobody knows."

Still not used to being this transparent when my facade has served me well, I flinch and become a coward again. "You don't have to give me a ride back to the bar. I've kept you away from home long enough."

"That wasn't an accusation, Jamie. Just an observation I couldn't censor after sleeping on a bench for a few hours."

"I didn't know how to let you leave. It was selfish to ask you to stay."

"The bench thing wasn't an accusation either," Mateo says, and he turns toward me slowly enough that I don't notice his free hand moving until he's already pushing his hood away from my head again. I don't know how much I look like Jameson Sinclair this morning, but it became too late to hide a while ago. When I close my eyes anyway, he combs his fingers through my hair. "I was properly warned about your selfishness. I'm glad I stayed. I'd do it all over again if you wanted me to. And you don't owe me an answer to a question I didn't ask."

We've been careful about that—asking things and answering them—but I look into Mateo's boundless brown eyes and I hate our caution. He might hate it too, but he lets go of my head and gives me time to put my words together.

"It's probably a lot more complicated than whatever you're thinking, but you're right. It's never been a thing for me—being *out*."

"Are you married?"

I laugh and wonder how far the wind carries the sound. "No, definitely not married."

Mateo chuckles too, but he quiets quickly. "You've kissed men."

"Mmmm."

"You've slept with some, too."

"Mmmm."

He stands then, gentle when he drops my hand and gives me all of his blanket. I stare while he stretches, just a sliver of his happy trail visible for a second I won't forget. I have the eerie sense that our prolonged goodbye is going to hurt no matter what hopeful things we say. When he turns toward the ocean to speak, I don't feel any better.

"You know, nothing about your life has to get more complicated because you rescued me from a bar fight and bought me tacos."

"Are tacos your big takeaway from last night?"

"I already told you, I remember everything," he says.

I fold his blanket to keep myself from reaching for him while I argue a point I think we agree on. "I want it to count."

"But the sun is up."

"Yeah. And I think that could be okay."

Mateo looks at me again. Studies me. Smiles and stays guarded. "Because you're arrogant, and you're ready for the whole world to see you?"

It's not the right time to tell him I never really had a choice. That I was still a child when strangers started to know my name. I'll be ready to talk about it someday, on this bench or anywhere he'll agree to meet me, but it's too much to promise this morning. I can hear decades of locker room slurs, and I'm afraid of my future no matter how long those doors have been closed behind me. I'm not lying about being willing to come out for him, but there's no good way to explain how messy it could get. That conversation will have to wait.

For now, I smile back instead. "You didn't get to try the wings at Kai's."

"No, I didn't," Mateo agrees. "And I probably won't have time to try them for a couple of weeks. It's a busy time of year for me. But if you—"

When he doesn't go on, I finish the thought I'd started. "I could give you my number. And you could give me yours."

Mateo takes some time to answer, but when I begin to peel his hoodie over my head, his hand covers mine. "If we're going to see each other again, you don't have to return that while you're still cold."

"No?"

"No."

"Do you only want dinner?" I ask, pulling my hand away to tuck it into the pocket he's let me borrow.

"I want hammocks and frozen lakes."

Fuck. My stomach turns with need, fear, and something as unfamiliar as hope. I breathe as though I feel nothing, but I'm sure I'm as transparent as I have been since I pinned Mateo to a stucco wall. Maybe he saw through me before that.

"We can figure out a good time to meet at the bar."

"Because Kai is safer than the whole world," he says.

I nod slowly and swallow around something that isn't supposed to hurt. "Kai has always been safe, yeah. But that's not—we can start at Kai's and then we can go anywhere."

"Anywhere?"

"Everywhere."

***

I keep waiting for something to hit. Regret or cold feet or a hundred questions about why this one man has made me want to crack open every closed door. How this one man could make me forget years of media training and handling meant to keep the public from spreading rumors too easy to believe. I expect anxiety, or just basic concern for my family and all the castles I've built in the sand.

Nothing ever comes.

Harper stays at her mom's until Sunday evening. I stay in Mateo's hoodie for more of the weekend than late summer should allow. She starts her first year of high school on Monday. I start a dozen texts I don't send but wish I could.

The unsent messages have nothing to do with regret or cold feet or questions or anxiety or concern. I'm still waiting for all of those things. No, I've only deleted those texts to give Mateo more time to deal with whatever busyness he'd warned me about.

I'll give him close to forever if he needs it. And then we can meet for beer and wings.

"So, like, it sucks to be back at school because—school? And we're just stupid freshmen, so whatever. But also, only one of my classes fully blows, and it's good to see people I didn't hang with all summer, and I still sorta can't believe that Mr. Z is exactly as awesome as everyone said he is, but that alone will make this year pretty bangin'."

"Mr. Z?" I ask, leaning against the kitchen counter that Wednesday afternoon and looking up from another message I probably won't send.

Harper rolls her eyes just before she opens the fridge. "And you think *I* don't listen to *you*?"

"That's true often enough for you to forgive me now." I set my phone aside and give her my undivided attention. "Mr. Z. He's one of your teachers, right?"

"Gee, fantastic powers of deduction, dad. Glad you never got checked hard enough to forget that two plus two equals four."

"Argument made. Tell me—*again*—about Mr. Z."

She closes the refrigerator door with her shoulder and hops onto the island, her legs swinging while she tears into the first of five string cheese wrappers. I bend forward to steal one and wink when she tries to glare.

"He teaches freshman honors English, though rumor has it he might take over the AP English classes once Schneider retires, and hopefully that happens by the time I'm a senior, but I guess it doesn't matter for now? Anyway, Lizzie's older sister said Mr. Z's really strict but also really cool and nice and funny, and I don't care about the strict thing because English is my best subject and I don't really get into trouble, right? But yeah, I don't have to worry about some terrible teacher making my favorite subject suck. And on top of all of that—"

"There's more?" I laugh.

"Um, yeah? Of course. He's also the soccer coach—for the girls, not the boys, obviously—so if I can make varsity as a freshman, then he won't make that suck either, and I'm okay with the strict thing there, too."

She pauses long enough to shove too much cheese into her mouth, and I narrow my eyes. "You don't have a crush on Mr. Z, do you? Because that would be really bad. You know that would be really, really bad, right?"

"Oh, so I'm not allowed to like boys?"

"You're allowed to like *boys*, yes. You are not allowed to like teachers and coaches."

Harper bursts into the same easy laughter I've lost over the past several years. "Oh my god, seriously? I don't have a crush on him, I promise. I'm sure some people do because he *is* objectively hot for a guy in his 30s or 40s or whatever, but Lizzie's sister says he's gay and, I dunno. I can see it, I guess? So, it wouldn't even matter because he's definitely not gonna look twice at me, and if I'm gonna drool over an old man, I'll pick one of your teammates and drive you super crazy."

"So, everyone loves this guy and nobody cares that he's gay?" I ask, missing several other points.

"I mean, I'm sure *somebody* cares that he's gay," she says. "Probably all the girls who *do* have a stupid crush on him and the boys they ignore because of it. But yeah, no. He's way popular. And being gay isn't a big deal to anyone at school, as long as they don't have their head up their—"

"Hey now."

With another quick laugh, Harper jumps back down from the island and throws her handful of wrappers into the trash. "I'm gonna go to Kate's. I'll be back before dinner."

"And homework?"

"I'll do it later."

She's already halfway gone, but I call after her anyway. "Hey, don't think I missed that crack about people in their 30s being old. Or that bit about my teammates."

"Bye, dad. Love you, dad."

"Bye, pixie."

I don't pick up my phone until I hear the front door slam. Then I distract myself from a few things by finally sending Mateo a text.

Definitely not bothering you while you're busy. Definitely not thinking about tacos or sunrises or kisses either

There's no response right away, and whatever I'd hoped, I honestly didn't expect one. Or I don't know *what* I expected. Hookups with men have never required chitchat. I've only needed an app or DM or help from a handful of people who've looked the other way afterward. Longer flings with women have been entirely public and predictable things requiring less effort than that.

Or significantly more effort in a dozen other directions, shared custody of a teenager among them.

I consider walking down to the beach. A lonely ex-superstar dragging his feet in the sand would be a more poetic spin on the drama most gossip sites preferred to sell with a tawdry pun. Then I realize

I'm not writing poetry anywhere, and my own backyard has been kinder to me than I deserve. Maybe healthy choices will make me the person Mateo deserves. Changing and grabbing a towel doesn't take more than a minute, though it's easy to imagine the crack of bone when I jog back downstairs. It's a reminder to slow down, and I hate it.

There's very little splash when I dive into the pool, an incredibly ironic observation given how often I've made my presence known. Because it became a habit, or because I need an easy win, I start with some basics from a rehab routine I haven't been assigned for a while. From there I ease into laps that clear my mind better than anything but alcohol and sex. I exhaust myself, but balancing my mental and physical health has never been my thing.

It's sheer luck that my head's above water when my phone vibrates against the ground. I lift myself from the pool and sit with some of my scar still submerged when I read the message.

Were the tacos and sunrises and kisses not good enough to think about?

I've thought about them plenty. Just wasn't gonna bother you with any of it today

What changed your mind?

I can't blow up Mateo's phone with a story about Harper and a gay teacher and being reminded of my age and teammates she'll tease me about even though they're not actually my teammates anymore. He only knows me as the pretty, arrogant stranger who made him spend the night on a bench. That can't change with a couple of texts.

I missed you

Another minute passes, and I almost take it back. I don't know whether you can miss someone you've been without for all but a single night, but Mateo must think so.

I've missed you too. Every day. And I wish I could see you

this weekend.

But you're busy this time of year

I'm going out with coworkers and then I have brunch with my best friend. Both are traditions.

Brunch should be everyone's tradition

Absolutely. But is it terrible that I keep daydreaming about brunch with you instead?

I pause before responding. Of course it's not terrible, but omelets aren't bar food and mimosas aren't on tap. For the first time in a while, I imagine the flash of cameras exposing me. Then I stare at Mateo's name until I remember what it was like to be held by him, and how much I want him to hold me again.

I love that you daydream about me. I pause again, but don't let it linger. *I guess weeknights aren't great for you?*

I go to bed embarrassingly early on weeknights. You'd laugh at me.

I would never. Well. Maybe I would. A little

I'm smiling now. I hope Mateo is, too.

I'm sure we can find plenty of other reasons to laugh. Maybe next Saturday night at Kai's?

For a moment, I consider pointing out that the bar will be at least as crowded as it was the last time he pressed himself close to me. I stop when I decide there's a better way to handle it—something I wouldn't be able to avoid even if I wanted to. And after all these years, I really don't think I want to.

Definitely. Just let me know what time works for you

I haven't asked about your schedule. I guess it's open?

Harper has a back-to-school night thing coming up, but that'll be on a weeknight. Haunting the rink will be a daytime activity, if it becomes an activity at all. Guest commentator gigs won't start for at least another month. Same with appearances at fan events. And binge-watching tv from my couch remains blessedly flexible.

My wild weekends are a thing of the past

Then I guess I'm lucky I got treated to beach night.

I think I'm lucky you said yes

Jamie?

Yeah?

It might take me a while to respond sometimes, but you can always say hi. You don't have to miss me first.

You can say hi too

He sends a smiley face, and I swim away from my phone, another few laps doing what they can to calm whatever just got kicked up again. My leg feels great, and I think the rest of me is getting there. By the time I climb out of the pool, I'm steady enough to spend a few minutes appreciating the ocean view I'd shared with Mateo, and I think Harper and I should have dinner out here tonight.

She brings Kate back with her, and the three of us enjoy the fresh air.

The next day I say hello to Mateo because he told me I could, and I'm helpless.

He says hello to me, too.

Our next several messages are so simple—boring, maybe—but nobody who's kissed me has ever wanted simple before. It's overwhelming to think about a future so unlike the one I had when millions praised or cursed me, and I let the heavy quiet of it keep me company each night as I fall asleep. It's as easy to hold on to as the blanket that shielded Mateo and me from the ocean air and my very famous name.

When Sunday morning rolls around, I decide it's as good a time as any to have a conversation that could've happened twenty years ago. On every intellectual level, I'm remarkably calm. Nothing will change for the worse after today, and maybe we'll both be relieved to stop pretending we've never kept this open secret.

Physically, though. Physically, my body's not entirely sure it wants to be upright long enough for me to shower. I'm shaking when I fasten my jeans and tug an old t-shirt over my head. I don't even consider trying to eat breakfast when my coffee barely stays down. My phone becomes dangerous company when I use it to scroll through years of escapades that have come and gone, but Harper isn't here to distract me from my worst habits, and it's not her responsibility in the first place.

I haven't let myself consider what this conversation would look like if I were having it with her.

Will. *Will* look like. *When* I have it with her. Because if everything goes well the next time I see Mateo, she and I will need to sit down with a lot more string cheese.

Intent on leaving some of my bullshit behind, I give up on trying to settle everything inside me before I go. I'm in my car before I think about it more than that, and blast one of my pregame playlists because it feels right. Parking near Kai's feels right too, even if another wave of nausea tries to convince me otherwise.

The bar isn't open yet, so I text when I'm headed toward the alley. I don't remember the last time I hung out with Kai with nobody else around, and I'm grateful for the privacy we'll have this morning. I'm also grateful he'll be busy with inventory and kitchen prep.

"Two weekends in a row?" Kai says, pushing the back door open just enough for me to catch it and follow him back inside. "What's the special occasion?"

"I've got plans for a third."

He's moving quickly, but I've said enough for him to throw a look over his shoulder. "Alone or with someone?"

"With someone."

"Keep talking."

Kai doesn't stop walking until we're in the bar's kitchen. I move to lean against a stack of food crates that seems to always be here, even if I'm sure they come and go, but he waves for me to sit on the counter. He disappears into cold storage, but he's back by the time I continue.

"It will probably be Saturday night, and I know you'll be slammed."

"Absofuckinglutely," he laughs, eggs, cheese, and bacon tossed next to me. "But if you're bringing a plus one, it doesn't matter what I'm up to, does it?"

"I meant 'you' as in the bar, not 'you' as in *you*."

"Ah, of course. Because if you wanted to talk to *me*, you've got my number, my email, my home address, all my socials, my passwords, my birth date, my blood type—"

"Some of those have nothing to do with talking to you," I interrupt. "But you've made your point, and I know I suck. I suck now and I've sucked for at least the past five years."

Kai laughs again and warms a couple of skillets. "At *least*. But seriously, you're here. Talk."

"Last week, after I left—"

"With your damsel in distress."

"He was definitely not that," I snort. "But yes, I dragged him with me when I ran."

He's busy with a few different things on the stove, but he could handle them in his sleep. "And then you didn't let him back in."

I nod because Kai knows this much. I'd paid him back for the half-drunk beers and the food Mateo and I never ate. And because I'd felt the need to explain something, I'd told Kai that Mateo and I had been mid-conversation and decided to grab tacos while we finished talking. It's strange when the truth fails to capture anything honest.

"We ended up at the beach, actually."

"The beach?"

"The *bench*," I sigh, pausing to appreciate the smell of bacon and ignore the rumble in my stomach.

Kai pulls a plate from the shelf in front of him and nods. "Your broken ass could've walked to half a dozen places from here—at least a couple of which have tacos—but instead you drove toward your house and ended up at the ocean."

"Yeah."

Before he can show off the puzzle he's put together too quickly, Kai hands me a plate stacked with a bacon, egg, and cheese sandwich. I look down at the food and back up at him, a frown enough for him to answer my unspoken question.

"You haven't stopped shaking since you got here. You're nervous about the story you're about to tell, which we both know is fucking stupid, but at least I'm not getting your selfie smile or media lies. And because you're nervous, you didn't eat this morning. Now you're going to."

I shake my head. "I don't even think I'm hungry."

"Bullshit. Eat the sandwich. If talking to me really makes you sick, you know where the bathroom is."

"You know it's not like that."

"And *you* know you won't shock me with anything you're about to say," Kai argues back. "I'll admit the bench was a slight surprise, but take a bite and tell me the rest."

I skip almost everything that matters, because even my best friend doesn't need to see every bruise and the boldest ways I want to heal them. I take a couple of bites too, because he deserves to see something.

"I wanted more time with him—Mateo—so I had him drive us down there. We ate tacos and talked, and it still wasn't enough.

He didn't recognize me, even when he couldn't stop staring, and I needed him to keep looking."

"Oh, come on, J," Kai says, stealing a bite of the sandwich he made and dropping it back onto my plate before he talks with his mouth full. "You've gone unrecognized before, even by people in your bed. That's not what made him different."

I nearly choke at the thought of Mateo in my bed, and how calm Kai is about my wanting him there. "It never went that far."

"Ah, so *that's* what made him different."

"Oh, fuck you."

Kai snorts. "I'm beginning to wonder whether you say that to everyone."

"But you don't care?" I ask.

"Not in whatever way you're still freaking out about, no. And years after one very specific rumor, combined with—oh, let's see—actually *knowing* you, you can't think this is news to me."

I give up on the sandwich with a couple of bites to go and set the plate next to me on the counter. "We've never, ever talked about any of that."

"We're talking now."

"Okay, yeah, but I don't know what to say. I don't know what it is about him. It was one night. And yes, I got to be Jamie, and hold Mateo's hand, and talk about wishes like I was a kid again, but it was still *one* night."

Once he's finished my sandwich, Kai starts in on the dishes he shouldn't have to do this early in his day and looks sideways at me. "How long did you stay on the bench?"

"'Til morning," I whisper, clearing my throat when there's more to say. "The thing is, I didn't want to let him go, but there was no hurry either. We kissed, but it felt like we'd have the rest of our lives for everything else. We didn't even say that to each other, and he would've let *me* go if I'd asked him to. He told me nothing had to change—that he didn't have to complicate my life—but it felt like we were making promises to each other. Like we were telling each other we want this to be the beginning of everything. And I don't think I believed in that sort of thing."

"Love at first sight?"

I wave him off quickly. "God, no. It's not *that*. It just matters. Wanting more than a night matters."

"Right, okay," Kai smiles. "So, now we're back to where we began. The bar will be slammed on Saturday. You're bringing a date anyway. Did you want me to run out and buy some fancy wine glasses for his Sam Adams or—"

"Actually, I was hoping you'd save a couple of stools for us. Which, yeah, is probably a bigger ask than fancy wine glasses."

"You know, even without throwing your money around, you could get a nice table for two—maybe a corner booth, even—in a place that doesn't specialize in beer and bad decisions."

"I know," I say, watching as Kai moves close to me again.

For two guys who have been best friends forever, we've never touched much. I don't know whether that's on me or him, though I'm willing to accept the blame. I think back to all my years on the ice and in locker rooms or at our hotels. Back then, I was surrounded by teammates who had few physical boundaries, and I was often the object of circumstantial affection. In the middle of a celebration because I was the one who'd scored. Arms draped across my shoulders because I was the one who'd draw the most women at a club. Embraced by men who'd never be Jameson Sinclair because breathing the same air might've been enough for them to believe they once came close.

And I can't say I didn't care. I've always loved to be loved, however I could get it.

But I'm not sure whether Kai noticed when I said I'd held Mateo's hand. If he did, I'm not sure he understood how foreign that kind of intimacy is to me. It's probably a difficult thing for anyone to imagine when years of internet chatter—and so many paparazzi pictures—have had me wrapped around one beautiful woman or another. But sex isn't the same thing as wanting someone who sees through you to press their skin to yours.

Kai reaches for my knee now, and it's enough to make me miss something that isn't mine yet.

"You're gonna pretend the two of you are just friends here," he says. "You're gonna pretend it *doesn't* matter."

The tip of my thumb grazes his. "No. I don't want to pretend anything anymore. I just haven't figured out where else to take this version of me."

"It's not a version of you, J. It's just you."

Chapter Four: Mateo

(I Finally Learned His Name)

A glance at the clock on the wall tells me I've been here for over twelve hours now, minus the quick walk I took with Sophie this afternoon. We'd both needed iced coffee as a reward for making it through the day, or a bribe to ensure we'd return for the rest of the night, but that high wore off a long time ago. I smile at a family waving goodbye from across the room, then look at the clock again. Officially, I've got twenty minutes left. Unofficially, probably another twenty minutes after that.

My phone vibrates in my pocket. Sophie. I think I wanted it to be someone else, but I haven't spoken to him since yesterday when I called to confirm this weekend's bar date, and we reminded each other that we'd be busy tonight.

After our first round of texts last week, Jamie and I sent a few simple messages back and forth—*good morning* or *hope your day is going well* or *thinking about the beach*. A couple of nights later, I took a chance and called him from bed, exhausted after a long day and wanting to hear his voice before I closed my eyes. Anything but selfish, he said goodnight and sweet dreams, and then he let me go. We've talked a handful of other times, sharing preciously brief fantasies of a future that would start Saturday if it hadn't already started two weeks ago. He won't call tonight, but it'll be fine if I don't hear him say my name again until I can see him smile at me, too.

For now, I need to stop daydreaming, and I read Sophie's message.

Might go out for margaritas after this

I chuckle to myself. *I'm still recovering from last weekend. I used to handle the start of the school year better*

We're getting old babe

One of my kids slips into the room with his parents close behind, so I leave my phone on my desk and greet them with the same grin and handshake I mastered in my first year of student teaching. This isn't my favorite part of my job—for all the hassle people give teenagers, I've found their families are often harder to please—but the conversation is pleasant, and I encourage them to look around the classroom. I've set up displays of some of what we'll be working on this year, plus the kids can show off the few things we've done so far.

Some students would rather keep talking, either to bullshit me or their parents, but this one nods to me and leads them away. Another couple of freshmen come in, but they're two of my shyest, and I'm not surprised when they bypass the introductions altogether and simply tour the room on their own, their families as quiet as they are. I smile and leave them to it.

My phone rattles on my desk, and Sophie's calling this time. With only about fifteen minutes left, most of my students have probably come and gone, but I still hesitate for a few seconds. Then I go ahead and answer.

"Since when do you call me during back-to-school night?"

"Since Miss Vicki showed up in my room with enough gossip to keep everyone away from me," she whisper-snorts.

That perfectly explains both Sophie's need and ability to escape. Victoria Gallagher has had kids at our school for almost as long as I've taught here, and she's quite the queen bee. The worst of the worst attempt to befriend her so they can get the latest dirt on teachers, parents, and students, too often forgetting that proximity won't save them if they become the subject of something juicy. Sophie and I have long suspected that Vicki's knack for tattling on everyone else is her best defense against anyone's attempt to tattle on her. Some sort of adulteress sleight of hand.

I don't have a Gallagher kid in class this year, but I'd do my best to avoid their mother either way.

"Ah, so you're calling to explain why you need those margaritas?"

"Actually, no," Sophie says, still hushed. "Vicki did have one interesting thing to say before I fled. Apparently, Jameson Sinclair is here, and rumor has it he's even hotter in person than when we've seen him sweaty and mouthy in a locker room interview—or when he's been positively slutty on the cover of those entertainment magazines I *definitely* don't read."

My heart stops. When it starts again, each beat comes too close to the one before. "Jameson Sinclair?"

"Hockey stud. Lusted after, envied, or despised by everyone who knows what a puck is. Once broke his leg in front of us—"

"Shattered," I rasp, so many messy feelings washing over me at once. Memories from several years ago, when my best friend and I watched Jameson Sinclair's career come to an end. Memories from a couple of weeks ago, when I watched a familiar stranger named Jamie limp on his way up a hill before he wished for a frozen lake. "He shattered his leg, and he never fully recovered."

"Yes, *shattered* his leg in front of us. Never recovered," Sophie amends. "His daughter is in your class this year, but I'm guessing they haven't made it to your—"

"Harper. Harper Sinclair."

She sighs. "Yes, Harper Sinclair. Jesus, I think you need the margaritas more than I do. I'll come grab you when I—"

I hang up on Sophie before she can finish the thought because my throat's gone dry. It's true that Harper hadn't made it to my classroom earlier in the night, but she's here now, her father a step behind her. And I think I want to be upset about a phone call that's turned me inside out, but I'm too grateful for the warning it provided.

Jamie—Jameson fucking Sinclair—wasn't blessed with the same, his blue eyes wide and his beautiful lips parted.

"Mr. Z! Sorry we're so late, but we stopped to talk to a bunch of people. Or a bunch of people stopped to talk to us, I guess? But we're here, and I told my dad about you, so now I can—oh, hi, Miranda. Bye, Miranda. Okay, sorry. Dad, come on, don't just stand there. Mr. Z, this is my dad. Dad, this is Mr. Z."

Harper is practically dragging him through a maze of desks, and it makes it painfully obvious that I haven't moved more than a foot away from the phone I'd set down seconds ago. He recovers before I do, years of practice with screaming fans reminding him to smile now, but I want to throw up, and it takes all my self-control to keep my iced coffee down when I smile back.

"Mateo Zavala. It's very nice to meet you, Mr. Sinclair."

Years of practice or not, he flinches at that. "Jamie. Please just call me Jamie."

"Yes, please call him Jamie," Harper groans. "I've been listening to everyone squeal *Jameson Sinclair* for the past two hours. Oh, wait, are you a hockey fan? I'm not trying to be mean about anything. He'll give you autographed merch if you want."

I could answer her, but one night with Jamie had taught me

that conversations *about* him haven't always *included* him, and I'm careful to avoid that mistake now. It's too late for it, but I hold out my hand and breathe easier when he takes it.

"It's very nice to meet you, Jamie," I say. My voice sounds weak, and I swallow in search of strength. "I'm a casual hockey fan. Not enough of one to recognize players on the street—or in a random bar—but I was at a few of your games. You don't need to give me anything though, and more importantly, I'm really enjoying having Harper in class."

Jamie nods. "She's told me so much about you, and I've heard your name a hundred times tonight. Everyone loves you."

"Do they?"

He finally lets go of my hand, and I hate it. He smiles again, and I hate that even more. "You can't possibly doubt that."

"Well, it's probably not a good idea for me to think about it too much. I have a job to do, right?"

"Right. And I guess I'm just the dad grateful that his daughter will get to spend so much time with you. You're the soccer coach, too? She's mentioned tryouts."

"I am, yes. But you're not *just* anything, Jamie," I argue, blinking hard before I remember I'm not on a bench anymore. "Harper, how about you show your dad around? You've written a couple of incredible things already, and I know you're excited about a few of the books we'll be reading this year. And we'll chat plenty about tryouts soon."

"Yes! Okay, so, I'm gonna tell you about everything," Harper starts, leading Jamie away from me.

I expect relief to fill the space between us, but nothing's there and the emptiness hurts. Sophie has texted a couple of times, but I swipe the messages away without reading anything. Then I tell myself to stop watching Jamie move around my classroom, his presence a sudden and sharp reminder that I learned so much about him and knew nothing.

My hands shake until I curl them into furious fists. Seconds later, I relax them because I don't want to live with half-moon scars. I'm logical, and I want so badly to reason my way past a problem I didn't know I had five minutes ago. It feels more like a tragedy though, and all I can see are the warnings keeping me from dragging Jamie to the bar right now.

The school administration could consider firing me. Vicki Gallagher and her lackeys would have horrible things to say about what I've done.

Even worse, fans and players could turn their backs on him. Media vultures would be outright cruel.

I'm spared a few moments of pain when another student pops her head through the door and waves at me, except that she's Harper's best friend, and the one person more important than both Jamie and me. Harper scurries toward Lizzie, and like goddamn magnets, Jamie and I end up next to each other. It's impossible to know where the attraction begins and ends.

Science is more Sophie's thing than mine.

"I'm sorry," he murmurs. "I didn't mean to—I would've told you this weekend. All about me. I wasn't going to hide anymore."

I shake my head, devastated by the whole damn world. "You looked familiar, but I couldn't make myself care. It was too easy to—"

"Be nobody."

"Yes," I sigh.

He glances over his shoulder, then returns his attention to me too quietly. "A few minutes ago, you said you didn't want me to give you anything, but I think it's going to take some time before I stop wanting to give you everything."

"Need, not want."

"What?" he asks.

"I said you didn't *need* to give me anything. I haven't magically stopped wanting our wishes to come true."

"But none of them will come true on Saturday."

"Sorry again, dad," Harper interrupts with a grin. "I'm back, but I showed you the good stuff and I can tell you more later, plus you got to meet Mr. Z, which was really the whole point of this thing, so we can go home now."

She's already backing toward the door, tapping the surface of the desks as she moves between two rows. I tuck a wayward piece of hair behind my ear, and Jamie takes a deep breath.

"Goodnight, Mateo. I look forward to seeing you around."

It's a lie, perhaps, but it changes nothing about my response. "I look forward to seeing you around, too."

They're gone a few seconds later, but it hurts to breathe a lot longer than that. I fall into my desk chair as a loud group tumbles down the hall, and I vaguely register someone yelling hello as they pass my room. I'm grateful nobody cared to get closer to me than that, and maybe nobody else will. I stare at a wall of favorite quotes and posters from teen movie adaptations of classic literature until one more look at the clock makes me wonder how many minutes have passed with no memory of them.

Stragglers will be around for a while, but I can close my door and reorganize the scattered show-and-tell families have admired over the past couple of hours. I'd rather leave it for the morning, but forcing myself out of my chair seems wise, and with as many students as I have, it shouldn't be that difficult to avoid anything with Harper Sinclair's name on it.

Shouldn't be, but is. Self-flagellation is a hell of a thing.

I sigh and kick at the leg of a desk that's done nothing to me, and

I force myself to move on.

Within the next several minutes, I'm mostly done putting my classroom back together, and I'm sitting at my desk again, my glasses on while I pretend to read a couple of in-class essays from earlier in the day. I give up when I'm too ready to escape the professionalism suddenly riddled with responsibility heavy enough to hurt. Then there's a halfhearted knock on my door before it swings open, and my best friend's appearance means my time has run out on a couple of things, good and bad.

"Okay, tell me, did you get to meet Jameson Sinclair?" Sophie asks, no real hello necessary when she has more important things on her mind. "I mean, you must've. They wouldn't be here and not see you. Everyone loves you."

"So I've heard," I say, picking up the stack of essays again just to keep my hands busy and my eyes down.

"You know what? Don't even tell me yet. It's tequila time, and you can give me the whole story while we drink. Not that there could be *that* much of a story when you probably shook his hand, introduced yourself, and smiled at him like he's any other parent, but still."

It's almost funny how she's managed to be very right and very wrong all at once, but when I take my glasses off and set the papers aside for the night, I don't comment on Jamie, nor on any of my behavior toward him. Instead, I appreciate how fiercely this woman loves me. It's a certainty that will keep me still when I can't figure out whether I want to run from or toward everything I've just lost. I only hate how abruptly I'm about to turn Sophie's mood upside down. I roll backward in my chair and force myself to stand, my fingers curling around the strap of my messenger bag when I finally look at her.

"I'm not going out, but if you want margaritas, come home with me," I say. "Spend the night."

Those last few words get her attention. They're enough to make Sophie understand a couple of important things and want to know so much more. She's watching me closely, but now that I've invited her to stay over, she won't ask for an explanation here, immediately aware my classroom isn't the place for anything I'll tell her tonight. She only pushes my limits when she steps around my desk to hug me, my eyes quickly filling with tears I won't shed on campus.

The Mexican restaurant we frequent will wait for a night we need stress relief—not a complete overhaul of a future I shouldn't have had time to imagine.

"Okay, let's get the fuck out of here," she mumbles against my chest. "It's been a minute since either of us has cried into a drink."

I nod as I gently push her away and gesture toward the door. We're parked near each other, but say nothing on the way to our cars, only the clack of her heeled boots and the unintelligible conversations among lingering teachers, parents, and students serving as a distraction. I don't pay attention to the music playing as I drive home, nor do I remember much about how I make it to my apartment complex. I think it's the vibration of my phone that finally brings me back just as I'm unlocking my front door, and I pull it from my pocket only to wish I hadn't.

I miss you already and I really am sorry

I'm close to dropping my phone on the floor just so it's not my problem anymore, but I make it far enough inside to kick off my shoes and hang my bag on the wall and ignore Jamie's text. I consider getting drunk in my untucked button-up and khakis, but I'm sad, not stupid. After another few minutes, I'm in sleep shorts and a t-shirt, my hair pulled into a careless ponytail. I make my way to my tiny kitchen, barefoot and thirsty and a little afraid of what comes next.

My phone stays face down and silent, and I'm stirring a full pitcher when Sophie arrives, letting herself in the same way she's done for years. We live in the same complex, so she's had time to change too, and she tosses a duffel bag toward my room without worrying about how it lands. It's been a while since a sleepover has been this spontaneous, most of them planned for movie nights or the need to bitch after a semester. I should be grateful life hasn't knocked either of us to the ground for a while, but I'm finding it difficult to muster a thank you tonight.

I salt the rims of our glasses and pour. Sophie joins me in the kitchen to take one, hums around her first sip, and takes a deep breath before she speaks.

"What happened?" Even as she asks, I can see her brain sifting through potential answers, and she voices a few of them. "It's not a family emergency, or you'd be with them already. You didn't get fired in the middle of back-to-school night, or I would've heard about it from Miss Vicki before it happened. Honestly, you look a lot like you did when you and Gabe broke up, even if we'd all seen that coming a mile away, but it's also—it's worse than that. You look so much *worse*."

"You've always been a hell of a friend, Soph."

"Drink. Talk."

I down half my glass embarrassingly quickly, refill the emptiness I've swallowed, and wander into my living room before I follow through with the rest of Sophie's command. As soon as I've settled onto my couch, she follows to curl into the corner of it, impatient but wise enough to give me the space I need to start my story. After another mouthful of tequila and triple sec, I leave my glass on the coffee table and stay leaning forward, my forearms against my legs to keep me close to upright.

"I met him two weeks ago," I say. "Jameson Sinclair."

"You *what*?"

I glance over my shoulder at her, then turn back to stare at the glass in front of me as I shake my head. "He wasn't—I didn't know. He was Jamie."

There's so much more to it than that, and I'll get there as soon as I have more of my margarita. I'm licking the salt from my lips when Sophie practically growls behind me.

"I get that you're big into story structure, character development, pacing, and all that good narrative shit English teachers love, but please consider less drinking and more talking. I can get drunk enough for both of us."

In the end, neither of us gets more than tipsy while I take forever to tell Sophie about the night I drove to a dive bar for the chicken wings she loves, and ate nothing until I had tacos by the beach. She's silent when I fall back against the couch and describe a man who had nothing to do with hockey and fame, and maybe even worse, nothing to do with being the father of a teenager. She refills our glasses around the time I tell her I'd noticed the lingering effects of an injury she'd witnessed at my side, but gave up wondering why he was hiding beneath his hat or my hoodie. She swears under her breath and refills them again as I talk about our first kiss, and we both pause for a long drink when I can't speak around the regret that Jamie and I never kissed goodbye. By the time I tell her how he and I left things—his decision to come out before I could've possibly understood what that meant for him, and our decision to meet back at the bar to chase shooting stars—Sophie is wrapped around me.

As close as she is, I've kept a few details about Jamie to myself because I have nothing else of him left. It means I've got little more to say, and I wrap up the story with my reintroduction to Jamie and the awkward goodnight following our acknowledgment that we want things we can't have.

"How did you not tell me about any of this? And how did I miss how different you've been these past couple of weeks?" she asks, her voice low enough to keep from jostling my broken heart.

"I didn't tell you about this because I don't *do* this—I don't let strangers into my car to drive them wherever they want to go and then promise I'd do it again and again. I needed one more night with him first, just to make sure it was real." I scrub my hand over my face and shrug. "And we're always busy at the beginning of the school year. Other than the night a dozen of us celebrated surviving week one, and our reliably sleepy recovery brunch, you and I haven't spent time together outside our respective classrooms."

She nods. "And you keep your personal life off campus."

"And I definitely keep my personal life off campus."

I think that would be true regardless of my actual job. My desire to keep my love life separate from my workplace doesn't feel predicated upon my position as a high school teacher and coach. I'm reserved by nature—and by nurture, too—and giving people less to gossip about suits me just fine. I've had a relationship with the aforementioned Gabe. I've dated in the years since that ended. Being gay means I capture the attention of strangers who are looking for something provocative to say, or people like Vicki Gallagher who always want to talk, but I rarely hold it for long when I don't bring anyone interesting around.

That would've changed someday, but I can't admit it tonight when *someday* has turned bitter on my tongue. Instead, Sophie lets go of me while I wash the taste away with the last of my third margarita.

"I can't believe you fell in love with Jameson Sinclair."

My glass misses the coaster when I attempt to set it back down, and I'm probably lucky its rough landing doesn't leave it with a crack. Or not one obvious enough to notice before I turn back toward Sophie.

"I'm not in love with him," I argue. "We spent *one* night together. It's more that we both wanted to spend a lot of nights together, and I never expected to lose that chance in such a spectacular way. We didn't do anything *wrong*. We never had the time to."

"So, that's it? You had one night together, and it's got you looking like this—" She uses her free hand to gesture wildly up and down my body, as if I could be confused about where she was flinging that particular pronoun. "Are you really going to walk away from a future with Jameson Sinclair?"

"Jamie."

"Of course. *Jamie*. Even better," Sophie says, her hand falling to her lap. "God, this fucking sucks."

I go back to staring at my empty glass. Two weeks ago, the rocks and sand beneath our feet were hardly stable, but where Jamie and I stand now has become unsteady in a way I've just begun to grasp. We'd been on the verge of promises we meant to keep, but circumstances have betrayed them for us. And it's not just that he's the parent of a student, which complicates everything enough for me to end this thing and break my own heart. It's that coming out in front of the sports world had already meant taking a chance that he'd break some of *his*, and doing it to date his teenage daughter's teacher would all but guarantee it.

Tequila hasn't made that any less true, even if I can barely swallow now. "It really does. And yeah, I have to walk away."

She doesn't believe me, but if there's an argument she wants to make, she'll save it for later. "Did Harper realize you two knew each other?"

"Not at all. Jamie knows how to bullshit under pressure, and I'm not sure she slows down often enough for it to matter."

I hide in my hands then, my head heavy and my heart wrung out.

Sophie peels herself off the couch to take our glasses back to the kitchen, unsteady on her feet, but in no danger of falling. We both need to be at work in the morning, no matter how much I'd love to call out and avoid one of my brightest students while I recover from whatever I feel for her father. Forcing myself up, I shuffle into the bathroom to pee and brush my teeth and splash my face with cold water that won't change my mood. When I open the door, Sophie's there waiting to do all the same things, and I crawl into bed and leave her to it.

A few minutes later, I'm lying on my side when Sophie tucks herself into the space I've left for her. I find her hand in the dark and hold on, and then I promise myself I won't ask her to stay again tomorrow night.

"Have you heard from him since he and Harper left?"

"Shit, I left my pho—"

"It's on your nightstand. Charging," Sophie says.

Of course it is. I squeeze her hand. "He texted me right when I got home. Said he misses me and he's sorry."

"What did you say?"

"There's nothing I *can* say. It's over."

It's abrupt, and maybe even rude, but I roll away from Sophie then and spend the next several hours wide awake, wishing it could be that easy.

It's a wish I'm already sure I'll make too often, because by defin-ition, one night should have ended in the morning.

It didn't.

Jamie and I didn't.

And I don't know what to do when *over* feels like the kind of thing reserved for hockey careers and summer breaks.

When the sun makes itself known, I start by making a greasy breakfast, the best way to apologize to our stomachs for an impromptu tequila night. I follow that up with a morning routine requiring very little thought or small talk with a best friend who's heard plenty, even if she had more questions after I stopped answering. Outside my apartment, I get a hug meant to hold me together, then Sophie and I go our separate ways, and I drive to school and teach a full day of classes.

When Harper Sinclair smiles up at me from her desk, I smile right back.

When I hear her dad's name too many times in the teachers' lounge, I take my lunch outside.

Another text doesn't come until I'm home again.

Can we talk?

I despise the way my body reacts to the sight of Jamie's name, a tangle of nausea and relief, and I can't decide whether I'd feel better if I change it in my phone or whether I need to delete him entirely. Neither will help now, and I exhale slowly when I sit on the edge of my bed and tap on the screen instead.

"Mateo."

"I don't know if you can keep calling me that," I sigh.

"But it's your—it's how you introduced yourself to me."

He could be referring to the alley or my classroom, but it doesn't matter. "It's too soft. Gentle. You say my name like you're taking care of it for me."

"Or like I'm afraid to let it go."

"We have to, though. We have to let all of it go."

He's quiet for several seconds, and I almost pull the phone away to see whether we're still connected. I don't, only because there's really no need. I know he's there, and I hate that comfortable certainty in the wake of everything else.

"Meet me at the bench," Jamie finally says, as tender with his command as he'd been just a minute ago. "Tomorrow night. Late, like before."

Like before is impossible, but I don't say so. "Is that a good idea?"

"Probably not, but I'm used to getting my way."

"Right up until the moment you don't."

Jamie chokes on a weak laugh. "Right up 'til then, yeah."

"Okay."

"Okay? You'll be there?"

"I'll be there."

The echo of hope in his voice—and probably the resignation in mine—is what keeps me moving forward the next 24 hours, and I still hear both as I approach the beach. After I'd hung up with Jamie yesterday evening, I'd considered canceling on him a dozen times, only to scroll through our texts and steel myself for any bad idea that could get me close to him again. The last time I read our messages was about three minutes ago, when I left my car on the street and began this short walk, but my phone is in my pocket now.

I'm close enough to the rocky shoreline to look for Jamie.

Just like that first night, it's dark and quiet this far away from the fire pits and smoother stretches of sand, but a house on the hillside has beautiful backyard lights, and they help me now. I'm cautious with each step while I search for the path that will bring me to a hidden bench, and pause to glance around again in case Jamie's near enough to lead me there. He's not, and I'm not sure whether I'm early or late, but I keep going.

I find the path.

I find the bench.

I find *him* standing just behind it and wearing my borrowed hoodie, looking at me like I'm a dream he didn't believe would come true.

"Jamie."

It's difficult to see, but I think his eyes are wet when he smiles. "You're as gentle with my name as I am with yours."

"I'm afraid to let it go."

He could tell me we have to. It's what I'd said to him. Instead, he moves around the bench and steps close to me. Arm's length, if it were a thing we were measuring. We should sit or talk or search the sky for something that will save us, but both of us breathe around the reliable rumble of the waves until I speak again.

"I guess you've been here a while. I was looking for you down by the rocks, but I—" I stop talking as Jamie tilts his head, the slightest frown there and gone when I glance over his shoulder. The houses of millionaires. One that helped light my way. And a path from there to here, because this bench belongs to *someone*, and it's only now that I realize we never trespassed at all. "I'm such an idiot. This is your—you live here. We're in your backyard."

"More or less," Jamie says.

"We can't go up there. I can't go inside."

"I'm not asking you to. This is where the rest of my life leaves me alone, remember?"

I nod. "Where the great Jameson Sinclair can pretend time doesn't count."

He ignores my tone and swallows hard. "We already made it count, Mateo. We made it count so much it hurts."

"So why did you invite me here?" I ask. "Because you're right. We made it count, and we can't pretend a damn thing. We can't keep meeting here like everything we might say and do won't spill into the rest of our lives. And if it hurts—"

"I've lived with pain for a long fucking time."

His honesty takes my breath away, and I watch as he finally sits on the bench. He's left room for me, and I don't take as long as I should to join him, my eyes on the ocean because I think I'll kiss him if I look anywhere else.

"I don't want to be the reason you're in pain," I say.

"You're not," Jamie huffs. "I can't imagine ever hurting when I'm with you."

We fall silent, careful not to touch, and I want to stay here until morning just to let another sunrise absolve us of sins we won't commit. As it is, we sit for a long time on a bench I already consider ours. It's unfair to consider anything *ours* when this feels like a prolonged goodbye, but there's something in the air that makes it okay, and I breathe it in.

"You're not going to come out," I finally say, too soft about it until I clear my throat and try again. "It was going to be hell for you anyway—all the wrong attention—but while you might've done that for me, and while you would've done anything to help protect Harper from the worst of the fallout, you won't put her in the middle of it by dating her teacher."

"I can't."

"You shouldn't, and *I* can't."

Jamie sighs and swallows feelings I know well. "You love your boring life. You might've given some of it up for me, but—"

"I won't put Harper in the middle of it, either. And the chance of getting fired over it—"

"Mmmm. Is this where I point out that she won't be your student forever?"

My head turns sharply at that. "You'd wait a year to be with me?"

"Four. She wants to play soccer."

"Jamie," I say, struggling past the lump in my throat.

"What if we still see each other?" he asks, hurrying on. "We could be friends, right? We could talk and get to know each other and hang out like friends do. Even if we do it quietly, so nobody asks questions.

We could have something else for these four years. We don't have to wait for everything."

"*Jamie*," I say again.

I don't know how to explain how I'm wounded by what he's just said, still far from recovered from seeing him walk into my classroom two nights ago. The idea of being nothing more than friends isn't something I can fathom yet. And doing it quietly feels so goddamn unfair that I want to drag us both in front of a press conference for the chance to ruin it all.

"It's—no, you don't have to—it was one night, and I—" He stops and squeezes his eyes shut. "It was one fucking night."

When I turn toward him on the bench, my knee lands against the top of his thigh. It should be enough for him to look at me again, but his eyes are still closed and I can't do anything but reach for the side of his head, my thumb tracing the curve of his eyebrow.

"You and I both know we're not here because of one night."

Jamie slowly surrenders to the eye contact we need. "Nothing really happened."

"Everything happened."

"And you still want hammocks and frozen lakes."

"In four years," I say, dropping my hand from his face.

I stand a second later because I don't want to stay here for more promises we shouldn't make. He follows my lead, but closes the distance between us, and I'm fiercely relieved we'll have to turn our backs on each other if we want to make it home.

But we don't go anywhere yet.

"Do you want to take your hoodie back now?" he asks.

"No," I answer, my fingertips already digging into the fabric at his sides. My hands cling to him there, and I think I'd scream if the ocean would care. "I want to kiss you. I want to hear all the different ways you can say my name. I want to tell you that you don't have to come out, and I don't have to worry about my job, and neither of us has to worry about Harper, because we can come back to this bench over and over again—to this place where real life will leave us alone. I want so *many* things, but no, I don't want my hoodie back."

Jamie hums and lets me see how much he struggles with his next exhale while he thinks of what else to say. I can't tell whether he's after pain or some relief from it, but then he reaches down to cover my hands with his, forcing me to let him go just as my first teardrop falls.

"Just remember, everyone loves you, Mr. Z. Or could, soon enough."

Relief. Pain.

"I know. And I could love them, too."

Chapter Five: Jamie

(I Told Him Not to Miss Me)

"**Y**es, Harper! That's yours! Go, go, go!"

I'm silent as I drink from my water bottle and listen to Mateo cheer for my daughter. She'd busted her ass to make varsity, and to say I'm overwhelmed watching her hard work pay off would be a massive understatement. The first game of the season is almost over, and Harper's just beat two opposing players to the ball. She's dribbling up the far side of the field and—

"If her coach thinks she's doing a good job, maybe he should've let her play more," Danielle mutters.

I side-eye my ex, then return my attention to the team's offensive push when I answer. "She's a freshman on a team full of talented players. She wasn't sure she'd be playing at all today, so these six or seven minutes are great. He'll probably give her varsity experience as a sub for a while, and she'll earn her way up from there."

"If she'd stayed in club soccer, she wouldn't need a few extra minutes of experience now."

"She decided to quit. *She* did," I say. "I wasn't going to stop her."

Danielle scoffs. "No, of course not."

I'm being baited, but while I'm no stranger to several versions of this fight, it's easy to distract myself with a glance at Mateo. It's been three months since he and I met—two and a half since he walked away from my hillside bench—and this is the closest I've been to him. Harper's success in his class has left me off the hook for the parent-teacher conferences others suffer. Picking her up from soccer practice hasn't required me to leave my car.

I'll be seeing him regularly now, from whatever distance will allow me to act as both attentive father and guarded egotist. Throughout my life, my selfishness has known few bounds. Now I'm afraid of being near the one man who could make me cross those last couple of lines. Harper deserves better, though. So does Mateo. He isn't ready for us to be friends, and I'm not sure he's wrong. I stay where I am and fracture from the inside out.

"He's kinda cute," Danielle muses. "The soccer coach. Maybe I could go talk to him about Harper after the game."

"You're not his type."

She crosses her arms defiantly. "Since when am I not someone's type? For fuck's sake, I was *your* type even after you hated me."

The whistle blows. Harper's team celebrates. I take a long look at Mateo while I know he won't be looking at me. There's a handshake line and a chorus of *good game, good game, good game*. Some parents and friends move closer for congratulatory hugs, and it creates a barrier I can approach without crossing into anything dangerous.

"You should try talking to your daughter about school once in a while," I tell Danielle.

And then I leave her there.

Harper's next game is mostly the same. My ex and I stand shoulder to shoulder while she complains that she knew everyone from club soccer, but doesn't recognize anyone here. I'm still not interested in a fight, especially not when it would draw attention to me so far from my backyard. I mumble a suggestion that she introduce herself to other parents. She goes nowhere, and when Harper subs in for the last ten minutes of the game, Danielle's comments about her lack of play time are unsurprising.

"I know he's gay," she adds after her little fit. That catches me off guard, no matter how much I'd led her there before. "You could've just *said* that."

I shrug, forced nonchalance something I've practiced. "Now you're all caught up."

"Lucky me."

The team loses that game. Whether it's that result or a lack of friends or the disappointment of not being able to seduce Coach Mateo Zavala, Danielle doesn't show up for the next one. Harper and I get separate but equally blithe texts with an excuse that means little. Danielle will make up for it by taking Harper shopping with my money. While Harper isn't stupid, she *is* a 14-year-old who enjoys having her mom's attention and something new to wear to school.

I'm just the ex, and I wouldn't care much about her absence except for how it leaves me exposed. It's early December now, so my hoodie—*mine*—gives me some cover, but more parents wave hello to me, and Mateo can't help but look my way. I wave back to strangers who will become familiar, if not friends. Then, from several feet away, I mourn the distance between me and a man I should've woken up next to weeks ago. His hair is pulled into a tiny bun, and it only makes his profile more striking as he moves up and down the sideline to yell a dozen different things to a dozen different players. Even ignoring my more complicated interest in him, I can tell Mateo is an excellent coach. It tugs at a different desire before I ignore it with the rest of them.

Harper's team wins that one, and two of the next three. Danielle stays away, and I make small talk with a few other parents. With an eye roll I know well, Harper reminds me I'm allowed to say hello to Mr. Z. I wave her off with the excuse that I don't want anyone to think I'm a hotshot athlete overstepping my bounds if I spend too much time chatting with the coach. She rolls her eyes again.

In the next game, Mateo calls Harper's name with about fifteen minutes left, and I smile at her while she stretches. Once she's subbed in, she makes a great defensive play, clears the ball, and her teammates score within seconds. When the whistle blows, they've won again. And after the post-game celebration, when the team wanders off to greet family and friends, I hear my favorite voice in the world.

"Dad! Think fast!"

She's struck the soccer ball hard, and it's headed for a space about ten feet to my right. Her shout obviously helped, but I think instinct moves me as much as anything. My water bottle is still in my hand when I run to stop the ball with the same leg that once shattered under pressure. It's cold out, and the contact hurts, but the pain isn't new, so I grin and dribble toward Harper. She doesn't hesitate to come after me—I assume it was her plan all along—and we battle for control of the ball for a minute or two before the applause starts.

Harper traps the ball beneath her cleats and giggles. I carefully turn toward Mateo.

"Hey, don't let me stop you," he says. "You're only in danger of inspiring me to hold an official parent/player scrimmage this season."

"I'm gonna pretend you're joking. It's been years since my very public retirement, and I think I'm finally adjusting to being a spectator."

Mateo nods, subtle conflict blinked away. "Ah, yes, Harper told me you two have already been to several hockey games this season. Maybe we'll put the scrimmage idea on hold."

I'm not surprised he knows about my time with Harper. They talk five days a week—in class and at practice or games—and I'm to blame for making her tired on at least a few mornings. I'm not sure whether he also knows about the nights I make more professional appearances, but as Mateo's noted, we've driven up to L.A. more than usual. I'm not prepared for him to dissect the reasons why.

I don't think I'm ready for *me* to dissect the reasons why.

Looking for a way out of this conversation, I reach toward Harper. Then a couple of friends yell for her, and she runs off before I can figure out how to explain that I'm in a hurry to be anywhere but here. A second later, I hope Mateo might be in a hurry too, because I know how to watch him go.

He's left me at the bench twice.

He stays now.

"Wasn't sure you'd ever come close enough for a hello. Harper said you didn't want to be all *Jameson Sinclair* about it."

"It was easier than explaining how badly I want to kiss you."

"Of course," he says, glancing around to see whether anyone's overheard me. They haven't. I'm not a stranger to this kind of caution. Mateo changes the subject. "Did Harper ever play hockey?"

"Nope. She skated around with me when she was tiny, but grabbed a neighbor's soccer ball when she was about four, and that became her passion."

"I guess she was probably too young to choose it out of spite," he teases.

I smile because he does. "Probably."

The ball Harper and I had been playing with is still close to me, and Mateo moves for it now. His practiced footwork means he's got full control when he slips behind my back, but I react before I can think it through, spinning to meet him there and strip the ball. He laughs, a sudden and beautiful thing, and easily steals it back, dribbling further away to see if I'll follow.

I don't, only because I can't. Not for another four years. I distract myself with my water bottle and wait to see if he'll be the one to close the distance between us again.

He doesn't, maybe because he can't. Not for another four years.

"Looks like you can take the man out of the competition, but not the competition out of the man," Mateo says.

"Looks like," I agree.

A couple of parents shout their goodbyes, and he waves while still playing with the ball. I stare, context making his soccer skills more mesmerizing than when he was a stranger with a pile of short-notice fun in his trunk. Harper remains entrenched in gossip with her teammates, and when Mateo passes to me, I pass it back as easily as I had the night we met.

"So, you were one of the best centers to ever play in the NHL, but your daughter's one hell of a back," he says. "Is that because any early soccer skills she practiced *with* you meant she had to learn to defend *against* you?"

"Nah. I think *that* was spite." I pout, but I know it's too fond to come across as anything but the adoration it is. "Even little Harper wasn't going to stand for me being an expert in something she could beat me at. If I remember correctly, she put her hands on her hips and said, 'I don't want to score like you do. I want to be the one to stop you.'"

"Well, she seems to have succeeded."

I want to believe Mateo is only talking about soccer, and it's possible he thinks he is. My next breath rattles in my chest anyway. Nodding gives me a moment to recover and a decent chance to begin an awkward goodbye, but now that he's had a second chance to watch me kick a ball around, I'm curious.

"When's the last time you were on ice?" I ask.

"On ice?"

"Have you skated before? Ever held a hockey stick? Shot a puck?"

Mateo's grin lands somewhere between mischievous and suspicious. "I *have* skated, though it's been years, and I'm sure I'd be wobbly now. And no, nobody's put a stick in my hands."

"Somebody should take you skating and put a stick in your hands."

"Come on, Jamie. I know you didn't miss the *wobbly* part of that."

"Okay, then somebody should take you skating and hold you steady before they put a stick in your hands."

Harper returns to us then, sweaty and energized in a way I miss. She's got her backpack now, and I barely realize I have the soccer ball again before she takes it from me and kicks it back to Mateo. As she wipes her forehead with her arm, she begs to stop for pizza on our way home, and I agree, even while too much of my attention remains elsewhere. I don't miss it when Mateo fixes his little bun and never quite looks at me as he responds to what I'd said moments ago.

"I hope somebody does."

Hope is a bitch, but it's all we've got.

The next couple of weeks pass amid contradictions I can't control. The days leading up to Christmas bring joyful chaos and seasonal depression. My house is full of chatter when Harper's home and nearly silent when she's gone. And her soccer games are colder and darker, both dragged out on long tournament days, but I'm welcomed by the bright smiles of other parents and warmed by one careful hello.

Mateo and I haven't had a conversation since the evening I practically suggested a date at the rink. It's enough to be around him for now.

I haven't seen Danielle at all, which is typical. I've seen several former teammates—and a few favorite opponents—at hockey games, and even more at holiday parties. There, among a crowd of people who only sort of care, I'm the center of attention until I become easy to forget. I'm not stupid enough to think it hasn't always been that way.

Coming down from my bullshit highs, I've found myself at Kai's on a few mornings after. I'd texted him back then—after back-to-school night—to say that Mateo and I wouldn't need those barstools anymore. Then I'd avoided him for weeks, and he'd let me. But for as many times as I've been lost, he has never failed to bring me home.

Back to something honest.

Back to the daughter who's laughed more in her childhood than I ever did in mine. I'm glad I did one thing right.

She's at her mom's until late on Christmas Eve. We both sleep in on Christmas morning, but wake up ready for gifts and waffles and far too much hot chocolate. In a few hours, we'll be expected at my parents' house, but for a while it's just Harper and me—and a text from Mateo.

Merry Christmas. I miss you.

I look up to find my kid busy with her own phone, giggling to herself. She and her friends entertain each other with stories about the presents they got, or the presents they didn't, and how much quality time their families will force on them in the name of holiday cheer. It gives me time to change Mateo's contact name to *M*—hardly a difficult code to crack, but slightly less damning at a glance—and then I tap out half a response.

Merry Christmas to you

Ignoring the rest, I mumble something to Harper and leave to take a shower.

Because there are some things I can count on, New Year's Eve comes days after that. Over the past week, I've been to a soccer game and a hockey game and to the bar twice. Now, Harper and Lizzie are at Kate's for the night, and I'm alone without believing for a second that it's a good idea. I try to get invested in any of the celebrations being broadcast from across the country, but nothing holds my attention for long. For a moment, I consider getting dressed just to take my clothes off with a stranger, but there are better levels of stupid within reach tonight.

I pour myself a strong drink. Then another. I watch old episodes of a melodramatic teen drama. A third drink is paired with the laziest version of a charcuterie board anyone has ever seen, and a fourth gets carried upstairs when I decide I don't want to fall asleep on the couch. I'm not drunk, but I'm not sober, and once it's officially January, I pick up my phone.

If I'm supposed to make a resolution about the man who isn't ready to be my friend, it'll have to wait until tomorrow.

Mateo doesn't answer when I call, maybe because he's busy partying in all the ways I'm not. Maybe it's because he's already asleep. A moment later, I swallow hard and wonder whether I'm *Jamie* or *Jameson Sinclair* or *Harper's Dad* in his phone, and why he's ignoring every version of me. Whatever the reason, he's telling me to leave a message, and I do exactly that.

Hey, I—it's New Year's Eve. Well, technically, it's New Year's Day, I guess? But it's the middle of the night, and I need to tell you—fuck—it's—you said you miss *me. On Christmas. You said you miss me, and you can't do* that. *I miss you every fucking day, but I will deal with it and pretend to be okay with waiting, but I need you to pretend, too. I need to believe you're okay. Because it hurts so much, and I don't want you to hurt like this. And I know—I know* you *do. We had one perfect night, and I was ready for a lifetime of everything else, but I can't—you can't remind me you feel the same way. It hurts.*

You miss me, and it hurts. I'm sorry. I don't think that's why I called you, but it's fine. Happy New Year, Mateo. I miss you, too.

By the time I wake up, I remember little of what I said, and he hasn't called back to fill me in. At Harper's next game, I get the same careful hello, and it's still enough to be near him for now.

My birthday comes and goes after Harper and I celebrate with dinner at my favorite seafood restaurant. As her soccer season winds down, she gets more playing time, even starting twice. Danielle reappears when they make the playoffs, a habit I'm familiar with from years ago. When she sulks at their defeat, that's familiar, too. I shrug her off from where I stand, closer to a few parents I've started talking to, and further away from my ex and the man who just feels like one.

Harper is upset by the loss in the way most competitors would be, but she's proud of everything she's learned. I'm proud of her too, and selfish when I count the nine months we'll wait to start again. It would be a good time to take Mateo skating, but my leg throbs and my chest tightens. A couple of weeks later, on the night of the soccer banquet, I do everything wrong. It's not the first time, and it won't be the last.

The banquet is an opportunity to recognize the team and everything they've accomplished over the past several months. Everyone gets a little dressed up, and there's a nice catered dinner, and the coaches give out awards. I take pictures of Harper with her teammates, and of Harper with Mateo. When she runs off for selfies with friends, I shake Mateo's hand and congratulate him on a successful season. His thumb brushes against my skin like it had on the bench, and I pull away before I can ask him to meet me there again. Then I find myself in a conversation with Melanie Bishop, the gorgeous single mother of the team's leading scorer.

We've talked at games, but there's something different in her eyes now. She's intent when she wraps her small hand around my elbow and laughs at something that isn't all that funny. Women have flirted with me since long before it was appropriate to do so, and I recognize it easily now. When I flirt back, I swear it's because I want her to be someone else.

And not because that same someone else is watching.

Nothing really happens—not there in the middle of my daughter's high school soccer banquet. But Melanie wants me to text her sometime, and she wants me to meet her for drinks sometime after that, and she's told me enough about where she lives for me to know she wants me to take her home sometime after *that*.

Nothing really happens, but ten minutes later, when Mateo barely waves goodbye to Harper from across the room, I think maybe I flirted enough to ensure that two of us will have trouble keeping dinner down.

There's no good excuse for me to see him after I leave that night. I only hear about his English class and consider revisiting the classic literature I dodged in my youth. With soccer behind us for now, I find myself waiting for a formal email requesting an in-person meeting about my daughter's academic performance, but none come. I hope for the kind of holiday when he might miss me again, but a look at the calendar confirms none of those are coming either.

If he finds a way to yell at me for talking to Melanie, that would be okay, too. Mateo doesn't pick that fight, and I don't know how I'd defend myself if he tried. I'd just be happy to hear his voice.

In the coming weeks, the mildly cool weather turns mildly warm. Los Angeles is making a playoff run. I've spent hours in my pool because it's the clearest overlap of what I should do and what I want to do. The only drinking I've done has been with Kai. I've got coffee in my hand now, and I'm in my backyard just to stare at the ocean I've seen a million times before.

"Dad, will you drive Lizzie and me to the carnival?"

I turn my back on the Pacific and look at Harper, just barely out of bed on her first morning of spring break, her eyes half open and ready for adventure. Danielle is taking her for a spa retreat in a few days, but she's all mine now. Well, except for wanting to ditch me for some thrill rides and junk food.

I take a sip and smile. "The one at her church?"

"That's the one," she says. "Her sister can pick us up later tonight, but if you could just drop us off—"

"What if *I* want to eat my weight in deep-fried Oreos and be flipped upside down while listening to Metallica from beneath a questionable harness?"

"Then you'll have to bring one of *your* friends. I'm a bratty teenager, remember? Way too cool to be seen with my dad."

"You know, about ten years ago, I was way too cool to be seen with you. It didn't stop the paparazzi from getting decent pictures of the time I won you a giant stuffed polar bear at the Orange County Fair."

She laughs. "And then when I tried to share my cotton candy with it, I added sticky pink streaks to the white fur."

"You sure you don't want me to win you another bear today?"

"I think the ride'll be fine, thanks."

It's a few hours before she's ready to go anywhere, so I work out and shower and mess around on my phone and make myself lunch. When I get dressed, I grab an old t-shirt, old briefs, and my favorite jeans, my service as a chauffeur requiring nothing fancier than that. Harper, of course, has made an effort, and I don't torture myself with the possible reasons why. She's a good kid with a good head on her shoulders, and she talks to me without much of a filter. Will she screw up a few times? Almost definitely. But I don't expect a crisis at a church carnival.

She does make a face at my clothes. "Are you ever gonna throw that shirt away, or are you waiting for it to disintegrate while you're actively wearing it?"

"It's comfortable and clean, and it won't disintegrate *today*," I argue, adding a worn baseball cap for good measure.

Harper shakes her head, but I don't think I'm embarrassing enough for her to find a different way to the carnival. We pick Lizzie up on the way, and I make the quick drive to the Catholic church that's hosted these carnivals for years, even if I was too busy to slow down for one until recently. The parking lot is expectedly full, and I'm not interested in being the asshole who blocks traffic. I mumble something about parking long enough to be out of the way and—

"Oh, hey, we're right next to Mr. Z," Harper says. "Hi, Mr. Z!"

I cut the engine and look through Harper's open passenger-side window because, yeah, we're right fucking next to him. Mateo's just getting out of his car, and I have no doubt he recognizes Harper's voice. Then he turns with the teenage-friendly smile he's usually paid to wear.

"Hi, Harper. Hi, Lizzie," he replies, his smile shifting into something calmly adult when he ducks his head and finds me. "Hi, Jamie. Do I even want to ask which of you three is the biggest thrill-seeker of the bunch?"

"Oh, it's not dad, that's for sure. He'll barf. But Lizzie and I will try everything. We don't care." Harper pauses for a breath. Barely. "But what about you? Are you gonna hit all the rides?"

She's already moving, opening her door enough for Mateo to back against his car while she tumbles out. Lizzie does the same from the back seat before she waves shyly and fixes her tank top. I stay where I am, and think it's probably polite to keep my eyes on Mateo until he answers.

"I'm actually here to help with one of the church booths," he says. "I might sneak in a ride or two, but I'll be working more than playing."

"Teacher, coach, and saintlike volunteer," I nod. "You're far more disciplined than I'll ever be."

"Oh, I don't know about that. I've been known to stay out past my bedtime when the mood strikes."

"Ah, of course. Does the mood strike often?" I ask.

"The mood? Yes," Mateo answers. "The opportunity? Not so much."

Harper bounces on the balls of her feet. "Okay, well, Lizzie and I are gonna go do some upside-down things. Bye, Mr. Z. Dad, I don't know what time I'll be home, but I'll text you later? And you should see if Mr. Z needs some help. Nobody will accuse you of being a hotshot athlete here."

"I'm not exactly dressed to hang out at a carnival, remember?"

"Oh, it's fine. Your shirt won't disintegrate *today*," she giggles, running off with her best friend without caring what I do next.

I sigh. "Sorry about that. She just—says things sometimes."

Mateo sighs too, and I catch it when he steps closer and rests his folded arms against the window opening. His t-shirt is nicer than mine, and his hair is pulled into a messy bun that never had a chance to contain the strands hanging around his face. I want to sweep them away, but my hands are curled around the bottom of the steering wheel. Even without being on a ride, I need to hold on when he smiles again.

"She says a lot of things, yeah. But we could use the help if you're up for it. And if you *are* worried about being recognized, I'll remind you your hat's done a pretty good job of hiding you in the past."

"I want you to remind me of so many things," I admit. "I'm just not sure whether a church fair is the place for it."

"Does that mean you're going home?"

"No."

Mateo takes a deep breath and glances around the parking lot.

"You know, if you drive away now, there's a chance we won't have to do this until soccer season returns. You could go home. You don't have to help, and I don't have to remind you of a damn thing."

"No."

"Okay, let's go," he says, slowly peeling himself away from the passenger door. "You're plenty familiar with tacos and tortilla chips."

I don't understand what he means until we've snaked our way past the crowd of young families and excited teenagers and no small number of couples on dates. We're not any of those, so we don't stop until we're at the carnival's food court. Church volunteers are selling hot dogs, chicken fingers, popcorn, shaved ice—and apparently, nachos and tacos. Stepping behind the cheap plastic table covered by a cheaper plastic tablecloth, I feel Mateo's fingertips against my back as he introduces me to the volunteers we're relieving.

"Jamie, this is Barbara, Eileen, and Rosa. They've all known me since I was a skinny little altar boy. Everyone, this is my friend, Jamie. He's offered to help me out, so all of you are off the hook."

"He says that like we weren't prepared to arm wrestle for the chance to spend the afternoon next to him," one of them mutters with an endearing wink. "But it's very nice to meet you, Jamie."

We all sort of nod and smile and rearrange ourselves, then Mateo and I say goodbye to the ladies, and I look around. We've got meats, cheeses, onions, and jalapeños, and so much of it is familiar to me, albeit from the other side. There are stacks of small paper trays we'll fill quickly. Nachos and tacos get assembled and handed to people who won't stick around long enough for more than a thank you. Our setup is no different from a food truck, but even as my stomach growls and Mateo nudges me with a grin, none of it's the same as the carne asada and guacamole down the street from my house.

It's better that way.

It's better if today is nothing like that night.

CHAPTER SIX: MATEO

(I SAW US IN THE MIRROR)

Regardless of where he lives or how much money is sitting in his bank account, nothing I've seen from Jamie suggests he's a snob about food. Still, it's fun to watch him light up when he pumps bright orange cheese sauce onto a pile of canned chili and tortilla strips. He grins around a ridiculous bite, then hurries to pull on a pair of disposable gloves before he helps me serve more of our hungry crowd.

We're in the middle of a rush, but it hasn't been like this the entire two and a half hours we've worked together, and I'm glad we've had a chance to talk around occasional interruptions. Our small talk means even more than it did the night we met, all of it coming with context we lacked before, and we learn more about each other without attaching promises to every word. I think everything about those hours at the beach crushed us with hope, and while I won't give any of that time back, Jamie and I both need this now.

We've got three more years to wait before our future starts.

"This is really your church, huh?" he asks.

"It really is—has been my whole life."

"Does your family still go here?"

"Most of them," I say, handing over two trays of tacos. "We could run into someone today."

His head whips toward me at that. "Your family? Here? Why didn't you say something?"

"Believe it or not, I wasn't that eager to see that look of terror on your face."

A group of five or six kids runs up to us then, food tickets in their hands, and we swap them for nachos they're likely to drop.

"Are you—I mean, does everyone here know you're—" Jamie stops and looks around until well-practiced composure replaces fear. He could come back with sarcasm and a smile, but I think he always saved his most caustic responses for the press. "Wow. Even at church."

"Even at church, yes," I say. "There were only so many times I could turn down dates with their beautiful, single daughters before they became concerned enough to push for more information."

"And they're fine with it?"

"What did you say earlier? 'Teacher, coach, and saintlike volunteer,' right?" I smile. "But no, I'd say there's been a range of acceptance. The people you met today are on the good end of it. And if Crissy and Isa are around—"

"Crissy and Isa?"

"Cristina and Isabella. My sisters. They said they might be here with their kids, but I haven't heard from them today, so who knows."

"Okay," Jamie says.

His tone makes me wonder whether it is, but I let it go. "What about your family—your parents? Have they ever suspected that you like men? I know there was a rumor a long time ago, but it was buried beneath stories of many beautiful women and no small amount of late-night trouble. What would they say if they knew about me?"

He goes back to his tower of chili cheese nachos for several seconds, then wipes his mouth and sighs from beneath his baseball cap before he answers. "My parents blasted all rumors, no matter what they were. It was easier for them to dismiss everything off the ice as nonsense—orgies, arrests, cocaine, brawls, men—even if it might be true. 'You need to *focus*, Jameson. Make them talk about what you do *on* the ice.'" He sighs again. "You? I don't know what they'd say. I really don't. I let them down when I broke my leg, so maybe I don't have much further to fall."

I'm close to pointing out that a freak accident and a shattered leg shouldn't be causes for parental disappointment, but I've seen worse as a teacher, and Jamie doesn't need a lecture today. I don't know what he *does* need once he's done licking salt from his fingers, and I've tried to push most of what I want aside while I study the sad blue eyes I see in my sleep.

"How much does Kai know?"

"Enough to understand why I'm at the bar alone these days."

I raise an eyebrow. "You were alone the night we met."

"But I hadn't been there in months," he says. "And I wasn't supposed to be alone after."

He isn't alone today. He's here with me, and now I need to figure out what comes next. Then Eileen returns with her husband in tow, and I don't have to ask why before she answers on her own.

"Our grandkids want to stick around for a while, and this guy was pouring our life savings into infinite attempts to land a metal ring around the neck of a bottle," she explains. "Thought I'd drag him back here to keep him out of trouble and give you boys the rest of your shift off."

I glance at Jamie because I'm not sure whether his plans include more time in a place he hadn't meant to be for longer than a minute or two. He glances at me because I'm supposed to speak on our behalf either way.

My response isn't much more than a flustered thanks as we switch places, followed by the press of my fingers against the small of Jamie's back. It means I'm guiding him away from something uncomplicated the same way I'd brought him toward it a few hours ago, and when we find some room to stop, I step away and let my hand fall to my side.

"So," he says.

"So."

Jamie ducks his head for a second or two, then his attention is on me again. "You want to do the rides and games and shit."

"If I have a friend to do them with, yeah," I shrug.

"What about Harper and Lizzie?"

"They already know we're here, and I think they understand two people at a carnival together are not inherently betrothed," I say, pausing a moment later. "Do you really get sick on rides?"

"Only the ones that look like literal death traps."

I chuckle and wave my arm toward one of the ticket booths. "Let's go buy wristbands, and then you can lead the way."

We do, and he does, and for a while, the two of us wander from one end of the carnival to the other. There's no hurry as we point out the things we'll return to soon, and there's no pressure to talk much either. We know how to be quiet. It's been true all along, and we walk with it now.

Our first ride together is the Tilt-A-Whirl, and it's almost unbearably sweet, this former hockey agitator and superstar opting to start with a simple carnival classic. It makes perfect sense somehow, and from there we go to the swings, our legs dangling in the air like we're better at fighting gravity than time. We trade a few silly shouts mid-ride, and the levity continues after we land, conversation more comfortable as we adjust to the idea of having fun together.

A break for games comes next. First, we toss wiffle ball after wiffle ball into chalices, a stupid amount of concentration at war with our grins. It's almost as though our respective skills could possibly come into play in this game of lucky bounces, and we tease each other endlessly about it. We shoot water into clowns' mouths after that, but both of us lose to a girl missing her two front teeth, and more laughter carries us to the next game.

It's one I know well. A favorite, actually. Sibling battles were fierce when I was a kid, but I could beat my sisters at this more than they beat me, even if there's probably luck involved here, too. We're going to roll balls into numbered holes, racing to move our horses from start to finish, and when Jamie rushes to sit down, I'm at his side quickly. I'm overwhelmed by the urge to tell him a hundred stories, but while we wait for more players to join—more people means bigger prizes!—I try to bite my tongue and look anywhere else.

I end up staring at his t-shirt.

Jamie's already acknowledged that he hadn't dressed for plans to get out of his car. He and Harper joked about it. And his jeans are great—I've admired them a couple of times today—but I'm not confident his shirt *won't* disintegrate. It's worn so thin, and while I'm not complaining about seeing more of him, I reach for a small tear at his side. My finger slips through and grazes his skin, and it doesn't escape me that I've never touched him here before. When he trembles, I think it hasn't escaped him either. I haven't looked up yet, but I don't think he's dared to look down, and I take another few seconds to find the weakest version of my voice.

"I could've looked in my trunk again. I could've found you something to wear."

"Will it make anything better if I have a closet full of your clothes?" he asks.

We're interrupted then, but it's probably for the best. I pull my hand away so I can play, and I swear the heavy beat of my heart is keeping time with childhood memories and nothing more recent than that. It slows me down though, and Jamie wins a stuffed penguin while I finish in the middle of the pack.

"Congrats," I say once we're a few steps away. "Are you going to give that to Harper?"

"I always have," he smiles, tilting his head when he lets it turn into a smirk. "You're not mad that I won, are you?"

"Why would I be mad?"

The smirk is slow to fade, but then he shakes his head. "I'm hungry."

With a stuffed animal in his hand and holes in his shirt, he leads us back toward the food court. We stop before we're anywhere near the tacos we abandoned, and I feel like I should've known where we'd end up long before we arrived. The funnel cake smells predictably incredible, but I pause incredulously when I catch Jamie studying the small menu.

"Really? Funnel cake and powdered sugar aren't enough on their own? You have to add *toppings*?"

"Mmmm, pretty sure powdered sugar counts as a topping."

I roll my eyes. "Okay, yes, but you're adding extra toppings."

"And mango chipotle wings were going to be your big end-of-summer adventure," he points out.

"Tough talk from the guy who will vomit if we go on a big-kid ride."

Jamie bursts out laughing—a literal eruption of sound that turns a few heads—and I'm proud of myself for making it happen. When he quiets long enough to order, he ends up with strawberries, Nutella, *and* powdered sugar. I'm content with my more traditional treat.

We look for a table nearby, but everything is taken, and I'm glad I know my way around. It's not much longer before we're sitting on the ground on the back side of several booths, a bunch of cardboard boxes and someone's golf cart keeping us company. I frown when Jamie stretches a leg in front of him, disappointed in myself for not thinking this through.

"It's fine," he says.

And I leave it at that.

Eating keeps us from talking for the next minute or two, neither of us making sounds more coherent than mumbled pleasure. We watch each other because it's easier when nobody's watching us, and I smile around a mouthful of sugar. Then I glance at the penguin in Jamie's lap and let myself feel too many things until I swallow comfort and reach for something else.

"So," I start, that single syllable dragged too far. "How's Melanie Bishop?"

He's sinful about the way he sucks the tips of his fingers clean, but I don't know whether it's aimed at me or just how he is. I wipe my fingers on a napkin and wait.

"You're good at a lot of things, Mateo—"

"Teacher, coach—" I interrupt.

"But you're shit at casual jealousy," he snaps back. It's gentle, mostly. An admonishment not meant to sting for more than a moment. I think I flinch anyway, barely looking at him when he goes on. "I haven't seen her since the banquet."

"She seemed interested in seeing plenty of you."

"She was," Jamie says.

"You didn't seem *un*interested."

Jamie goes back to eating, but I think I've had enough. I set my paper plate on the grass and close my eyes, the many sounds of the carnival giving me something to focus on while I scrape the rest of an argument off my tongue. We don't get to spend much time together, our long wait for each other crowded with distance. It would be stupid to waste this chance we've got.

He touches me, a careful, barely-there thing, and it's a lot like his pinky reaching across a blanket at the beach. I'm at least as far gone now as I was then.

"Does the Scrambler count as a big-kid ride?" Jamie asks.

I look at him again when I playfully shove him away. A minute later, we're walking across the fair to the chaos we'd left behind, and I'm as excited to get back to this as he is. If the Scrambler is a bad idea with a stomach full of funnel cake, neither of us worries about it now, but maybe we should've worried about the physics of the ride itself. Once it hits full speed, we're pressed together with no finesse at all, and the giggles consume us before and after Jamie uses his stuffed penguin to block the next unintentional hip check.

We go from there to the giant slide and a pile of burlap sacks, a couple of small children the only reason we're careful not to race. Then it's off to darts and underinflated balloons, and a few more tries with wiffle balls, even more ridiculous about our competition now. Jamie's earlier win remains the only one of the day, and he taunts me with it because he knows he can. After we wander a while longer, I point to another ride.

"How do you feel about Ferris wheels?"

"Sitting next to you while we enjoy fresh air and a nice view?" he asks. "It's familiar."

I glance toward the sky, then return to him. "It's certainly some-thing."

Whether it feels good to joke around the hollow ache in my chest, I don't know, but Jamie is studying me as if he might figure it out. It won't do either of us any good to stand here though, and I walk toward the line because I know he'll follow. Within minutes, we're tugging on the lap bar and ignoring instructions we don't need, then moving further from the ground to a hard rock soundtrack that fades as we rise. It's all start and stop for as long as it takes to load several more riders, and I'm lulled by the rhythm of it.

We become nearly invisible the higher we go, and I hold his hand because I break my own rules sometimes.

He lets me, but I think he's crossed lines since people learned his name.

"Tell me more about your family," he says, his voice just louder than the music.

"It's a longer story than we have time for up here," I warn, frowning a little because I know it's the opposite for him, an only child who sought off-ice comfort at a bar owned by his best friend's dad.

Jamie squeezes my hand. "The short version?"

"Ah, let's see. My mom was young when she had me, and she didn't know my biological father. Not even his name. She met my dad just before I turned five. He and his mother—my grandmother—took me in as their own from the very beginning. His father never really has."

"What'd he have against you? You were *five*."

"I wasn't his family," I shrug, the Ferris wheel finally full and moving without interruption. "Worse than that, I was clingy with my mom. Soft-spoken. Weak. He's every macho stereotype, and I wasn't someone he thought worthy of being my dad's first-born—literally or otherwise. Once I started school, and my sisters came along, I adjusted to being around more people and I changed, but he never stopped thinking of me as a mama's boy—or calling me that outright."

Jamie nods. "And being gay didn't help."

"No. So, I've lived my life, but I've also kept a low profile. No trouble. No reason for anyone to regret making my mom and me part of their family."

"Boring as self-defense."

"Something like that," I agree.

"But you're close to your sisters."

"Very. I'm close to everyone else, really. My grandmother, my parents, my sisters, their husbands and kids. I have no complaints about my life. I really don't."

Unspoken rebuttals stay that way, and Jamie lets go of my hand. Untethered, we enjoy the fresh air and the nice view as we go around and around, music and laughter louder on every downswing, and then quieting again. I push away most of the noise in my head and appreciate where I am, stupidly grateful he stashed the penguin on his other side while we're in no danger of crashing into each other.

The space between us is plenty.

By the time we're back on solid ground, it feels very little like it. Nothing under our feet has been stable since the first time we stepped from the sidewalk to the sand, but we keep walking anyway. The back of my hand brushes his now and then, and I think we're making a lap around the carnival to avoid making decisions about anything else.

"You called me your friend today," Jamie says after another minute. "Twice."

I remember introducing him that way and forget when else I might have said it, but I trust his ability to count to two.

"Is there a better word for what we are right now?"

"I suggested that once—that we be friends. You weren't sure you could do it." He doesn't waste more time reminding me of things I already know, but he slips further away from my side. "We don't really talk."

"We don't. You said I'm not allowed to tell you I miss you—that I'm not allowed to tell you I hurt like you do. And sometimes it's hard to know what else to say."

"Is that what I left on your voicemail? On New Year's? I know I called you, but I didn't—it was late and I—"

"And you were drunk."

"It was New Year's," Jamie says again. "But you stopped saying those things anyway."

"Probably because you were right."

"So, we can be friends as long as we lie about how we feel?"

I stop short at that. There's an omission technicality, but I don't point it out. "Do you think we've lied today?"

"I haven't," he tells me.

"Good. Neither have I."

A couple of toddlers run past us, chased by their tired parents. I smell popcorn and fries. Then a mob of teenagers—Harper and Lizzie nowhere among them—giggles and pushes and shoves and laughs as they tumble by. It's all so normal, and as soon as there's room to do so, I follow, speeding up like I can have more of that and less of whatever made me stand still.

Nothing is wrong. Jamie and I are no worse off than we were before. But after we've walked another several minutes in relative silence, it makes perfect sense that we find ourselves in front of the funhouse without having spoken about it first. As long as we're unsteady, we might as well get lost in an attraction designed for it.

The darkness is abrupt, but it could be good for us. The narrow halls put Jamie just behind me, and the first moving walkway is enough reason for his free hand to land at my hip. He takes it back just as quickly, and we climb wobbly stairs before walking through a spinning tunnel and past mirrors that stretch us out or squash us down. There's a ladder we can barely trust, and more metal plates shifting beneath our feet, and then we run into another series of mirrors—literally, actually—a maze welcoming us with maniacal laughter piped through a speaker overhead.

I think I laugh too, collisions impossible to avoid when we don't know where else to go. Some kids scurry past us, and then we're alone for another minute, Jamie using those precious seconds to push his body against mine. With his chest to my back, we're facing a mirror we'll need to sidestep eventually, but for now, I freeze. It's the first time I've seen us together, and even this blacklit visual is enough to choke me up.

We're gorgeous like this. We're *right* like this.

Jamie moves us anyway.

We land further away from the exit, staring at each other in a corner that will do no good for fair-goers who want a way out. We're still in public, but nobody could capture a decent picture among the mirrors and darkness, and it leaves us with a bubble I'll deny we're in, and makes it so the time we spend together doesn't count.

Again.

My back is pressed to the glass, and I'm the one more likely to break when Jamie reaches for my head and uses one hand to pull my hair tie free, a stuffed carnival prize still dangling from the other.

"I like when it's down like this," he says, his voice heavy from a day that should've been weightless.

I try to smile. "Not a fan of the ponytail? Or the tiny man bun?"

"I'm a fan of everything. But when it's down, it's like you've let something go. Like you've stopped caring so much."

"I care about everything."

Jamie nods and tugs on my hair, watching closely to see what I'll do. My hands move to his waist, and he whimpers when one of my thumbs finds another hole in his t-shirt, brushing bare skin there for the second time today. The speakers continue to crackle with something almost hysterical, and my thumb keeps moving. I know I need to push him away, but he grabs my wrist.

"Please don't," he begs. "Not yet."

I look over his shoulder in time to catch a glare from someone too focused on us to have fun getting lost. I'm glad Jamie wasn't the one to see it, and I opt for the most selfish way to forget, burying my face in the warm crook of his neck. I whisper something he can only feel, and I'll swear later it wasn't a kiss. Leaving one small patch of skin behind, I reach for him everywhere, and he arches into me, our hands roaming until they curl into fists and hold nothing. We hiss and swear and fall silent so we don't say the wrong things, all of this more than my boring life will allow.

Eventually, Jamie finds words when I have none.

"I know it was my idea first, but I don't know how to be friends with someone like you. I barely know how to be a friend at all. There are people I've played hockey with, and there's Kai, who might as well be my brother. But you—" He's almost panting against my ear before he trails off to pull my hair again. He only goes on when I look at him. "We haven't lied today, but there's still so much time between now and the rest of our lives, and this mirrored maze isn't ours to keep."

Jamie's kind when he ignores the way I shiver, but I succeed in pushing him away this time, the tension between us dangerous when we're surrounded by glass.

"That was poetic," I say roughly. "Have you been helping Harper with her homework?"

Cracking a joke might be callous or clever, but after staring at me for several more seconds, Jamie takes the out I've offered. We hear the squeals of a group catching up to us, and I blink myself out of what might have been a funhouse fever dream, hurrying to follow him past the last couple of mirrors and down the spiral slide that returns us to the ground. The evening light is striking when we land, and Jamie's there to help me up, the smile on his face one I've missed since our last round of midway games.

"Where are we going now?" I ask.

"I think I'm gonna go home," he tells me as we wander away from a few different crowds. "This day has been—it was unexpected. Seeing you here at all, and then deciding to stay, and whatever just happened in there."

"Okay, yeah. I should probably go back and see if anyone needs help before I leave. But then we can—maybe some other time—"

"We can be friends and liars?"

I nod, my next exhale far shakier than I'd like it to be when I can't find a way to keep him with me. "Goodnight, Jamie. Thank you for the unexpected."

He doesn't smile then. He doesn't say goodnight or leave me either. Instead, he steps forward and pushes a stuffed penguin against my chest.

"This is for you."

I cling to it, but I'm on the verge of giving it back. "You told me you were going to give it to Harper."

"No, I told you I always *have* given them to Harper," he says. "Nobody else was ever worth it."

"What about her mom?"

Jamie swallows a quick laugh. "Danielle? Ah, no. I showered her with expensive gifts that meant nothing. In hindsight, some carnival prizes might've helped lower a few of her expectations."

"Are you trying to lower mine?"

"Would it work?"

"No."

"Didn't think so. It kinda feels like a ship that might've sailed while we watched from the beach." He sighs then, and glances toward the parking lot before he returns to touch the top of the penguin's head and stare cautiously at me. "Sorry. That was probably poetic, too."

"Don't apologize, Jamie. Just try to be friends with me."

He waits until the next day to text. I wait longer to call. Sophie's on a trip with college friends, but I interrupt her vacation long enough to update her on my day at the fair, and I wonder whether Kai has heard anything new about me.

It would make sense to hang out with Jamie again—as friends or liars—while I'm still on spring break, but spending time with him so soon would tempt me to look for our reflection again, and I'd pretend I can't see the reasons to wait.

It's not until I've returned to work that he admits Harper went away with her mom the second half of the week, and we could've seen each other without him having to answer questions about who and where and why. His decision to keep that distance between us is no different from mine, and I don't know whether I'm more mad or sad or resigned that he hasn't forced my hand.

Maybe it'll be safer to hang out when I can't remember the view from a Ferris wheel, and Jamie has responsibilities to call him home, but I decide I can't wait that long.

A few weeks after spring break, I ask him to go on an easy hike with me—more of a nature walk, really—along a trail in a nearby canyon, and he agrees before the invitation is fully out of my mouth. Meeting there earlier than he's usually out of bed means fewer people to examine the degree of our friendship. We have little company as we come together and fall apart until we simply stay shoulder to shoulder and talk about some of the most innocent things. As was true for most of the carnival, we're not crossing any lines. And as was true by the end, there's a time limit on everything, including our self-control.

We return to where we'd left our cars at the trailhead, and when I open my back door to grab an extra water bottle, Jamie steps close enough to pin me in that space. He could be eager for a drink, but the tip of his nose is against the back of my neck, just beneath a bun he might take away. We're sweaty, our t-shirts clinging to us on such a warm morning, and when I turn to face him, our curious hands are tempted by damp fabric. We pull the shirts over each other's heads and stand there breathless and stupid until I remember to shake my head and he remembers to back away.

Our goodbyes come quickly after that, and several days pass before either of us says more.

Once the school year ends in the middle of June, it would make sense for us to try again. Harper isn't in my class anymore, having finished with an A that was never in question, and with soccer still months away, she's an easier obstacle to ignore. But she's also *the* obstacle, more so than my current job and Jamie's former one, and we react by staying apart. Or I react by telling him we should stay apart, and he agrees because we don't know how to fight about it instead.

In those weeks, I meet up with my sisters and their families, and I go to my parents' house for dinner, and I make the long drive to visit my grandparents because it's worth it to see the smile that used to coax me out from behind my mother's legs.

There's an English department get-together one weekend, and Sophie and I stroll the farmers market and go to the movies often. We run into a few parents, students, and coworkers throughout the summer, and it's a reminder of how easy it is to be recognized in public, and why the promise of privacy exists only at home. She and I also have the luxury of snuggling on my couch or hers. We share a bed, and we hug all the time. I'm an affectionate person, and being affectionate with the people I'm close to comes naturally to me, but

I know it'll be different with Jamie. He had said he doesn't know how to be friends with someone like me, but I'm not convinced I know how to be friends with someone like him either. We've done it poorly twice.

Possible things continue to feel impossible when I think we can't go out because of him, and we can't stay home because of me. I do my best to explain it to him without the lies our friendship doesn't deserve. But fantasies, even consistently kept to myself, become restless nuisances when I forget how he tastes and do everything I can to remember.

And I'm nowhere naive enough to believe he hasn't done the same.

Still, I can come with Jamie's name on my tongue, and it won't matter as long as he can't hear me. That's the thing about fantasies—they're not real; they're just all we get for now. I moan into my pillow that night because it's probably better than screaming.

We talk the next day, and plenty after that.

We don't see each other again until the first soccer scrimmage of Harper's sophomore year.

CHAPTER SEVEN: JAMIE

(I WENT TO NEW YORK)

My first games of the season had always brought about a thrum of energy. That combination of excitement and nerves. A lot of "I can't wait to get back out there" and "Am I ready for this?" Most of it was eager anticipation. There'd always been a hint of fear that it could all go wrong. And a lot of those feelings have returned sharply today.

Things can change from one year to the next.

So much stays the same.

As I watch Harper take the field—she's a starter now—I think I feel Mateo's eyes on me. I also think it can't be true when he has a team to worry about, and he could've looked at me a dozen times over the past few months if he'd wanted. Instead, we greeted each other minutes ago with a friendly handshake and clapped shoulders.

A *friendly* handshake. Because we're friends.

Or we're friends enough to text and call and share stories and learn more about each other, even if we're not the kind of friends who go out to eat or visit each other at home. I get it, though. I really do. There's never been a time I've seen him and not come close to begging for another five minutes or one more touch. Mateo won't invite me to dinner just to listen to me go hoarse with need.

Hearing his voice or remembering his smile is enough to push me over the edge when I'm hard and wet and wanting, but that confession won't earn me another invitation either. Friends probably don't want to spend happy hour trying to forget about the shooting star that made them dream of being hard and wet and wanting together.

Harper's team wins that scrimmage. The season continues to go well for them after that. Danielle shows up a few times. Melanie and I talk more than once. Mateo and I see each other at least a couple of times a week, right there on the sideline. Christmas and New Year's pass with sober texts omitting half the truth. I turn another year older and spend it watching a hockey game while my leg aches.

"You know you could ask *him* out," Kai growls, fed up with my sulking on a random Wednesday night in early February.

I look around the mildly busy bar, then down at the stupid fucking mango chipotle wings I ordered. "You make it sound like we're dating."

"What you two are doing is so much worse than that. Waiting *years* for each other? That's some freaky tragic romance shit."

Over the next few days, I think about asking Mateo out to dinner. Or we could meet for drinks. Or just a movie. I could wear my hat pulled low, or his hoodie pulled up, and everything could be like the night we met, when we weren't friends at all.

But whether those feel like dates or freaky tragic romance shit, I do nothing but kick a wayward soccer ball his way when I see him again.

At the end-of-the-season banquet, we spend more time together than we did the year before. It would be unnecessary if we could remember how to do it anywhere else. Harper receives the Most Improved Player award, and I'm reminded the night has nothing to do with me. She has two more years of high school soccer to play, and I can't wait to see the ways she succeeds before she graduates. I won't wish away time with her, but it doesn't stop my heart from keeping more than one beat.

In the weeks that follow, I'm scheduled for autograph signings with other former NHL stars because the things I touch are still worth something. I continue to appear during a handful of game broadcasts because my name still gets attention and my face still keeps it. I get asked to pose for pictures everywhere, and I love it because I'm wanted and wanted and wanted.

Mateo and I text between obligations. We talk a few times a month. My leg throbs with pain I wanted gone a long time ago. My chest aches for things that haven't happened yet. Another notification appears on my phone, and I smile at the *M* I put there more than a year ago, doing my best to ignore how much I still hurt about it, too.

Spring break comes around again, and Harper's just turned 16. We get an invitation from Taylor McKeon, my fiercest rival-turned-acquaintance. He offers to host us at his sprawling vacation home in upstate New York, and Harper agrees to the trip because she thinks Taylor's son is hot. I agree because it's three time zones away from home. She and I arrive, and it's gorgeous in this different world. More than a dozen of us—mostly former players and a few gorgeous women—are spending the week together. We forget about the rest of our lives as much as the rest of our lives will allow.

Of course, it's the end of the regular season when we're in New York, and most of us are watching the playoff race closely. During one game, we're surprised and unsurprised by the secret Taylor spills in the privacy of his own home. He hasn't played in years, but he's no better at staying away from the game than I am, and I feel the sting of envy when I hear the news we've all promised not to repeat until the story breaks. I'm never far from hockey, but the lake has thawed and Taylor's extra skates remain piled in his garage. My wishes have to hold for another day.

There's other fun to distract me, especially because this group of adults isn't known for following rules. Those of us with kids are aware enough of what's happening to be considered responsible. When the few teens aren't on their phones, they're pushing boundaries, but they're as safe as they can be under this giant roof—or within a loud whistle—and we leave them to it. I'm probably laughing and drinking more than they are when my phone rings.

"Hey," Mateo says after I answer. "Do you want to guess where I am?"

I pull my phone away from my ear and squint to read the time. Math is mostly beyond me, but I'm just okay enough to figure out that it's still afternoon in California. Then I remember I spent one of those with him a year ago.

"Are you sitting in the shade, enjoying several toppings on your funnel cake?"

"Ah, I knew I forgot to do something before I got on this Ferris wheel."

"Oh," I say. Maybe it's a sigh. I move toward the patio doors, a beer in my hand. "You're really on it right now?"

"I really am. The view isn't quite as good as I'd hoped."

That stings. Mateo could have almost any view he wants, and mixed with alcohol, his comment makes me bitter tonight. "Guess you're in for a real disappointment when you reach the funhouse maze."

"I'm not sure I want to get lost alone," he says, and that's definitely a sigh.

"Even if I want to believe that's some sort of sideways invitation

from a man who hasn't seen me since a soccer banquet in February,
I can't run into you at the fair today. I'm in New York with Harper
and some friends."

"So, you have those now?"

It's borderline cruel, that question, and more my style than his,
but it has me turning to look around anyway. Harper and the other
kids are upstairs playing video games. Everyone else is spread out
around the family room and kitchen, louder and more fake than
Mateo's been a day in his life. I'd easily agree to catch a game with
half of them, but we wouldn't talk much. What would we even say
when we're not bullshitting a crowd?

"You know I don't," I answer, stepping further away from people
who don't notice. "Even the one I thought was different—"

I don't know how to finish my sentence, and Mateo fills the
silence. "I am different."

"But you don't want to spend time with me."

There's noise then—the distant clatter of metal and the mumbled
thanks signaling the end of his ride—and Mateo returns with a
derisive laugh. "You can tell me you're arrogant and selfish all you
want, but I don't believe for a second you're that stupid."

"It's been almost a year, unless you think sharing a sideline brings
friends closer together."

"Almost a year, but I've *never* stopped wanting to spend time with
you, and I've *never* stopped being your friend," he hisses. "We get too
comfortable when we're together. It's too easy to be near you, which
makes it so damn *hard* to stay apart. And I know you're willing to
keep trying, but I can't keep being the one to stop us. I'm not that
strong."

"There are things we can do—"

"And we could get away with it," Mateo finishes. "We could stop
waiting and sneak around and cross all those lines. We could stop

lying to each other and only lie to the rest of the world. But it wouldn't be fair to Harper. It wouldn't be fair to Sophie and Kai, who'd almost certainly have to cover for us at some point. And it sure as hell wouldn't be fair to *us*. We deserve an actual chance at this, and Harper's almost done with her sophomore year. We're almost halfway there."

I think I was going to suggest ways we could be actual friends, without sneaking around, but I'm too tired to make those promises. I gulp at my beer before I pout for nobody.

"So the next two years will be spent on the phone?"

"I don't want them to be."

"But?"

"I don't know," he says.

There's more fight to pick, if fighting is what we've been doing at all. I could apologize for being the way I am and try to explain that this is why nameless encounters have always suited me best. I could plead for a chance at friendship and swear that I can stop us, too. But Mateo won't talk all night, and Taylor's sister approaches me now, swapping my empty bottle for a full one right after she takes a sip and winks.

I wink back, then squeeze my eyes shut. "We'll be home next week, so I'll text you then."

"I'll have more free time once the school year's over. And I'm guessing you'll be all over the L.A. games until their playoff run is up."

Maybe I should be excited by the implication that he's caught any of my on-air appearances, but I only hear the excuses he's making. Taylor's sister scrapes her fingernails over my chest, and I think I'm wanted and wanted and wanted.

My goodbye to Mateo is barely a breath. When he's gone, I glance toward the family room, and whatever everyone's busy with there.

Swallowing more beer is a challenge around the lump in my throat, but I manage eventually when I'm just drunk enough to smile.

"Hey, there's that pretty face," she coos. Her name might be Bailey, but I'm not sure I care when she curls a hand around my side. "You didn't look happy during that call."

Indignation flares, but she's probably right. "It's over now."

"Good, then come down to the basement. My friend and I are bored, and she'll like your pretty face a lot."

I go. They both like a lot of things about me. I give far more than I take, by choice or by default, but it can't last forever. Nothing ever does. And when I finally return to my guest room, I take a shower and jerk off to thoughts of the man who missed me enough to call from the middle of a carnival.

Mateo is busy until the end of the school year. I'm busy with Stanley Cup hype amid some unexpected success and the reminder that L.A. hasn't done this well since the year I won the Conn Smythe. I text him and he texts me, but little of it makes a difference.

As soon as it's officially summer, and hockey's behind me again, Danielle takes Harper to Hawaii for a couple of weeks. I swim more laps than I can count. A few days later, I drive to Vegas for a bachelor party and a few nights in clubs that offer a very different kind of therapy. It takes me a while to recover after I'm back home, and I turn to the pool again, swimming naked this time because I was too lazy to go upstairs for swim trunks. I'm feeling as dramatic as the night I ran away to Kai's, but once I'm underwater, I'm not sure I want to give up my house anymore.

I'm not sure I want to give up the bench.

I'm just pulling myself out of the pool when I hear the doorbell through the patio doors I left open an hour ago. I'm not expecting anyone, but I hurry to pat myself dry. Then I fight with cotton sweatpants that don't move well over damp skin. Once I'm halfway decent, I consider finding my phone to check my security app, but a scavenger hunt doesn't interest me.

The doorbell rings again as I pass the kitchen, and I swear out loud. I'm not convinced I'll actually answer the door, but I've got a peephole for a reason, and I shuffle close enough to use it. After blinking and refocusing, my first reaction is confused elation. My second is skepticism. My third is something pathetic, and it clings to me when I open the door.

And then I wait too long to speak.

"Can I come in?" Mateo asks, after I've done nothing but stare.

My hair is dripping onto my shoulders, and I look down at my bare chest and gray sweatpants, the fabric darkened by the spots where I wasn't completely dry. Then I rub my hand over the scruff on my jaw, fully aware he looks better unshaven than I do. He waits patiently, and uses the time to look at my bare chest and gray sweatpants too, close to sheepish when I shrug and back up.

With the door closed behind us, I wave him toward the rest of the house. "I should probably get dressed. Or more dressed, I guess. If you're staying."

"I'd like to."

I nod and let him help himself to my kitchen or the great room or wherever else he'd like to be. In my bedroom, I dry my hair better and find a t-shirt to wear. I'm careful to check for holes Mateo could be tempted to touch, because I know that's not why he's here. Then I look down at my sweatpants and realize I'm hurt and confused enough to want to tempt him somehow, so I stop before changing into my jeans. He showed up unannounced. If he sees more of me than he wants to, he can leave unannounced, too.

When I get back downstairs, I find him facing the patio doors to stare at my backyard—or past it, to a horizon we know well—and it finally hits me he's never been in my house before. It sucks that it's taken so long, and I don't know what Mateo wants from me today. I watch him comb a hand through his hair, and I do the same to mine.

"Didn't feel like climbing up from the rocks?"

"Seemed even more presumptuous than ringing the doorbell without an invitation," he answers without turning around.

"You don't need an invitation. Ever." I pause and cross the room. "How long did you sit in your car before you made it to the front door?"

"Long enough to think about throwing my car into reverse and never telling you I was here."

"Why didn't you?"

He huffs. "I wasn't sure whether you'd catch me on a security camera."

I'm close enough to stare over his shoulder, but I keep several inches between us. "You're not here to go skinny-dipping with me."

"I'm not here for the view either."

"Are you here to end this?"

Mateo whips around to look at me, his brown eyes ready to swallow me whole. "End this? I—is that what you—"

He stops talking, and if I'm supposed to finish his sentence, I fail, dropping my gaze instead. There are too many directions this conversation could go, and at least half of them would haunt me. Whatever low moments I've had, most of them have happened away from home. I'm not eager to bring one inside today.

His shorts show off muscular thighs, not unlike the ones I've seen in a lifetime of locker rooms. I look away to study a scar on the palm of my hand.

"Got this when I was nine. Grabbed a teammate's skate, blade first, because I wasn't thinking. I do that a lot—not thinking things through. I've never learned."

"And you're the one who bleeds and scars," Mateo starts, surprising me when he takes my hand and presses his thumb to a 30-year-old wound. "I assume your teammate was fine."

I swallow all the sounds that will remind him we're not supposed to touch. I frown because I think I was trying to make a point about how my recklessness hurts the people around me. He's still holding me like he knows I'm about to fuck up again, and with my warning ignored—and my impulsivity still high—I stumble toward another mistake.

"You know Harper isn't here, don't you?" I ask. "You know nobody is here to catch us. You know we could close our eyes and jump and fuck it all up. You know that if you're not ending this, we have enough privacy to get away with things we've waited two years to have."

"Yes, I know. But I'm not here to close my eyes and get away with anything, and I'm not here to end this. Not really."

"Not really?" I echo, pulling my hand back while my heart screams.

"My grandfather is sick, and my grandmother needs help around the house. They live about two hours away, and I'm on summer break, so I'm—" He pauses to take a deep breath and never looks away. "Everyone else has kids or work, but going away right now won't mess with my job. I can stay there for a while."

"You're leaving."

"For a while," Mateo says again.

"And you came over to tell me in person."

"I came over to see you before I go. I miss you and I'm tired of not saying that."

I look toward the backyard, and a bench I can't see. "I miss you too, but what happens if we're not going to lie about that? We're friends who haven't spent any time together—"

"In a year, like you said when you were in New York."

"So what changes if we tell the truth?"

"I'll be gone the rest of the summer," Mateo says, and I don't care that he's ignored my question when I'm distracted by hair I want to tuck behind his ear. "There's a chance I won't see you again until after school starts."

"Harper will be a junior."

"It should be a good season for us."

He's talking about soccer, but I want the *us* to mean more. Almost two years ago, we drove away from Kai's and toward the rest of our lives, and it still feels so far from where we are now. Something good would be great, but I expect Harper's team to succeed where Mateo and I can't. I shove my hands in my pockets to keep from reaching for the man I so badly want to stay.

Of course, his plans to leave mean I have little to lose by asking for exactly that.

"Don't go."

"Jamie—"

"I don't mean to your grandparents' house," I say. "But now. Here. You're gonna walk away anyway, so spend the day with me first. Give us something more to miss. Give us a different way to hurt. Let us fuck up with our eyes wide open."

There's so much happening when a few expressions play across his face, and I can't predict what he'll do. He's mad at me for wanting to cross this small line. He wants us to cross them all. He's sorry that this will be the last time we see each other for weeks. Months. He's hopeful an afternoon at my house will lead to fewer regrets than whatever happened among mirrors and canyons. He knows very few people say no to me. He thinks he should be one of them, even when he's desperate for the same delicate pain he already knows.

Mateo looks me up and down, then glances over his shoulder to squint at the summer sun. I can't take my eyes off him right away, this man close to surrendering to borrowed time because I've asked, and we both know he could've said goodbye on the phone.

"Let's sit by the pool," he finally says. "We can talk."

I slip past him to open the door and lead us into the backyard. I'm not sure what he had in mind—there are patio chairs around a table or lounge chairs lined up poolside—but I lower myself to the stone surrounding the pool. I tug my sweatpants up to my thighs before putting my feet in the water, and it exposes scars I hadn't expected him to see like this. There's more than one way to fuck up an afternoon together.

Mateo sits next to me and looks at my leg without pretending otherwise. "I guess swimming helps, even after all these years. Low-impact, as a physical benefit. Almost meditative, as an emotional one."

"Maybe I just like being naked out here."

"Maybe you do," he smiles, his feet slowly kicking back and forth. "So, did you really spend spring break at Taylor McKeon's house?"

"Did you really look me up online?"

"I wanted to know who your other friends were."

The bitch in me wants to say something about still not having those, but if I can't let Mateo go, I at least need to avoid old arguments with him. Then there's a flare of panic when I remember Taylor's sister and her friend and a basement nowhere near as warm as the shower I took afterward, but I don't think I've been lured into a trap.

"What did the internet have to say?"

"A lot about your rivalry, on and off the ice. A recap of how he set records about ten years before you came along to break them, and how his success with women might've been the one way he had you beat, no matter how much the league plastered your face everywhere."

"He and Danielle slept together once."

Mateo's quick huff of surprise is gentle. "Really?"

"Really," I say. "He'd retired. I was still playing. There was a gift basket in my hotel room that night with a card that read, 'You scored just fine on the ice, but I did even better in your bedroom.'"

"Holy shit."

"It was whatever. By that time, scoring on the ice mattered more to me." I look up at a cloudless sky and push away the past. "Was there anything about Taylor's big announcement?"

"That he'll be coaching for New Jersey next season? Yeah, I don't follow hockey news closely, but it sounded like it had been rumored for a while."

"It had been."

He's quiet after that, and I don't believe for a second it's because he's bored with the conversation we're having. We've talked about my hockey career enough times, and Mateo is only slowing now so he can navigate around the bruises we've already leaned on. Then he reaches for my hand, and our fingers slide together. I'll let him lean against whatever he wants.

Mateo knows it, too. "You've never mentioned wanting to coach before. You've only talked about how much you miss playing."

"It's not much more likely than another run for the Cup."

"Why not? Taylor McKeon wasn't a saint."

"He was always a dick, but I was the known troublemaker. Like you said, women were the only place he had me beat," I say. "Not much of a liability when I was leading the league in points and getting us into the playoffs year after year, but I can't think of many people who'd take a chance on me to be a responsible coach."

"You're a responsible parent," he argues. "And it's not like you're causing any problems during the live broadcasts you join, or when you're taking pictures with fans. Hell, most of your teammates praised your leadership as captain. Would it be that hard to believe you still have all the knowledge and talent, and less of the attitude the league and press loved to market for their own good?"

"I don't know. Are you going to call the owners and GMs to ask?"

Mateo sighs, but he's still holding my hand too tenderly for me to think I've lost him.

"You really never took anyone down the hill from here?"

"Mmmm, not the way you're thinking, no."

"Harper?"

"She was the exception, but she doesn't actually know it's there," I say. "I'd take her for walks on the beach when she was a baby, and then use the shortcut to get back up here. Sometimes I'd just sit there with her and slow everything down."

"But you stopped as she got older?"

"I don't need my wild child and her friends playing on the side of a cliff, no matter how small it might be. I'm not stupid—if she finds it, she finds it—but it's difficult to see from here if you don't already know where to look, and they rarely hang out on the rocks below."

"Danielle lived here a long time, right?" Mateo asks. "She wasn't a fan?"

"Danielle's not really the hiking type. And *you* know that's not an actual hike, and *I* know that's not an actual hike, but she never cared to see for herself. I never cared to change her mind. She wasn't—" I shake my head, a sad laugh escaping before I go on. "She was a one-night stand who took years to leave."

"Isn't that what I am now?"

"You're the furthest thing from it."

"Because you brought me there."

And yeah. Probably because of that.

"Do you want a beer?" I ask, letting his comment fall to the water untouched before I scramble away from him without waiting for an answer. "Oh, hey, did you hear Harper has a boyfriend? Aidan? Brayden—"

"Stop," Mateo interrupts with a laugh that catches me at the patio door. "It'll take you forever to get there that way. It's Zaiden."

I grab a couple of bottles from the fridge and pop them open before I return to his side. In the thirty seconds I was gone, he took off his shirt, and since I'm at least as bold as he is, I hand him the beer and do the same.

"He's a good guy?" I ask instead. "Zaiden?"

"Yeah, I think so." Mateo takes a long pull from the bottle, then drifts from story to story about Harper and Zaiden, together and separately.

Minutes later, I'm telling him about the girls who'd come to the rink and flirt with my team when we were young and too dumb to flirt back. He laughs through memories of his own high school mishaps and then returns to some of the funniest teenage dating disasters he's seen as a teacher.

"What's the wackiest happy ending you saw from any of those stories?" I ask, stupidly in love with moments like this.

"Ah, well. There was this kid who wanted to ask his crush to the homecoming dance, and to say he had a flair for the dramatic would be an understatement. He wasn't my student, but the girl was, so he interrupted my second period class dressed as Dread Pirate Roberts from *The Princess Bride*. He launched an amended monologue about beauty and true love—accent and everything—and I'm pretty sure his endgame plan had something to do with—"

"'As you wish'?"

"Exactly," Mateo laughs again. "Anyway, he had two big problems that day. One, the slits in the mask were too small for him to see through properly. Two, his crush looked a lot like her best friend."

I nearly choke on my beer. "Oh, no."

"Oh, yes. His very theatrical invitation was delivered to the wrong girl. A girl who happened to have a crush on *him* and said yes immediately. But this poor guy's best friend had a crush on *that* girl, and the best friend was in the class watching it all unfold, so he turned to the original crush—the one who was supposed to be invited to homecoming—and *he* asked *her*. Basically, two sets of best friends swapped would-be dates for the dance, all in the span of a couple of minutes during second period honors English."

"But there was a happy ending?"

"That was almost six years ago, and last I heard, both accidental couples were still together. Almost inconceivable."

I do choke on my beer that time, and Mateo and I are doubled over for a long time, wiping away tears as quickly as they fall. The temptation to kiss him is as strong as ever, but then I yawn unexpectedly and start to sober.

"Sorry," I say, covering my mouth with the back of my hand and quieting us both.

He takes a few deep breaths, facing the ocean we can't see from where we sit. "We'll still talk—when I'm with my grandparents, I want us to talk."

"I've never wanted us to stop."

"I know."

"How do you feel about going to take care of a man who probably wouldn't do the same for you?"

"*Definitely* wouldn't," he corrects. "And it's for my grandmother more than anything. Being around him will mean taking more verbal abuse than I'd accept from anyone else, but there's little I wouldn't do for her, and my being there will give the rest of my family a break, too."

I sigh. "If he's used to being strong, and now he's not, that'll make everything harder for you."

"It's all harder on her. I'll be fine."

"Will you tell me if you're not?"

"I don't remember whether we're supposed to lie to each other anymore," Mateo says, pressing his bare shoulder against mine.

"No more lying."

"Then I will tell you if I'm not fine. Will you tell me what else you want to know?"

"When you're gone?"

I don't get an answer right away. Mateo cocks his head when I yawn again. "Are you okay?"

"Yeah, I just haven't slept much the past few nights."

"Then let's go back inside. I saw that sectional, and I've got no doubt it's as comfortable as it looks."

Just like I'd done before fetching the beer, he stands without waiting for me to respond and uses my towel to dry his legs before he puts his shirt back on. I follow his lead, and then we go inside together. Mateo moves to lie on his side with enough space left for me.

"What are we doing?" I ask, my voice barely a rasp as I look down at him. "I don't actually want to fuck this up. I want you to come back when the summer is over."

"I'll come back. But lying hasn't worked for us, and staying apart hasn't worked for us, so maybe we can figure out how to do this right."

I've been carefully silent about how I've longed for this closeness more than anything we could do while wearing nothing at all. He doesn't need me to say I miss the casually intimate contact with teammates more than years of sex with strangers. He doesn't need me to tell him that the memory of this afternoon will help get me through the next few months.

But maybe he's seen right through me and will give this to me anyway.

"The right way is cuddling on my couch?"

"I'm still not trying to get away with anything," he promises. "But I want to hold you, and you want us to tell the truth. So, what else do you want to know—now, not when I'm gone?"

I blink once or twice, then grab a nearby throw blanket and lie down, my back pressed to his chest. Our legs slot together with no real effort, then he wraps an arm around my waist and nuzzles hair that must smell of chlorine.

"Do you believe in love at first sight?"

"No," Mateo says.

"No?"

"I think love requires a little more time."

"Why did you agree to drive me to the food truck that night?"

"Because I think love requires a little more time."

I'm grateful to be facing away from him when I squeeze my eyes shut and do my best to breathe. "And you stayed until morning."

"Just like today, you asked me to."

"What will happen when the waiting is over? When we can always stay, and we don't stop at a kiss?"

Mateo's lips graze the back of my neck, or maybe I'm imagining broken rules. Either way, the heat of his answer raises goosebumps on my skin.

"We can do anything you want, but I want you to be loud. I want to *make* you loud."

"I want us to go slow," I tell him.

"Okay. We can do that. We can be loud and slow."

"You think about it a lot, don't you? I'm not the only one?"

"Of course not," he murmurs. "I think about it all the time."

It's simple and honest, and now that we've said that much, I don't feel his mouth anymore. I'm curious and aroused, and I want details from a man who's probably done it all. I also know we have to stop talking about a night that's still two years away. The rest can stay confined to my dreams, or the nights I'm wide awake and stroking myself off. I'm worried we've pushed today's boundaries as far as they will go.

"Do you like disaster movies?"

"Sure. Are we going to watch one?"

"If you'll stay a little longer."

"I will."

He stays long enough for us to watch a few. Pizza gets delivered somewhere among them. I find better pillows for us. Mateo borrows a pair of sweatpants. He massages my leg. I try not to cry.

He stays until morning because we want to believe it's that easy. We won't remind each other why it's hard.

Chapter Eight: Mateo

(I Listened to His Confession)

My grandfather dies six weeks after I said goodbye to Jamie on another oceanside morning.

I have complicated feelings about everything I experienced during the summer away from him, but mostly I mourn with the rest of my family in deference to their loss. My grandmother leans on me—physically as much as anything—my parents handle the Catholic rituals and splendor, and my sisters cry. People I've known forever surround us with prayers and food. And a man I've known for two years keeps his head down at the funeral, but makes sure I know he's within reach.

The school year starts before I'm fully ready for it, too much time away from my apartment leaving me unsettled in a way I hate. Sophie helps as much as she can, in the classroom and over plenty of margaritas, and she encourages me to see Jamie and forget as much of everything else as I can. I want to see him, obviously. He wants to see me, too. We talk all the time and make time for one quick lunch, an outing milestone we acknowledge with cautious grins. The restaurant is surrounded by office buildings, and is pretty damn empty this early on a Saturday, but Jamie has his back to the room just in case. Beneath the table, he and I steady each other, our sneakers pressed together where nobody else will see.

It's the only contact we need here.

"It doesn't feel as fragile now," I say.

Jamie looks up from his menu. "What doesn't?"

"Our self-control. This is more like those first few hours at the fair. Or the start of that hike."

"Before we had our hands all over each other," he says with a smirk. "But what happens at the end of this lunch? It won't break then?"

"No. I spent the night with you, and if we had that once, we can have it again. We can touch each other again."

"And we don't have to touch each other today."

A smile spills over when I tap the side of his sneaker with mine. "Not at all."

In November, soccer season starts without fanfare, and it's great to see Harper in action again. She's been contacted by a couple of Division I schools already, and I'm looking forward to helping her through the recruitment process. For now, it's only her junior year, and Jamie makes it—as always—to every game. I kick a ball around with him after a couple of wins, and we act like I'm only smiling because I'm delighted to have the parent of one of my best players around.

Harper doesn't seem to care that her dad and I are getting along. I get along with a lot of people.

On Christmas Eve, my family goes to midnight Mass, and I listen to stories about my grandfather I've heard several times. I wake up at Crissy's house when my nieces and nephews squeal about Santa, and it's a while before I check my phone.

Merry Christmas. No more pretending. I miss you

And I miss you. No pretending.

It's a ridiculous exchange, and maybe that was true the first year, too. We're still in the middle of soccer season, so Jamie and I saw each other in the days leading up to the holiday, and we will again days after. I'm grateful for the text though, and then I feel abruptly guilty when I receive one from someone else.

Hope you and the family are doing okay. Miss seeing you around the neighborhood

Shit.

Logan.

I'd never stopped thinking about Jamie over the summer, but he and I had been two hours apart from each other and two years away from everything else. I'd ached, so damn lonely and tired, and Logan had been right there. I've spent the past few months ignoring the few weeks I let myself get close to the man living across the street from my grandparents—or across from my grand*mother* now. Returning home had meant leaving him behind, but now I need the memories to stay there too, and a sincere Christmas greeting does nothing to help.

I can't miss anyone else.

We're doing well. And I hope you have a wonderful Christmas.

At first, Logan and I had only exchanged pleasantries between one driveway and another. He'd been curious about who'd moved in with his older neighbors, and I'd been curious about the awkward young man whose suit and tie were always a little bit askew. Then we'd run into each other at the pharmacy, and I'd straightened his collar, and I'd felt fully in control and wildly out of it when I asked him if he wanted to keep me company for a few other errands.

He did. And when it happened again a week later, we had dinner together, too.

Living with my grandparents all those weeks had been difficult, but when it became increasingly clear my grandfather wouldn't survive to see the end of the year—if he'd even see another month—they'd needed time alone, and I slipped away. On those nights, in an unfamiliar place, I hadn't known where to go. The house across the street made as much sense as anything, and my knock was answered with a shy smile.

I'd still been tired after that, but a little less lonely. I'm not sure how I'd describe myself today, but Logan has nothing else to say, and I don't have to try.

Merry Christmas to me.

A few days later, during the most liminal week of the year, we have an all-day soccer tournament about an hour away, and the first game is almost unfairly early for anyone's holiday break. Most of the kids have carpooled, only a handful of parents planning to hang out from beginning to end. I've been at the field for a few minutes when a hot cup of coffee is pressed into my hand.

Jamie smiles. "I really, really didn't want to get out of bed this morning, but it was worth it to see that look on your face."

"Can everyone else see the look on my face?" I ask, my eyes still on his.

"There aren't enough people here yet, and it was my very loud and very kind daughter's idea that I bring you something hot and caffeinated."

"Is this where I point out that you're hot and caffeinated?"

"That's such a terrible line, and I hate how much it's working on me," Jamie laughs, his eyes surprisingly bright this close to sunrise.

I look around at where the girls are already starting warmups, my coaching important, but unnecessary for another minute or two. Another look has me gauging the interest of any other early arrivals, but Jamie and I aren't doing anything wrong, and I take a long sip from the coffee he brought.

"Wait, how'd you know what I like?"

Jamie stares, another smile pulling at the corners of his mouth. "Sometimes friends notice things. And sometimes they remember them for later."

One of my co-captains shouts for me then, and he and I have run out of the time we've got today. We're still chasing the time left ahead, and I hate how much it frustrates me to wait.

After the new year, weeks pass quickly and slowly, and I self-soothe with a rotation of homemade broccoli cheese soup, baked ziti, tomato bisque, and white chicken chili. Sophie and I aren't spending as much time together because she's on a hot dating streak and spares me the sordid details. I only hear from Logan once, but I see Jamie at Kai's a couple of times because those barstools are almost as safe as the bench. Harper has better things to do than hang out at the church fair over spring break, and Jamie doesn't owe me another afternoon on a date that isn't really that. We're brave enough to meet for brunch once instead, and we tell ourselves it's the same thing.

He and I are less shy about what we want when we talk, but we haven't made it back to his giant sofa again, and I want that to be okay. I once chose him in an alley and outside a taco truck and in a backyard I didn't know was his. I'm still choosing him, and will for as long as it takes to make wishes come true.

It's why I don't expect the jolt of betrayal that hits in May of that year. On prom night.

Or actually, it's a couple of days after that, when I find out what happened the night I was in a nearby ballroom, chaperoning hundreds of dance-happy juniors and seniors, including Harper Sinclair.

It's dumb luck—or a curse of some kind—that I'm in a position to overhear anything. A case of being in the right place at the worst possible time. But it's the Monday after prom, and I have to stop by the front office to speak to one of the guidance counselors, and it means walking past a cluster of parents to do it. Presumably, they're on their way to a meeting to discuss graduation preparations, but I've been working here long enough to understand that Vicki Gallagher will open her mouth wherever it suits her best. And today, an audience of one handsome gay English teacher will do just fine.

"She finally did it. Melanie Bishop finally got Jameson Sinclair."

I look up and scream at myself not to care, but I'm not sure my forced incredulity gets me far. I move past Vicki and her minions at the pace of someone nightmare-crawling through molasses, and she keeps talking while her smirk is aimed in my direction.

"There's been plenty of flirting before, of course. But with both of their daughters dancing the night away at prom, I guess they took advantage of an empty house and a big bed."

"What did she say afterward?" one of the other moms hisses. "I mean, was he as good as we've all imagined?"

I'm down the hall now, but the guidance counselor is finishing a phone call, and I'm trapped while I wait, Vicki's voice carrying as well as it always has. I'd guess the smirk is still in place, but I do myself one small favor and don't turn to look.

"I was a little worried that the old rumor about him might be true, but Melanie says no way. Apparently, he was very, very good. Attentive, if you know what I mean. And *that* was a bit of a surprise, given his well-established ego, but isn't she a lucky little thing?"

"So, she'll be seeing him again?"

I get waved forward then, and I don't get to hear an answer to a question that's already made me sick. My stomach is no better by the time I leave, but the echo of Vicki Gallagher's voice is only in my head. Sophie has other plans, so I can't drag her out for too much tequila, and I don't think Kai can help with this one. After a lonely drink at my apartment that night, I almost text Logan. I think I might be willing to drive two hours to ruin so many things.

In the end, I don't go anywhere, but it takes me until the weekend to text Jamie.

Will you please meet me at the bench tonight?

He's there before I am, and I'm not surprised. His response to my request hadn't been met with the flurry of questions I'd expect from someone who didn't know what I might have to say. He hadn't asked me to come to the house instead, nor had he begged for a meeting on neutral ground. Jamie had simply suggested a time—after dark again—and there's a chance he's been waiting here for a while.

But he's wearing my hoodie, and I hadn't seen that coming.

"Do you want it back now?" he asks, his voice complemented by the waves below.

"No."

Jamie nods and lifts the blanket draped over his lap so I can join him beneath it. It hadn't occurred to me to bring one, even on a night that calls for it, but he's prepared for this. I sigh and make myself as comfortable as I can, stopping short of taking his hand when we're pressed close together. Then neither of us speaks for a while, my ears catching muted sounds the wind could've carried from anywhere, though I'm curious about whether Harper is home tonight. I stare at the ocean and don't ask.

"I slept with Melanie Bishop."

There it is.

And already knowing helps nothing. Nor does my equal share of guilt.

I still can't turn to him. "On prom night."

"Yes." It wasn't a question for him to answer, but he keeps going.

"That was the only time. I know you've worried about it before, but there wasn't—it was just this once."

"So far?"

Jamie reaches for my jaw, rough with me in a way that holds my attention when he forces me to meet his somber blue eyes. The moonlight leaves shadows just beneath them, but it's possible he's been sleeping as badly as I have been, and maybe the shadows were already there. When he seems certain I won't look away, his fingers roam selfishly and soothingly, over my lips and across my cheek and into the hair I've left down because I know he likes it that way.

"My kid went to prom, and it was so—it was such a milestone. I kept thinking about how fast she's growing up, and I wished for a second that time would just slow down." He frowns and his grip on my hair tightens until he reminds himself to relax. "But I also don't want it to slow down at all, because I want to be with you. And it's stupid because I don't have control of it either way. Time will pass no matter what I want."

"It will, yeah."

He lets his hand fall away as he takes a deep breath. "After Harper was gone, I showered, and I had a couple of drinks, and I was just *restless*. I knew you were at the dance too, and Kai was slammed at work, and I felt like I was crawling out of my skin. Then Melanie called with this sad, lonely drawl that made too much sense. When she invited me over, I went."

Whatever conflict Jamie felt about time passing was unlikely to have been true for Melanie. Her daughter's a senior, and unless there's someone special she's been waiting for, she had nothing to hold her back. She'd had her sights on Jamie for years, and prom night gave her little to lose.

Still, he's here with me now.

"You needed each other," I tell him.

Jamie rubs at the shadows under his eyes. "What are we doing?"

"Waiting."

"Are we? Have you been out there waiting for me as well as I'm waiting for you?"

"I'm not sure waiting for each other ever included a vow of celibacy," I say. "In a perfect world, maybe. But we're imperfect adults who keep talking about what we want, and imagining what we want, but not actually getting what we want. Four years was always going to be a very long time."

His next exhale is full of resignation. "Fuck. You slept with someone, too."

"We're imperfect adults," I say again. "Not characters in a rom-com."

"Anybody I know?"

"No."

"What's his name?"

"Come on, Jamie. You don't need to—"

"Please," he interrupts.

"Logan."

"Are the two of you still a thing?"

"No."

"He'd be stupid not to want more."

"Melanie Bishop isn't stupid," I murmur.

"Melanie Bishop wanted orgasms and clout."

"And who better to provide both?"

That's unfair of me, but Jamie doesn't argue the point, cautious but intentional when he finds my hand under the blanket and holds me there. It's different from the first time we were here, but so much the same, and we're silent for a while before either of us disrupts this painful peace.

It's Jamie, using my hoodie as his armor. "It's been three messy years. What are we doing?"

He's already asked me that, and I've already answered, but there's another question if I listen closely, and I squeeze his hand when I respond again.

"We've got one more year left. Do you still want to wait?"

"We're back to that morning," Jamie says. "When we admitted we wanted everything, everywhere."

"But back then, I didn't understand why it was going to be so hard for you. Now I know who you are, and I may not be familiar with your fame, but I've heard all the slurs before. I know how headlines work. Those problems won't be solved by Harper's graduation. That'll only let *me* off the hook."

Jamie snorts. "No, it won't. Everyone will be all over you and the boring life you love. Fame by proxy."

"What if I love something else more? Someone else?"

I'm looking at him when he swallows, slow to make eye contact with me, even in the dark. He doesn't pull away, but I wonder if that's because he doesn't know where he'd go. We need to talk, and escaping to his gorgeous house won't take care of that problem unless he wants to bring me with him.

It might be less intimate than this bench, but our words are better drowned down here.

"Do you? Is that even possible?"

"Whether it was possible that first night was a fair question, but now? Of course it's possible. I don't need to have slept with you to know how I feel about you." I pause and comb my hair back from my face, a pointless act when the wind insists on knocking it loose. "But if you're asking, I guess that answers the question of how you feel about *me*."

"It answers nothing, and I hate that you think it does."

I drop my head back and stare at the sky for a few seconds, just to clear my head. "There will be people who support you, too. It won't all be bad, right?"

"Sure."

"Do you still have an agent?"

"Nah. When I couldn't play, and all my endorsement deals ended, there wasn't—I didn't really need an advocate, right?" There's a pause, but I know Jamie wants that question to be rhetorical, and I fight myself to let it go. "I've got an attorney who can look at paperwork when I need her to."

"But your fans. And your team."

"I don't *have* a team," Jamie snaps, frustrated by a loss he's mourned for years, and finally taking his hand away from mine. "And I don't know. There are Pride nights, and more than one player has spoken up to support those, but the actual fallout of Jameson Sinclair being a confirmed bisexual? Which, of course, people won't say—"

"You'll be gay to them, and the Melanie Bishops of the world will weep."

"Exactly. So, there will be a frenzy about that, no matter how long it's been since I was in a locker room. Questions about teammates and secret apps and who knew about me and who else might be gay. Digging into any inappropriate thing I ever said or did. What lines I crossed. Will I still be invited to signings? Eh, probably? Whatever the reason for it, I'd continue to draw a crowd for a while. Being a guest commentator? It'll come down to the money I make them or cost them. The press will be reliably terrible to me, except for a few more reputable journalists who have always been kind. The league? They'll remain officially uninvolved in the private life of a former player who hasn't done a little dance for them in years."

I sigh. "Without a team—without a contractual obligation and the ties either side would risk severing—you'll be in the middle of a public tug of war. Stuck between the fans and teammates who stand by you, and those who love your name but will only use it until they want to distance themselves from it."

"I *wish* I had that obligation, though. Fuck, I just want to be in the middle of it again. I want the sounds and smells and love and hate and a *choice* about losing it all. I never had a choice."

My stomach winds itself into an ugly little knot when his voice breaks, my blood running cold in a way that has nothing to do with a late night at the beach. It hits me hard that the night I last saw him play—the worst night of his life—is the only reason I'm sitting next to him now. Without that injury, he would've been preparing for the season instead of drinking at Kai's. His appearance at Harper's back-to-school night might've been possible that September, but a relationship with me? All the wanting and waiting we've shared for the past three years?

Jamie would've had his choice back then.

And it wouldn't have been me.

I almost say so out loud, but I choke on it, and wonder whether I could risk everything right now for the chance to have a single night in his bed, rules be damned. It already feels like I'll regret staying where I am.

"One year to go," I start, clearing my throat and seeking a middle ground. "And if we're doing this, I don't want to hold back anymore. Not if it's only about protecting ourselves from feeling too much. I want to hold you, and you want the truth."

"Like the day you came over to tell me you were leaving for the summer."

"That night, too."

"You want more of those."

"Yes."

"Without getting away with anything."

"Without crossing lines in the first place," I say. "Not the ones that would mean we've given up on each other."

He turns toward me then, and while we're huddled under the blanket—and while it feels like that first night—I pull him into my lap. Jamie's strong thighs are on either side of mine, and he's quick to readjust the blanket like he had back then, the pure longing on his face something I wish I could kiss away.

Jamie presses his forehead to mine. "This isn't giving up?"

"This is close. But it hasn't done me any good to keep my distance from you. I don't love you any less just because we don't touch like this."

"I don't love you any less, either. But in public—" He trails off and eases back so we can see each other clearly.

He's so goddamn pretty.

"We'll be careful then, but it's what I want—I want to go out more than we already have. Just the two of us, or with Kai or Sophie or anyone else."

"What about Harper?"

I tilt my head and can't figure out what he's asking. "What about her?"

"I still don't want her to know about us. Not everything, anyway," Jamie sighs. "I don't want to put her in the position of having to keep our secret."

"Okay, how do you feel about her knowing we're friends?"

He's quiet for a moment, his hands clinging to the blanket while mine are at his waist. I want to feel the warmth of his skin, but even after telling him I'm okay pushing up against a line that will make me ache, I hold back. His answer matters. After all, Harper is why we're hiding in the dark.

"Let's wait until soccer starts again," he finally says. "It'll be easy then. She's mentioned that I should take you to L.A. for a game, and maybe she was half kidding, but I don't think she'd blink if I actually followed through. I don't think she'd care."

"And then we hit it off at the game, talk a little more at soccer, decide to hang out again—"

"Exactly. And when she's with Danielle or at Lizzie's or Kate's—"

I smile. "I can touch you again."

"I want you to touch me now," Jamie whispers.

My hands are moving before I can think it through, my fingers under a hoodie that hasn't belonged to me for three years. He's watching me, his arrogance flashing where everything else is dim, and I pause.

"You're daring me."

He shakes his head. "I'm trusting you."

I'm curious what Jamie would do given the same free rein, but he hasn't let go of the blanket yet and shows no signs of doing so now. On another night, in a different place, he can have it all, but we're on his bench and my only limits are the ones I don't want to talk about anymore. My hands slide higher, over a body slightly softer than the last time I touched it like this, and my own body reacts immediately. Everything is familiar when it barely has a reason to be, but the attention I pay to his nipples is newer than that, and I earn an unexpected sound, lower than the whimpers I've been blessed with before.

Arrogance fades into desire I know well.

With my hands still under our hoodie, I brush my thumbs over his nipples one more time, then flatten my hands as they travel over his rib cage and around to his back. The move has Jamie arching into me, dangerous and nothing I plan to stop. A second later, he curls forward, his face buried in my messy hair when he says my name. I say his name too, and memorize the moment for when I'm alone.

When I scrape my fingernails down his spine, he trembles, and

I ignore the slight thrust of his hips. Then I do it again, and for a moment, I feel damn near arrogant, too.

My heart is pounding, and it works in tandem with the slow roll of the ocean to make me think of another night, still more than a year away. We're in public here, but it hardly matters, and with Jamie's blanket or mine, we'd be able to do anything without the fear of being caught. Next summer might be so much like tonight—so much like *then*—but with him in my lap, and nothing between us anymore. He'd sound the same, too. Little moans and promises made against my ear each time he takes me deep.

Without realizing it, my hands have dropped to his waist again, tight there. I'm the one to thrust this time. "God, Jamie."

"I know. Me, too."

We're both in sweatpants, and it renders any other words unnecessary. Our situation isn't unlike the night I'd spent with him at his house, when he'd loaned me something more comfortable to sleep in. We'd woken with morning wood, unsurprising on any day and less so when we'd stayed tangled together while we slept. But we hadn't talked about it then because we hadn't been so close to do something about it.

We don't talk about it now, either.

Jamie trusts me.

"I can't kiss you."

"No, you can't," he says, his mouth hot against my neck. "We're doing all we can."

"But it's just over a year," I tell him. "If we're still waiting, it's just over a year."

"We're still waiting. Of course we are. We're almost there."

CHAPTER NINE: JAMIE

(I WAITED OUTSIDE HIS DOOR)

This time, I'm the one to take Harper on vacation after the school year ends. The two of us start with a week in New York City. Our trip is loaded with incredible food and incredible shows and incredible museums. I'm only met with a small amount of attention from the hockey world when I stop by the NHL store in Manhattan. When we move on from there, we spend a week in Boston. We visit a few old acquaintances of mine, eat more amazing food, and explore historical landmarks until Harper tells me she's tired. I know she's giving me a reason to rest my leg.

In both cities, we tour universities that would like her to commit to playing soccer for them. Harper isn't sure she wants to go to college so far from home, and I'm going to struggle with her going anywhere. She has a little more time to decide, and I'll support her regardless.

While we're gone, she calls her new boyfriend—Zaiden has been replaced by a swimmer named Dean—as often as she can. I send Mateo dozens of pictures, but he and I don't talk, and I miss his voice more than I should. He sends me dozens of replies and tells me he misses me, too.

Harper and I get back to California at the beginning of July, but by then, Mateo has gone with Sophie and a couple of other teachers up to Lake Tahoe for the holiday. I watch fireworks from my backyard.

After that, though—

After that, we have some of the best months of our lives.

For the rest of that summer, we keep Harper in the dark, just like we'd planned. The bar remains a relatively safe place for us to go, but we're ready to try spending time anywhere else, however cautious we are at first. I hold excuses for the public on the tip of my tongue the night I'm finally introduced to Sophie, but Mateo's favorite Mexican restaurant does me the favor of serving great food under shitty lighting. From a table in the corner, the three of us get tipsy on the same happy hour margaritas he tells me he once ditched for a sad batch of his own.

We catch an outdoor concert after sundown, and most people around us are too drunk or high to care who we are. We wander further from potentially curious fans or students, and drive up and down the coast for miles and miles. Sometimes we find something to do in either direction, and sometimes we're happy simply talking to each other or singing along with somebody's favorite songs. When we stay close to home, we meet at the mall or the pier and walk around from there, prepared to explain it away as a happy accident when we run into anyone we know. If we're captured in a stranger's picture, the space between us will fit a few denials.

In between it all, we talk. Sometimes I keep him up too late on a weeknight because it's hard to say goodbye. Sometimes he wakes me early on a weekend morning, when my voice is still gravelly and Harper is sound asleep.

It's nice to tell the truth more often. I enjoy getting my way. It's also nice when Mateo gets his, and he holds me.

When we want to be close to each other, we do it on the nights Harper is at her mom's or out with friends. My house is obviously larger and fancier and full of high-end bullshit as far as the eye can see, but I almost always go to Mateo's apartment just in case she returns unexpectedly. And it's fine, really. He and I mostly end up wrapped around each other, so I'm not sure it matters how big the couch is. His queen bed is fine, too.

I still react too strongly when he touches me, but I'm not sure that matters either.

"I love it—knowing how I make you feel," Mateo murmurs against my skin before he pulls back to be friends again. "I'll want to know for the rest of our lives."

It's unfair how much I want to kiss him for that, and I bite his shoulder instead.

In the middle of the summer, Harper gets a part-time job because she wants to save her own money for when she moves out. I tell Mateo about it on another one of our nights together.

"She's a hostess at a restaurant on the water, and she loves it so far. Gets along with everyone she works with. Chats with everyone waiting for a table."

"I'm not even a little surprised."

I laugh. "No, I didn't really figure you would be."

"And I'll probably hear a lot about it from her throughout the school year."

"Juggling a job, a boyfriend, and soccer should be interesting."

"Juggling a job, a boyfriend, soccer, *and* class with the new AP English teacher," Mateo smiles.

Vaguely, I remember a conversation in my kitchen, when Harper had gone on and on about her first week of high school and someone she'd called Mr. Z. She'd said something back then about him taking over the AP class when another teacher retired. I was busy being head over heels for a guy named Mateo, and so much of that time was lost to daydreams. I blink hard now and push bittersweet memories away.

"Does that change things?" I ask. "Between us, I mean."

He reaches for me, gentle and honest. "I don't think anything could."

Closer to the start of the school year, he gets busy again, and I'm swept up in Harper's excitement. She's close to deciding about college, and she'll be reuniting with friends she hasn't seen much over the summer, everyone comparing schedules as soon as they're released. She squeals, of course, when she sees that she'll be in Mateo's class again. She has an entire school year ahead with her favorite teacher and coach.

And I hadn't thought about it before, but because he's her teacher again, I see him at a back-to-school night. I'm prepared for his gorgeous grin in a way that hadn't been true three years ago.

"Mateo Zavala," I say almost teasingly, my hand outstretched. "It's been a little while since my first visit to your classroom."

"It has been, but having Harper in class is as much of a pleasure now as it was back then. Fewer surprises, though—among all the kids in the AP class, I mean. I taught a lot of them as freshmen, and now I'll be getting them ready for graduation."

"Ugh, I can't *wait*," Harper says. "Not to be, like, rude about school or anything. But once I get through all of this, I'll have so much *freedom* and chances to do so many new things, and I'm just really freaking out about it? In a good way? So, yeah, this class will be cool and soccer will be awesome, and then I'll graduate and everything will be sooooo—I just can't wait."

"Be careful about wishing away time, pixie," I warn, as hypocritical as anyone has ever been.

"Okay, yeah, I know."

I tug on her ponytail once, then turn my attention back to Mateo. "Speaking of time, if you have some to spare, I may be looking for someone to go with me to a hockey game or two this season. I know Harper offered you my autograph the last time we stood here, but I always get tickets. She's busier than ever, so I'd be happy to take you if you're interested."

"I am. Unless it's weird for you?" he asks, his eyebrow raised in Harper's direction.

"It's very mildly weird, but not like, *weird* weird?" she answers. "And he's right that I'm busy. Plus, he should get used to me not being around, for next year when, you know, I won't be around. So, yeah. It's good. Go to some games."

She nods. I nod. Mateo nods. And it's as easy as that.

Mateo and I go to a game the second week of the hockey season. It's probably sooner than we should, but it feels like a step we could've taken a long time ago. I tell myself I've been to games with Kai, and with lesser-known ex-teammates, and this shouldn't look any different. Still, on our way to the arena, I remind him it'll be the first time we're surrounded by people likely to recognize me. I offer him the chance to turn around and know he won't take it. He chuckles, and when he points out that he'll have to get used to it eventually, I silently count the months ahead.

Eight. There are only eight months left before a crowd just like tonight's sees my name in a headline and asks questions about my future I once never expected to answer.

We go to another game in November. We've each got a beer in our hands and L.A. is up two, but my focus has been drawn to where Mateo sits next to me. He's chanting something with the rest of the crowd, but my eyes follow the sexy stubble on his jaw up to the strands of hair falling free from his ponytail. I'm in love. Then, just a few minutes before the third period starts, I remember an afternoon on the soccer field when we were just learning how to talk to each other without naive promises making it easy.

"Has anyone taken you skating and put a stick in your hands?"

Mateo's smile is subtle, but I can see it in the tiny crinkles next to his eyes. "Not yet."

"Somebody should."

"I hope somebody does."

So, that's our next date. With the high school soccer season and Thanksgiving weekend complicating our schedules—not to mention the precious time I spend with a daughter who has several better things to do—it's mid-December before we make it happen. It works out though, because Los Angeles is on a four-game road trip, and I'd always made nice with employees at the practice facility. We get the place to ourselves for an hour I'd be willing to pay for ten times over. I stand back to watch while Mateo laces up his borrowed skates.

He glances up at me. "This really won't mess with your leg?"

"You think I'd be doing this if it would hurt me?"

"Yes."

I shake my head, but don't argue when we both know he's right. "Come on. Time for me to steady your wobbly ass."

This isn't actually my first time back on the ice. Besides, he and I won't be doing anything vigorous enough to piss off my broken leg. If I'm sore at all, it'll be from working to keep him upright. Then it doesn't take long for me to realize he can skate just fine. He's lacking finesse and speed, but he's fine.

It doesn't stop me from reaching out for him when I can.

After several minutes of skating the perimeter, I grab us a couple of sticks and a bucket of pucks. His years of soccer make him no stranger to anything I have him try now, but I have a great time teaching him the finer points of the game I love. We pass back and forth, and he gets better at maneuvering around me. I'm as happy when he scores now as I was back when my own goals counted toward something real.

"Someday we'll do this on one of your frozen lakes," he tells me.

I really want that to be true.

A few weeks later, Christmas Eve passes with only a few texts. I'm not bothered by it, because for the first time ever, Mateo and I will have the chance to celebrate together. We have to wait until Christmas night, after Harper has gone to Danielle's and Mateo has fulfilled a much longer list of family obligations, but then he's at my door. I'd be mad about the wrapped gift in his hand, but I have something for him, too. I step aside with a grin that feels like it belongs to him these days.

My house is only lit by the strings of lights I have everywhere—on our giant Douglas fir and the garland draped over the patio doors and wrapped around the banister—but it's enough for me to see him well. I appreciate his thick sweater and messy hair and the stubble pressed to my cheek the moment he sets the present on the coffee table. We hug for a long time, mostly quiet about it when the sensation itself is overwhelming.

When I finally take a step back, I leave him on the sectional while I pour Bailey's and hot cocoa for both of us. Christmas music plays softly enough to keep us company without interrupting whatever conversations we'll have. Once we've taken a few sips, I nod toward the gifts.

"I kinda hate that we've never done this before."

Mateo touches two fingertips to my lips. "Stop looking back. We're doing it now."

"Mmmm, yeah, okay. Open yours first."

He drops his hand and reaches for the present I wrapped earlier, but he studies me, too. I'm sure he knows I'm impatient and that I love being given things. Wanting someone else to open anything before I can is wholly unlike me. I also think he knows he's the exception to at least a few rules, so he slides his finger under the tape and tears as gently as anyone ever has. When he gets to the box, he's careful with it, too. I'm close to yelling that nothing I could give him is that precious.

I'd be lying, of course. This present means something, and he already understands that much.

"Oh. God. This is—Jamie," he chokes. There are questions he wants to ask when he lifts my jersey and brings it to his nose without thinking. His eyes fall closed and I give him time. It's clean, nothing about the scent giving him an answer, but it's obviously worn, and he cradles it for a while. When he looks at me again, Christmas lights dance in tears that don't fall, and he shakes his head. "When? What games?"

"Don't worry. It's not what I was wearing in the last one. I'd rather not give you a reason to imagine that broken version of me."

"But I was—" Mateo stops and frowns, then shakes his head.

"You were what?"

"No, it's—I don't want you to hide any version of yourself from me," he says, shaking his head one more time before he takes a deep breath. "Tell me, though. Please. When did you wear this?"

"Throughout the playoffs, the first year we won the Cup."

"Are you serious?"

I am, and I deflect with a small huff of laughter. "It wasn't my Conn Smythe season."

"I would've been happy with something you wore for a ridiculous photoshoot. This is so far beyond anything anyone has ever given me. Thank you."

"You're welcome, and I'm glad you like it, but I'm gonna guess this is more than a board game or a holiday sausage," I say, pulling the other present into my lap.

"It is."

It is.

For someone who once gave me shit about trespassing, Mateo doesn't seem to have hesitated to climb halfway to my backyard without my knowledge. I run my finger around the simple black frame, unwilling to smudge the glass. I don't look up yet because I'm unable to speak. The photo is matted, and I stare at that blank space for several seconds before I refocus on the details captured by the man waiting silently next to me. He took the picture at night, but the moon might've been full, the bench lit up beautifully even as it's guarded by the brush surrounding it. There's a blanket there too, folded neatly where either of us could sit if I took his hand and walked him outside right now. It's where we started. It's where I told him I'd wait for him. It's where both of us confessed we hadn't waited as well as I wish we could have.

But nothing has ended there, and maybe this is a promise that it won't.

"Thank you, Mateo," I say. "I love it."

His fingertips touch my cheek, painfully light there. "And I love you."

<hr>

That holiday high lasts for a while. We don't spend New Year's together, but we escape to Santa Monica for an amazing birthday dinner. The restaurant is the kind of place frequented by friends as often as lovers, and we keep our hands to ourselves until we're back in his apartment. Then Mateo holds me all night.

The soccer season wraps up, the team falling short of a championship. They fought hard until the end and will be proud of themselves once the sting of the loss fades. Harper isn't the only senior who will play in college next year, though she is the only one headed up to Seattle. There are some tears at the banquet when those distances sink in. She wins a couple of awards and takes pictures with everyone who stays still long enough. Mateo congratulates her with a smile I know well.

I'm quiet that night because my loss will become my gain. Harper's impending graduation is the only day likely to leave me feeling even more conflicted than I am now.

If I'd stopped to predict the future, I would've expected those last months to drag on forever. Instead, so many things are happening as the end of the school year approaches. Harper's AP classes are preparing for exams, she's picked up extra hours at work, she flies up to Washington for spring break, and she weeps briefly over the end of another relationship. I make a couple of local appearances for charity and get invited to L.A. for several more broadcasts. I also take long-distance calls from people who want to talk about an opportunity they think may suit me well. I'm surprised, but I don't disagree. When meetings are proposed, I travel to them without thinking.

In hindsight, I should've wanted everything to slow down.

Mateo and I remain so close, still sneaking away if our schedules allow, or curling up at home whenever it's possible. We've kept our promises about the lines we can't cross, but it's easy to get lost in him when he touches me in ways nobody ever has. There are nights I think I need to pull away, for his sake.

I stay where I am for mine.

"I'm chaperoning prom again this year," he tells me in early May.

I want to tell him he doesn't have to worry about me, but I'm not sure that's ever been less true. I force a smile instead. "Harper will be there, too."

Those next couple of weeks are a whirlwind, anticipation leaving all of us to hold our breaths. Things are about to change, and it feels like sparks are flying in so many directions. As much as everything about them is beautiful, I'm worried about how soon they'll start a fire.

As it turns out, the answer is the morning of prom. Someone I've known for a while offers me the only way to hurt Mateo more than I did one year ago, and I take it.

I tell myself I don't have time to dwell on my decision when I've promised to take Harper to brunch. We relax there, and I hear more about the group of friends—a dozen adorably platonic pairings—who will share limos and a dinner reservation. She reminds me of their plans to spend the night at Lizzie's house after they've danced for hours, her parents braver than I am. We run a few errands after that, picking up last-minute accessories she swears she needs before she goes anywhere tonight. When we return home, she blasts music and showers while I fuck around on my phone, looking for headlines I won't find until Monday. I consider calling Kai, but he has the bar to deal with. I think stopping by to see him tomorrow morning will be better for both of us.

"I'm gonna go. We're getting our hair done in, like, twenty minutes?" Harper says, hurrying down the stairs. She's holding a garment bag and a small suitcase because Danielle never taught her to pack light while I was on the road. "You've been crawling out of your skin all day, so do you need to have a whole 'dad moment' about this, or can I promise to send you a million selfies to calm you down?"

I ignore the observation and answer the question. "A million selfies will do. Text me when you get back to Lizzie's after the dance. Text me again whenever you wake up tomorrow."

My phone is still in my hand when she drives away. I think about talking to Mateo before his night gets as busy as Harper's. Unfortunately, I'm no braver about that than I am about hosting a prom night sleepover, and I decide therapy is probably a smarter option. Within the next several minutes, I'm in my pool, swimming laps that once healed me.

I hate that I need them now, while the sun is shining on what should be one of the best days of my life. I'm close to staying underwater too long just to feel my lungs burn.

As long as I don't come up for air, I can't speak another word.

I'm not sure how long I swim, but eventually my body is worn out and my stomach demands to be fed. When I'm dry enough to raid the kitchen, I grab my phone and thumb through the pictures Harper's sent so far. I'm pretty sure there are meme references being made way above my head, but I'm just happy she's smiling like she is. I catch myself smiling too, because I deserve that much.

It's a really, really great day for me.

It really, really is.

Then Mateo texts me, and my smile changes, and the leftover lasagna I've just reheated will have to wait another minute. He's sent me a picture from his bathroom, where he's facing a foggy mirror wiped enough for me to love several things at once. The wet strands resting against his shoulders until he pulls them back for the night. The beginning of a mustache and beard I don't expect him to shave. The enviable hair on his chest, more than I've ever had, calling for my touch. The happy trail disappearing beneath the towel wrapped around his waist.

That's calling to me, too.

You're a tease

Mateo responds quickly. ***Hardly. You know you're welcome to come over and watch me get dressed.***

And then have to watch you leave? Sounds terrible

The thing is, I *will* go to his apartment later. I don't tell him that now.

You flatter me.

Do I get to see what you're wearing tonight?

Ah you want me to put clothes ON? You flatter me less.

I don't say anything else then, shoveling food into my mouth before my stomach turns more than it already has. I pour myself some wine too, my unannounced visit still hours away. In another ten minutes, I've received enough pictures to be sorry I asked.

Mateo's wearing a dark blue suit and a burgundy button-up, his tie and handkerchief bringing both colors together. His hair has been pulled into the bun I expected. His grin is full of mischief he'll have to smother when it's time to be the responsible adult. He's so fucking gorgeous. And it's been almost four years.

I just choked on my pinot noir

The flattery is back.

Neither one of us texts after that. The time suggests Mateo should be on his way to the hotel hosting tonight's festivities, doing whatever the chaperones do until the students arrive. I get more pictures from Harper, all dressed up and on her way to dinner. Then *at* dinner. Then at the dance. I get a warning after all that, telling me she's done with me until it's slumber party time. I sign off with a simple *I love you*.

I'm lonely—and yes, crawling out of my skin—until midnight has come and gone, and I can go to Mateo's to tell him about my day. I shower and change into black joggers and a dark green henley. Then I roll my eyes because nothing I'm wearing matters. I'm shaking, probably obviously so, and that continues when I arrive at his apartment before he's returned. I sit on the ground with my back to his door, and I wait and wait and wait.

We've done so much of that. I wonder if promises can become

indefinite things.

There's plenty of ambient sound, but I swear I know his car when it purrs through the parking lot and comes to a stop. The chirp of his key fob comes next, and I know that, too. Then I see him, and he sees me, and I imagine our expressions change a dozen times when we take each other in. Mateo's suit jacket is in his hand now. I'm thrown off by the sight of suspenders hidden from me before, his tie and top couple of buttons undone. That I'm here at all throws him, but I push to my feet and don't wince when my leg unfairly reminds me of things I could never forget.

"Watching you come home was nicer than what you offered earlier," I say, my voice low for at least a few reasons.

"I didn't think this was an option," he chuckles softly. "It's the middle of the night."

"And you need to sleep."

Mateo shrugs. "I just had a drink with a couple of other teachers. I wouldn't mind another one with you."

He unlocks his door, and I follow him into his kitchen, our shoes kicked aside and his jacket draped over a chair on our way. The only light is from the dim lamp he'd left on in the living room, his apartment small enough for him to keep everything else off for the night. I watch as he reaches for a bottle of bourbon. I say nothing, fine with anything that will help dull what happens next.

I can't be nobody anymore, but just for tonight, I could do without feeling all of Jameson Sinclair's highs and lows.

"How was prom?" I ask as he pours.

"Incident-free, which is pretty much the measure of success on our end." He passes me a glass and takes a sip from his own. "Harper looked beautiful."

"*You* look beautiful."

He smiles almost shyly. "I assume she's spending the night at a friend's?"

Her last text came about ten minutes before Mateo pulled into his complex. I nod. "She is."

"So you can stay?"

"I won't."

He wants to ask me why—I can read that much in the tilt of his head and the quick crease between his brows—but he stalls with another sip. Honestly, I'm not sure *I* know why anymore. I should say the things I came here to say, but they make less sense now. I'm standing in a mostly dark apartment with liquor in my hand and Mateo staring at me, and I consider taking this in the opposite direction, just to let us have this one night together. We'd know what it was like to see and hear and taste and feel everything before I ruin it with my happiness. I was raised to focus on a singular goal, but maybe I can have two tonight.

Maybe I can hold on to Mateo now and let him go tomorrow.

I don't beg for the chance because I've learned to live with the bruises he'll touch without trying. Sometimes I think the nearness of pain motivates me as much as anything.

"Dance with me."

I startle at that, the request falling from Mateo's lips and not mine. "You were just at prom."

"It wasn't *my* prom, Jamie." He's teasing me, but sobers quickly. "This *is* my apartment. Dance with me."

The bourbon is smooth when I swallow, and I hope it will keep my heartbeat steady. For almost a minute, neither of us moves except to lift our glasses to our mouths. Then I step forward and pull his phone from his pocket.

"Pick a song."

He does, and it's a U2 song I know well. It doesn't need to be loud for me to know I'll hear it for the rest of my life. Mateo may have been the one to ask me for this, but he hesitates as the song plays. I assume he's still curious about why I showed up just to tell him I have plans to leave. I'm not going anywhere yet though, and I reach for one of his suspenders. With my fingers curled around it, I back toward the living room and drag him with me. I don't know how to do the rest of this—I couldn't guess when I last slow-danced with anyone, and I definitely haven't done it with another man—but he seems to understand. He takes me in his arms as we start to sway.

Minutes pass, and I only know because the songs have changed. I'm locked in an embrace I still want forever, and I'm remarkably silent as I press my nose to Mateo's neck. I've heard scents are closely linked to memories. He doesn't stop me, no matter how careless I am, and it reminds me of something else. Slowly, I pull away until my mouth is just a few inches from his, and I find his bun with one hand, tugging until I can drop the hair tie to the floor.

"I care," he whispers, because he's been reminded, too.

"We're friends."

"*Friends*. It's the faintest line I've ever drawn," Mateo scoffs, shaking his head. "I've never known how to be less than everything when I'm with you."

People lie to me all the time. I'm an easy mark with a big ego. Bullshit does its job for as long as I let myself believe it. I've had things people want—money and a pretty face now; breathtaking talent and a pretty face long ago—so they've always told me what I need to hear. But while held captive by Mateo's soft stare and clumsily dancing in his arms, I know this is different. That just like that first night, when we could've said goodbye after dinner from a taco truck and careless kissing by the beach, *he's* different.

Years later, he's still telling me the truth, and I'm the fucking liar.

We take a deep breath together as if we can reset both. Then Mateo guides my hand to where his tie remains loose around his neck.

Tossing it aside is easy for me, but he doesn't stop there. He finds my other hand now, and moves both to his shoulders, humming his encouragement when I push the suspenders down his arms. There's nothing to add to the pile this time. In search of something else to do, I untuck his shirt and swear—even in the dim room—that I can see his brown eyes bleed black.

"I'm not staying the night with you," I say, gentle when I work my way through his buttons. "I won't touch you everywhere."

Mateo's shirt is open when he wraps his arms around me again. We sway, his mouth next to my ear. "You've stayed before."

"Not when we've been like this."

"We weren't like this when you first said no to spending the night. You'd probably decided that before you left your house."

He's right, and he knows it, and he only holds me closer, almost grinding against me to a song that doesn't demand it. It's agonizingly slow, and I let it happen because I've never stopped wanting to be wanted. And by this man more than anyone I've ever met.

"I don't know how to be less than everything with you either."

"We're going to have to wait longer than a few more weeks, aren't we?" he asks, his question pressed to my temple before he drops his head to bite at my shoulder, frustrated in a way I'm unable to fix. "It can't be right after graduation, because everyone would know."

"Yes, we'll have to wait," I rasp.

One of his hands slides down my back and stops just below my waistband. The pressure there keeps me in place when he knows I'm about to run. I'm weak enough to stay for another terrible, wonderful minute, and if he pushes any harder, I might stay forever. Then I remember a year ago, on the bench, when I was in Mateo's lap and rocking forward and more aroused than I'd been in years. Even my prom night mistake with Melanie couldn't compare then, and he and I are closer to trouble now.

"Go."

For the second time tonight, he startles me, that single word almost a kiss left on my cheek. I nod because the hair on his face feels so fucking good against me. Then I press my hand to his chest as I back away, his heartbeat as wild as mine always has been.

I'm still fully clothed, my shoes, phone, and keys all I need before I leave. Mateo doesn't move from the middle of the living room when I walk toward the door. Actually, his head is tipped downward, like I've given him a reason to pray.

I step outside and pull his apartment door closed behind me. The night greets me with a haunting hum of near-silence, and I start walking to my car with a prayer of my own—unspoken, but so loud inside my head.

Don't stop being everything.
Don't stop loving me.
Don't stop waiting.
Then I stop and turn around.

Chapter Ten: Mateo

(I Asked Him to Let Me In)

I should jump when I hear the knock at the door less than a minute later, but I don't. Maybe I'd noticed the footsteps, or maybe I'd just hoped hard enough for Jamie to return. I look down my body, where my shirt is still hanging open and my legs are now bare. My pants have joined the pile on the floor because my entire body is vibrating with need that hasn't allowed me to be tidy. I give myself a couple of quick strokes over the pale blue boxer briefs left behind and pause at the small wet spot that would give my secrets away if I had any to keep.

I step forward and remind myself to be careful because that faint line hasn't gone anywhere, and even if Jamie has changed his mind about spending the night, it hasn't changed anything else. I'm so hard I think I could cry, but I've ignored it before and I can do it again. There's a month until graduation, and so much unknown after that, so for tonight, we'll continue to be friends.

Being everything has to wait.

It's so late—early, really—and while I don't expect anyone to be wandering past my door at this hour, I only crack it open, confirm it's him, then duck out of the way before the rest of the apartment complex can see me half-naked. Beautiful and bothered, he falls against the door as soon as it's locked again, and I won't pull him any closer. I stay a foot or two away and don't apologize for standing in front of him with a dick weeping for attention. Jamie doesn't apologize for failing to meet my eyes.

"Are you going to stay?"

"No."

That surprises me, I think. If we can't cross lines, and he won't spend the night like he's done before, there aren't a lot of options left for us. I watch as he turns his head toward the kitchen, and the empty glasses we left on the counter when I asked him to dance. I can't drink any more bourbon, but I won't stop him if he's thirsty. My phone is still there too, the playlist nowhere near over, just in case he'd like to dance again. Maybe I could take his shirt off this time.

When he gives up on the kitchen, he makes eye contact for a moment before he looks past me instead, finding the dark suit pants crumpled on the floor. Then his big blue eyes open wide.

"You weren't in your bedroom yet. You weren't getting ready to sleep. When you took off your pants, you—you were right where I left you."

"I was feeling pretty desperate. Didn't think I'd make it any further."

"Your bedroom's only twenty feet away."

I shrug. "My couch is right there."

"And I interrupted."

He didn't really, but the thought of it makes me twitch. I take a slow breath while Jamie continues to look at me, seeing more than he ever has, and I want to ask him why he's here. I'm not sure I'd get an answer, and I decide not to try.

"No," I tell him, a confession or a dare. "I hadn't started yet."

Jamie nods and accepts both. "Are you still desperate?"

"Of course I am."

"Your couch is right there."

"And where are the lines?" I ask.

"We're right on top of them."

It's such a quiet answer—*everything* is quiet except the songs I'll never hear the same way again—and I move away from him, certain he'll follow and curious what will happen after that. We could watch each other get off. We could help each other get off, though that seems a step past "right on top of," even in the middle of the night when everything's a blur. Either way, I lie down for him, my boxer briefs still in place when I wait to see what Jamie will do next.

I was stunned when I returned from prom to find him sitting with his back against my door, and I'm stunned now when he sits on the floor, his back against my couch. He reaches for my hand over his shoulder, clasps it in his, and doesn't turn to look at me.

He just holds on.

I'm foolishly delirious, and too love-drunk to be afraid of turning the wrong things upside down over the lines he says are beneath us. I've needed this relief since I told him to go, and it feels so fucking good to finally pull my cock free, those first couple of strokes causing me to make a sound like one of his. I shift until I can push the fabric a little lower and tuck it beneath my balls, cupping them before I return to the same reckless rhythm. When I'm noisy again, Jamie squeezes my hand and I arch into my fist, wet and whining.

There are things I should say. At the very least, I think I should remind him I love him, but the relative silence around us almost makes each sensation better and my staccato breathing loud. Besides, maybe if we don't speak, the most dangerous parts of our night won't be real. This won't take nearly as long as it has thousands of other times, and I won't disrupt anything to tell him that either. I briefly wonder whether he's getting off too, but his body remains still when I slow down enough to check, and the pressure of his hand only responds to the things I do. When I'm almost lazy about teasing my tip, Jamie's thumb brushes gently against my skin. When my grip is unforgiving and I speed up and another moan slips free, he tightens his hold on me.

I tremble, and he vibrates with my need.

He still hasn't turned around to watch what I know he must want to see, and I won't explain it away with a simple lack of experience or the relationship we can't have yet. This is an eager, hungry man who's lived through rumors full of truth, but he's got hold of the control I've lost, simply because he knows I can't do anything but race toward an inevitable end. I want him to talk me through this, and I think he could be filthy about it, but asking Jamie to speak will break the only spell that will protect us for another minute or two. He came over with more on his mind than some bourbon and a slow dance, but pushing for those answers might hurt in a way this doesn't. We once confessed to wanting a night that would be loud and slow, but this moment is full of other things we've dreamed of and can't have, and I don't worry about how many more years that might be true.

Something is wrong, but the intimacy is exactly right, and if this fragile thing will shatter, I want to appreciate the beauty for the short time we have it.

Jamie can tell me everything later. I'm going to come now.

Every ragged breath and needy moan tangles together, and I feel my stomach muscles contract. As one of my hands works furiously around my dick, the other is curled around a promise, so afraid to let it go when the rest of my body surrenders to pure pleasure. My release ripples through me and leaves my chest messier than it's been in a while, Jamie's closeness as effective at ruining me as anything ever has been.

I close my eyes and will my heartbeat to quiet so I can hear the rest of what neither of us will say. In the few seconds after that, my hand is free, and his head remains turned. I tuck myself back into my boxer briefs, and while I hadn't imagined I'd be here when I got dressed hours ago, I use the loose sides of my shirt to wipe my body clean and ignore how much I'm still shaking. Sitting up takes effort, though it's less than what Jamie has just used to stand, and if I thought he'd accept, I'd invite him to stay while I massage the ache away.

Instead, I watch the rise and fall of his shoulders as he sighs, and when he walks toward my door, I prepare myself for a wordless goodbye. I'm not even sure he'll turn to look at me before he goes, but my legs won't allow me to give chase.

He does, though. Jamie turns around in the open doorway, and eyes that have always been a little sad make me want to cry.

"Mateo, I—" His voice breaks, and I'm too softened by liquor and an orgasm to fully register the cracks it leaves in me. "Call me tomorrow?"

"Of course."

Of course.

Of course I agree to call him tomorrow. When I throw my dirty clothes in the hamper and pull on a pair of sleep shorts and stare bleary-eyed at my reflection in the bathroom mirror, I can't figure out a reason I wouldn't want to talk to him. I'm worried about the conversation itself, but if I don't call him, how will I know what I'm most afraid of? I brush my teeth and crawl into bed and only wonder how early he'll be awake when he's been up so late tonight.

Then I sleep far too well and roll over mid-morning, already thinking about him when I reach for my phone. Those first several seconds of my day are lazy bliss, and then I see two texts from Sophie.

The first is a simple question. ***Did you know about this?***

The second is a link, and I pay little attention to it until I land on a relatively reputable sports media site. I'm not sure knowing where I was headed would've helped me dodge the shock of the headline. I read it quickly, and my stomach turns faster than that.

Broken No More: Former Phenom Jameson Sinclair to Join Rival Behind the Bench in New Jersey

This breaking news has yet to be confirmed, but reliable sources have told our site that the team plans to formally announce on Monday that they've hired Sinclair. He's expected to serve as an assistant alongside Taylor McKeon, who just wrapped up his second successful season as New Jersey's head coach. The two men never got along on the ice, and were thought to dislike each other off it as well, the superstars' egos colliding over multiple NHL records and even more beautiful women. Since suffering the horrific injury that ended his stellar career, Sinclair has made numerous appearances as an on-air analyst, his talent there apparently drawing the attention of McKeon. The two of them were spotted vacationing together at McKeon's home right around the time an announcement was made about McKeon's new position. One has to wonder if the two Hall of Famers may have first discussed the idea of working together then, but regardless, the entire NHL community should be eager to see the sparks fly between them now. We will have more for you once New Jersey confirms the news and we have the opportunity to talk to both Jameson Sinclair and Taylor McKeon about their future.

I want to throw my phone across the bedroom, but I have to respond to Sophie first.

I had no idea.

When I don't call Jamie by midday, he tries calling me. I don't answer.

I get a series of texts throughout the afternoon.

Are you awake?

Can you call me?

I need to talk to you

I should've talked to you last night

I guess this means you know

Nobody was supposed to say anything until Monday

Please Mateo

Call me

I ignore those, too.

Sophie comes over and we watch terrible movies that don't remind me of love. Other than her apology for sending me the hockey link without thinking it through, she says nothing about Jamie's new job, nor does she tell me I need to talk to him. I already know that.

I consider calling in sick on Monday, but then Harper would tell Jamie I wasn't there, and I don't need him showing up at my door. I'm a little surprised he hasn't done that already, but maybe he knows holding my hand and turning away will only get us so far. In class, I make myself as busy as possible, but Harper's already talking to a small group of students around her, and I get pulled in. Dragged, really.

"It's so perfect. The timing? I was a little nervous about moving away for school, but if he's moving away too, we'll both have big adventures. And yeah, it means he'll probably only make it to a few of my games early in the season, which definitely sucks because he was gonna fly up a few different times, but he's missed being on a team, so I know he's really excited to be back." She pauses and looks at me. "Did you hear, Mr. Z? My dad's gonna be coaching? He'll be on the ice again. I mean, not like, *playing*. But you know."

"I heard, yeah," I say. "And I know."

Over the next few days, I think about how much I know now, and always have. Two years ago, we sat with our feet in his pool while we talked about Taylor McKeon, and how much Jamie missed hockey, and the idea of him coaching someday. Then it was only a year ago that we sat on the bench, and I realized he'd only chosen me because I wasn't competing with an arena full of everything he'd lost.

That isn't true anymore.

As the nausea fades and something like exhaustion settles in, I finally pick up my phone.

"Mateo," Jamie breathes, his relief washing over me more than I'd like it to. "Thank you, I—fuck, I didn't—"

"Please stop," I interrupt.

"Okay."

"I don't want to do this over the phone."

"Okay," he says again. "Can we meet on the bench?"

It would be so easy to say yes to him. It's where we started, and if our story has to end, I think it should happen there, too. But we spent that first night together because neither of us wanted to walk away from feelings we barely understood, and I don't want to walk away from the bench now that I understand everything too well.

"No, let me come over. When Harper is at work or with friends or whatever. Let me into your house."

"You say that like you haven't come over any other nights," Jamie sighs. "Or like I haven't wanted you to stay until morning after every one of them."

"I won't stay this time."

"That's fair. I didn't stay on prom night."

I rub my tired eyes, and nothing becomes clear. "Is that a yes?"

"Yeah, she works tomorrow night. I'll be home."

Our goodbyes are quick and quiet after that. I have one more day of teaching to get through before I'll see him, and that's quick and quiet, too. When I make it home, eating is a challenge, but I successfully shower for the second time that day. In the foggy bathroom, I lament the pictures I can't take for Jamie tonight. Then I pull on a t-shirt and jeans and take a picture for myself without knowing why.

I park in Jamie's driveway, and he's waiting for me at the front door by the time I get there. I'm not sure he's slept much all week—it's a feeling I know well—and the shadows under his eyes make me want to apologize for things I've only sort of done. Instead, I stop a few feet short of where I could reach out to sweep the darkness away.

"Congratulations," I say. "I guess that's probably overdue, huh?"

"You owe me nothing."

"I'd rather give you everything."

He nearly winces at that, so close to what he'd said to me the second night we met, but then he turns to walk further into his house, leaving me to lock up behind us like I've done before. Jamie's wearing nothing but pajama pants that hang too low on his hips, and I'd ask him to put a hoodie on if I weren't afraid he'd pick up mine again. When I catch up with him in the kitchen, there's an unopened bottle of bourbon on the counter, and I raise an eyebrow.

Jamie shrugs. "Impulse buy. You can take it home if you want."

"A consolation prize?"

"Mateo."

"When did you know?"

"Officially?" he asks. "The morning of prom. I went to your apartment to tell you, and then I—it wasn't right."

"But holding my hand while I jerked off was fine?"

"It was as close to perfect as I could get."

"When did you *unofficially* know?"

He leaves the liquor alone and reaches for his water bottle. "We've been talking for the past few months, off and on."

"We?" I echo. "You and Taylor McKeon?"

"He doesn't get to call all the shots, no matter what he thinks," Jamie snorts. "But yeah, he was part of it. Most of it was the GM, or other front office people."

"Did all of this start at McKeon's house? When you were there for spring break?"

"Nope, that's just a rumor. All of it happened recently."

I shake my head. "You still had time to tell me."

"Yeah, I did," Jamie agrees. "But at first, it felt impossible. Like I was dreaming, and at any second, I'd wake up and be in the hospital again, and have nothing. Then even after a few meetings, my attorney reminded me none of it was a sure thing until they put something in writing. But then they did, and it still wasn't supposed to be announced so soon. It shouldn't have been a big deal anyway. I'm just an assistant coach, for fuck's sake."

"You're *you*, for fuck's sake. You're Jameson Sinclair."

He tosses the water bottle toward the sink, the landing louder than the throw was hard, and he marches past me and through the great room. For a second, I think he'll go into the backyard—maybe even to the bench from a path I still haven't approached from this side—but he stops at the patio doors, his back to me. I want the distance between us to lessen the pressure in my chest, but it does nothing to help, and I follow him because I'm hurt enough to want to share.

"It wasn't just you—I didn't tell *anyone*. Not Harper, not Kai. I didn't want to jinx it."

"Sure. It wouldn't be a decision you'd necessarily have to talk through with us, right?" I sigh and hope my breath against the back of his neck is why Jamie has goosebumps. "Harper will be away at school and doing her own thing even more than she already is. Kai's watched hockey take you away since you were kids. And I'm just the guy you said you'd wait four years to be with."

"I didn't lie to you."

I think he means he wasn't lying about waiting these past four years. He might mean he wasn't lying when he remained silent about his new coaching position. Or it could be about loving me. It doesn't really matter, and I'm only angry when I curl a hand around his waist, my thumb brushing against his bare skin because I've never been able to help myself.

"I can't move to New Jersey with you," I say. "I've got my family and my job and—"

Jamie tenses, and I'm not sure if I caught it in his reflection or against the palm of my hand, but either way, his reaction forces me to take a step back. He whirls around immediately, his fist in my shirt because I've already let him go.

"Please don't leave."

I laugh, and it's so ugly, and I'm so tired. "Pretty sure that should've been my line. Especially because you weren't going to ask me to go with you. You don't want me there."

"What I want and what I can have are not a circle. They never have been, and maybe that's true for everyone, but hockey has always meant sacrificing other things."

"I think it's mostly meant *compromising* other things," I argue. "So much time away from home—away from your family. Fewer lazy weekends full of pizza and beer with your friends. Less anonymity when you want to spend a private night out with someone you care about. But you never actually had to give up your relationships. Not until now."

Jamie still has a grip on my shirt, and he goes after me then, spinning us until my back hits the patio door hard enough to rattle the glass. It's a shame he didn't check me like this when he took me skating, but my mouth falls open and I barely remember the man who'd held my hand and kept his head turned away while I came all over myself. His eyes don't leave mine, and I get hit with the most absurd battle of arrogance and need, and I don't know how much either has to do with me until he speaks.

"Hockey was the first love of my life. The first. Yeah, maybe my parents pushed me more than they should've, but the rink was home. I wanted to be there more than I wanted to be with my family, or have a lazy weekend, or spend a private night with anyone. I loved hockey with everything I was, and it loved me back. Then it broke my heart, and I have spent years *desperate* for another chance. I've said yes to every opportunity I've had to be close to it again. And then just last week, I was asked to say yes again, and I *did*, and I'm not sorry about that. But it fucking kills me to hear you say that I'm giving up on *us*. Hockey was my first love, but it's not my only one, and I'm standing here begging you not to give up either."

It's impossible to know what's in his expression when he falls forward against me, but I assume need has won for now, a second fist at my side. Without thinking, I wrap my arms around Jamie and bring him even closer, his skin warm and his heart pounding. One of his hands moves to my head and pulls my hair tie free. I growl and reach for his hair, too. Nothing is going to happen right here, but everything could, and I want to remember how it feels for him to be mine before he leaves and can belong to anyone.

"We'll already be across the country from each other," I murmur in his ear. "And coaching doesn't come with a four-year expiration date. If we're not giving up, what are we doing?"

"You love me. You told me you love me."

"Loving you doesn't change anything about my question."

Jamie shifts until his mouth opens against my neck. "Just keep loving me."

"Okay, yes, but—" I gently peel him off me, and the shadows under his eyes are still there. This time, I pretend I can wipe them away, my hand cradling the side of his head while I brush the darkness with my thumb. "Will it ever be over? The waiting for more?"

"My contract includes a clause about behavior 'outside the scope of my duties as a member of the coaching staff.' Basically, I got away with being a pain in the ass as a player, but being a captain isn't the same as being a coach. The late-night antics that were reprimanded back then may be cause for dismissal now."

"Coming out as bisexual and admitting to the world that you're in love with me are hardly *late-night antics*."

"To them they might be," he says, leveling me with a stare I expect. "Please, just give me time to figure that out. Let me see what's changed since I've been out of the locker room. Let me get to know everyone there. Maybe behind the bench, I'll be nobody. And while I'm gone, you and I can still have the friendship we have now."

I laugh weakly. Sadly. "*Gone* and *the friendship we have now* sort of contradict each other, no?"

"We'll have a couple of games down here, so I can see you then. And in the offseason, obviously. And talking and texting, and I don't—I don't want to have to choose, 'Teo."

"You already did, sweetheart."

Jamie's eyes are wet, and I know he wants to defend his decisions all over again. He sighs instead. "Does that mean you won't wait for me?"

I couldn't begin to count how many times I've thought about the promises we once made on top of wishes, but I'm overwhelmed by the memory of them now. For two men who'd lived full, independent, successful lives before we met, we were incredibly naive that night. Maybe we've been naive every day since. Jamie and I have been waiting for something we've never had—keeping secrets about things that haven't happened—and tonight's our best chance to make a clean break from it all. Tonight is our chance to decide we made promises we couldn't keep on top of wishes that won't come true.

But with my hand still pressed to his cheek, I hold Jamie still and kiss him.

He's surprised at first, but it doesn't take him long to realize this is another shooting star, and insisting on my answer now will only give it time to disappear into the night. His mouth opens easily, and I can't believe it's been almost four years since I've felt the drag of his tongue against mine. There's so much space behind him, but we don't move away from the door separating us from the ocean and the moon and the bench I suddenly and fiercely miss. Briefly, I wonder whether he'll sell the house, and whether I'll ever see the bench again, but then he moans and I can't care about anything but him.

Our kiss feels endless—or it ends and restarts a hundred times, just like this thing we have between us—until I know I need to answer Jamie's question. I give myself another few seconds to memorize something I'm afraid I won't have again, then finally pull back to mumble something foolish against his lips.

"Of course I'll wait for you. I already made my choice, too."

***

A few weeks later, Harper graduates. I get invited to the party celebrating her, and when Jamie finds me in the backyard, we both stare down the hillside and go nowhere.

He doesn't sell the house because he doesn't need to, and he wants to make sure his daughter has a place to call home no matter what Danielle does with her own empty nest. He'll rent something small and meaningless in New Jersey, where other things will mean plenty. He gives me a spare key for the house, just in case.

In case of what, I don't know.

There's no party for Jamie before he leaves, though he tries to spend time with the people who want to see him, his parents included. They're thrilled about his new achievement, the best they could expect after he lost all he had. He sees Kai too, and that goodbye has nothing to do with achievements or loss. It's just love.

Jamie and I don't meet at the bench. We don't talk about why we're avoiding it, but I figure he's afraid of the same things that have kept me up at night. He suggests one more drive up the coast. I agree. We don't make promises. We don't say *I love you*. We barely talk at all.

And then he's gone, and we begin to wait all over again.

Part Two

(We Waited Until the Wedding)

CHAPTER ELEVEN: JAMIE

(I SLEPT IN MY OWN BED)

A decade ago, if anyone had told me how well Taylor McKeon and I would work together one day, I would've rolled my eyes. If anyone had told me we'd have a decent chance of becoming friends, I would've laughed and told them to fuck all the way off. Now, as my first season of coaching begins with him at my side, both are true. I'm breathing more easily than I have since the night my playing career ended.

During the first week of October, I stop in one of the empty hallways of our practice facility and lean against the wall with my phone in my hand.

I keep waiting for him to be a dick to me, but maybe we'll actually make it to opening night without an argument worthy of a headline or two

It's early morning for Mateo, but it means the school day hasn't started, and I get a quick response. **You have less than a week to go. And I could do without any more McKeon/Sinclair headlines tbh.**

Well when you put it that way

Are you still nervous?

You know I am. Are you still watching the game at Kai's?

You know I am. And Sophie said she'd come with me.

That makes me feel better and worse, knowing they'll be together while I'm so far away. And Harper will be with her soccer team, their season already underway and going well, so the loneliness hits hard. The good news is that I rarely have time to sit with any feeling long enough to be bothered by it. Coaching in the NHL is a full-time job on top of a full-time job.

Let me know how I look in my suit

I can already tell you how pretty you'll be in your suit.

My smile comes easily, or maybe it's been there since the first message from him. I use old PR skills to hide it when footsteps round the corner, and tuck my phone into my pocket.

"Ah, here you are. I was wondering whether you'd finally realized there are fewer groupies for middle-aged coaches than for 20something phenoms," Taylor huffs. "But seeing that look on your face? I'm guessing you're not looking for groupies at all."

I scoff, also a skill picked up from a press conference or several. "There's no look on my face."

"And your phone?"

"I have one, yes. Even use it occasionally to keep in touch with my daughter and my friends and a few old teammates who'd still love the opportunity to kick your ass."

"Somehow I don't think your conversation was about *my* ass," he says. "But whatever. I don't care who you're fucking. Never did, except for how I could use it to get under your skin."

We're on the same team now, and several of his records have been mine for a while, so I know he has no reason to mess with my head. I don't point out how rarely it worked even then, all those years ago when I wanted hockey more than I wanted anyone. I don't point out that it could work now, if I weren't so intent on making sure I can love two things at once. Our friendship may come sooner than expected, but I won't tell him about Mateo. I can't.

That friendship matters more.

That friendship *is* more.

We win our first two games. We lose the third. We start a road trip and win the fourth. Taylor and I have great things to say about the team. The team has great things to say about us. Mateo tells me I'm just as pretty as he'd imagined I would be. I imagine him in the boxer briefs he wore on prom night.

My parents are proud of me again, and I hate how much I care. Harper and Kai remain my north stars, even while they shine in a busy, busy sky.

I'd say I'm getting settled in New Jersey, but that's not entirely accurate. I'm traveling with the team, which makes hotel rooms home as much as the small house I've rented. When we have a homestand, my early mornings and late nights are spent on the ice, or close enough to it. There's little time for me to want someone in my bed, no matter how often Taylor drops hints about all the women in his. I don't have a spare minute to miss Mateo, but he's on my mind every day. I feel like it's all those years ago when I wanted to pretend that wasn't true.

I have trouble falling asleep after a tough overtime loss. *I miss you*

He juggles conferences and a soccer tournament and his second year of teaching AP English. ***I miss you too.***

We have a night off, and Taylor and I go out for dinner and drinks, and he wants me to get laid. *I'm eating garlic parmesan wings but I'd rather have mango chipotle with you.*

Mateo goes out with Sophie and some of the other teachers, and someone tries to set him up on a blind date. ***I haven't forgotten the taste of your mouth.***

That turns me on more than eight simple words should. I almost bring up the idea of phone sex, and not for the first time. The years we've waited for each other have been built upon months built upon weeks built upon days, and more than a few of those were lonely. I stop myself now because Mateo and I have lines we won't let ourselves cross, even if the exceptions have been exceptional. I'll never forget the broken little sounds he made when he jerked off behind me. I'd brought a mess of contradictions to his door that night, and they excused the bourbon and dancing and orgasm that followed. And we've only kissed twice—at the beginning of something that made perfect sense and at the moment I was afraid I was ending it. Making each other come from across the country would be normal in a way nothing else has been. I won't break Mateo's rules to ask for that tonight.

I don't actually say anything else to him, but I hope he says no to the blind date.

Harper's team loses in the second round of the playoffs, but it means I can fly her out for a quick Thanksgiving visit. We catch up when I'm not at the arena. She asks about Taylor's son and half my roster before I remind her she has a new boyfriend. Then she asks about Mateo.

My kid wants to know if you and I still talk. I guess we can't hide from her forever

She's 18 now. She'd still have to keep it quiet, but it's not the same as when I was her teacher and coach.

So you think I should tell her?

I think she's your daughter. You'll know what to do and when to do it.

If only it were that easy.

Christmas comes, and I cling to a framed picture of a bench I haven't sat on since the day I left California. Mateo and I could've said our goodbyes there, but I'd made peace with the ocean alone that morning. I could've flown home for a turnaround holiday hello, but I wasn't going to find any of the relief I needed if I couldn't spend more than a few hours with the man I love.

There's a game on New Year's Eve, and we win it. I call Mateo before I've left for home. Taylor sees me, but he only winks and waves and believes things about me that aren't true. For the first time since my arrival on the East Coast, I wonder whether his sister visits often.

Mateo asks whether I plan to make any resolutions, but I can't imagine why I'd bother.

Harper surprises me on my birthday. We're playing later tonight, but she's at my door absurdly early after her red-eye flight, and she takes me out to breakfast.

"You really don't mind that I'll be busy all day?" I ask.

She smiles, and I've missed her so much. "You didn't mind when I made you follow me all over campus in August, and I don't mind now. I'll be perfectly happy being introduced to Nikolai, Roman, Erik, and Jonathan before you have actual work to do."

"You mean, before they have an actual game to play. And you and Simon are still together, right? I didn't miss some big breakup news?"

"Yes, we're still together. Everything is great. I also think you have a really hot team."

"Just what every dad wants to hear on his birthday," I tease. My phone vibrates against the table, and I glance down as if all texts are created equal. After a second of letting my heart kick at my chest, I take the opening I've been given. "Hey, so, I know we talked about you coming to the game when we're back in California next month. Are you still up for that?"

"Yeah, of course. I'll be able to see you there, plus catch up with a bunch of friends who stayed close to home. And mom. She'll probably want to have a spa day or something? Are you getting two tickets? I'm sure I can find somebody who'll want to go with me. Lizzie might be home then, but I don't know for sure yet."

"How would you feel about me giving the second ticket to someone?"

She looks at the phone in my hand, then back up at me. "Was that Mr. Z? Did he text you for your birthday?"

"It was, and yes," I say. "Would it be okay if I give the other ticket to him?"

Harper pauses, and I can't tell whether it's about Mateo or all the friends she could take to the game instead. Then she shrugs and gives one of her shortest responses ever, mostly because she has a forkful of pancakes in her hand.

"Totally fine."

Harper's here. We're having breakfast. You think you'll be okay going to the game with her next month?

I don't have time to reach for my bite before Mateo texts back. ***I'll be totally fine.***

Two peas in a fucking pod. I shake my head, and my daughter and I talk until my game-day routine begins. She gets to meet Nikolai, Roman, Erik, Jonathan, and everyone else. Taylor has at least as many responsibilities as I do, but he takes time to show Harper around, and I'm grateful for all the ways the past is the past, even while I miss it with everything I am.

If I look around the arena for Mateo, it's not because I'm comparing one love to another.

Southern California feels downright warm compared to winter back east, and stepping through my own front door is the kind of heaven I believe in. There isn't much time to relax when we've got a couple of games down here, but I breathe in the Pacific Ocean for as long as I can. I stop by my parents' house because I have to. Kai meets me in the bar kitchen for a hug we didn't use to share. Harper is everywhere with everyone for the few days she'll be home.

I'd expected to have as much time with Mateo as possible, but it doesn't happen that way. With so many people asking for a chance to say hello, he and I are limited to texts we could've exchanged on any other day.

As much as I can, I shift my focus to coaching. We beat the team I played for my entire career, and I'm more emotional than what I let the world see. It's been that way since I was first propped up on skates and told to smile for the camera without fear in my eyes. We celebrate in the locker room and unwind and pack our things. When everyone else heads back to the hotel, I head home. Both Harper and Mateo had texted me after the game.

Going to Lizzie's for the night. I'll find you tomorrow before I see mom

Not sure whether you'll be able to sneak away, but I'll be outside

I take a deep breath when I step into my house and lock the front door behind me, still adjusting to the idea that I don't really live here anymore. Sure, as a player I was on the road too, but only for half of each season. It's not the same now, and I'm worried about how much time I have left before this doesn't feel like home. Tonight it feels like exactly that—almost painfully so—and I hurry upstairs to change before I find another way to remind myself of what I've left behind.

I'm wearing track pants and a hoodie when I get to the kitchen and make some hot apple cider. With a full thermos in my hand, I open the patio door and move to the middle of my backyard, staring at the moon while I consider going back inside. It's been months, and as much as I love what I've done in that time, every single night has hurt, too. It's been months, and I want to forget about them now.

In another minute, I'm sitting next to Mateo on the bench, his blanket across our laps. I help myself to a sip of the cider, then hand it to him. "Nice jersey. Did you wear that to the game?"

He looks down at the gift I gave him over a year ago and shakes his head. His fingertips are gentle against material used to so much worse. I catch the hint of a smile just before he combs his hair back from his face. Then he takes a long pull from the thermos without asking what's in it and finally meets my eyes in the dark.

"I did not. Your daughter is too curious and too clever," he says. "But there were a hell of a lot of Jameson Sinclair jerseys in the crowd. More than when you were the one sitting next to me. So many people were there for you tonight."

I want to say something about that, but I save it for later. "I'm sorry I didn't get to see you before this."

"I understood you were going to be busy."

"You're a higher priority than *busy*."

"Sometimes I am," Mateo agrees. "And you're here now."

"Mmmm." I accept the thermos when he passes it back to me, glad to have something to hold. There's so much for us to talk about, but nothing we need to say, and I've never minded the quiet down here. Still, while I've mostly acclimated to the colder weather, Mateo hasn't, and there's an entire house just behind us. "Not that I don't love the way our lives change every night we're out here, but it's warm inside. Will you come with me?"

"What about Harper?"

"She's gone for the night."

"It's pretty late."

"Don't leave."

Mateo drags the blanket away and stands slowly, but he's looking at the water when he tries to tame his hair again. "I've never been."

"To my house?" I ask, confused. Even if he's talking about my bed, he's spent the night in it before.

"On the other half of this path," he says. "I've been between here and the shore. I've been in your backyard, in your kitchen, on your couch, and in your bedroom. But from here to there—it's the missing piece."

I stand too, and reach for his jaw, turning his face toward me. "It's *a* missing piece, yeah. Do you think that'll be enough for tonight?"

With the wind playing with his hair and my jersey covering his body, Mateo first answers with a deep breath. Then he nods, his longing and resignation things I know well. I lead the way, though I have no doubt he could move the missing piece into place on his own. The top of the path doesn't stop at the back edge of my property, skirting the side instead, and we follow the wrought-iron fence to a gate. Most people assume it's used to access the backyard from the front of the house. They're not wrong, but tonight we approach from my long-hidden sanctuary.

Our long-hidden sanctuary, maybe.

We could stop when we first get inside—grab something to eat in the kitchen or make ourselves comfortable in the great room before we watch a movie—but like Mateo said, it's pretty late. At least for now, neither of us will waste time playing games. The thermos and blanket get left behind. He and I go upstairs without talking about it first, and in the middle of my bedroom, I'm the one to touch my jersey too gently. Before the moment turns dangerous, I back away from him and offer him sweatpants. Then I lock myself in the bathroom so I don't have to watch him change from one of my things to another.

He's half in bed when I return, almost unbearably comfortable in space someone as selfish as I am shouldn't want to share.

"I told her she could call me Mateo."

I cock my head. "Harper?"

"Yeah. Instead of Mr. Z—or Coach, I guess. Now that she's graduated, and if we're—I don't know. It just felt strange for her to be formal with me while we sat there and watched you."

"Watched the game, you mean."

He's too serious when he smiles. "No. We watched you."

That's a lot to take in about him and my kid. I give myself a moment while I close the distance between us, crawling under the covers. The domesticity is a lot too, but I turn off my bedside lamp and lean into it anyway. Our heads are on our own pillows while we face each other and can barely see.

"How'd my curious and clever daughter react to that? She must have had questions."

"She did. She asked how often you and I talk, and I kinda shrugged and said you're busy these days, but that we text when we can."

"That's true."

"We let her know about our friendship for a reason, right?"

"I guess we did," I say. "Did she push for any other answers, *Mateo*?"

"Nah, she was easy to distract. I asked about school and soccer, and I got to hear all about Simon, plus she agreed to come down to help me out with a workshop after her season's over."

"Ah, yeah, all that tracks."

We shift closer to each other then, or it could just be him reaching for me. His hand is in my hair, like mine is so often in his. My eyes fall closed for a few reasons, but then I hear Mateo chuckle and I open them again.

"Your hair. I was trying to figure out what was different, but it's—you've got coach hair instead of player hair."

"What the fuck is that supposed to mean?" I snort. "I wore a helmet when I was playing. Of course it's different now."

It's funny, but it's not. I can feel his fingers at the back of my head, and I need him to feel something, too. Our conversation is almost silly, and it makes it possible for me to touch him back. We're friends. We've said it a million times. So I bring my hand to his bare chest, and then slide it around to his side and hold him there, and I wait for more teasing to cut the intimacy of whatever this is.

"Relax. You're still pretty."

"Shut up."

He does, even if we both know I'd listen to him talk forever. Our legs are slotted together now, though we're practiced and careful about it. I don't make a sound, still hungry for his touch but quiet about it tonight. And even though my body is rocked by time zones and a very long couple of days, I think Mateo may be about to fall asleep. It's okay, though. His steady breathing gives me a chance to say what I'd been thinking when we were outside.

"I don't know why—it's stupid in hindsight—but I hadn't thought about the crowd before I heard all the cheers," I start, sighing and fidgeting until Mateo soothes me by softly scraping his short nails against my head over and over again. "We played them already, back in New Jersey. I was a disaster about it. And really, only three of the guys were playing back when I was, but I spent all those years still hanging around the games after I got hurt. Having to coach against them was a big deal. Then I got through all the emotions and refocused, and it felt like a huge moment came and went, and I was still standing."

"But tonight you were back home," he says, slow and sleepy. "Why didn't you expect the crowd to cheer?"

"It's not that I didn't expect them to *cheer*. I forgot to prepare myself for them at all. After already playing a team full of guys I got to know pretty well, my focus was on finally being back in an arena I know inside out, but as a visitor this time. I knew it was gonna fuck with my head—wrong locker room, wrong bench—but I was so hung up on the place that I didn't think about the people in it. The fans."

"*Your* fans."

"I've heard people yelling my name everywhere we've played. Booing me, too. That love-hate relationship I had with them way back then? It's quieter now, but it's still there. I just forgot that it wouldn't be the same here. My fans here haven't stopped being loud."

My voice breaks, and I start to roll away from Mateo, but he's still holding me and won't let go. "Don't leave."

It's what I'd said to him when I asked him to come inside and spend the night, and I'm sure he knows that as well as I do. A tear rolls over the bridge of my nose. A few seconds later, his fingertip is there to trace whatever is left behind. He touches my lips next, and my eyes have adjusted enough that I can watch him watch me. My hand remains curved over his ribs, and I feel each steady breath before he speaks again.

"Did the cheering make things harder or easier for you tonight?"

"Harder."

"Why?"

I sit with that—lie with it, technically—and think about how to walk this tightrope. I've been trained on it, and I've been told not to look for a net when the media hits me with question after question. Of course, I don't take those questions these days. Official attention is directed at Taylor while I keep busy with anything else that needs to be done. But Taylor isn't in my bed, and after four and a half years, Mateo wants to know more about me. I want to tell him without leaving too many more tears on my pillow.

"It was so *frustrating*. My response to them. Why do I need them so badly? After all this time, why does it matter so much that they still love me like they did before?"

"It was your parents who first got you into hockey, right?"

"Yeah, my dad was a fan, so he suggested it when I was little," I answer. "My mom drove me to practice. Both of them were at my games."

Mateo nods, a subtle thing. "And what did they say to you when you went out on the ice?"

"What did they *say* to me?"

"Sure. I assume they didn't just open the car door and kick you into the parking lot with your gear. I don't even think they kept it to 'See you later!' So, what did they say to you? What things did you hear most often?"

He lets me roll away then. After another minute, he rolls away too, leaving to use the bathroom and give me time alone with my past. I'd prefer him with me in the present, but sometimes Mateo reads me too well and I'm stuck with what I need instead. When he returns, I'm on my back, staring at the ceiling. He keeps distance between us, looking fucking sinful in my pants, and I sigh.

"You know you're allowed back in the bed, right?"

"You know you don't have to have this conversation with me, right?"

I hold my hand out until he takes it, but as soon as he's under the covers, he turns his back to me and pulls me with him, my big spoon to his little one. There's so much of me that hates this—that we're still here after all this time—but part of me knows I'll always want this with him. The quiet contact I've never had with anyone else. Love that feels different from how it's been given to me before.

Ever before. Even when I was five or six or seven, and my parents loved their little hockey player.

"They told me to score the most goals. To win the game. To be the star. To get all the awards and hear the crowd chant my name. They told me I could be the best there ever was, and everyone would adore me."

Mateo pulls me more tightly around him, almost as if I'm his blanket instead of being the one whose blood runs a little too cold. "They didn't bother to point out that you could be adored regardless. That love never had to be contingent upon how well you played a sport."

"No," I say, the answer to a question he didn't actually ask.

"You've chased it your entire life. That crowd and how loudly they cheer for you. You've chased the proof that somebody loves you."

"Why can't I stop wanting that?"

"The cheers or the love?" he asks. "Because I think you *should* want to be loved, and it's fine to want the cheers, too. But only one of those is something to chase. Only one of those is supposed to be earned by the things you do."

"And the other?"

"You needed to be told that love is unconditional. I'm sorry your parents made it seem like it results from winning a goddamn game."

With my nose pressed to his hair, I breathe him in. "Remember the love-hate thing, though? Pretty notably, I've also had a lot of people *not* cheer for me. Or only want me for other reasons."

"They wanted you, though," he says. "And there's a fine line there, yeah? Hero. Villain. Heartthrob. Menace. All tied closely together. All tied up in one hell of a career."

He's right. They feel like the same thing now. They've been the same thing forever. Hockey and hatred and cheers and love, all mine for as long as I hold on to the habits I've had since I first understood what a habit is. As long as I stay as close to center ice as possible.

"I don't know how to let it go. If it's all tied together and I drop one thing, what will I have left?"

Mateo becomes all tension and fear in my arms. Anger maybe. Bad things that give him reasons to get out of my bed and trade my pants for his. I'm not sure what he'd do with my jersey, but I don't get to find out when he stays right where he is.

"You won't know until you stop running after everything and look around."

"I wasn't running much after I stopped playing," I argue. "Until I got the job offer, it seemed like I was standing pretty fucking still."

"Well, if that's true, then I guess there wasn't enough worth looking at."

"Come on, you know that's not what I meant."

"I know it's really hard to see past your first love," he murmurs.

"Please, Mateo."

He still doesn't leave me. Instead, he turns in my arms and kisses me on the forehead. "You'll be busy again tomorrow. You should get some sleep."

"It's not my only love," I remind him, waiting until his eyes are closed because I don't want him to go searching for lies in mine. "I love you."

"I know."

Chapter Twelve: Mateo

(I Told Her About the Nice Boy)

I don't sleep much, and just after sunrise, I slip away from Jamie while he continues to snore softly from beneath a duvet I miss already. In the bathroom, I change back into my jeans and the sweatshirt I'd worn under his jersey, and then I toss the borrowed pants in his hamper and tell myself it's not weird that I know exactly where it is. It can't be weird that I still have a toothbrush here either, but I don't think much about it once I'm distracted by my messy hair and tired eyes.

Leaving like this is a mistake, and I know that already, but there's something about forgiveness and permission that makes it okay for now.

Gentle with the jersey I may not wear again, I hold it to my chest and grab the rest of my things. Once I'm downstairs, I have to think for a moment before I decide which way to go from here. I'm not parked in the driveway this time, having never expected to go further than the bench, but I'm not sure I want to make a sudden appearance on the rocks below when I don't know who else might be there in the morning light. In the end, I go out through the front door because everything feels backward already.

Jamie doesn't text me when he wakes up, and I don't know whether that counts as his mistake or another of mine. We often go days without texting, but when I hear from him another couple of games into their road trip, he sends a message that could've gone to anyone. The following night, when they don't have a game, he leaves a drunken voicemail that I get in the morning. I think about him sitting alone in his hotel room when he goes on and on about the things he has and the things he's afraid to lose, then I worry he might not be alone at all.

I leave him a voicemail while watching him on tv, and I tell him I'm afraid, too.

I'd love to know how often Harper hears from him these days, but even if we're on a first-name basis now, it's not the kind of thing I should ask.

When he's back in New Jersey, and there are miles of nothing between us, I refocus on work, and our conversations return to a lighter shade of normal. The texts don't come as often, and when we talk, there seem to be as many pauses as words. More than once, I think maybe this is it—that our relationship has reached its end without ever getting the beginning it deserved—but then Jamie calls me again and his voice is soft and I realize this is as quietly as he's chased anything.

But it's a chase, nonetheless.

Spring arrives, and it should bring about a fresh start of something, except that we don't get true seasons in this part of California, just a push toward the end of the school year. Of course, my AP exam prep is nothing compared to Jamie helping coach his team to a playoff berth, and we send voice notes in between days of silence. When I call him during spring break, I definitely don't expect him to answer.

He does.

"Hey."

"Hey, yourself," I say. "I wasn't sure I'd catch you the week before the playoffs. Rare day off?"

"Nah, I'm working, but I haven't heard your voice in a while." Jamie almost sounds like he's smiling into the phone. "So, Ferris wheel or funnel cake?"

I glance down at the plate in my hand, then up at the ride looming behind me. "A little of both, actually. How'd you know that?"

"Lucky guess. Don't suppose you found any other volunteers to spend the afternoon with you?"

"I wasn't looking for anyone. I haven't been since the year I found you."

There's a lot to dissect about such a simple sentence, and Jamie takes long enough to reply that I think he might attempt exactly that. I lick powdered sugar from my fingers and watch others have the fun I covet. The fun I could have if—like Jamie suggested—I found another man to volunteer.

"Why?" he pushes. "Why not look? What are we doing while we're this far apart?"

"I'm sorry."

"Sorry?"

"For leaving that morning." I sigh loudly because it's not what he asked for, but I'm not stupid enough to think walking out on him has nothing to do with his questions now. "We've done this for so long—back and forth and close and not and wait and screw it all up and try again—but I don't think I should've come inside with you. We were both so fragile, and one of us was going to break, and I still don't even know which one of us did. But I had to go. I wasn't ready to look into your eyes and see what damage was done."

"And you thought sneaking out of my house would do less damage?"

"Of course not. I just didn't want to do any more."

"I didn't want—just a sec—" Jamie's voice is muffled while he speaks to someone else, and I throw half my funnel cake away. I catch the end of a mumbled goodbye, and then he clears his throat. "Mateo? I—Taylor needs me for a meeting, so I've gotta go. But I—I'm glad you're not looking, okay? It's really shitty of me to say that, but I'm glad."

He hangs up before I get the same mumbled goodbye he gave a few moments ago, and before I can ask him to finish his sentence and tell me what he didn't want. For what it's worth, I hope he's not looking for anyone either, and if that's equally shitty of me, so be it. Jamie and I simultaneously owe each other nothing and have promised everything. Glancing down the row of rides ahead, I think about going through the funhouse, but I leave the carnival instead. I don't need those mirrors to remind me how much it hurts to be here alone.

Sophie and I go to Kai's for the first playoff game, but the bar is loud and crowded, and Kai's too busy to catch more than a face-off or two. It'll be better for me to stay at home for the next one. Something about that little bar backing up to that dark alley is as intimate as a hidden bench facing the gently roaring ocean, and I might need a break from both for a while.

We're at my apartment for game two, my mouth full of pizza when Sophie nudges me with her elbow. "Do you think Taylor McKeon knows about you?"

"No," I mumble.

"That was fast. Do you know that for sure?"

"You asked if I *think* he knows, not whether I *know* he doesn't."

Sophie rolls her eyes. "And Harper still doesn't know?"

"Not yet. We've talked about it, but right now, there's nothing for her to know. Not really. Jamie and I have only seen each other once since he left last summer. We call and text here and there, but it's not like it used to be." I toy with the pizza crust in my hand and look sideways at her. "He asked me why I'm not looking for someone else."

"He *what*? When? *Why*?"

"Last week, when I called him from the carnival. He asked what we're even doing anymore."

"But when he took the job, he asked you to keep waiting," she says. And yeah, I know.

I eat the crust and nod. I watch several seconds of the game and nod again. "He still wants me to wait, but I—it's possible he's not doing the same. He sounded tired."

Sophie waves her hand toward the tv, which is fair. I'd be tired, too. But then she pokes me again. "How closely are you watching the gossip sites for any mention of the playboy returning to his playboy lifestyle? Is he out with a dozen different women again? What about the rumor he enjoyed the company of a man once upon a time?"

"The only rumor I've seen recently is something about him spending time with Taylor's sister, but that's not—I don't doubt how he feels about me, I just think he'd almost prefer if I give up on us and tell him the fantasy's already let us go. He doesn't know how to, and it must be exhausting to want so many things."

The opposing team scores then, and the camera pans across the New Jersey bench in time to catch the frustration on Jamie's face. It has nothing to do with me, but I shake my head as if I can clear it away.

It mostly works, at least for that night.

I rarely go long without thinking about the shades of blue in his eyes.

By the end of the following week, after the series has gone seven games, Jamie's first season as a coach comes to an end. His team played well, but they'll be disappointed, and I send him a stupidly long voice note when I know he'll be away from his phone. I keep myself from asking how soon he'll be able to come back to California, my body aching with need I'm sure he feels as often as I do.

As other teams move on to the next round of the playoffs, Jamie keeps busy with meetings and whatever behind-the-scenes house-keeping sort of stuff happens at the end of a professional hockey season. I imagine it's like wrapping up the high school soccer season, dialed up several notches, and while he's still there, I bury myself in classroom responsibilities here. AP exams are right around the corner, and I don't have the energy to chase conversations I've never chased before. I spend time with Sophie and some of the other teachers, all of us counting down to the end of the school year as much as any of the students do.

I'm sitting at my desk on a Friday night, staring at essays that have begun to blur, when my phone rings. It's late for me, which means it's too late for Jamie, and I'm on edge before I take my glasses off and touch my thumb to my screen.

"Hey, are you okay?"

"Yeah, I'm—I wasn't sure if you'd be a couple of margaritas deep by now, but it sounds like you're somewhere quiet."

"My classroom. I bailed on everyone tonight so I could get caught up on grading," I tell him, still wary. "Did you *want* me to be a couple of margaritas deep?"

"I don't know. I guess. This isn't—I'd rather have you pressed up against my patio door for this, I think. It would be better than only having a phone call."

"Are you breaking up with me?"

The choked sound he makes is one I'll hear for a long time. "What the fuck is there to break up, Mateo? And since when have I known how to quit running after things that should be too big to want?"

"Right. Of course," I sigh. "But when I was pressed to your patio door, you were saying goodbye before you moved across the country. So, what are you saying now?"

"That I'm staying here."

"Staying," I echo.

"Yeah," Jamie says. "I mean, not forever. And I promised Harper a week in Alaska, so I'll be home for a minute, but—"

"But only for a minute."

"I need you to know it's not because of anyone else. This isn't—I want to put more time in around here. Team stuff and just—I feel like I buried myself in the job, but didn't consider that part of my job is building relationships around here. I barely learned my way to and from the arena. I haven't done any touristy shit. And this summer, I want to be here to do that."

None of what he's saying makes me feel any better about his *not forever* comment, especially after his loyalty to a single team kept him in place his entire playing career. And the thing is, I don't think he's wrong to want to stay and meet people who will greet him with the cheers he loves. I don't think he'd be wrong even if he didn't need the cheers in the first place. I don't know how to encourage him around the selfish lump in my throat, and I don't really try.

"I understand."

"Would you let me fly you out here?" he asks. "We never really talked about that. And I guess during the season, it wouldn't be a lot of fun for you. But yeah. Over the summer, maybe?"

"Over the summer, while you're learning your way around, which means I'd have to be a friend and nothing more."

Jamie hums, thoughtful for a moment. "Isn't that the way it's always been?"

It is, of course, though I've never known how to stop hating it. That steady ache overrides the potential blow of his offer to pay my way, obviously helpful but technically unnecessary. I lean back in my desk chair and stare at stained ceiling tiles. For a few seconds, I think I should blame Sophie for talking about those damned chicken wings so much that I wanted to try them myself. Then I'm mad about the strangers in a bar fight who forced Jamie and me into an alley, and even further to a food truck. And finally, I take a deep breath and remember that everything happening now is because Jamie and I couldn't leave one night behind us, even when sunlight gave us a reason to.

"Does Taylor know about me?"

"No."

I should be satisfied that I was correct about that, but I ignore the sensation and move on. "Are you sleeping with his sister?"

"No. Stop reading that shit."

"You're just mad you can't search for dirt on me."

Jamie laughs softly, and it heals a dozen things inside me. "I could always give Vicki Gallagher a call."

"God forbid," I say as he yawns.

"It's getting late."

"It's *been* late."

"And you have to finish grading," he reminds me. "Go. Be safe getting home. We'll talk and I'll let you know when I'm coming home. Maybe we can go for another drive."

My smile is weary. "You don't trust me to stay all night with you."

"A drive would be really nice."

Jamie and I take that drive. We take two of them, actually—one just before his trip with Harper, and one after they return—and he was right about them being really nice. There are other places where we can be alone, but the car isolates us differently. Or maybe it's the fantasy that we could run away entirely—keep driving and never look back.

We never say that out loud, but a few heavy silences leave space for those daydreams.

I don't see his bench or his bed while he's home, but it keeps our latest goodbye free from the promises we've already made too many times.

My school year ends right after Jamie flies back east, and Sophie and I go away for a few days once final grades are turned in and our classrooms are empty. I reach out to my family too, all of them used to my schedule and my desire to unwind once I have the time to do it. It's only when I have dinner at my parents' house that I realize I've been more out of the loop than usual.

"Your grandmother hasn't been doing well," my mom tells me. "Nothing is specifically wrong, but she's lonely and it's taking a toll on her. We've asked her to consider moving, but she won't leave that house."

I look back and forth between my parents. "She spent Easter weekend with us. And I thought everyone was visiting pretty regularly."

"You know as well as anyone that our own lives can carry us away from other responsibilities and relationships. She doesn't drive much anymore, and there are only so many times the rest of us have been able to travel two hours for a brief stay, but she's too stubborn to ask us to try. To ask *you* to try."

Guilt comes easily to me, and I have little doubt it was my mom's intent when she summarized the situation so succinctly. Yes, I have most of the summer off, and I'll take the hint that's been dropped on my dinner plate, but there's been so little actually keeping me from my family. Everyone else has spouses and children and their own jobs and friends, and I have happy hour with my best friend and a million minutes of texts and voice notes and phone calls to someone who's only sort of mine.

Much like my grandmother, I've been alone without acknowledging that I'm getting lonely.

"I'll go out there again. I'll stay, like I did before."

I almost add that I have nothing planned for the summer, but that's not entirely true when Jamie's invitation to visit remains loud anytime I get quiet. It's so loud that I don't hear any of the whispered reminders about my grandmother's neighbor and the warnings that should come with them. My mom smiles at me, satisfied with her work. My dad grunts his approval. I go back to my apartment and figure out what needs to be done before I spend most of my summer away from home.

Telling Jamie is something I put off until my grandmother is taking a nap a week later.

"Is she sick?" he asks, soft and worried.

"Not exactly. She misses my grandfather and won't ask for the company she only sort of wants. I think she's fading away more than anything."

"But now her favorite grandchild is by her side. That has to make her feel better," he says. "It's always made me feel better to have you close."

I want to tell Jamie he has a terrible way of showing it, but that's not a fight I'll pick under someone else's roof. After glancing down the small hallway, I move toward the living room window and try not to look across the street.

"A visit to New Jersey isn't off the table. I volunteered to spend the summer here, but I'm allowed to leave. I'm allowed to see anyone I want."

"*See.*"

"Is there another word I should use?" I ask.

His pause is as good as a shrug. "It's fine. It just sounded like maybe you weren't talking about me."

"Come on, Jamie."

"I know. It's not fair that I keep wanting it all. I do know that."

It won't change anything though, and my next thought is unrelated. Or maybe it's my turn to want it all. "I wish you could meet her. My grandmother. I hate that you haven't met any of my family. I know you sort of saw them at my grandfather's funeral, but you stayed away, and that was—it wouldn't have been the same."

"If I remember correctly, you threatened me with their presence at the carnival that first year."

I chuckle. "It could only be considered a threat if you were actually afraid of it."

"You don't think I was afraid?" he asks, his voice nearly cracking. "All that acceptance and love and probably immeasurable displays of affection? And they know about you, so then they would've known about me? And they might've been glad to meet me anyway?"

"I mean, I *have* introduced them to straight people before," I tease. "Their hugs wouldn't necessarily have come with a bunch of preconceived notions about why you and I were spending the afternoon together."

"But they would've hugged me?"

"Almost certainly, yes."

"And meeting them eventually is probably inevitable, huh?"

It doesn't matter how many times I remember I'm one of the dreams he's chasing—it takes my breath away every time. "I hope so."

"Okay, I'm gonna let you go," he says. "Keep me posted on things there, and then we'll figure out a time for you to fly out here?"

I agree, and we say our goodbyes, and I turn at the sound of quiet footsteps behind me.

"Was that a nice boy on the phone?"

"It was," I smile. "How long were you listening to me talk to the nice boy?"

"Only long enough to hear you say *I hope so*, but you were so sad about it. Do we need to pray for him? Should we pray for you both?"

"He needs to find some peace. Once he does that, I'll be okay."

She nods, then shifts her focus to the window I've tried to ignore. "What about that nice boy?"

"Logan?"

"Yes, *Logan*. Are there so many boys outside my house that I was unclear somehow?"

"No, ma'am," I say, ducking my head to hide my grin. "And I haven't spoken to Logan since I've been here, but he's—"

I trail off, but my grandmother doesn't miss a beat. "Not the one who makes your voice so full of love on a phone call."

"He's not. That was Jamie."

"Okay, you are going to make me some tea and tell me all about this *Jamie*. I do not have new stories of my own anymore, so I would like to hear this one of yours."

I take her hand and lead her to the kitchen, and while waiting for the water to boil, I talk.

It makes it easier when I finally run into Logan a few days later. My heart still knocks restlessly around my chest, yearning for more than the fleeting intimacy Jamie and I have shared for years, but telling my grandmother our story made it more real than it has been since my tequila-soaked confession to Sophie.

And that was a goddamn lifetime ago.

So, now two of the most important people in my life know about the man I love more than I probably should, and having those memories surface means I choke on them when Logan waves. I've been out front for a while, taming overgrown shrubs and pulling weeds, and he walks across the street wearing tiny shorts and a t-shirt that barely makes up for those long, bare legs.

"I noticed your car here—is everything okay with Maria?" he asks as I stand. "I haven't seen her in a while."

"Yeah, she's—she and my grandfather lived here for over twenty years, and she won't leave now, but it's also—sitting alone with so many memories isn't great either."

"So, you're here to sit with her for the summer?"

"Most of it, probably." I look over my shoulder at the house, then back at Logan. "How have you been? I guess we haven't really talked lately."

"We haven't *really* talked since you left last time," he says, far from unkind about it. "Do you think you'll be available sometime soon? You know, as long as you'll be here most of the summer."

"I—" There are so many answers I could give, and very few of them would be wrong, but I flash back to Jamie's comment during our conversation the other night. *It just sounded like maybe you weren't talking about me.* I'm allowed to see anyone I want, and I'm not sure whether I was referring to Logan then, but I don't want to promise him anything now. "I don't think I'll be available in the same way I was before."

"Ah, you're notably *un*available. Congratulations to you both."

"It's more complicated than that."

"Isn't it always?" Logan laughs, quieting a few seconds later. "Listen, I wouldn't mind hanging out while running errands again—or a friendly dinner. Nothing else, just a chance to catch up."

"Friendly?"

"Mostly friendly. Also, slightly tinged with jealousy because I'd love to be unavailable too, but definitely mostly friendly."

"In that case, I would love to run some errands with you. Text me whenever. You know where I'll be."

He smiles. "Right. Most of the summer."

So I hear from him when he has to go grocery shopping, and I decide I might as well make a list of the things my grandmother and I need. It's a relief to exist at his side without worrying about whether we might run into someone we know or what we'd look like to them if we do. Logan and I are nobodies, and standing in the middle of the produce section, we're nothing more than friends.

We're nothing more than friends anywhere we stand, but being more wouldn't make a headline, and I think I'd forgotten what that freedom feels like.

The week after grocery shopping, we hit the library together and stop somewhere to eat once we're satisfied with stacks of books. We make plans to hang out at his house soon, so I can show him how I meal prep during the school year, but Logan gets slammed at work and my grandmother has a string of doctor appointments, so it takes a couple of weeks to make it happen.

The evening we get together, I lean into his side while we portion the rice we've just made. He nudges me with his shoulder, and neither of us shies away from the contact that follows. It's friendly in a way I'm used to, and I'm confident it won't go further than flirting in his kitchen, but I like it, and I tell him I'd like to come back again soon.

Not long after, I get a call from Jamie, and so many things change.

Some are obvious right away. Some I don't realize until later.

"How would you feel about spending a few days up at Taylor's lake house instead of staying at my little rental?"

I glance at my grandmother, who's sitting in her favorite chair and staring at me far too intently while I talk to this nice boy she's never met. If she were anyone else, I'd turn my back and walk far away, but I'll let her watch me like I'm one of her nightly shows.

"Did you—does he know now?" I ask.

"No, no. Sorry, it's not—" Jamie pauses and clears his throat. "He invited me and a couple of other guys out there. I wasn't sure I wanted to go, and mentioned that a friend of mine was going to be visiting from California. I figured it would be a good excuse to stay where I am, but then he said I should bring you."

"Why didn't you want to go?"

He's silent long enough for me to wonder whether he's about to lie. "Partying by the lake doesn't have the same appeal it used to. But it really *is* gorgeous there, and if you're with me—"

"It won't be much of a party?"

"It'll be better than that. We still won't be able to—I mean, I think we might even sleep in separate rooms, but—"

"Yeah, right, of course." He's not Logan, and we won't be at the store.

Jamie sighs. "I want you to come to the lake with me. I want you to meet Taylor, and I want to pretend this is a little vacation for us, and I—I want to see you, 'Teo. I just really want to see you, so if you'd rather stay with me here, I can blow him off, and we can—

"No."

"No?"

"No, don't blow him off. I'll go to the lake with you," I say, my voice lower as I continue. "I'll go anywhere with you."

Chapter Thirteen: Jamie

(I Left the Team Behind)

I borrow one of Taylor's cars to pick Mateo up from the airport. He presses his hand to my bouncing leg to reassure both of us that this trip is a good thing. We've been bullshitting the world for five years, so it should be fine. We've never had to bullshit in such a concentrated group for a few days in a row, so maybe it won't be.

The introductions go smoothly, though there was no reason they wouldn't. Mateo doesn't have the same PR experience I do, but he's been in the trenches with the parents of teenagers for a couple of decades. I think that's probably trained him at least as well. We're at the lake house with one of the other assistant coaches, one of our trainers, and a friend of Taylor's who has nothing to do with hockey as far as I can tell. I don't know. I'm careful not to pry into his personal life. I very defensively don't want him prying into mine.

Our plans for the entire stay are about as casually undefined as any getaway can be. Tonight, we're grilling out back and lounging near the dock. We'll eat and drink around the fire pit while we talk shit about anything and everything. The days are warm, but the nights are cool, not unlike my oceanside backyard. I'm wearing Mateo's old

Baja hoodie because it's as much as I can get away with for now.

I've got little doubt he'd wear my jersey if he could, but he'll be even more careful here than I am.

"Soccer, huh? Are you the guy responsible for making Sinclair's kid a Husky?" Taylor asks.

Mateo smiles easily. "I think Harper's responsible for making herself a Husky. I'm just the lucky guy who got to coach her along the way."

"How about her mom? Pretty lady."

"She's beautiful, yeah. But she never seemed all that interested in talking to me, so I don't know her well."

"Not like you know Harper's dad."

Everybody looks at me, their expressions so much the same and all at least a little different. Some kind of bait has been dangled, though I can't tell whether it's about our relationship. Whatever it is, Mateo barely raises an eyebrow before he responds.

"Jamie and I talked a lot more often. Not quite so much since you lured him to the East Coast, though."

Taylor laughs. His friend does, too. "I'm not sorry about that. First, he's a hell of a coach, and our team is better with him behind the bench. Second, it couldn't have fucked with your friendship that much if you were willing to fly all this way to see him."

"You're right," Mateo says. "Nothing has been fucked."

I take a long, long drink.

The subject changes with no effort on my part. Everyone has plenty to talk about, and none of them have an interest in doing genuine harm to Mateo or me. I think they like Mateo a lot already, and none of my once-famous personality conflicts have followed me here. My reputation for late nights with beautiful women has lingered more than I'd like. At least a rumor or two has caught Mateo's attention, but I'll work on that.

I'm curious about how much of my reputation still catches Taylor's attention when tells me I'll be sharing a room with Mateo. He says something about the other three guys already claiming rooms. Then he insists it'll be fine because the one we'll be sleeping in has a bed and a futon, and "there's not a single piece of furniture in this lake house that isn't worth more than a high school teacher's paycheck, actually."

I don't roll my eyes because it's not the worst thing Taylor's said in the past fifteen minutes, much less the entire evening. I assume Mateo doesn't roll his eyes because he knows what his bank account looks like.

"I guess since I'm the one who can't afford this futon, I should be the one to sleep on it?" Mateo chuckles once we're alone. "Or did you want to let me have the bed after the long flight I took just to see my *friend*?"

"And here I was thinking his carpet is pretty soft. You could just toss a pillow and blanket down there, and you'll probably sleep like a baby."

Mateo pauses as if he's considering it. Or something else. "I wonder how much room Taylor's friend has in *his* bed."

"Taylor's friend? Wyatt?"

"Yes, Wyatt. Let's just say he'd be unlikely to turn down overnight company from someone like you or me."

My eyes widen. "Are you serious?"

He just shrugs, then gestures toward the bedroom door. "Do you think anyone will notice if we use that lock?"

"They don't have any reason to," I answer, though I'm not sure it's an answer at all.

Without another word, I lock the door. Mateo makes up the futon so it looks slept in. Then we get ready to crawl into bed together. There are bitter things on my tongue—reminders of what happened the last time we fell asleep in each other's arms—but tomorrow he'll still be here, no further than the dock, even if he runs from me.

And I don't expect him to run from me.

"Do you still think about sneaking around—trying to get away with it all?" he asks. His lazy fingertips trace the length of my spine, my bare back turned to him.

"It wouldn't be that easy."

"The sex could be. Maybe not right here, under Taylor McKeon's very expensive roof, but you know we could break the rules and have *something* while we wait for the rest. We've come so close. And how many times have we asked each other what we're doing?"

"A lot," I admit. "Too many, probably."

"I wonder whether we'll stop asking someday, and let ourselves have that much. While we're still waiting, I mean," Mateo says, his hand finally resting against my waist. "Once. What if we decide to lie even more loudly to everyone else just to have one night together?"

"Only once?"

"Only once."

"I don't think I could. The rules and lines are there for a reason."

"You hate the rules and lines."

I roll over and pull him closer, kissing him on the forehead and taking far too long to move away. He's always so warm. Without his hoodie on now, I shiver and want more.

Which is exactly my problem. I always want more.

"But it would break me, I think. Having all of that and not being able to tell the world."

"It doesn't break you already?"

We're tangled together, the way it usually happens when we get the chance to be close. Both of us are wearing shorts, but they leave so much skin within reach. We take advantage of the time we have to hold each other, but Mateo asked me a question, too. I try to find the right way to answer him.

"Right now—having what we have and keeping our secret—it's like the day after a great game against a tough opponent. When I played hard and fought for the win, and loved every second on the ice. Then I woke up the next day and felt it everywhere, that perfect ache. It doesn't break me. It never did. It's more like a full-body bruise. Sure, it hurts if I lean on it the wrong way, or for too long. But otherwise, it's just a wonderful reminder of the night before. An ache that won't go away until I can do it all over again."

"But if we fuck?"

I shiver again, having nothing to do with being cold. He's always been nicer than I am when we talk about this—far less crude—and my dick reacts quickly to hearing the word *fuck* from Mateo's well-educated mouth. And he knows it, too. I can almost feel his smile against my neck, at least until I keep talking.

"Fucking you will change everything for me. Everything I want and everything I need and everything I am," I say, my voice laced with pleas for so many different things. Patience. Understanding. A promise that the feelings turning me inside out are still mutual. "Fucking you and walking away like it didn't just alter our lives in one final, irrevocable way? That wouldn't feel like a bruise. That would be another shattered leg."

Mateo growls and noses at the underside of my unshaven jaw. "You're putting a hell of a lot of pressure on an orgasm, sweetheart."

"It's not about the orgasm."

"Yeah, I know," he sighs.

"So we wait?"

"So we wait."

As far as I know, nobody notices the locked door. After Mateo and I wake up to a greasy breakfast and plenty of coffee, all six of us go out on Taylor's boat to soak up sunlight that feels different from California's. Someone's playing music. Someone else brought a deck of cards. We enjoy a little of everything while doing almost nothing.

Once we're docked again, most of us are hungry. Taylor has pizza delivered so none of us have to put on a shirt. When we stop shoving slices down our throats, some of us talk about the team. It's probably only natural when four coworkers spend time together, even in the offseason, but it means there are two outsiders today. Mateo and Wyatt follow the conversation for a while—however long it interests them, or long enough to be polite—and then Wyatt's hand is around Mateo's arm, tugging him out of his patio chair.

I try not to panic, but I'm only familiar with being the one drawn away from the crowd for a private moment. I know I freeze mid-sentence.

"Relax, Sinclair. It's a vacation, not a horror movie. I'm sure they'll both return safely. They're just bored because the rest of us don't know how to take a break from our jobs like your daughter's teacher does."

It's at least a little like a horror movie, but eventually I remember to be nonchalant about the man Mateo suggested is less than straight. Wyatt grins, and I feel like it's mostly directed at me.

"We're just going for a walk."

They do put shirts on for that, and I'll take what I can get.

"You were jealous," Mateo teases me later that night.

We're in bed, and I'm more possessive of him than I ever have been, however fair that is when he still doesn't belong to me. My arm is wrapped around his chest and one of my legs is hooked over his. My teeth find his bare shoulder without caring about the mark I could leave behind.

"What if he wants you?"

"It doesn't really matter if I don't want him back."

I bite him again, and safe like this, we both fall asleep quickly.

The rest of our time at Taylor's is more of the same—food and drinks and the lake and no small amount of giving me shit—but a few days of this group is probably all anyone can take. I'd love a lifetime with Mateo, of course, but I have to take him back to the airport so he can return to his grandmother.

For a minute or two, I wonder if I could ask to go with him. He wishes I could meet her, after all. But then he's saying goodbye to me, and I'm saying goodbye to him. It becomes one more thing that will wait for another day.

Home again, I'm not sure where the summer has gone. I've done a lot of what I wanted here. I've found my way around and dropped by tourist hotspots in New York City and asked the right questions to learn where the tourists *aren't*. I've met local fans and people who have no idea who I am. I've stayed on top of the work that needs to be done for the team ahead of the new season. I've made my rented house slightly more like a home because, as unreal as it still is, I live here for now.

Hopefully, Harper can stay with me again soon. Hopefully, Mateo can see it for the first time.

Regardless, the summer is as productive as I could've hoped it would be. And now, while I never had a truly long break from work—like I'd told Mateo in the spring, there's always more to do—we're getting closer to training camp, and I'll be even busier soon. Harper is already back in Washington, busting her ass ahead of another great year. Mateo will be with his grandmother for another couple of weeks. Then I assume he'll bust his ass too, his job far more important than mine.

All of us have responsibilities. I don't talk to any of the people I love as often as I'd like to. Weeks pass, and it's school and soccer and hockey and three different states and teammates and staff and life.

And death, apparently. Because it's the one thing that we can count on, even if I hadn't seen it coming. Weirdly, I'm grateful for the abrupt text I get shortly before a gentle phone call.

My grandmother died. Can't talk right now but I thought you should know.

I swallow hard. Mateo had *wanted* me to meet her. He'd only *thought* I should know she died. I can't decide how I feel about his choice of words, but they feel important. Then my phone vibrates in my hand.

"Hey, pixie."

"Hey, dad, this is—I'm on my way to class, but I just heard from someone back home that Mr. Z's grandma died? He bailed on practice and said he might not be back for their game tomorrow? And I don't know—you guys are still friends so maybe you'll want to call him?"

Her habit of making everything sound like a question would make me smile any other day, but now it makes me bleed. I take a deep breath and mumble something stupid. Or a few somethings stupid.

"He was with her most of the summer. We never met. I shouldn't have taken him away."

"Mr. Z?" Harper asks. "You took him away?"

I sigh and think this would be easier if I'd told her before. "He came with me to Taylor's for a few days. He'd been spending time with his grandmother—she wasn't doing well alone—but I invited him, and he came."

"It's almost December now. That was months ago? I'm not sure one has anything to do with the other."

"Maybe not."

I hear a burst of voices, and assume Harper's closer to class now, but she's got another question for me, quieter than the rest of them. "Is there a reason you would've met her?"

"They were really close. Maybe if she'd lived nearby—" I stop because I need to avoid an honest answer. Neither of us has time for a confession. "Listen, I've got a meeting coming up, and your class is about to start. Thank you for telling me. I'll call Mateo soon."

"Mmmm, well, please tell *Mateo* I'm sorry about his grandma."

Our goodbyes are brief, and I really do have a meeting to get to. I also need to respond to the text staring up at me from the phone still in my hand. Nothing I can cram into a message will matter the way it should, but I have to try.

I'll be here when you're ready to talk. I don't care if it's the middle of the night. I know she loved you so damn much and I'm sorry

Some of it's a lie, but he'll know that. I see no need to remind him I might not be here to talk if I'm still in my meeting. Or tomorrow, when there's a game. Or anytime between when Taylor needs me to take a call he doesn't want to take, or give an interview he doesn't want to give.

Whether it's intentional or not, his next text arrives between the first and second period of our next game.

I just wish you could be here for the funeral.

Between the second and third period, I duck away from the team long enough to text back.

I wish I could be there too

It's not until the morning, after our fourth straight win, that I realize I could be. Probably.

"I need a day off—maybe a day and a half. Personal reasons. Death in the family."

"Anyone I know?" Taylor asks, sympathy a thing he doesn't convey well.

"No, but I need to be at the funeral. In California," I tell him. "I don't know when it'll be yet, but I should be able to catch up with the team in Texas or Colorado."

"Will you draw any media attention?"

"At a funeral? You've gotta be fucking kidding me. The only rumors since I got here have been about me and your sister—none of which are true, by the way."

Taylor laughs, then sobers quickly. "Yeah, I know they're not true. But I also know people are still waiting for you to fuck up. Just don't do it while dealing with a 'personal matter,' okay?"

It would make sense for me to call Mateo then. Ask him for the details about the visitation and Mass and burial. Find out whether it'll be the same as when his grandfather died three years ago. But I'm just worried enough that something will keep me away at the last minute, and I stay silent for now.

I stay silent while I search online for the information I need.

I stay silent while I book a flight and update Taylor.

I stay silent the morning I put on a charcoal gray suit and slip into the back row of the same Catholic church that hosts a carnival I think I love and hate. Someone hands me a funeral program, and I look at a picture of the woman who welcomed a scared and lonely little boy into her family without reservation. I hadn't been close enough to notice on the day she buried her husband, but now I can see Mateo has her eyes. I'm not sure that's how the nature versus nurture argument works, but I'm distracted by the deep brown kindness in them. That kindness looked down at me once, at a crowded bar that might as well be home. I'd love to believe Mateo's grandmother is looking down upon me today.

Believing she's looking down upon her family is easy.

Mateo is a pallbearer, his hair pulled back into the tightest ponytail I've seen him wear, and his profile stunningly stoic as it passes me by. He doesn't glance my way, nor did I expect him to. I'm trying to keep my head down as much as possible because I've never wanted to be recognized less than I do now.

I haven't attended Mass since the last time I was here. From the corner of my eye, I admire the stained glass and statues surrounding me. My parents certainly didn't make time in my schedule for religion—or anywhere I wouldn't have had the opportunity to shine—but former teammates and coaches have married and died, so the rituals aren't wholly foreign. There are a lot of people here, evidence of a life well-lived, I suppose. The Zavalas are far away, and I won't have to worry about being hugged by people who might love me before they find reasons not to. I spot Sophie a couple of rows behind the family, but she hasn't seen me.

There's a single eulogy, delivered by Mateo and his sisters. I don't fight the tears demanding to be shed. The music has been beautiful all along, but "Amazing Grace" nearly ruins me. I want to laugh at how many people would be surprised to see me like this, dressed up and weeping over a hymn. I'm so far away from being Jameson Sinclair right now.

I'm just Jamie. I only *want* to be Jamie.

When Mass is over, I blend in with the crowd and read the back page of the program still in my hand. She'll be buried next to her husband, with a reception at someone's house following. I know how to get where I'm going without the help of the small map. In my car—one I left behind when I moved across the country—I check my reflection in the rearview mirror and pretend I don't look fucking exhausted. Things are better for me than for almost anyone I'll see today. I shake my head before I drive.

As soon as I'm parked again, another look in the mirror confirms nothing has changed. A look toward the burial plot confirms far fewer people are expected here. There are a few rows of folding chairs, some mourners settling there while others hover nearby, but all of it's too intimate for me. I find a large oak tree some distance away and lean against the trunk. Then I close my eyes when I can't quite make out any of what's being said.

I daydream or I grieve, but time passes quickly either way. When I hear the crowd stir, a dozen conversations kept to a respectful buzz, I open my eyes and search for the Zavala family. They've separated some, all greeting different guests with the expected smiles and tears. It's no surprise that I only have eyes for Mateo, but when I watch him leave Sophie's side and wind past a handful of others to greet someone new, I'm close to looking away.

This man doesn't resemble the Zavalas enough for me to assume he's related to them. With Sophie heading in a different direction, I doubt he's another coworker. He could be anyone else—a former student or a college friend or someone at the apartment complex who doesn't slow dance in his living room—but the way they touch makes me feel hot and cold at once.

Mateo's fingertips are playing with this other man's tie. The other man's hand has slipped past Mateo's open suit jacket. They have a conversation with plenty of eye contact until they step further into each other and hug tightly. The other man presses a kiss to Mateo's temple.

I let my eyes fall shut again and daydream or grieve until I have a reason to stop, his footsteps muffled by the grass, but my goose-bumps quick to warn me I'm no longer alone.

"You have a game tonight."

"They do," I say, slow to stare straight ahead while Mateo crowds my side. "I'm not sure I'll make it in time."

"Taylor's okay with that?"

"Okay enough."

"What did you tell him?"

I turn then, unwilling to spend too much time looking at people who might decide to look back. "Death in the family."

"You never even met her," Mateo says, and it sounds like an accusation no matter how softly it falls from his tongue.

"I'm sorry."

He nods. Whether it's an acceptance of my apology or not, I know he understands I'm referring to more than a single missed opportunity. We've sacrificed a lot more than that, mostly because I've silently demanded it or very loudly pleaded.

"Are you coming to the reception?"

"I don't think that would be a good idea," I huff, only adding to the list of things to be sorry for. Then I pick at the scab. "Who were you talking to?"

"When? Just before I came over here and found you with your eyes closed?"

"Obviously."

I half expect him to tease me for being jealous again. He sighs and hurts me instead. "Logan."

"Logan, as in the guy you slept with?"

"Logan, as in the guy I slept with," he confirms. "For what it's worth, he's here as my grandparents' longtime neighbor more than as a friend I once fucked."

"Once?"

"*Once*, general past event. Not *once*, specific event count."

"Neighbor?"

"He lives across the street."

I stop myself from growling. "So you saw him this past summer?"

"Saw him, yes. Spent time with him, yes. Only ended up in bed with you."

"Is he going to the reception?" I ask.

"Probably," Mateo says. "Does that change your plans?"

"No. I'm still Jameson Sinclair."

"That you are."

Rubbing my tired eyes makes nothing any clearer. "I know you said you wished I could be here, but I—should I have stayed with the team?"

"I always want you with me more than I want you with the team. *Always*," he hisses, dark eyes on fire under the cool December sky. "It just sucks that this is the one time you made it happen."

That's probably fair, and I drop my head back to stare at the sky. "I'll try to make it happen on a better day."

"Stop."

"Stop what?" I ask, staring at him again.

"Stop talking about a future that may not be ours to have."

My gaze wanders, taking in the peacefulness of the cemetery around us. It's then I realize how many people have already left for the reception, and how close to alone we are now. Mateo's grandmother is nearby. So is his grandfather. But they're gone and we're here, and I frown at him now.

"Is that some kind of mortality thing?"

Mateo shakes his head. "No, it's a you and me thing."

Laying us to rest here is poetic. Tragic too, but mostly beautifully poetic. The only better place to do it would be on the bench where it all began, but it's too late to ask him to join me there.

"This is it, then? It's all over?"

He shakes his head again, his gorgeous face twisting into a sad smile. "Oh, I'm not sure either of us is stupid enough to believe it'll be that easy."

"We wouldn't let ourselves say goodbye that first night."

"And I don't expect us to do it now."

"But we're not waiting anymore," I murmur.

"I just don't know what we're waiting for."

Chapter Fourteen: Mateo

(I Didn't Have to Do It)

I spend the night at Isa's the night of the funeral because going back to my apartment seems like a level of lonely that would leave scars. I'd stay at Sophie's, but I've leaned on her all week. I would've followed Logan home, but I've done enough damage for the day. And I think I'd crash on a barstool at Kai's, but I may not be welcome there anymore.

I'm still not sure how it all went so wrong, so fast, but I don't know how to take it back when I meant everything I said to Jamie.

I meant everything, but I don't want to stop waiting for him. I've never wanted that, and I never said it either.

Why couldn't he have held on to the fact that I always want him with me? That, at least, was something I did say.

But Jamie left, and I felt so damn detached from myself all day. I know I was fortunate to have my grandmother as long as I did, but losing her hurt, and I've been spiraling since I got the call. At least some of the pain had been simmering since the summer, when I realized how much time I'd spent away from her, my parents right to lay that guilt on me. My brief trip to New York hadn't been a problem—my grandmother had encouraged that wholeheartedly, and more or less kicked her feet when we caught up upon my return—but the years before, especially after my grandfather died, had been wasted.

My throat closes around something bitter when I think about how much Jamie kept me from her, but only because the reality that I'm at fault is a much harder pill to swallow. Staying near home and making myself available for dates we could never call dates wasn't something I could blame him for, but today it was easier, and it made seeing him more difficult.

I *did* want him to come to the funeral, but spotting him in the back row of the church reminded me of why he shouldn't have been there. The distance was worse than if he hadn't been there at all.

And then there was Logan.

He and I had been in touch the past few days—as much as Jamie and I had been—so I'd known he'd be making the drive to pay his respects. I'd also known I'd be glad to see him, so I certainly wasn't sorry that we'd had a chance to talk, and the hug had felt so good. But then Jamie had seen us together, and I suppose I'd known that would happen, too.

My payback was that Jamie and I didn't touch at all before we went our separate ways.

On the bed in my sister's guest room, when the rest of the house is asleep, I consider sending him a voice note. Several, maybe. Even after all these years together, it feels like there are so many things to say. I thought we'd have a lifetime for that, and I'm still not convinced we don't, but right now my chest is hollow, the beat of my heart lost in an empty room.

I put my phone down and fight my way through a terribly restless night.

Checking hockey scores in the morning shows me Jamie missed

out on a huge win.

In my classroom, I flip through my desk calendar, grateful I only have a couple of weeks of teaching before the holiday break. Even with soccer to provide some distraction, it'll be an emotional Christmas with my family, and I won't try to guess whether I'll be in touch with anyone else by then. Regardless, nobody will look too closely if I drink a little too much and hide more than usual. I don't have a grandparent left to visit, so I'll keep some guilt at bay.

Until we actually reach our break, and on nights I'm not coaching, Sophie and I pass time with a couple of happy hours, a few movie nights, and plenty of bitching and moaning. I cry about Jamie, and she wipes my tears away, but she doesn't let me dwell on that ache. I'm not sure she believes Jamie and I will stay apart any more than I do.

One night, I wake from a dream that must have been about him, and I reach for my cock and make myself come, clenching my pillow while I wonder how I can simultaneously yearn to go back in time and be desperate for a peek into the future.

Is Jamie still there? Where am I?

Everything at school is wrapped up the week before Christmas. I leave my classroom behind with a pile of gifts and treats in my arms, and I'll rely on them to soothe me as long as the sugar high lasts. Unlike all the evenings that we find an excuse to drink cheap margaritas, most teachers are eager to start their vacations, and Sophie has a red-eye to catch. My family doesn't expect me until tomorrow, when I'll spend the day making cookies with my nieces and nephews, so I'm left alone and nostalgic for nights I've never had.

Jamie's team doesn't have a game for me to watch, so I don't have a way to watch *him*, and it makes me stupid in a way I should be able to quell by now.

I know it's not Christmas yet, but I miss you.

It's late in New Jersey, and I figure he's either asleep or working or doing things I'll read about online someday. Things I'd read about Jameson Sinclair long before I met Jamie at a bar. He shouldn't have his phone in his hand, and yet—

You're not supposed to tell me that. Remember?

I sigh. *I thought we stopped lying years ago.*

I'm pretty fucking lonely when I stop

Then chase me, I almost type. Chase me, chase me, chase me, chase me, *chase* me. It's what Jamie's done his entire life, and I know how easily he could do it now, but I think there's something about our shared intimacy that works against me. I love him like nobody has before, and this lonely, needy man understands that what we have is unconditional as much as it's unfamiliar to him. It also means he understands he can stay where he is, trusting in us more than he fears the damage any distance could do.

I trust in us too, but my eyes well with tears anyway.

What are you doing for Christmas? They don't have a game. I know that much.

Harper will be here for almost a week

Good. I almost say more, but delete the words nearly as quickly as they appear. There's so little that will help either of us feel better tonight, and I might as well let us go. *If you and I don't talk…Merry Christmas and Happy New Year, Jamie. Everything has changed, but nothing has.*

Yeah, I know

And just like that, we've said goodbye without a goodbye. Again.

The rest of December comes and goes, and guilt lingers or builds anew when I'm grateful for the chance to say goodbye to my family. We'd welcomed January together after a month in which we were only apart when any of us had to work, and I've barely slept off the New Year's celebration, much less a month of complicated losses.

I nap as soon as I'm back in my apartment, but when I'm awake again, I press a hand to my chest and hate the pain that rattles on each exhale.

I don't have to be back at school until Monday, so I have some time to breathe. It means I also have time to breathe by the ocean, somewhere quiet and perfectly alone. I'm aware it may be cruel—to one or both of us—and I sure as hell haven't been invited. Still, some petty part of me argues that I have as much right to it as he does, and it's not like there's any risk of running into him today.

After a quick shower, I change into layers of warm and comfortable clothes and reheat a tomato basil soup from a few days ago. With it poured into a thermos for later, and my blanket already in the trunk, I waste no more of my day, parked about twenty minutes later. The wind is already colder when I start walking, but I ignore it and almost close my eyes, just to prove how well I know my way to a place I've mostly seen in the dark.

In the end, I'm glad I've kept my eyes wide open. It gives me the several seconds I need to realize I'm not alone. I wonder whether it's too late to turn around, decide it definitely is, and then smile as I take those last few steps.

"You know about the bench," I say, the surprise in my voice clear no matter how hushed I am by the ocean behind me.

"Pretty sure that's supposed to be my line," Harper replies with a playful smile that looks so goddamn much like her father's. "*I'm* the one who lives here."

I hadn't forgotten that—I've never been less than fully aware that it's her home, too. It's more that I figured she'd still be in New Jersey with Jamie or up in Washington with Simon or running around with friends for the rest of her winter break. I certainly didn't expect her to be sitting right in front of me, wearing a Husky hoodie and what looks like pajama pants.

"Aren't you cold?"

She laughs. "Yeah, a little bit? Up at school, it's like, 15 degrees colder than it is here, except that sitting by the beach is always cold, and I wasn't really thinking about that when I walked down here. Looks like you came prepared? Is that hot chocolate?"

"Tomato soup." I nod toward the bench. "Do you mind if I sit?"

"How willing are you to share your little snack?"

I join her and unfold the blanket enough to drape it across our laps before I open the thermos and pour some soup into the lid. She thanks me and takes a sip, and then we both face the ocean.

"Did you have a nice Christmas?"

"With my dad? It was very good to see him," Harper says. "He was busy again right after, but we ate a stupid amount of food and watched movies all day. I got him a bunch of soccer shit—oops, sorry, soccer *stuff*—and he got me a bunch of 80s music because he likes oldies and thinks I should start liking 'em, too."

Her comment makes me remember songs I should forget, but I shake my head for a different reason. "You don't have to apologize for swearing. You're not in my classroom."

"Ah, yes. And I'm supposed to call you Mateo now."

"You're not *supposed* to call me anything. I told you that you *can* call me Mateo," I argue. Then I take a drink from the thermos and glance at Harper. "How's he doing?"

"He looks about as good as you do."

It's not a compliment. I wait for her to go on, knowing all too well she's never been short on things to say, but she continues to enjoy her soup and a view she's had her entire life.

"Last I heard, your dad didn't think you knew this bench was here."

"Found it when I was a kid. Google Earth," she shrugs. "It wasn't an exciting place to hang out back then—the excitement was in the discovery, I think—but I've appreciated it more as I've gotten older. It's quiet. Private."

"It's definitely private. Right up until someone shows up unannounced with a blanket and some soup."

"I'm not mad you're here."

"Nah, I didn't think you were," I say.

"And it's not your first time."

I raise an eyebrow. She tilts her head. I answer. "No."

"Am I allowed to ask when you first came here?"

"A while ago."

She sits with that, and I can't decide whether she's pieced together the truth of what Jamie and I are to each other, or whether she's still working it out. Honestly, if it's the former, I'd like to ask for her help. I've been lost for weeks now, and if he looks as rough as she's suggested, I'd love to know what the hell we're doing. Of course, that's been the question all along.

"I'm glad he has you," she murmurs, as quiet as I've ever heard her. "You're different from everyone else."

"I'm a friend."

I could go on. Defend myself and this ride I've been on for years. I could argue that we're barely friends now, and may not get back to the way we were. I could confirm that he very much does have me, and will forever, mostly because I will never again be that guy who tried to order takeout and didn't expect to watch the sun rise. I'm only the guy who fell deeply in love with Jameson Sinclair and doesn't know how to crawl back out.

And I'm not sure I would if given the chance.

But it doesn't matter what I could say. Harper waves me off.

"I don't think my mom was ever his friend. Even when they confused lust with love, or used each other for whatever, I don't think they really liked each other all that much."

It's very matter-of-fact, and from what I know, she's not wrong. Still, I hurt for Jamie and Harper. Maybe Danielle, too. I tuck a few stray strands of hair behind my ear and try not to think about why her first comparison was to something supposedly romantic and definitely sexual. Then I redirect my thoughts and her words.

"What about Kai?"

She grins, but there's a crease between her brows. "Tricky. I mean, sure, he's definitely a friend, but Kai was around *before*—before hockey became all of what my dad did, and most of who he was."

"Before Jameson Sinclair became more than a name reserved for roll call in a classroom full of kids."

"Exactly, yeah. Like, he was just J back then? And to Kai, he's still just J, so they're best friends, but they're basically brothers. He'll always be around, no matter who my dad is or was, and it's not the same as anyone my dad met after he became That Hockey Player." She stops and studies me. "I probably don't need to ask whether you've met Kai."

"You don't."

Harper snorts and shakes her head. "Anyway, my dad's also been friends with lots of teammates. We've vacationed with them. Spent some holidays together. Honestly, I grew up around them more than my grandparents. But they only sort of count because they're all part of that world."

"They all met Jameson Sinclair, and probably never spent time with him as J, even after he stopped playing. Same goes for Taylor McKeon."

"They never spent time with him as J *or* Jamie, and wouldn't be sitting on this bench today even if they knew it existed," she says pointedly. "And Taylor McKeon is in sort of a separate subcategory. Only friendly when egos don't get in the way, or when enough alcohol makes them stop caring? There are a lot of guys like that.

I'm sure you saw it when you were at the lake last summer."

I nearly choke on the last of my soup. "I didn't realize he told you about that."

"I was a little surprised he invited you," she says. "McKeon can be a bit of a dick, and you deserved a better getaway."

"It was gorgeous there."

"It's gorgeous in lots of places. Tell my dad to take you somewhere better next time."

That causes a frown Harper doesn't need to see. "I'm not sure there will be other trips in our future."

"Because of your grandma?"

"My grandma?"

"Yeah, when she died, my dad felt guilty for taking you away from her," she explains. "He knew you were close, and that she needed you, but then he invited you and—yeah."

"Did he say anything else?"

"That he didn't get to meet her."

Jesus. I hold too tightly to the thermos and swallow hard. It would've been absurd to predict where any conversation with Harper could have led, but even with the last month barely a memory, I didn't think she'd bring me back to the funeral so smoothly. I chance a look at her now, and she seems to know she hurt me somehow. But as much as I've been surprised a couple of times already, I don't think Jamie told her about our argument.

The fact that he and I both look terrible could be caused by anything, really.

I gesture toward the empty lid in her lap and smile when she hands it over. "I should probably go soon. Leave you to your peace and quiet."

"If you want to," she says. "But what about *your* peace and quiet?"

The ocean calls to me, and I think I turn toward it in search of an answer to Harper's question. She waits me out while she folds my blanket, and I'm close to telling her to keep it. There's probably a hoodie of mine left behind in a drawer not far from us, and there's no reason I shouldn't fill an empty house with a few more of my things. I wonder about the picture I gave him for Christmas—the one year we let ourselves share a moment of it—and hate that I never saw his new home to know whether it's hanging there.

I hate a lot of things I've never done.

Then I shake my head. "I'm just missing my friend."

Harper helps me out with practice over the next week and a half, before she flies back up to school. We finally exchange numbers too, and I feel like I'm drawing nonsensical lines in windswept sand. I don't think I've given away anything about Jamie she hasn't already heard from him, or figured out herself, but I don't want him to think I'm using her to tie myself to someone drifting so far away.

If he's finally learned how to keep from turning around, I don't want him to think I'm using his daughter just to make sure he looks back when I call his name.

If I call his name.

As winter shifts into spring, Jamie's team is making another push for the playoffs. I watch more of the games than I should, but none of them at Kai's. Los Angeles is having an incredible year, and when anyone around school talks about hockey, it has nothing to do with New Jersey. I keep my head down as much as I always have, focused on my students when I'm working, and sprawled on the couch with Sophie on a handful of nights in between. I'm spending more time with my family because my parents tug on the strings that will always guide me home, but when spring break comes around, I skip out on my volunteer work altogether.

And I go camping with Logan instead.

He'd texted me a month ago, our first contact since December, and asked if I'd mind a phone call.

I hadn't minded at all.

When we'd talked, he mentioned his plans to get away for a while, and coincidence or not, he'd made reservations for a campsite the same week I'd be off work.

"No strings attached, I swear," Logan said. "But you're good company, and I figured you might like to be off the grid for a while."

He'd figured correctly.

"I've got a sleeping bag, but not much else."

"I've got everything we'll need. And I'll even drive us there and back."

"It's out of your way," I pointed out.

"Eh, it's slightly out of the way. Worth it for the good company I mentioned."

And without thinking too hard about it, I'd let the church group know I'd be out of town, and I'd explained to my parents that I could be reached through the park rangers in case of emergency, and I'd told Jamie nothing. It's a long drive from home, and just before I lose signal on my phone, I stare at it from Logan's passenger seat and second-guess a little of everything. Then I turn it off and toss it into the backpack at my feet and do my best to forget.

Setting up our tent goes surprisingly smoothly given that my last camping trip was probably thirty years ago. Logan apologizes for the large mat we'll share—one he borrowed from his brother and sister-in-law without thinking—and I wave a hand at the sleeping bags that will keep us apart. I set up chairs next to the fire pit, and he sets up a small propane stove nearby. We eat and we drink. Before, during, and after, we talk and stare at the stars. Logan and

I go to sleep separately and together, and other than a few distant voices from other sites and crickets closer than that, I only hear him breathe. I'm awake to notice because my tossing and turning never stops.

I'm on edge most of the night, physically more comfortable than I expected to be, but anxious enough to consider going home in the morning.

"Give it another 24 hours," Logan murmurs, pressing coffee into my hand as I drop into a chair. "If you still want to leave tomorrow, we will."

I don't think I said anything out loud, but maybe there are bags under my eyes giving me away. My free hand attempts to keep my hair out of my face, a hair tie left somewhere in the tent, and I force a smile weaker than what Logan deserves.

"I'm sorry."

"For?"

"Not being the good company you expected," I say, shaking my head at my coffee.

Logan reaches down, his fingertips under my chin until I look up at him again. "Everything was fine until you couldn't sleep. Let me wear you out today, and we'll see how tonight goes, okay?"

There are easy ways to interpret what he's said, and I have no doubt he's done it intentionally, almost a bitter and kind game of chicken. We're only friends, but the definition of friendship has been blurry to me for so damn long. I've been promised no strings attached, so I could take any of the things being offered and go home without a debt, but I don't know what I want.

For now, I simply nod.

While I use the communal bathroom and change into jeans, Logan makes us breakfast, and it surprises me because I know we're both used to grabbing coffee and running out the door in the morning. I take the time he gives me to keep breathing and watch the campground stir. There's no way for me to check for texts or hockey scores, and I make peace with that as well as I can.

Later, with our boots on, and Logan looking better than I could've imagined in his flannel and beanie, we go for a hike around the lake just out of sight from where we slept. It's a beautiful morning, and there's no need for us to talk about it or anything else. I get lost in the sight of the water and think about the last time I vacationed next to a lake, also with a man who knows what I sound like when I come. I must make a noise, because Logan turns to look at me, but I can't explain, and he gives up on me after a few seconds.

We stop several minutes later for water and shade, and while Logan drinks, I watch a droplet of sweat slide down his neck. I want to taste it, but it's unfair of me to want things here, so I only trace its path with my finger and stop when I reach the collar of his shirt.

"Sorry," I say again.

"For?" he asks again.

"Thinking you're pretty."

It sounds like I'm apologizing for the mixed signals, and I suppose that's true. But I'm angry with myself for using that word when it belongs to someone else. It has since the night Jamie and I met.

I push off the tree I've been leaning against and continue walking.

Back at the campsite, we make sandwiches for lunch and eat our weight in fruit. He's set up two hammocks, also borrowed from his brother and sister-in-law, and we let the food settle while we read books we'd brought along. Then, because we're camping or because he knows how good he looks doing it, Logan crouches next to my hammock and asks me to go kayaking with him. And sometimes—maybe too often—it's unfathomable to say no to him.

So, we spend the afternoon in the sun as it reflects off the chilly lake water. We talk about our families and our jobs and other safe topics we've covered before. On some level, it's all bullshit, but it brings us back to the afternoons we ran errands and the evenings we went out to dinner. It allows us to ignore the nights we spent in his bed, and how easy it would be to do that when we're on a camping trip we might not have thought through.

After kayaking around the lake, we return to the shore. After returning to the shore, we splash each other senseless. After splashing each other senseless, we return to the campsite. And after returning to the campsite, we change into something dry and we make dinner together and we rest. It's only when we're side by side in our chairs, warmed by the fire and made safe by the night sky, that we talk about something real.

"Was that Jameson Sinclair at your grandmother's funeral?" Logan asks, a mug of spiked hot chocolate in his hand.

"Yes."

"He's not a family friend."

It's a statement, not a question. I drink, then respond. "His daughter was in my freshman honors class, and then in my AP class as a senior. She also played varsity soccer all four years."

"How many other students' parents were there that day?"

That one's a question, but it doesn't need to be. "None."

"But you and he had become friends."

"I know him better as Jamie, yes."

If Logan's lining up dominoes, I've already knocked the first couple of them down, and everything else will fall quickly. He pauses as if he might walk away before he witnesses the mess he's asked me to make, but then he goes on.

"It was hockey season. I'm not a big fan or anything, but I know enough to understand that he was supposed to be in Texas that night."

"You know enough to have recognized him, too."

Logan makes a face at his hot chocolate. "I may have jerked off to his underwear ads a time or two."

He and probably a ridiculous number of other queer men who were paying more attention than I was. Of course, that puts him an important step ahead of me, and I wonder whether getting off to Jamie *before* we met might've been enough reason to keep from wanting impossible things with him after.

"Yes, he was supposed to be in Texas," I say when Logan's looking at me again. "I had told him I wished he could be there, but I didn't expect it to happen. That was a surprise."

"A good one?"

I raise my eyebrow. "I just said I wished he could be there."

"Right."

"We're not together. We're not—a *couple*."

"I didn't ask that, but—"

"But yes, he's the reason I wasn't available over the summer."

It's a lot to say to someone who could spill to all the gossip sites tomorrow, but I trust Logan more than that. Maybe even more so when he slowly swallows more liquor and chocolate, and then makes gentle, gentle eye contact.

"It's not like whatever you and I had, though. The casual fucking we did, whenever it worked out that way. You and Jameson Sinc—*Jamie*—are different."

I want to laugh or cry at how perfectly he's understated that, but I just smile sadly. "Yes."

Logan changes the subject then, and going to sleep separately and together is a lot like the night before. It's also not much like it at all, despite the distant voices and more crickets. Logan had set out to wear me out, and he's done just that, so when I listen to him breathe, I only last a few seconds before he'll have to listen to me instead.

In the morning, I tell him I don't want to leave. We spend the next few days busy with a mix of the same activities—hiking and reading and kayaking and drinking by the fire—and I have *fun* for the first time in a while. I love getting sweaty and dirty, and washing it away with a shitty campground shower. My hair is usually pulled into a little bun, but I'm as careless as I've ever been, the rest of the world kept inside a phone I haven't turned on all week. I breathe easily every morning and sleep dreamlessly every night, and the decisions I make are guided only by how I feel in that exact moment.

It's why I'm facing Logan now, in our tent on our last night here. We're looking at each other, unafraid of all the things I think we should fear, and I barely blink as I begin to unzip my sleeping bag. The sound would be embarrassingly loud if I were embarrassed, this silly thing giving away my intention with every inch it's lowered, but I don't stop until it's somewhere around my knees. It's cold, but there are blankets nearby if we need them later. I'm not all that worried about the temperature at the moment.

I reach for Logan's sleeping bag next, and we haven't looked away, but he's the first to speak.

"You don't have to do this."

"I know."

He licks his lips, then sighs. "I don't want you to stop."

"I know."

Neither of us has shaved since we arrived, and when we're finally too close to keep staring, his face feels so fucking good against mine. I ease back only to spit into my hand before I reach for him, and he doesn't hesitate before he does the same and reaches for me, the two of us still fully covered except for where the waistbands of our sweatpants have been shoved out of the way. This will be fast and messy and mostly silent and entirely selfish, but Logan takes what I can give, and we kiss until I don't need him to be somebody else.

We kiss long after we both come.

Chapter Fifteen: Jamie

(I Reminded Myself Who I Am)

Sorry. **I was camping. My phone was off.**

Camping's new. They must've missed you at the carnival

The break was good for me.

Did you go with Sophie? Your family?

Logan.

Oh. Well. I'm glad the break was good for you

Good luck next week.

Thanks

I press the heels of my hands against my eyes like they'll help erase a conversation I memorized almost immediately after I walked away from it. Next week was seven days ago, and the playoffs start tonight. I can't keep worrying about whether Mateo will watch the game with Logan. In the past, he's gone to the bar to be near Kai. He's spent plenty of game nights with Sophie. Once, Harper was at his side. Groaning, I remind myself not to text him now, and then I decide I don't care who he'll be with.

The only thing that will wreck me is the idea of him not watching at all.

I need to believe he still looks for me when he's sitting next to someone else.

My phone remains face down on my desk when two players stop by to talk. However much the public was fed stories of my arrogance—stories about how my place at the top of the league kept me from being within reach of anyone who needed my support—I was always a great teammate. If the media cared to ask me about it now, I'd tell them I'm an even better coach. Over the past two seasons, I've especially connected with younger players. They're professionals thrust into the spotlight for this chance to make lifelong dreams come true. They're also overwhelmed in ways they're not encouraged to admit.

The guys sitting in front of me today are nervous about the game, and I've given them the space to be honest about that. The closed door in our organization belongs to Taylor, and nobody is surprised. Anyone *could* knock and be let in, but I've made it easier for our players to come to me. I'm glad these two have.

Several hours later, they both play great, two goals and two assists between them. We win the game, and I feel good. It's fine that this time, it's my phone that's turned off.

I turn it off again four games later, when we're unexpectedly knocked out of the playoffs. I don't need pity from Kai or Harper or Mateo. It doesn't matter that none of them would dare offer it. Over the next several days, we wrap up the season and say goodbye to the team until September. I go out with a bunch of the staff to get wasted as inconspicuously as possible in a city where at least a couple of us are pretty fucking conspicuous. There's a headline about it halfway down a few different sites the next day. We're forgiven by people who have also gotten drunk to forget about our loss, and by most of management.

The hangover lasts longer than anything having to do with alcohol. I want to rehab in my pool, but I'm not in my real house with my real backyard, and laps would require a trip to the gym. There are always old tv shows to watch or greasy food to eat. I'm mad both remind me of the night I was halfway through a beer and a conversation when a bar brawl broke out.

Caught in the middle of a bunch of options I don't like, I'm grateful when Harper calls to interrupt. As usual, she's walking across campus. I hear the chatter of university students who'd prefer to procrastinate than prepare for finals.

"Hey, dad."

"Hello, Harper. Hello, Simon."

She giggles. "He's not here right now. I'm going over to his place after class, but I figured I'd talk to you first because I know we've sorta mentioned doing something this summer, and I wanted to know whether that's still a go or—"

"His place, huh?"

"Really? You wanna talk about *that*?" she shrieks. "I'm 20. He's 22. You barely freaked out about anything when I was a teenager, but you're worried about me going to my boyfriend's house now?"

"Not worried at all. Just being a father for a minute. Do you go over to his place a lot? Do you *stay* over at his place a lot?"

"You know, you weren't much older than Simon when you had me."

I snort at that and pour myself a glass of water. "Fine, don't tell me. Are you still bringing him with you on the trip? Are *you* still coming on the trip, or was this call a way to bail on it?"

My tone is still light because I know Harper's busier than ever. I'm not counting on another 20 years of dragging her with me on summer vacations. But while soccer and school and Simon keep her schedule full, she's got a break from one of them now, she'll have a break from another soon, and I've encouraged her to bring the third along. She and I have tossed out ideas about where we'd like to go when the semester is over. Because I'm not actually unreasonable about where she spends the night, I chuckle at what she says next.

"You're not gonna make us sleep in separate rooms, are you?"

I promise her I won't, and then we go back to narrowing down our choices to a top three she can discuss with Simon later. After trading my water for a slice of cold pizza, I leave the kitchen behind and shuffle from room to room. We talk about the pros and cons of New Orleans and the Caribbean and the Mexican Riviera. I'll be happy with anything, and I let my mind wander as Harper continues to talk, only a little concerned about whether she's running late for wherever she needs to be. It's just a coincidence that I'm standing in front of a framed picture of a bench when she clears her throat and stuns me into silence.

"Is there someone special you could invite to join us?" she asks. "Anyone who will have some time off when we do? You know, just to keep it even?"

"What, like Taylor?"

"I said *special*, dad."

She did, and I heard her. Not only was I fortunate enough to be blessed with exceptional looks and exceptional athletic ability, but I also have half a brain, so the point she's trying to make is perfectly clear. I'm only struggling to figure out why she's asking now. She's spent her first two decades on this planet being curious about everything except my love life. I want to know why she's—only barely vaguely—suggesting I bring Mateo as my vacation date.

I don't ask because it's not a conversation I can have without lying several times, either to Harper or myself. At least for today, both of us deserve better.

"I'm not inviting anyone, but I'll make sure I'm not in your way too often. You and Simon can have a very nice time without your father looking over your shoulder."

"And I—it's not that I don't appreciate that, but—" She huffs and clears her throat again. I'm entirely reinvested in this conversation because she's never had this much trouble speaking. "Can I ask you a question?"

I laugh just loud enough for her to hear me through the phone. "A lack of permission hasn't slowed you down yet. I'm not sure why you think you need it now."

"Because this isn't—" She stops there, and I play with ways to finish her sentence. *This isn't any of my business. This isn't the kind of thing we talk about. This isn't a question I think you'll answer.* As it turns out, she gives up on whatever she'd started to say, and takes my breath away instead.

"Are you not inviting him because you think I'd have a problem with it?"

Fuck.

"No, pixie," I say softly. "It's because I think *he* would."

The thing is, Mateo and I still talk. We exchange texts and a short voice note or two. We're friends, so everything feels almost right, even on the nights the sharp edges sting. I listen to him until his voice is absorbed into my marrow, and I think there's a chance he can heal the most broken things between here and there.

When it's been a couple of weeks since my team's abrupt playoff ousting, and the pain of it isn't so fresh, I give Mateo a call. He sounds relieved to hear from me, and we stay on the phone for almost an hour, just catching up. We're consciously careful about it, because he doesn't tell me about Logan. I don't tell him nobody's held me since he and I shared a bed at the lake house. But I hear about all the work he has ahead before another class of seniors graduates—he has freshmen finishing their first year, too—and about a soccer clinic he's going to run for the district in early July. He mentions the idea of asking Harper to help if she'll be home. I encourage him to reach out to her. It's easy then to tell him about our upcoming vacation and warn him that Simon may come as part of a package deal. Mateo laughs, and just like his voice, it's a hell of a balm. By the time I confirm that I'll be staying where I am throughout another summer, we're both as ready for it as we can be.

"Do you think that'll ever change?" he asks. "Or is that home now?"

"Does it matter?"

There's something ugly I've left unsaid, and it sounds a lot like *If you're fucking your grandparents' neighbor, why do you care where I live?* It's loud enough that I'm sure he heard it, too. Maybe his answer takes care of both.

"Whatever else has happened, I've never stopped missing you. I'd always rather have you here with me."

More balm, but my leg aches and I couldn't say why. "So, maybe we should make plans for you to visit again. Maybe you can see where I live."

"Maybe we should, and maybe I can."

But then we don't. And so he can't.

Harper, Simon, and I go on our trip and return home before Mateo's even done with his school year. She's agreed to help him with anything he needs while she's in California for the next several weeks. I don't get involved in the arrangements they make, nor do I question the relationship they're building without me. I find trouble while they stay out of it, suddenly eager to accept when Taylor offers to set me up one night. Then another. And another.

"Look at you, Sinclair," he smirks. "It only took you two years of being my assistant coach to decide you might like to have some fun outside of my basement. I was afraid the player I once knew had suffered more than a broken leg."

Two years of being his assistant. Four since I let Bailey McKeon introduce me to her friend. Lara or Lena or Lana. Almost six since I craved greasy food and a friendly face, and kissed a man I might've loved before believing something that magical ever happens outside of fairy tales.

"Look at me," I say. "I'm hardly broken at all."

Amazingly, I don't actually sleep with the first woman. I couldn't say why. She's exactly the type I used to show off at awards dinners or official team parties. On our date, I take her out to dinner, and she makes it known she'd be happy to follow me home for dessert. I charm her as I turn her down, and get a kiss on my cheek for my efforts and make promises that will remain unfulfilled. Once I've returned to my house alone, I crawl into a hoodie that I shouldn't need in this heat. I get off while wearing it, and I shouldn't need that either.

The next woman and I meet at a bar in the lobby of her hotel, and fucking her takes very little effort. A short elevator ride and a condom are all we need once we've had a couple of drinks and a few forced laughs. I don't think she's any better or worse than the last woman I went out with, but I arrived knowing I can't go home with a hard dick again. I want to come with a stranger's name on my tongue, and she's the ex-wife of someone Taylor played with years ago, so I don't think I'm supposed to fall head over heels or anything. The sex is nice.

I like the third one more than I want to. She's a teacher, and we meet up at a silly street fair. We share funnel cake and talk about oceans and lakes. There are only a few rides here, but I mumble something about heights when she asks me to go on the Ferris wheel, and we keep both feet on the ground. She talks about her family and doesn't really give a shit about hockey. I'm relieved when she doesn't give a shit about soccer either. Strands of her dark hair fall free from her ponytail, and I resist the urge to tuck them behind her ear. Then she smiles and asks me if I'd like to go home with her, and I say yes because I think I would. I do. That sex is nice, too.

It feels good to be touched again.

She's pretty.

It's a lonely morning. I have a mug of tasteless coffee in one hand and my phone in the other. I squeeze my eyes shut at Mateo's text as if that will make it disappear when I open them again. It doesn't, though I've done a decent job blurring it some. I don't know which woman he's referring to—which probably says a lot about how little I've changed—nor do I know where he saw me with anyone. Cameras are everywhere. He and I are lucky we spent time together after I'd been mostly forgotten, and before I was remembered again. Far fewer people cared.

But he cares now, and my next exhale is shaky. I try to be funny. Or something.

Prettier than I am?

Impossible, sweetheart.

I don't respond to that because I'm too close to ending up with tears on my face or a mess on my hands. I want to be drinking coffee with him, one of us in the other's lap, sleepy and lazy about it when we kiss. My hands would be in his hair, soothing until I need to pull his head back and suck at his neck. He'd keep us rocking together, both of us soft for a while because everything is so slow and so gentle.

I'm horny enough to know I need to fuck Mateo someday. I'm pathetic enough to know I'd rather fantasize about just *being* with him this morning.

After I've set my mug on the counter, I refocus on my phone, my texts closed but a new search open. I quickly type my name and land on sites Mateo might have found. I read and shake my head and marvel at the manipulation of public perception and the passage of time. Gone are the days of *Jameson Sinclair Scores Five-Hole at a Las Vegas Nightclub* next to a picture of liquor-soaked me, several half-dressed women, and at least one slutty man. Now there's a candid of sober me standing behind date number three, my arms wrapped around her far too sweetly, and the words *Two for Holding? Why the List of Hockey's Hottest Bachelors May Be Down a Man.*

Even back then, when everyone loved to hate me for being unstoppable on and off the ice, I could've been found in quieter places if anyone had thought to look for me there. Now I'm a few years past 40, and I'm not sure I'd be in any VIP lines, but I'm not against the idea of being drunk in a club, especially if a very specific slutty man is next to me. I frown at the images on my phone. Where I am and where I've been don't change the fact that it's always been a show. A version of the one my parents made me rehearse as a kid.

I give myself a few minutes to lament the loss of things I've surrendered. Then I set my mask aside—only here, in the privacy of a place I don't really call home. Sighing at the terrible puns in the headlines, past and present, I wonder what words they'd use to write about Mateo and me, if given the chance. Something about backchecking? Stickhandling? Anything about the crease or the slot would be fair game, I suppose. Two-man advantage almost makes me smile, but I remember it will be easier for the media to be cruel than kind. Then I close the search on my phone and walk away.

I miss my view of the ocean, and everywhere I dream about being is closer to there than here. I stop myself just short of wondering what Mateo can see from wherever he is now.

A few days later, another search results in another flurry of photos of me, this time from date number two. I roll my eyes at any of the articles suggesting they were taken after the adorable embrace candids at the street fair. I roll them again when some aren't sure whether it's the same woman as before. Or not before. There's a picture of us at the bar, our knees touching as we lean toward each other to talk. There's another one once we've stood and are saying goodnight to the bartender, my hand resting against the perfect arch of her lower back. A third captures us while we're waiting for the elevator. I'm surprised to see her body pinning mine to the lobby wall.

I remember a lot about that moment. How she smelled like perfume instead of cologne when I breathed her in. How her cheek was smooth instead of rough when I brushed mine against it. How she was all softness and curves and lace instead of the taut lines and broad shoulders that had once stood in front of me wearing nothing but boxer briefs and a wet spot I've never been able to forget.

But if anyone had asked, I would've sworn I had pressed my body against hers.

Mateo texts later that night. *Having fun?*

I'd tell him no, but those two letters are difficult to type.

Over the next month or so, I go out another five or six times, and sleep with none of the women. I wake to five or six pictures of me touching them in five or six different restaurants or bars or night markets. Nobody in a position to fire me cares that there's been an uptick in my social life because I've been caught with successful women on dates ranging from cute to classy. Harper knows better than to go looking for things she doesn't want to see. If Simon's half the man I want him to be, he'll keep his mouth shut about anything he finds. I tell myself the hum of guilt I hear is only because of them.

The voice note I receive suggests I'm wrong.

It's late, and I hope you're already asleep by the time I send this, but I don't know. Maybe you're up. Maybe you're out with someone again. But I—is this because of me? Is this because of Logan? He and I aren't—we went camping, and I'll answer anything you want to know about that, if you really want to know it, but it's not—we're not together or anything. We're just friends. Or maybe—that's probably a shitty word to use, right? Friends. You and I have said that for years, but it doesn't really come close to describing us. What we are. Or what we were. But Logan and I are—maybe we're doing the same thing you're doing with all these women. Are we all reaching for the closest warm body? I don't know what else I'm allowed to hold on to. I don't know the right way to be close to anyone else when I'm still in love with you. But that's not—I want you to be happy, Jamie. And if you are—fuck, why do I feel like the only person who doesn't think you're happy? Why do you look so much like Jameson Sinclair again?

I want to drop my phone to the floor. I also can't stop listening to him, his voice no longer a balm when he sounds this tired and this disappointed in me. Part of me wants to defend myself by saying that I probably haven't had any more sex with these women than he's had with Logan, but I don't think that was his point. And I could argue that he's the one who gave up on me, but I've never been convinced that's true when I'm the one who moved away.

Still lying in bed in nothing but my briefs, I glance at the time and wonder whether he's awake. I don't want to talk to him, but I'm just frustrated enough that I need to respond. The only question is whether I text it or say it out loud. I decide my raspy voice would give him a way to torture himself too, and I start recording.

I've always been Jameson Sinclair.

Whether Mateo's quiet accusation got to me or not, I don't go out with anyone for a while. Swimming laps at the gym becomes a priority again. I talk to my parents more than I have in a while. I spend hours on a video chat with Kai while he preps the bar for the day. He tells me he hasn't seen Mateo in almost a year, and suggests that I stop being a fucking idiot.

It's what it sounds like, anyway.

He really says, "That man's the only choice you've ever made for *you*, J."

"Hockey," I argue weakly. "I love hockey. I've chosen that for me, too."

"You chose hockey because your dad told you to try it, and your mom cheered you on, and it came so damn naturally to you. You stayed with it because everyone around you made it your entire identity, and you didn't have to be anyone else. Even off the ice you've been hockey player and playboy, or hockey player and girl dad, or former hockey player and current coach. You love hockey, and it was easy to love because until you ran from here one night, it had given more than it's taken. But you met Mateo, and he was easy to love too, and he was all yours. Only yours."

I've always been Jameson Sinclair.

"Kai—"

"You've never been anyone but J to me," he says, pausing in front of his screen with a couple of bottles of vodka in his hands. I don't think he's read my mind, especially when we're almost three thousand miles apart, but I can't ask when he keeps talking. "Then the rest of the world learned your name, and you started making decisions with them in mind. The choices didn't stop being for *you*. They just stopped being for J—or Jamie."

I swallow hard and blink away tears before they fall. "We've never talked about this."

"Guess we've gotta add it to the list."

He's not wrong. I try to keep myself from feeling terrible about it by remembering how many important things we *have* shared. Who cares that I didn't tell him about my attraction to men, or that my name carries pride and loss everywhere I go? We've spent countless hours mourning his dad and bitching about my mom. We've cried when dreams have come true and laughed when it's all gone wrong. We've pulled each other from fights and cleaned each other's wounds, and gone weeks without speaking and picked up right where we left off.

When we have to, we'll get a little pissed off that there's something we've ignored—maybe even hidden—and then we'll be best friends again. And I need my best friend now.

"I'm scared, Kai. Really fucking scared. What will happen if everyone finds out?" I ask, hushed in case a fear spoken too loudly will have a better chance of damning me. "What will they do to me?"

"If nobody ever finds out, what will you have done to yourself?"

I don't answer Kai. I can't, in part because the right words sit heavy at the back of my throat, and in part because I get a string of texts from Taylor in the next several seconds. It will be safer to respond to him. I already know a quick goodbye will be forgiven by the man who can see that I'm still reeling. In fact, he nods and waves me off, gesturing to a bar I can't see but could navigate in my sleep.

As I scroll through the messages, I figure Taylor is probably bored and ready for more of my internet-exaggerated antics. We haven't had any meetings at the front office recently, and we've still got some time before camp. He's asking whether I'm in New Jersey now, and whether I have plans for next week. There are a few insults thrown in for good measure. I think he sends them out of habit more than anything.

Too eager to hear another voice today, even if it's his, I respond to his texts with a call and several prepared excuses for why I'm not interested in another date right now. Taylor interrupts me not long after I've begun, telling me he's just glad I'm finally getting laid. I don't bother explaining to him that it's only happened twice. In the next breath, he invites me to the lake house for the third time. When I say yes, he asks whether anyone will join me this year. Even planning for a group trip, I feel so fucking *alone* in a way that can't be solved by blind dates or coworkers, but Kai has the bar and Harper will start her junior year soon. And if Mateo thinks I look too much like Jameson Sinclair in some pictures, I don't want to know what he'd say when faced with the real thing.

The man he fell in love with isn't the same one going to Taylor's for a week.

Taylor grunts while I stare at my reflection in a hallway mirror. I'm not sure I actually respond before he hangs up on me. Days later, I'm packing my bag.

Our new goalie coach—a guy named Oskar, rumored to drink, swear, and fuck more than the rest of our staff combined—joins us at the lake. I'm irrationally annoyed to find out Wyatt is back. I greet Taylor's son for the first time since he and Harper engaged in an assortment of underage fun, and I look forward to teasing her about those memories later. I end up in the same room I had last year, the futon an unnecessary prop now. The sun calls us to the dock for beer and a boat ride almost as soon as we've arrived.

That first night, it's just the five of us, drinking too much and laughing too hard. For fleeting moments, I feel like everything is exactly the way it should be.

I've always been Jameson Sinclair.

However much hockey takes from me now, I haven't stopped loving it. The scrape of ice beneath my blades and the stillness on the rink before anyone else is there. The energy in a locker room as the team prepares for a big game or celebrates a big win. And yes, the cheers from people who are excited to be there with me and get to see me at my best and maybe even be proud of me for a couple of hours. I'm not playing anymore, and I still carry phantom pain everywhere, but this is only my second offseason as a coach, and I just need a little more time.

Hockey will start giving to me again if I wait.

We're sluggish the following morning, all of us getting older and slower about recovering from a late night. We devour grease and coffee and don't bother showering before we tumble toward the lake. We spend most of the day on the boat again. That afternoon, we're joined by Bailey McKeon and a friend of hers I recognize too quickly. They bring a couple of others, and we sprawl everywhere, more beer in our hands. The warm afternoon drags on, and Lara or Lena or Lana clings to me as intently as her bikini clings to her.

She hasn't let go by the time the sun goes down. I haven't asked her to. The women have their own place to stay, but I already know none of them will turn down a request to stay with one of us. I also know I've had more to drink than is smart with a mostly empty stomach and a pathetically needy body. The likelihood of making smart choices is ticking away. Still, after a failed round of pool on a table that didn't use to be here, and a few successful rounds of a card game I've never played before, I tell everyone I'm going to bed.

Alone.

At least a few people look terribly disappointed in me. Taylor seems intrigued.

I almost promise them it's just for the night. That I can feel my restraint fading. That the man in the headlines hasn't gone far, no matter how misleading any of those articles or pictures have been. Lara or Lena or Lana can wait one more day.

Mateo once waited years.

Chapter Sixteen: Mateo

(I Went to New York)

"I should go there."

Sophie rolls toward me and squints. She spent the night in my bed after we got wine-drunk and watched too many sappy movies, but the sun is cutting through my closed blinds, and what I've said makes no sense until she looks at my phone.

"You want to go on a boat ride?" she mumbles, and maybe it still doesn't make sense.

"No. I mean, I would. And I have. But I don't really care about the boat. Just that Jamie's on it. That's Taylor McKeon's boat."

"When was the picture taken?"

I shrug as well as I can while I'm still lying down. "Yesterday? The day before? It doesn't say. But according to a 'source,' they'll be there all week."

"So, he's on vacation again."

"Apparently."

"But he didn't invite you this year."

"Apparently not."

"And you think you should go there anyway."

I sigh. "I don't know. Everything is wrong between us now, and it would probably be so stupid to show up at one hockey superstar's lake house just to make things right with another hockey superstar."

"Probably *so* stupid," Sophie echoes. "But?"

"But maybe it's my turn to chase proof that somebody loves me."

She shoves me sideways and then leaves me, still talking when she stumbles into the bathroom and shouts from there. "We both know he loves you, but if you really want to fix whatever got fucked up at your grandmother's funeral, wouldn't it be easier to knock on Jamie's own front door? Like, when he's not on a trip with his famous coworker?"

"Yes, but no," I shout back, finally sitting up. "Surprising him at his house means I risk interrupting him and any of a dozen women. Maybe a couple of them at once. At best, the risk is that he doesn't come home at all."

Sophie reappears and leans against my doorframe. "And if you surprise him at Taylor McKeon's house, you only risk interrupting his fourth or fifth beer."

I look at the picture again, three of the five men recognizable to me even when only two of them are named. It's not unlike the time I spent with them on that same boat, probably full of the same obscene jokes and incredible views. If I arrive unannounced, it's entirely possible I'll be turned away with a derisive laugh, but I may also be welcomed by someone who thinks I'm just the idiot Jameson Sinclair befriended when hockey didn't keep him busy enough for higher standards.

"Will you give me a ride to the airport tomorrow?"

"Is this the dumbest thing you've ever done?"

"Oh, I don't know about that," I sigh. "I think some people would question that first decision to wait four years for someone I'd known for less than four weeks."

"Do you regret it?"

"No."

She nods as if it was the only way I could've answered. Maybe it was. "Yeah, of course I'll give you a ride. Just let me know what time."

Sophie leaves a few minutes later, her apartment close enough that she doesn't need to raid my kitchen when hers is probably better stocked. Before I can think everything through and make better choices, I go online to book a flight at a price that should humiliate me, and forward the confirmation to her. For a brief—and even dumber—moment, I consider giving Harper a heads up just so somebody in Jamie's family has been warned, but I drop my phone onto my nightstand and take a shower instead.

I jerk off under the near-scalding water, a straightforward means to an end when I need to relax. At least some of the tension returns quickly when I rehearse all the ways I can say a couple of casual hellos—an apologetic one due to Taylor McKeon before I offer something hopeful to Jamie—and I wonder whether either could be helped by a small gift of some kind.

Then I remember the hit my bank account just took, and I decide my words will have to do.

A day and a half later, I'm navigating an unfamiliar road to an unfamiliar home in an unfamiliar state. I rented a car to keep one element under my control when so little else will be, but I've been shaking since I boarded the plane in California, and I don't expect that to stop soon. It's already later than I'd like it to be, three time zones and a layover working against me, and even given a long summer day, the sun is already down. I want to lean into the darkness and trust it to keep me safe, but my heartbeat suggests something more foreboding, and I'd turn around if I weren't afraid that would be worse.

When I park, there are more cars than I remember from a year ago, but nothing registers as a problem for me yet. I go back and forth about whether to leave my duffel bag in the back seat. I've booked somewhere else to stay in case I offend anyone beyond repair, but I'm unfairly praying I don't have to leave before I've said all I need to say.

We. I think *we* need to say things.

I walk away without my bag, and I become more concerned when I hear laughter from somewhere closer to the lake, at least one woman's voice among others. It has me looking back toward the cars before I frown about how wrong I might've been. Five men had been on the boat, but the party has grown beyond that now. I pause and listen for Jamie, but it's impossible to tell whether he's out by the dock or the fire pit or giggling in the grass with a handful of admirers.

He could be inside, recording another voice note for me. Maybe he misses me tonight.

After another step, I pause again. I don't know whether I should walk around the house to see who is out back, or just knock on the door like any other visitor. It doesn't escape me that my terrible indecisiveness might have served me better before I booked my flight, but I'm here now, and I finally force myself to march toward the front door.

I ring the doorbell. Someone swears inside. If there's still a chance to leave, I don't take it. Seconds later, I'm face to face with Taylor McKeon, and I realize my boring life became a little wilder when I wasn't paying attention.

"Ah. Mateo. From California," he says, his head cocked as he licks his lips. I feel like his prey, and maybe that's exactly right. "This is unexpected. Were you in the neighborhood?"

He hasn't welcomed me in, nor has he opened the door enough for me to see who else is inside. There's music playing somewhere and the sounds of people shooting pool, though I don't remember a table being here before.

"Is Jamie here? Jameson. Sinclair. Obviously." I stumble over everything, and Taylor smirks.

"You must already know the answer to that. It's a hell of a fucking trip to make otherwise, even if you've missed your friend while he's been gone."

"I do. Miss him, I mean. But I—if I could just talk to him."

Taylor looks me up and down. I'm wearing decent jeans and an old INXS t-shirt under an open flannel, and I've only got my phone and the rental car keys in my hand. He leans for a view over my shoulder, though I'm not sure he can see much without better lighting, and then he meets my eyes again.

"Did you bring a bag?"

"I—yes, but I don't have to—contrary to whatever this looks like, I wouldn't demand that anyone let me stay."

"This looks like a few different things," he says.

"I miss my friend. We've covered that much."

"Of course. And after you've said hello to your friend, I could introduce you to some of the beautiful ladies who've come to spend a few days with us."

My eyes fall shut, but I'm quick to open them again. "I appreciate it, but you don't need to go to any trouble for me."

"No," he says, that single syllable dripping off his tongue. "I don't suppose I do. So—no women. Just one man. By all means, come on in."

Taylor waves me through the door and says nothing else when he leads me upstairs. I can still hear noise from downstairs, but there are voices in front of us too, and we stop just outside the same door Jamie and I had once kept locked. I'm not stupid enough to believe it's unlocked now, and I'm only distracted from my brutal imagination when Taylor knocks loudly enough to startle me, and probably the two people inside.

"Later, you will have to tell me whether it was worth it," he says.

I can't answer before I realize I'm wrong about the lock. Taylor cracks the door open without waiting for an invitation, and I guess that's his right as a host, however dickish he is about it. I'm just off to his side, thrown by how stoic he can be while I'm feeling too many things—at the very least, I would've bet he'd be excited to have a front-row seat to this show—but I'm content to study him for another second or two.

My step closer to a room full of heartache comes just as he speaks.

"Lena, how about you go see what Bailey's doing downstairs?"

A woman—Lena, apparently—scoffs. "Bailey doesn't need me to check on her."

"No, but I need you to leave."

"Come on, Taylor," Jamie groans. "We're just—"

"You're not *just* anything. Not anymore. I need her to leave."

Taylor pushes the door further open, and while both Jamie and Lena can see me now, only one of them gasps. Only one of them remembers what happened on a late-August night six years ago. Only one of them understands that tonight might become more impossible to escape.

Lena's in his lap, the same way Jamie's been in mine, though the bench has been replaced by a futon, and I try to tell myself it matters. I watch carefully as she touches him, and feel my blood burn at how thoughtlessly she does it, as though she has before and knows she can again. Wanting to replace her hands with my own keeps me where I am, and Jamie blinks, closer to breathless than I'd like. His grip on her waist tightens, and I hate how vividly that will feature in my memories, but I take solace in the fact that they're both still clothed—and that he's starting to separate them while staring at me. She's confused, and more than a little pissed off, her kiss-swollen lips eager to help her pout.

"Who's he?"

"Taylor's right. You should leave."

She stands and smooths the front of shorts too short to need her attention. "Fine, yeah. I'll go see what Bailey's up to. You boys have fun."

"Thanks for letting me in," I say to Taylor just after Lena's disappeared down the stairs.

I don't thank Jamie for anything yet. I'm not convinced he won't throw me out soon, and I'm not sure he's eager to let me talk before that, no matter how far I've traveled for the chance. Taylor seems to have more faith than I do, and his eyes lock with mine.

"You're welcome to stay for as long as Sinclair would like. I'm sure it's been a long day, so I'll make sure nobody bothers you tonight." He holds out his hand. "Give me the keys. I'll get your bag."

I almost remind him I wasn't demanding a place to stay, but then I realize he isn't someone who responds to demands anyway, and I nod. With the keys in his hand, he lingers, staring down at where Jamie's still sitting without bothering to look at me again. It feels, oddly, like Taylor's got my back here, and I can't examine that too closely. It's easier if he remains the villain in this story, at least until I know how it ends.

Then he's gone, the bedroom door closed behind us. I lock it because I'm not Lena.

It was the goal all along, but now I'm left alone with Jamie—really privately *alone*—for the first time since we shared the bed just in front of me now. He's visibly tired, and more than a little ashamed by whatever I've seen, but he's so fucking gorgeous, and I can't help but tell him so.

He ignores what I've said, and he stands and walks toward me. I don't have anywhere to go to get away from him, but the trouble I've gone to so far makes it clear I don't want space. Jamie's wearing a loose tank top and gray sweatpants I've seen before, and it's easy to stare at them before I take another chance on falling for pretty blue eyes. He pulls the hair tie from my messy bun and drops it on the floor.

When it's down, it's like you've let something go. Like you've stopped caring so much.

I still care about everything, but I don't remind him of that. I haven't even said hello.

"Did he call you?" he asks.

I frown a little and shake my head. Of all the things I'd imagined Jamie saying tonight, that wasn't one of them, though it means I'm invited to answer after being afraid I'd lost my voice.

"No. God, no. Did you think he was pulling another gift basket stunt? Looking for a way to get into your head? Trying to start drama?'"

"It feels pretty fucking dramatic."

"Yeah, and for once, that's on me."

"For *once*?" Jamie asks. "Getting off while I held your hand wasn't exactly boring."

"That was a while ago. You still think about it?"

"Every damn day. You don't?"

"Every damn day," I say. "But you're the one who surprised me at the door then, and you don't look like you were short a hand to hold tonight."

"If Taylor didn't call you, how'd you know where I was?"

I shrug. "You're not that hard to find. But it's more crowded than last time. That was a surprise."

"I hadn't seen Lena in years, but she and Taylor's sister and a few others showed up yesterday. It's been all beer and boats. Lots of music. Less clothing—"

"More sex," I finish.

"Not for me. Not yet. But I guess tonight was a sure thing until you showed up."

"Well, you brought her up here. That's about as sure as you can be."

"I asked her if she'd like to go down to the dock while others were busy with the fire pit, but either she's not into semi-public sex, or she thinks I'm not."

"Right," I say. "Plus, you have a perfectly good futon here, and it would've been a shame not to take advantage of that."

"It made me feel like I was nineteen again, taking a girl back to my dorm room."

"You didn't go to college."

"Maybe I missed out," he spits. "You're not here for the futon, though. And you've already been quiet too long if you were here to break some sort of terrible news. So, what exactly made you blow a chunk of your savings on a trip like this?"

For a second, I'm terrified he'll offer to pay me back, and I swallow my preemptive fury before ignoring his question and asking mine.

"Who is she to you? Lena?"

Jamie laughs humorlessly. "She's nobody. They're all nobody. But what about Logan? Did you leave him home all alone?"

"Fuck you."

"I mean, I can't stop you from camping with him for the rest of your life, right? We gave up on each other."

"No," I growl. It's quiet, but I fucking growl. "You gave up on *me*. At my grandmother's funeral, all I said was that I didn't know what we were waiting for, and you walked away and decided we weren't waiting for *anything*."

"Where the fuck else was I supposed to go? Did you really want me to follow you to the reception? Should I have been waiting at your apartment for another slow dance before leaving you again? I don't know what else you wanted from me if being there wasn't enough."

"I didn't want to be so easy to give up on," I say. "It's always been hockey. It will always *be* hockey. But you left that day, and it was the first time I felt like maybe it wasn't *me* at all."

Frustrated, Jamie grabs his hair with both hands, and I wish he'd get that rough with mine. "Do you even hear yourself? You're telling me it's all about hockey and maybe not about you, but I left them for you that day. I chose *you*."

"That day," I echo. "And there's been nothing but distance between us since."

"So that's why you're here? To be close to me while we finish an argument we started eight months ago? Or did you want to show me you chose *me* over your adorably boring life?"

I'd told Sophie I was chasing proof that someone loves me, but I've always had that and didn't need to be standing in front of Jamie to know it's still true. Whatever else happens tonight, we're going to love each other for the rest of our lives, because the pull of the ocean and the promise of the stars won't let us go. It's relief and torture all in one, and all I can think about now is how to make both feelings bigger than they already are.

"Lena is nobody."

"Yeah," Jamie says.

"The other women—the ones from the pictures—they were nobody."

He doesn't say something as quickly this time, wary about the accusations I could throw at him as if I've ever called him a whore. I try to make it better when I catch the hem of his tank top and tether myself to him, but my fist around the fabric isn't kind. His response is to scrape his fingernail against the band letters on the front of my t-shirt, the touch as casual as it is arousing, and it's not going to be enough for much longer.

Jamie's gaze doesn't meet mine. Not then. "Everyone has been nobody. Everyone except—"

"No," I interrupt, my voice loud and low. "Don't say it."

"You don't believe me?"

Our breathing has synced, but nothing about it is peaceful. I'm angrier than I have any right to be when I'm the uninvited guest, and I harness it instead of letting it go. The longer I take to speak, the more Jamie gets desperate for it, and I don't think I'm playing a game with him, even when I'm rewarded with a shaky plea for something. Anything.

He could be playing a game with me. I'm shaking just as much as he is.

"I believe you just fine, but it's not—" I don't mean to demand eye contact by trailing off like that, but when I take several seconds to keep talking, black ice stares me down and leaves me with goosebumps that make me a liar. I let go of his shirt and knock his finger away from where it's touching mine, only to palm his dick roughly over his sweatpants. He's half hard and still vibrating with unfinished conversations that won't end tonight, and I exhale against his ear. "Is this for her or for me?"

It's for both of us, I think, but as much as I need that to be true, my impatience won't hold for an answer. I claw at his clothes, from his tank top to his sweatpants and back again. Jamie's pissed off and confused and so goddamn eager to touch me as much as he can, so he doesn't hesitate to fight back, my chest completely bare before I can figure out how it happened. He's working at my jeans now, unconcerned about a house full of people who will wonder why Lena was sent downstairs, and I'm frantic when he reminds me I'd asked him a question.

"She's nobody," Jamie hisses. "I fucking told you, you're the only—"

I cut him off with a brutal kiss, so unlike anything we've shared before, and I pull back just to fight again. "Please. Forget who I am. Just for tonight—just with you—I want—"

"To be nobody, too."

He understands. I don't need to explain because he understands. I don't need to explain because, once upon a time, in his best friend's bar, he wanted to be nobody, and the same anonymity that shielded us through sunrise is what's damned us ever since. I don't need to explain because he's ready to wield anonymity as a weapon now, just as surely as I am.

We'll be devastated by morning, but at least we'll have this first.

I kiss him again, or he kisses me, and I reach past his waistband to stroke him for the first time, his cock thick and wet and *mine*. The sound Jamie makes is dripping with sin, and the saint in me swallows it whole. He fumbles for a grip on me too, but even unzipped, my jeans and boxer briefs are still in the way, and I'm not interested in making this part easy for him. I walk him backward until he falls onto the bed, his sweatpants bunched around his ankles while he waits for me.

It's the story of us, made ugly by need, but neither of us is going to look away. I issue a command to this beautiful man and note how quickly he moves in response, even when he's shaking his head, awkward and perfect when he scoots up the bed to leave room for all the mistakes we're about to make.

I'm desperate to get his dick down my throat, but I crawl further than that first, grinding against his bare thigh while our tongues take more than they give. Jamie's hands are in my hair, far from gentle when he tries to arch into any contact he can find.

"She didn't taste like you," he pants. "None of them ever taste like you."

"I'm not me tonight. You don't know me. You haven't already memorized the way I taste and the way I sound and the way I feel. We'll fuck, and then we'll forget."

"I hate you."

"No, you don't," I say, stealing one more filthy kiss before I slide down his body. On any other night, I'd spend forever devouring him from head to toe, but we don't have the luxury of things like time or tenderness. "This would be so much easier if you did."

A second later, my mouth is around his cock, and a pillow is over his mouth. It's a sharp reminder that there are people everywhere, and I can't be nearly as enthusiastic as I'd like to be. That knife twists a little when I realize he wouldn't bother with a pillow if Lena were still here, and I go back on my word because I don't want to forget a second of a night I'm not allowed to have. Jamie's heavy on my tongue and I'm unsurprised by it, and the perfect fit of his balls in my hand is something I've imagined, too. He leaks more than anyone I've been with in a while, and in a different daydream, I'll tease it out of him until he cries.

There's no teasing tonight. I tell myself to remember how I suck and hum and choke, and how he can't stay still beneath me, his fingers curled into my hair again while he thrusts into my mouth. Then my mind races ahead, thinking about what happens next. We once told each other we wanted to be slow and loud, but the clock is ticking and we'll have to be silent. I let him go and disappoint us both, painfully hard when I scramble off the end of the bed and pull his sweatpants from where he's been cuffed by them.

He's naked and needy and stunningly scarred and still simmering with the fury left behind when I interrupted something that would've been so easy for him. What we're doing now will fracture Jamie, me, and *us*, and those cracks will never fully heal, no matter how much we promise to love each other forever or wait for even longer than that.

We only get one first time, and the tears pooling in his eyes all but promise me it will be our last.

"Nightstand," Jamie says. It's closer to where he lies, but he hasn't stopped staring up at me. Maybe there's no reason to put effort in when I'm so willing to be the one to ruin us. "Taylor keeps the bedrooms well-stocked for weeks like this. Help yourself."

I don't move from the foot of the bed right away. I furiously rake my fingers through my hair and shiver when I drop my hands to my hips, pushing at my jeans and everything I can drag away with them. Downstairs, the music is thumping, and the smack of pool balls punctuates laughter I almost envy. Nothing is funny up here, and my heart pounds relentlessly when I meet the challenge in Jamie's eyes.

It'll haunt me someday, how close I am to changing my mind. I flew all the way here, but I don't think it was for the chance to bare myself to him so literally. Maybe if I put my clothes back on and kiss Jamie like it's just us and the ocean, it won't matter that I sucked his dick for a few minutes first. He once heard me come, but we held on to something like friendship long after I cleaned up my mess, and I want to believe getting dressed and walking away could save us now.

I want to believe it, but it doesn't matter whether I do. I can't leave him now. I don't think I ever could.

"Roll over."

My voice shakes when I tell him what to do, but we both need to hurry, no time to waste when I've heard at least a couple of voices in the hall. I'm overwhelmed with lust and preemptive regret, but I'm thinking just clearly enough to grab his sweatpants from the floor and shove them into the space between the headboard and the wall. Whether Taylor McKeon's luxurious guest bed will make enough noise to give us away won't be answered until we're on our way to a precariously private moment, but my restraint has frayed and I simply won't care by then.

Raiding the nightstand drawer, I ignore that Jamie's head isn't even turned to look at me, his back arched as if he's made a blind offer like this a thousand times before. It leaves him on display, some version of that true his entire life, and there's so little I can do to keep from taking advantage of it now.

But I can silently remind him how much this nobody loves him.

My tongue touches him first, my hands holding him open for me, then holding him still as he bucks in my grip. When I sit back, slick fingertips circle him for a few seconds before I make everything wetter and more obscene. He should be tense, I think—guarded against something inherently intrusive—but I suppose that's another thing the years have stolen from him, and he sounds almost relieved when I push forward with two fingers at once. I don't know what else he needs from me, and I'll barely find out, but I shift until my weight can press him into the mattress and he squirms for more of a touch I'd give him forever if I could.

Someone in the next room speaks, and Jamie moans into the same pillow that smothered his sounds a while ago. I give up wishing we could be anywhere else, and I slide my fingers free just in time to hear him smother something new. Clumsy and very much not, I nudge his legs apart with my knee and pour enough lube into my hand to make stroking my dick as loud as anything else I've done, and I think it only makes me angrier about secrets I don't want to keep. A smeared handprint mars an overpriced duvet, and then I'm crossing every line I ever drew.

Jamie either heard me open the condom wrapper before I fingered him open or he doesn't care whether I'm wearing one. The idea of being bare inside him has me biting his shoulder until I imagine I can taste blood, but then I imagine nothing and feel everything as I rock into him with one long thrust after another, hardly gentle and hopelessly in love. This position limits the tattletale slap of skin on skin, and we find our rhythm sooner than anyone should. His body is tight and begs for mine while I answer with something like *yours yours yours* on every exhale.

Then I realize I need to fight with him, if for no other reason than to prove I have an ounce of willpower left in me.

"C'mere," I grunt, my arm forced under his abdomen to lift him a few inches off the bed and away from the contact that must feel so good against his weeping cock.

He's the professional athlete, but I'm plenty strong, and Jamie lets me have the win for a minute before he fights back, swearing at me when he grabs his pillow and shoves it past my arm. His quick thinking changes two things for us, and I'll remember both for as long as I live.

One, it means he can unabashedly hump his way to an orgasm while I admire something so wildly vulgar that I almost come inside him right then.

Two, it means there's nothing to keep Jamie from crying out until I cover his mouth and fuck every noise he makes into the palm of my greedy hand.

We're chaos now, that perfect rhythm faltering as we wear each other down. This warm room has grown hot, and I let myself love the sweat between us before he makes me realize I'm not covering his mouth as well anymore.

"Don't stop, 'Teo," he breathes. "Please don't stop."

I couldn't if I tried, but I have to make him stop talking, and I slip my fingers past his lips, unsurprised when he sucks them hungrily. With him closer to silent again, I get rough, intent on making him forget every nobody he's had since prom night with Melanie Bishop. My thrusts speed up and the angle is so fucking good and his body won't still beneath mine. He's needed me since I gave him a ride to a taco truck within walking distance of his front door. He's needed to know I miss him when he tells me I'm not allowed to. He's needed to know he can find me in the quiet spaces between strangers' cheers. It's possible he's needed to know I'd show up—wholly uninvited—at a hockey legend's vacation home for the chance to put an end to us once and for all.

But I don't think I've ever needed him to need me like I do now.

I'm wrapped around him while I bury myself deep and plead for him to keep me there. Jamie's still fucking the pillow, and as he's madly sucking on my fingers, he finds where my other hand is pressed to his heart and covers it tightly. He's going to come within seconds, and I don't know why I know that without knowing this part of him at all.

When it happens, Jamie shudders beneath me and bites my fingers hard enough to hurt.

When I come a minute later, the hand over his heart curls violently and cuts him open.

I leave him because I have to, almost responsible when I hide the condom in a couple of balled-up tissues. He rolls over slowly, staring at me when I attempt to assess the damage we've done. I think we might've kept quiet enough that nobody in the house heard us break promises to ourselves, but I'm not sure what can be done about the state of anything else. The bedding is stained with lube and sweat and blood and cum. At least a couple of those will leave the room smelling of sex for hours unless we open a window soon. My fingers will heal fine, but they hurt now.

And Jamie's been left with a wound that could've been avoided if I'd just stayed home.

CHAPTER SEVENTEEN: JAMIE

(I KNEW SOMEONE NAMED LOGAN)

He stays.

Mateo *stays.*

I'm not stupid enough to believe some part of it isn't because he has nowhere else to go. Then again, this is Mateo, and he makes lists of his lists and plans for his plans. If I ignore how absolutely unlike himself he's been tonight, I can assume he made a reservation somewhere. Or maybe he'd be happy sleeping in a rental car. He does like camping, after all.

Still, he stays, and we don't say a single fucking word to each other while we do what we can to hide the evidence of love we've kept secret for years. I retrieve my sweatpants from their position behind the headboard and look for my tank top. Mateo is already wearing his boxer briefs again. He gets a washcloth from the adjoining bathroom and goes to work on the worst of anything we did to the duvet. I open a window and don't worry that everyone who'd been outside has made it in. The pillow is probably beyond saving, and I'll wait to trash it when nobody else is looking. Mateo takes a deep breath, peeks into the hallway, and grabs his duffel bag from where it was left next to the door.

The dim lamp in the corner of the room has allowed us to see plenty tonight, but I think both of us were done with that a while ago. We spend those last several minutes navigating the dark instead, and crawl into bed with matching sighs.

We lace our fingers together, but never say goodnight.

We don't say good morning, either.

I wake up much earlier than usual. In all fairness, I'd fallen asleep much earlier than usual. There's a persistent ache whispering for me to stay still and keep my eyes closed, but I know most of it isn't a physical concern, and I was never all that good at being gentle with myself until I was forced to be. Barely careful, I stare at the ceiling. A second later, I flex my hand against the mattress and realize I'm not holding on to Mateo anymore.

It's worse than that, though. Of course it's worse than that.

He's not here.

My eyes fly to where he'd put his bag last night, but it's gone, too. It makes it harder to imagine that he could be in the bathroom, just taking a piss or brushing his teeth. I listen for him anyway, and lie when I tell myself I'm not surprised to be alone.

The same persistent ache yells at me now. I squeeze my eyes shut.

When Mateo was fucking me, somewhere between one perfectly excruciating thrust and another, I'd begged him not to stop. I didn't mean for that to have anything to do with sex. I'm not sure whether he thought I did. We haven't been on the same page for a while, except for how endlessly we've loved each other. And I want to scream until he understands that's all I meant. Even with a mess of mistakes and misunderstandings littered over years and miles, I just don't want him to stop loving me.

I refuse to cry about that now, sitting up in bed and feeling it everywhere. The window is still open, and it carries a chill to match whatever Mateo left behind. Every new breeze causes the curtains to flutter, and waves of sunlight rise and fall across the room whenever the patterned linen lets them pass. I want to say something about sleeping with the window open—that we should've done it last year, probably—but he's not here to agree with me. Maybe next year I can invite him back, just for a chance to do it then.

It's too quiet, and I don't know where I'm gonna go, but I can't stay in the middle of a bed I almost want to set on fire. I move too fast, then slow back down, and shuffle toward the bathroom. It takes me a minute to raise my eyes to the mirror, and I'm sorry when I do.

Or more angry than sorry.

Or more devastated than angry.

I wonder why I didn't see them last night until I remember that we turned off the light and got ready for bed in the dark. Mateo could've said something to me, but we hadn't talked. And I might've zeroed in on the pain, except that everything hurts and they probably look worse than they are. Three deep scratches over my heart, with shallower ones on either side. Claw marks, more or less, left by a man who hadn't wanted to let me go last night.

My fist slams into the mirror. I think I cut myself. I definitely cracked the fuck out of the glass, and it's just one more thing I've destroyed. For several seconds, I listen for the sound of anyone awakened by my tantrum, but when everything stays quiet around me, I stare at my fractured reflection. I'm unrecognizable there, and then I make myself nearly hysterical at the thought because when has that ever been true?

Once I've recovered, I consider showering, but don't make it further than washing my bloody hand and pulling myself together like I have a press conference to attend. It's too cold for the tank top I'd worn last night, but I find a long sleeve t-shirt in my bag and tug it on, my sweatpants comfortably low on my hips. I'm sure my hair is a disaster, but nobody in the house could possibly make me care. I need coffee and an idea of what I'll say to Lena when I see her again.

I can't quite jog downstairs, but I make it there eventually. The coffee pot isn't as full as it should be, and my brain is too clumsy to piece together the reason why. The house is so still when I take my first sip, but that only means I'm easily startled when I hear footsteps behind me. Coffee sloshes over the side of my mug and lands in all my new wounds. I could scream, but I've made enough of a scene this morning, and I bite my tongue instead.

"You spilled," Taylor says dryly.

He's only a few feet away from me, and the chill that forced me into a shirt must not bother him because he's wearing nothing but plaid boxers. He's in his mid-50s now, but he knows he's more attractive than almost anyone here. I'm the exception, but he doesn't hate me for it as often these days, and I don't have the energy to remind him of old feuds. I'm still stunned to see him up so early. I look stupidly between the mug in his hand and the pot that had confused me a minute ago.

"You're awake."

Taylor sets his coffee on the counter and grabs a couple of paper towels, wetting them at the sink before he steps toward me. He pulls the dripping mug from my hand and wipes me clean. It's the gentlest I've seen him be with anyone, even after two years of coaching at his side. I'd ask what he's doing, but my voice won't work. I'm left to watch as he finds a large travel mug and pours my coffee into it. A moment later, he tops it off with the rest of his own and secures the lid, pushing it into my curious grip.

"It's a beautiful morning." He almost smiles, but he's looking too closely at me, and it keeps him serious. "You should go down to the dock and enjoy it for as long as you can."

I don't want to enjoy anything right now, but Taylor's not in the habit of making suggestions he doesn't expect people to take. I nod and mumble something like a thank you. There's a pile of flip-flops and slides and sneakers by the patio door. I don't care which ones are mine when I step outside in a pair and let the cool air help with my first deep breath of the day.

Then I'm not breathing well at all, a short walk all I need to catch sight of the person already appreciating the view. He's sitting on the dock, his legs dangling over the lake. If I were feeling playful, I'd sneak up and pull his ponytail. His jeans are probably the same ones from last night, and without him turning around, I know the high school's logo is embroidered on the front of his jacket, just opposite the side that reads *Coach Zavala*.

He could be at the airport by now—maybe even on a plane—but Mateo's here. I'm not sure why, but it seems like Taylor's encouraged me to find out.

I take careful steps across the wood. It feels like everyone is asleep for miles, giving us the privacy we've only ever had on the California coast. I take a long sip of my coffee to prove it isn't a dream. I already know I can turn it into a nightmare on my own.

"Don't sit," he says, pushing himself off the dock without looking at me. "It'll be hell on your leg."

There's nothing about my approach that should've given me away, but I'm not surprised he sensed me coming because I'd know him anywhere. I press my shoulder against his as soon as I can, and I pass him the coffee. It takes another minute before I say anything, mostly because I want to say everything.

"I thought you were gone."

Mateo nods.

"You will be soon," I continue.

He nods again.

"Are you sorry?"

His head whips toward me, dark eyes pleading for things I'd give him if I could. "Do you want me to be sorry?"

I asked the first question, but I don't even know what we're talking about. Then I shake my head because Mateo shouldn't be sorry for anything. Not this morning. I don't know if we'll have another one like it.

"I should've invited you here," I murmur. "It was—I don't know why I thought you'd say no."

"Things have been weird for a while."

"Yeah."

"We've kept too much to ourselves. We're at least supposed to talk about things. We're supposed to be friends."

"Friends," I echo. "Yeah."

There's a beat of silence. Several actually, and I remember when they used to feel right. Discomfort stirs between us now, and I fidget next to him, shaking out a leg that's doing just fine. Mateo sighs, and I should've used those last few seconds to brace myself.

"I was there. That night."

I'm glad he has the coffee because I think I would've dropped it. "That night."

He doesn't drag those two words into a longer sentence. I don't need him to. Eleven years ago, *that night* began to mean one thing. Five years after that, it meant a second thing too, but I already know he was there for that one. I frown and lean away because there's been a lot of fucking time to have this conversation. I almost sit on the dock out of spite. Then my cheeks warm, and I close my eyes as I seethe over the injury that left me alone in my best friend's bar the night I met Mateo, and gave him the power to ruin my life every single day since.

"Sophie and I were there," he amends. "It was the only game we went to that season, and I can't believe we saw—actually, no. I barely saw it at all. But the sound you made. I think I knew even then that I'd never, ever forget that sound."

"I've always been too loud."

It's a hell of a thing to say to the man who figured out how to keep me quiet with a couple of well-placed fingers. He probably isn't interested in swapping one set of memories for another.

"It wasn't the volume. It was the sorrow."

I want to argue Mateo's choice of words, but only because I'm pissed he's spent so much time remembering me that way. "You should've told me."

"Maybe," he says. "But it seemed like an awkward thing to bring up at back-to-school night."

"And every night since?"

Mateo shrugs. "I didn't want to bind myself to the night you lost the love of your life, especially if I was going to spend forever competing with it."

"You're not competing with it."

"Yes, I am."

Yes, he is. I should apologize, but it won't matter much when he's going to fly home and I'm going to return to arenas full of people who know me by my full name. I should apologize, but I'm still unhappy, so I take the coffee back from him and soothe myself with it while he admires a view I don't think he'll have for a while. I should apologize, and I do, but I make sure it hurts us both.

"Sorry this isn't a Mai Tai," I say, holding up the mug.

"Sorry the lake isn't frozen."

He walks away from me then. I can't help but turn to watch him because he's the view I won't have for a while. When the dock is over more land than water, Mateo makes the small jump off the side and moves toward the lake again. The sun isn't high enough in the sky for him to enjoy wading right now, but that doesn't appear to be his goal. He squats when he's close enough to touch the water. Maybe he just needs to confirm my wish has no chance of coming true today.

I call to him from where I stand. "You have something else to say."

Mateo slowly pulls his fingers back and wipes them on his jacket. He's even slower when he stands to face me. I don't like that I'm above him like this, but maybe he's felt like I've had the higher ground all along. I'd bet millions the opposite is true.

"I think Harper knows. About us."

"About *us*?" I growl. "What the fuck does that mean?"

"New Year's Day. You and I weren't talking, but I'd just spent so much time with my family, and I needed—I went to the bench. It was as close as I could—"

"Yeah," I interrupt. "I get it. I've done it."

"She was there," he says. And if I want time to process that detail, he doesn't give it to me. "I don't think she was nearly as surprised to see me as she should've been. And then we talked about you and about me, and she was so—I don't know—*calm*."

Calm. A lot like she was when she asked me whether I'd thought about bringing someone special on vacation. And when she asked whether I was avoiding bringing Mateo because I thought she'd have a problem with it.

All of that could've been about my good friend. Whatever she said to Mateo could've been about his good friend. But he thinks Harper knows something, and I don't think he's wrong.

But I've been in pain since I woke up and I can't let it go.

"We're *friends*, Mateo." I spit the word and become stupidly soft around his name. "She knows we're friends. She's calm about us being friends. That's a good thing. And unless you plan to tell her you just became the first man to fuck her dad, there's nothing else to know."

Whatever other points he was going to make get lost before they make it to his open mouth, everything derailed when he sputters. "The first? That's not—you said you—there were others—"

He looks past me, toward the house. I'm not sure whether he's worried someone will overhear us or whether he's just remembering what it felt like to fuck me into the mattress. It felt pretty amazing to me, and if we weren't so busy saying goodbye, I think I'd beg him to do it again. We are busy though, and I wave my hand dismissively.

"Yes, there were others, but I—I was being literal," I explain. "It was always easier for me to—with anonymous hookups, I'd never—just you."

Whatever I've barely said covers a lot of our relationship. He's heard enough to understand that I've drawn meaningless lines with meaningless men for the sake of something I've called simple. Blowjobs have gone both ways, but nothing else ever did. Until last night.

"*You* should've told *me*," Mateo hisses.

"Maybe."

He's so frustrated with me, and he scrubs a hand over his face. "Is there anything you want me to do about Harper?"

"There's nothing *to* do. Nothing. We have waited and waited and waited, and after all this time, you think my daughter knows something? About *what*?" I'm deeply in love with him, but he showed up here and let us take things from each other that weren't ours to have. For just a second, I hate him for it. I exhale as slowly as I can before I go on, but I can't stop my voice from cracking. "Mateo. There's nothing to know."

It takes an impressively long time before he looks away from me. When that happens, he leaves the rest behind, too. His steps are measured—not quite a dead man walking, but it feels suspiciously close enough. I stay where I am because I can't chase him today. I'm still watching when he reaches the opposite side of the dock, closer to his way out. He needs to leave, and I don't think witnessing it is any better than when I thought he'd disappeared in my sleep, but it means I see the moment he stops and turns around.

The scratch marks on my chest sting, but he can't see them. Maybe he thinks I'm due a little more pain. He walks back to me, and those seconds take forever to pass, but I don't have anywhere else to be unless Taylor's waiting for a recap of my morning. I raise an eyebrow, cockier than I have been all week.

Then Mateo breaks me when he wraps me in his arms and holds me there. My sob stays between us, and he presses his mouth to the side of my head.

"I love you."

"Yeah," I choke. "I know."

We don't talk at all after that. We don't call each other. We don't record voice notes. We don't even text. For the first time since we met, I'm not sure whether I'll see him again.

And I don't know how to make him promise he'll come back when I'm the one so far from home.

Anyone looking closely enough could tell I've always been needy, despite the crowds who called me arrogant my entire career. My ego came with raw talent and near-flawless looks, but I've surrounded myself with people wearing my jersey or wearing nothing at all because I love the attention I get. It's loud, or it's quiet, and it feeds me so I don't have to go hungry. But these days, the wrong things are quieter and worse things are growing louder. I consume it all out of habit because otherwise I feel like I'm starving.

And really, most people have never looked.

I pick up my phone and pretend I'm close to the one who did.

Mateo always paid attention to me, but it was never quiet or loud or about hockey or how hot I am, even when he called me pretty. Before he knew I was needy, he wanted to know everything else. Then he stayed, and he waited. After I begged him a hundred times, he kept me around for a hundred more.

I put the phone back down because August becomes September, and September becomes October, and another hockey season starts. Mateo's been busy with school for a while. There's time for me to catch a couple of Harper's games, and she catches a couple of mine. On a road trip that includes a swing through California, I spend as much time with Kai as I can. I haven't always been a good friend, and I'm running low on those these days. I see my parents when they want to see me.

October becomes November, and November becomes December. Taylor and I are the first two and last two at every practice or meeting or game, and I'm grateful for something to rely on. That morning at the lake house, when I slipped back inside, he was in his bedroom again. Our mugs were clean and a new pot of coffee was brewing as though nobody had been in the kitchen at all.

We've never talked about why Mateo showed up late one night. I don't have a good enough answer to give him, and saying thank you wouldn't make much sense.

I love my team. I have a decent relationship with most of them, but the stars—the ones who make highlight reels and headlines like mine—gravitate to Taylor on the days they need more than a teammate or friend. I stay on the ice with players who won't set records or get selected to an All-Star team. While they're comfortable with their roles, they still want to get better. They lean on the veterans more than they lean on me, and that's how it should be, but my time with them reminds me of things I loved way back when. The buzz they carry to and from the locker room is a feeling I've lost and found.

December becomes January without the holiday greetings I used to count on. I wonder if he's worn my jersey since the night I saw him in it.

January becomes February, and February becomes March, and when March becomes April, it's time for spring break. Harper and Simon decide to follow me to three road games, in time to watch us clinch home-ice advantage for the playoffs. I'm curious whether he'll wait for her to graduate before he proposes. I hope he does, but I'm not exactly a relationship expert. And I almost start a conversation about carnival rides and midway games, but maybe I'm not an expert on those either.

April. May. June kicks off the Stanley Cup Finals, and we're still playing.

Then we're not, despite the athletic wet dream pairing of Taylor McKeon and Jameson Sinclair. We fail to coach our team to a victory, our own championships worth little to a group of guys still seeking their first. I hear from Harper and Kai and a dozen former teammates, all of them offering condolences one way or another. I hear from my mom, who offers criticism she thinks is constructive. My dad doesn't bother, and it feels worse than being told what I did wrong.

I don't hear from Mateo, and I would need an English teacher to help me find a word worse than *worse*.

And yeah, I know I could call him. If only I weren't so afraid he wouldn't answer.

Harper helps him with his soccer clinic again, and I leave them to it. To keep from confirming things Taylor suspected were true last summer, I ask whether he knows anyone who might be up for a blind date. He promises to get back to me, and then he doesn't. I stay at home and drink too much vodka instead.

I'm not sure which night it is when Harper texts me.

Mateo says you haven't talked in months. What's going on?

I think I'm drunk enough that if she were anyone else, I'd start talking about boats and futons and Lena and kisses and pillows and docks. She's my daughter, though. She doesn't need to know that sex with Mateo was everything I wanted at the time I wanted it least.

We're both busy and far away from each other. Sometimes Kai and I don't talk for a while and it's fine

Mateo isn't Kai

I know

I'm not sure when I'll stop counting the months since I hugged him goodbye, but it's been almost a year. Then she sends a message that turns June into July, and July into August.

I read it over and over and over again. I will for longer than I can imagine.

Do you know someone named Logan?

———

I don't go to the lake house with Taylor. I get more shit about it from the other guys than I do from him. One afternoon, in the middle of their trip, my doorbell rings and there's something left outside my door. It's a gift basket, and I suppose I should've seen that coming. When I look through the ridiculous arrangement, I find it full of hangover remedies, a bizarre movie mix of cheesy rom-coms and filthy porn, and a box of tissues that could probably be used for either, depending on my mood.

The notes reads *Snap the fuck out of it. If you really need that much help getting laid, we'll get you laid. I'm glad you're not all over the gossip sites these days, but sober up for the season. The Cup is going to be ours.*

I sulk like a kid who's been sent to his room to think about what he's done, except that I barely understand the reference when I was only ever sent to the rink. The more I stare at Taylor's note, the more obvious it is that he's taken a page from my parents' handbook.

If it's weird that my punishment and my safe space have always been so intimately entwined, I don't dwell on it.

If it's weird that I think of my relationship with Mateo then, I don't dwell on that either.

Another school year starts, and the hockey season follows. I don't know that I'm exactly sober, but I take coaching seriously. I'm not seen in public doing anything wrong. Then again, I'm not really seen in public doing anything right. Nobody sees me much outside of airports and arenas, and the hotels I stay at in between. Nobody except for a new collection of nobodies—women I pay for discretion and a touch that feels so little like the one I crave.

Do I know someone named Logan? Yeah, I fucking do.

I'm at a Westin in Detroit in mid-November, reading several of Harper's texts again. She had explained little that night. Just that a guy named Logan stopped by the summer soccer clinic to bring lunch to Mateo, and that he'd brought enough for her to eat, too. The same daughter of mine who used to comment on every hot guy in her classes or on my teams, had nothing to say about a man I know is attractive. Whether her decision was made with Simon or me in mind, I don't know and didn't dare ask. I'm still curious about the two-hour drive he would've had to make just to do a favor. I'm waiting for that bitterness to dissolve on my tongue.

There's a knock on my door, and it's one of my fourth-line wingers, not a nobody. I smile—genuinely—because it's why I'm here. I will be whatever this kid needs me to be tonight. Tomorrow, I will hear the perfectly unkind roar of an opposing crowd. I will listen closely for the whisper of my name as I pass.

After too-little sleep one night, and a grueling game and overtime loss the next, we get on a plane. I need to close my eyes, but I'm playing with my phone. I scroll too far back in my texts, and I fire off a new one without thinking.

Everything has changed and I hate it

I'm about to toss my phone into my bag, but it vibrates in my hand. Maybe Logan's around, or maybe he's not, and I'm not sure I care either way.

Nothing has changed, sweetheart.

Chapter Eighteen: Mateo

(I Answered Her Call)

The texts that changed everything had come about ten months ago, and the fact that it just happened to have been Jamie's birthday was absolutely not lost on me.

Hey stranger, can I take you out to dinner next week?

I'd blinked a couple of times at Logan's question before tapping out a response. *You'll be nearby?*

I will

Sounds great. Just say when.

I'd held on to my phone for too long after that, so close to calling Jamie to say something. Anything.

Hi.

Hello.

I'm sorry.

I've missed you.

Happy birthday.

I want to go back to being the kind of friends who stay in touch and aren't afraid of a night in New York that should have happened a thousand other times but might have ruined them instead.

I'm still waiting.

Then I'd convinced myself that hearing from Logan wasn't a good reason to reach out to Jamie, and I'd said nothing at all.

The following week, I'd shared a bottle of wine, a caprese salad, and a wood-fired pizza with Logan, and he'd told me he was around for a few days because he was looking for a place to rent. Then he'd told me he'd be around all the time because his company had offered him the opportunity to transfer to their Orange County office. I'd been just tipsy enough to ask him whether his decision to relocate had anything to do with me. He'd said no, because he wasn't looking for ways to fall for someone who couldn't be his.

I'd had enough experience with that to hope he'd be stronger than I ever was.

That night at dinner, he'd bribed me with a few more meals, and I'd agreed to help when it was time for him to move. Those payoffs fit nicely into days we spent together, me showing him around and Logan reminding me why we've always had fun together, just running silly errands and stopping to eat where anyone in the world could see us.

After we'd gotten him settled into an apartment, Logan had been busy adjusting to his new position and getting to know new coworkers. I'd been heading into the spring semester and still hitting happy hour with Sophie. Logan and I didn't spend *that* much time together. And when it was time to watch Jamie coach in the playoffs again, I wasn't stupid enough to bring Logan with me to Kai's. I knew he wasn't that much of a sports guy, so maybe that was my excuse.

Of course, Sophie and I had been at the bar for plenty of games before, and probably would be again, but I was feeling guilty or tender enough to spend those playoff nights at home with my best friend.

"Holy shit. The finals," Sophie had said from my couch, the conference series over, and Jamie and Taylor on the ice to shake hands with the team they had just beaten. "They could win it all."

They could have. They didn't.

I hadn't been sure whether that would be a good time to finally text him, just to let him know I was thinking about him, then and always. I'd decided against it because it felt a little like I'd be gloating that his love had let him down. And given the space Logan was starting to occupy in my life, I probably had little room to talk.

Not long after Jamie's season ended, so did my school year. I shifted my focus to the second year of my summer soccer clinic, thrilled to have Harper's help again. Seven years ago, I'd taught myself to keep her separate from her father, at least as much as it's possible to untie a knot without seeing the slight kinks left behind. I'd remained decent at it until Logan surprised me with lunch one day, and I froze like I'd been caught doing something wrong, her blue eyes suddenly so much like Jamie's that Logan was left to introduce himself while I gestured helplessly between them. He'd brought plenty for her to share, and the quick hitch of her eyebrow as she thanked him suggested she had questions for both of us. Logan distracted her with questions of his own for as long as he was there, and they both ignored me when I kicked a soccer ball hard enough to lose it to the roof of the nearest building. Even after he drove away, Harper stayed blessedly quiet.

He texted me that night. ***Sorry if I made anything difficult for you. I wasn't thinking.***

It's not something you should have to think about.

Still...

Still nothing. Thank you for bringing us lunch. Next one's on me.

Logan and I were friends, and I was happy to return a friendly favor, but I didn't make good on my promise right away. By the time

I did—friendly or not—it was only an excuse to see him again. I told him I wanted to make him dinner, but we both knew he had the better kitchen, so I arrived with a couple of grocery bags and a smile. Logan poured us drinks and leaned against the countertop while I cooked. We talked then and throughout our meal, never short of things to say to each other, and when he asked if I wanted to do the dishes together, it was so easy to say yes. We washed and dried, and I was at home in a place that would never stay that way for longer than a night at a time. I fiercely missed a kitchen I hadn't seen in two and a half years, and it was a terribly weak reason to reach out to a distant friend, so I left my phone in my pocket and startled when Logan ran a fingertip along the underside of my jaw.

"Hey," he murmured. "You okay?"

"No, yeah. I'm sorry. Did you say something?"

"No, but I splashed you," he said. "Got careless with a spoon. Water ended up on your face. You know how it is."

I looked down at my clothes, but everything was dry, and I would've preferred his hand on my face either way. Logan's t-shirt was obviously wet, but taking the time to check him out meant an extra few seconds to stare at his short shorts, always a perfectly ridiculous choice for someone with his long legs. With a dish towel still in my hand, I resisted the temptation to reach for anything he was wearing, and met his eyes when he decided there was no good reason to keep touching me.

Except that there was often a good reason, and we both knew it.

"You'll need to change," I said.

"Not really. When you leave, I'll just take everything off."

"Logan?"

"Yes?"

"Do you really want to wait for me to leave first?"

His breath caught at that. Visibly so. It confirmed that I was behaving terribly—selfish in a way I should abhor—but that was true at Taylor's too, and in Logan's kitchen, I was willing to bring that particular sin count to an even two.

"No."

It should've been fast then, our kiss and everything that followed. Instead, Logan pulled the towel from my hand and set it aside and pinned me against the refrigerator with his body.

I couldn't help but laugh. "Now you're getting me all wet."

"I guess you need to take everything off, too."

Then we kissed, and every familiar thing about it told my dick to react accordingly. I left in the morning with fewer regrets than I deserved.

For a couple of weeks afterward, we didn't quite ignore what had happened, but we didn't quite talk about it either. August was already creeping up on me, and all I could think about was the trip I had taken the year before. On an unbearably hot Saturday, Logan and I spent the afternoon at the community pool in my complex, and then we stumbled into my apartment, sun-drunk and barely dressed. I grabbed him, unfairly hungry, and he grabbed me back, pleading silently until he gathered the energy for a few words.

"Are you using me to forget him?"

"I don't know," I growled, most of it ending up in Logan's mouth. "I mean, yes, but it won't—I can't forget him. I don't think I want to. But it hurts to keep thinking about him all the time."

"Okay. Yeah, okay." He stopped to kiss me again, his tongue desperately deep inside my mouth. "Can you think about me while I'm here? While we fuck—can you please think about me instead?"

I told him I could. It was the only correct answer.

Tonight, over three months after I made that promise—and after many, many nights with Logan's endless legs wrapped around me—I don't know whether I've kept my word. Probably not. Probably not even close. It's why I respond to Jamie the way I do.

Everything has changed and I hate it

Nothing has changed, sweetheart.

Those two messages aren't enough to make everything right between Jamie and me. I keep an eye on his games and look for a reason to say something important to him, but *awesome win* or *tough loss* or *does Lena ever come to see you* don't feel right. I stay busy with teaching and coaching, and Logan and I weave friendship and sex into something almost real. November becomes December, and because his family isn't around, I bring him everywhere with mine.

We bake cookies with nieces and nephews who should be too old for silly traditions, but welcome us with faux eye rolls. We help my mom with last-minute Nativity play preparations at the church. We join everyone for a walk through a neighborhood known for outrageous light displays, and I refuse to acknowledge that the hot apple cider I drink reminds me of a night with somebody else.

It makes sense when my parents encourage me to bring Logan to midnight Mass, and it's even less of a surprise when they tell me to bring him to my sister's house on Christmas Day. I do both, but I break somewhere in between.

Merry Christmas. I still miss you.

There's a chance he's asleep—I won't guess much about his schedule these days—but he responds quickly enough to keep me from imagining anything that hurts.

Merry Christmas. I hope you have a great day with your family.

I set my phone down next to the bathroom sink and step into the shower, frowning at the ways Jamie's words made me feel worse, not better. He should know my family by now. He should tell me to give my mom an extra hug from him or joke about how my dad half-grunts at every present instead of looking as pleased as he is. He should have an inside joke with at least one of my sisters that he brings up just to annoy me before I have to spend the day with them. He should be *here*, but even if he has to be with his team, my family should at least know who I'm missing.

Instead, I'll have Logan at my side, and everything will seem just right to them.

It's a great day though, and on New Year's Eve, I'm officially Logan's date to his company's fancy party. He swears it means nothing more than an open bar, decent music, and a few hours of eye-fucking before we get to the real thing. That's a great night.

I don't know whether Harper spends New Year's Day on the bench. If she does, I wonder whether Simon is next to her this time. I haven't met him yet, but he sounds pretty amazing, and with Harper's graduation only months away, I'm curious about what comes next. She's talked about becoming a teacher and coach, and I couldn't be prouder. I could probably make arguments about why she should focus on that more than a college boyfriend, but I'm too in love with love to think I could ever speak out against it.

She's actually the next Sinclair to text me, firing off something too innocent on Valentine's Day, when she lets me know she's visiting Jamie for a few days. I don't know how I'm supposed to respond to that. *Great, please let your dad know there hasn't been a single day during which I've forgotten to be excruciatingly in love with him.*

I keep it simpler than that. *Have a great time and keep him out of trouble.*

Harper sends a string of emojis, and I just shake my head.

But over the next few weeks, I watch a couple of games and I look at the standings and I realize I should've been more worried that the *team* is in trouble. After being so close to a championship the year before, they're in danger of not making the playoffs at all. Sophie blows up my phone about it, and I don't know what to say to her either. *I guess Jamie coached better before I broke all my own rules and flew across the country to ask him to love me more than he can?*

Realistically, I know there's only so much I could've affected the team when I mostly destroyed *us*, but the weight of blame sits heavy against my chest and keeps me still. More and more often, I let Logan crawl just beneath some of it, where it's warmest and safest, and I don't put a name to the feelings we find there.

Our Southern California winter fades into spring as much as it ever has in a place without proper seasons, but I'm watching the calendar work against a group of guys who are fighting back amid a series of injuries that may have crippled them. With a little more than a week left before the playoffs, it doesn't look good for them—they have to win their final four games and hope the team just above them loses two—and I decide I can't watch. I focus on all the classroom work I have to wrap up before spring break starts. After saying my goodbyes that Friday afternoon, I spend almost the entire weekend at Logan's, grateful for time off and made breathless until I know I'll sleep soundly. I don't check any of the apps or sites on Monday morning for confirmation that last year's runners-up won't make it past the regular season.

It means I also don't see the comments—some concerned and some derisive—about New Jersey's assistant coach missing the last two games.

I only find out that night, when my phone rattles on the night-stand next to where I'm lying in Logan's bed. We're warm and relaxed and talking softly while we draw mindless patterns on each other's bare skin. It's too late for a phone call that isn't a wrong number or bad news, so my heart knocks around in search of an answer, and it doesn't quiet when I roll away from Logan's touch and read the name on my screen.

"Hello?" I say, somewhere between stupid and scared. "What's going on? Are you okay? Is he—"

"He's not—I don't know—shit, sorry." Harper stops and takes a deep breath, loud enough for me to hear. "He's sick. Really sick. And they said he'll get better, but I need you to check on him because I'm still up here, and I've got like a month left before I graduate, so I can't just leave, but you—please, I don't want him to be alone right now."

I slide out of bed and find some boxer briefs, unwilling to have any more of this conversation without them. "Sick with what? Is he in the hospital?"

"Double pneumonia. And I wish, but no, they let him go, and I hate it. He never gets sick. I've never heard him like this."

"Okay, yeah, I understand. It's probably pretty bad, and I know why you're scared. But I'm sure they have him on antibiotics, and I can't just get on a plane—"

"He's not in New Jersey," she interrupts. "He's at home."

"Here?"

"Yeah."

"But they played last night." I think. I still haven't looked.

Harper sighs. "They did, but he wasn't there."

"Because he's home."

"Because he's home."

"But how did he get there?" I ask. "He couldn't have flown with double pneumonia."

"He *shouldn't* have flown," she corrects. "But he's a stubborn idiot who isn't used to being sick and thought he knew better until he wanted to die somewhere over the Mississippi."

"Jesus."

"We can both yell at him later. What about now?"

"Listen, I—I want to go—I do. But he and I aren't—I told you last summer that we hadn't talked in a while. Maybe Kai? Or your mom?"

"I'd beg you to do this for me, but I don't think that would work as well as begging you to do this for him," she says, ignoring options she either already exhausted or refuses to consider. "There's no way your friendship is over. I don't care how much you are or aren't talking right now. I heard how you answered the phone. I heard you, Mateo. *Please*."

Her voice weakens, and it's new to me. It reminds me she's her father's daughter, all smiles and sass until the vulnerability slips through. This isn't some cute ploy to reunite two friends, and her manipulation's only goal is to make sure Jamie isn't alone while he suffers. I scrape my fingers through my hair and pace, my heart still pounding, even if some reasons have shifted sideways. But turning means I'm facing the bed again, and for a long while, I'll feel terrible that I forgot Logan was right there the whole time.

He's sitting now, a book in his hand, but his eyes are on me. I remember I have to say something to Harper, and doing it with an audience is probably shitty for everyone, even the man who doesn't know I'll be at his front door soon.

"Yeah, okay, I'll check on him."

Logan doesn't look away. Harper sighs with relief. "Really? Tonight?"

"Tonight," I promise her. I try to remember whether I've promised Logan anything recently.

She sighs again and asks me to text her once I've seen Jamie. I agree and cling to the phone once she's gone, standing in my underwear and waiting for Logan to ask me questions that won't require an answer.

He saves us both the trouble and skips that part. "Go."

"I'm—"

"Just go. He's sick. His daughter is worried. You won't be able to sleep until you've seen him, so go. I won't wait up."

I feel like I should argue, but we'd both lose in our own ways, so I nod and leave to find my joggers and t-shirt. I pause with my clothes in my hand, wondering whether I'll be forgiven for visiting Jamie while I still smell like another man, but I forgo a shower and get dressed instead. Pulling my hair into a messy bun only takes a few seconds, and with my phone in my pocket and everything else in his living room, I have nothing keeping me here. I'm at the bedroom door, and it feels like the effort it would take to cross the room and kiss him would be a lie.

He shakes his head.

The drive to Jamie's takes me about as long as it would from my apartment, though I'm coming from a different direction, and it feels strangely foreign. After that, nothing does. I park in his driveway and take a deep breath of the ocean air, and then I knock on his door because it's the nice thing to do. He doesn't answer, and I already have my key—*just in case*—in my hand. When I let myself in, it's almost frighteningly dark and still, and it's the first time since I saw Harper's name on my screen that I've been afraid. I call his name as I nudge my shoes out of the way, but I'm met with nothing but silence.

I make my way further into a house I didn't know I could navigate in the dark, and I try again.

"Jamie, it's me." I pause to listen, then I look toward the great room and a sofa I can't see. It's possible he crashed there, unwilling or unable to make it up the stairs, but there's so little sound and so much darkness, and I turn my back on it. "I'm coming up to your room. I need to make sure you're okay."

Finally, I hear an endless, ugly cough, and I realize *okay* is probably aiming too high for whatever I'm about to find. Barefoot and gentle, I make my way up, calmer now that I know where he is. Jamie's cough shifts into something like an uncomfortable groan just as I reach the bedroom door, the light spilling in from his bathroom allowing me to see him for the first time in a year and a half.

He's blinking up at me like he's not sure whether I'm something his fever-ravaged mind has conjured in the middle of the night. I move closer, and don't know whether it helps, but he's coughing again before I can reassure him with anything else. Jamie's tangled in his covers and so, so small in his bed, and I text Harper before dropping my phone on the duvet so my hands are free. I'm more careful when I sit next to him and reach down, his forehead so obviously hot beneath my palm before I slide my fingers into his damp hair and look at him until he's focused enough to look back.

"Mateo?"

"Yeah," I answer, swallowing hard. "It's me, sweetheart."

"Why are you in my bedroom?"

"Because Harper called to tell me you're sick. Why are *you* in your bedroom?"

"Because I'm sick," he says.

The little laugh that bubbles out of me is so unexpected, but I was trying to ask why he didn't see a doctor back east and stay there to recover, and his answer adorably misses my point. I let my fingers trail over his face, and the growth that suggests he's gone nearly a week without shaving. He's beautiful, though—I can't imagine there will ever be a day when he won't be—and I'll do anything to keep myself here for as long as he'll let me stay.

"Do you know when you're due to take your meds again?" I ask. "Your fever seems pretty bad."

"Was almost 104° earlier. What time is it?"

I glance at where I'd left my phone. "Just after 11:00."

"At midnight. I can have Tylenol and antibiotics at midnight."

I'm about to ask whether he wants to get some rest for the next hour, but another coughing fit hits hard, and Jamie's body curls to lessen the strain on his stomach muscles. There's a trash can next to the bed for him to spit into, and when he's ready to lie down again, I help stack his pillows to keep him elevated. He closes his eyes, but reaches for my hand, and I sigh as he coughs all over again. This should be awkward—my appearance in his bedroom and everything since—but after all this time, we've never learned how to be anything but comfortable finding ways to hold on to moments that won't last.

Everything would hurt less if we had, but letting go has been unimaginable for too long to do anything about it now.

I swallow hard and look away from him, only to swallow harder a few seconds later. There's a bottle of water on his nightstand alongside a box of tissues, the pills he can't take yet, and a lamp I leave off, but it's bare otherwise. A quick glance around the room shows that it's mostly empty too, clothes spilling out of a small suitcase further proof that Jamie doesn't live here anymore. I frown and immediately correct it, then gaze down at him again, using my free hand to brush hair back from his forehead.

"Do you want something to eat? Or anything other than water?"

"No."

"What else can I do?"

I'd love for him to answer, but the terrible wheezing sound Jamie makes with every exhale is terrifying, and I turn toward the emptiness again in search of an idea of my own. I find one almost too easily, and as abruptly as I think I can't do it, I think I have to.

As soon as I realize how badly I want to, I wonder if I should call Harper and tell her I'm too in love to do this right.

Jamie tugs on my hand. "What's wrong?"

"A hot shower—the steam. It'll help with the congestion. It'll help you breathe. And I—we can go in there together. You don't have to be alone."

Another round of coughing slows to something riddled with rattles and hums, Jamie's eyes cloudy but locked with mine. "You want to shower with me?"

"I think it would be good for you."

He nods clumsily, his head turned sideways on his pillow, but he says nothing else. I don't either, leaving Jamie where he is long enough to get the hot water going, the bathroom door closed behind me until I realize it takes away the only light we had. Cracking it open again, I return to the bed and peel the duvet from around and on top of and under him. He's wearing a sweatshirt and briefs, as if his body was trying to find the Goldilocks space between hot and cold, and as soon as he sits up, I pull the sweatshirt off him and drop it to the floor. I choke at the sight of pale scars my heart recognizes before my head, but swallow before I make a sound.

Jamie shivers, and I was stupid to undress him first. I hurry to catch up, my shirt and joggers left behind when I hold out a hand and lead him away from his own bed. Other than the coughing that still won't stop, we remain silent on the walk to the shower. Then we remain silent after that, once I've closed us in and dragged my boxer briefs down my legs and given him my hand to hold while he drags his briefs away, too.

If he's bothered by being naked with me, he can work through it when we ignore each other for another year or two.

Before we step into the shower, I adjust the temperature to something just shy of scalding, and take a deep breath in the steam with the hope that he'll do the same. He looks awful, dark circles under his eyes and pale skin that may be the product of the northeastern winter months as much as anything else. I don't know what I look like, freshly fucked and here to be something resembling a friend, but Jamie's eyes close as soon as we're under the water, and what he could've seen doesn't matter.

I'm still watching him as his coughing calms, but I'd only thought about how to get us this far, and I need a minute to think about what else will help. I don't get that much time though, Jamie deciding for both of us. Sick and sleepy, he wraps his arms around me and pulls me into him, and we hug and hug and hug.

And he sobs and sobs and sobs.

Crying brings back all the coughing that had barely quieted, but this isn't something I'm willing to interrupt with logic. I stay close to him and make unintelligible promises and rub his goosebumps away. I'm not sure whether his tears were brought on by a lack of sleep and fluid-filled lungs, or years of needing this kind of contact and being denied it far too often. I only know mine fall because I've never been as willing to wait for him as I am tonight.

We're pressed against each other as intimately as we ever have been, but as the minutes pass and the sobbing subsides, I move just enough to grab his shampoo and pour some into my hand. Being unwilling to untangle us makes the angle awkward, but I scrub it through his hair and listen to him moan. Something in me unfurls at the sound, and I ignore it while I get Jamie clean, finishing with his hair before I reach for the soap and wash as much of his body as I can from where we stand. I forgot to look for a washcloth when I was getting the shower ready, so it's only my hands and the suds that give me an excuse to touch him like this. He coughs again, and we pull apart, and I don't keep myself from letting my fingertips find him everywhere while we hold the eye contact we should have made in Taylor's bed.

Once he's rinsed off, I trust the shower wall to keep him upright, and I wash my own hair and body as quickly as I've ever done. The bathroom is full of steam when I turn the water off and pull two towels from the rack, and I wrap Jamie in one before I worry about myself. And there, while he's propped up against the sink and breathing better than he has since I arrived, I caress the side of his head and sigh.

"Why did you get on a plane? Why did anyone *let* you?"

"It was a charter. They didn't care," he says. "And I couldn't get the team sick, so Taylor told me to go home, and I just—I went."

"Jesus. I don't think he meant 'fly across the country with double pneumonia.' Your home is—what? Twenty minutes from the arena?"

His blue eyes have been reddened by exhaustion and tears, but they flare with indignation now. We've had pieces of this conversation before—I've asked him where home is—but I'm not sure he's spent more than a month here in the past four years combined, and it feels like that's answered everything just fine. Jamie must feel differently, his body stiff even when he can't help but nuzzle further into the palm of my hand.

"This is home."

I shake my head, confused more than anything. "But you're so far away. And with both you and Harper gone, it feels so damn empty. How can this be anything but the place where you used to live?"

Jamie's indignation gets replaced by weary wisdom he's yet to share, and I think I want him to fight with me somehow, if only he could find the energy for it. This *should* be his home, but he should be mine, and I should be his, and so little feels like it's turned out the way it's supposed to be.

I brush my thumb over his lips, but then he wraps a warm hand around my wrist and pulls me away.

Chapter Nineteen: Jamie

(I Wasn't Surprised He Asked)

I turn my head to stare at my shower because it's not him, and also because I want to be in there with him again. Those two things make little sense together, but I'm full of contradictions like that. A cough hits hard after minutes of some relief, and I think it must be close to midnight by now. We'll stand here a while longer, and then Mateo can help me back into bed. I should apologize for my breakdown, but he seems to have moved on. Instead, I answer the question he's asked.

"You and I have led very different lives," I start. The whistling from my chest sounds as terrible as it feels. "And I'm really not—yours hasn't been perfect. I know that. But you're close to your family. Physically and emotionally, and home—it didn't have to be a single place for you. It was everywhere. It's always been right *there*, and so full of—" I'm coughing again, and when I glance at him, he's watching me with so much fucking concern that it makes my point for me. "That. The way you're looking at me. Like you care."

"I do care. Maybe more than you've ever understood."

I understand just fine, and I'm probably pouting about it. "That everywhere kind of love? It was built all around you. For you. But I didn't grow up with those things. That care. That love. My parents weren't cruel to me, but they weren't warm. They weren't kind. The closest I had back then was Kai's house and his dad's bar, but I didn't get to stay there. They weren't mine. Nobody built that home for me."

"So you built it yourself," Mateo says. "Probably for Harper, first and foremost, but you needed it, too. And when you got sick, it was the only home that mattered, no matter how far away you were."

I almost mention that I'd once wondered whether I still belonged here, but that was so many years ago on a night I don't want us to remember now. I start coughing again anyway. I take off my towel and push it against his chest. Then I return to my bedroom and dig through my suitcase for anything to wear. Packing hadn't been a priority when I was self-medicating with a heavy pour of cough medicine. Even now, I'm clammy and shaky and desperately need to lie down. Careful not to whine, I find sweatpants and a t-shirt, and I pull them on without briefs. It must have taken me a while to do that much. I turn around to find Mateo wearing his joggers, water and meds in his hands, and my bed so much neater behind him.

I take the pills and water from him and swallow with one large gulp. "I don't think the emptiness was intentional—Harper and I just aren't here as much anymore—but I won't pretend it's unfamiliar."

Mateo looks frustrated by that. Then I shiver, and he reaches for me like I can't make it those few feet on my own. I let him get me settled, propped up on a couple of pillows and the covers pulled up to my chin. He sits on the edge of the bed and pushes his fingers through my hair again, and it feels so fucking good.

"Do you think you'll be able to get some sleep?" he asks. "Do you want tea or anything?"

"No. I'm not even sure we have any here."

It's the whole *empty* thing. He nods. "I can pick up some stuff tomorrow."

Even buoyed by the thought that I'll see him tomorrow, my breathing takes a turn for the worse. I curl up as I roll onto my side and cough again, losing his touch when I move. Blinking up at him, I find his hand and almost beg him to stay as close as possible. I need to ask the questions that have been on my mind since he walked into my room.

Or since last July.

"Do you still talk to Logan?"

"Yes," he says, his fingers tight around my hand until he relaxes to hold me there.

"Does he visit a lot? Or do you go to see him?"

Tighten. Relax. "Actually, he—" Tighten. "His job relocated him a little over a year ago. He's closer now, so we can—it's easy to visit whenever."

"Are you guys together?"

"Yes and no."

"Where were you when Harper called tonight?" I ask.

Relax. Mateo takes a deep breath I envy. I slowly tug his hand higher so it's back on my head. I'm needy, and he'll touch me the way I want him to, and even though he doesn't have to tell me the truth, I can't think of a time he hasn't. For a second, I almost let go and take my question back, but it's already too late. I wait instead.

"I was at Logan's."

I close my eyes and focus on how much my chest hurts. I think everything will be okay as long as neither of us says anything else. It's tempting to fall asleep like this—and I know I need the rest—but I'm so fucked up. I make one miserable sound after another. Mateo doesn't pull away from me, and I'm shaking again, ruined by a fever or the fear that he'll be gone as soon as he thinks I won't notice.

Everything might be okay if we don't say anything else, but I can't keep him here that way. "Does he know where you are?"

"Yes."

"Does he expect you to come home tonight?"

"It's not my home," he murmurs. "And no, I don't think so."

I nod beneath his hand, but I feel myself slipping away. Antibiotics and Tylenol won't knock me out—they haven't been in my system long enough to do *anything* yet—but the combination of the hot shower and Mateo's presence has relaxed me more than I could've imagined. I cough some, but even those are weaker now. While I'm suddenly having trouble finding my voice, I panic less when he stands up. Now that I know he's not expected back in his boyfriend's bed, I can listen to him return to the bathroom without trying to follow him there.

I'm not convinced I could get out of bed even if I wanted to.

He's probably only gone for a few minutes, but I haven't opened my eyes. Mateo crawls into bed, still shirtless and destined for a night of very little sleep by my side. He's spooning me as comfortably as he first did years ago, and he presses a hand to my forehead. I don't know whether he's satisfied by whatever he feels there, but he kisses the back of my neck. I feel the chill from a dock in Upstate New York when I mumble just loud enough for him to hear.

"Please don't leave me again."

***

He leaves eventually, but only so he can crouch next to the bed and nudge me awake with more water and meds. I fall back asleep after that. When I wake up again, Mateo isn't in my room at all. There's a mug of tea on my nightstand, hot enough that I can see the steam.

He hasn't gone far, and I strain to hear him above the nasty sounds from my chest.

I give up when I cough for about a minute straight, but my chaos is enough to bring him back to me. I look up to see him leaning against my doorframe. Attempting to read his expression gets me nowhere, and I say the first thing that comes to mind.

"Nice shirt."

Mateo looks down at where my team's logo is splayed across his chest and cracks a smile. "I needed something to wear to the store."

"You have a shirt of your own."

"I grabbed this one first," he shrugs. "How are you feeling?"

"You're here."

"I am. Drink your tea."

I roll my eyes and do as I've been told. I'm not feeling great, but that's still better than yesterday, when I'd stumbled off a plane and into urgent care. There'd been no need for Mateo to reprimand me for flying with pneumonia. Everyone who'd seen me had done that just fine, and I've suffered the consequences since. I haven't been this incapacitated since I literally couldn't stand on my own two feet. I stay helpless in bed now because I don't know where else to go, even in the place I call home.

I'm still holding the mug when I realize I haven't coughed since Mateo reappeared—less because he's here, and more because he was up early enough to give me medicine and tea. I take another sip, and he watches from the door.

"You didn't get much sleep, did you?" I ask.

He makes a face, still mostly unreadable. "I don't think I expected to. I can nap later."

"Are you leaving now?"

"You asked me not to."

"I did, yeah," I say, quiet and at least a little ashamed. "But I didn't—"

Mateo waves his hand to interrupt. "I only left to go to the store. We should have enough to eat now. We'll have to figure out the whole clothing situation because—well, I'm not sure we can both live out of a single poorly packed suitcase, and I haven't ransacked your closet to see how much you left behind four years ago. But yeah, no, I—if you still want me to stay, I—"

"I want. I always want."

I want, and he stays. And for a while, it's that easy.

At Mateo's suggestion, I take another blazing hot shower. He doesn't join me because the daylight has reminded us of boundaries the nighttime forgot. When I get downstairs with my tea, he's in the kitchen, so at home here I want to cry. I'm about to tell him I'm not sure I can stomach much after not eating for 24 hours. He turns around and nods at the closest stool and pushes a bowl of freshly cut fruit across the island.

"Start with that," he says. "I'll make us oatmeal when your hunger kicks back in."

He'd already texted Harper with an update. I give her a call and hear her tired relief through the phone. From somewhere nearby, Simon wishes me well and promises to take good care of her through her last month of school. With soft smiles, Mateo and I talk about them. I send a quick message to Taylor, loud about my diagnosis and silent about the company I'm keeping. I don't ask whether I still have a job because of course I do.

Nothing that has ever been taken from me has been something I wished I could give up.

It occurs to me that Mateo must have talked to Logan while I was asleep. I'm not sure I want to know more about them than I already do. It's unfair of me to believe he's betrayed a relationship we never really had, but I feel it too deeply to do anything about it now.

The coughing comes and goes. My body aches everywhere. My lungs feel less like they're about to end up on the floor. I think the early dose of Tylenol has kept my fever away. Even if it's only dulled the rest of my pain, I'm grateful that I'm no longer sweaty and freezing. My bowl of fruit tastes fucking amazing.

I want oatmeal already, and I want to hate that Mateo knows me well enough to have prepped it so I don't have to wait long. We eat side by side and don't need to say much. My labored breathing is loud enough to distract us. When he cleans up, I move to a sectional I miss when I'm in New Jersey.

He joins me, and I reach for his hand. "Time for that nap?"

For a second, I think he's going to laugh or give me shit for wanting to sleep so soon after I woke up. He only turns the tv on to something we'll quickly tune out and pulls a blanket from where Harper probably left it folded nearby. We curve around each other, a sideways embrace that feels too natural for something I left behind long ago. It's what should have happened at Taylor's—it's *all* that should've happened at Taylor's—but my hand has barely curled into a fist when Mateo is smoothing it into something he can hold again.

"I'm sorry," he says, his mouth warm against my head. "For the scars on your chest. I know I did that to you."

"I can live with scars. The memories are the harder part."

"And I did that to you, too."

"We did that to each other," I argue. "I could've said no to you that night. I could've told you we needed to keep waiting until the time was right."

Mateo sighs. "Was the time ever going to be right?"

"I don't know. Do you think I would've made us wait forever?"

"I don't know."

I cough over his shoulder. He doesn't let go because—aside from one stupid, reckless, beautiful night—he's been the one I can count on to keep me steady. I don't understand everything that's happened between us, or where he and I can possibly go from here, but Mateo has been mine since the night we met. I can't make that any less true this morning. I'll look for a way to make it more true tomorrow. For now, the deep breath I take is the best I can do with lungs that hate me.

As I drift off, I mumble against his cheek. "I'm sorry I said there was nothing for Harper to know. There's always been something."

Mateo sighs again. "Sleep, sweetheart."

I do. So does he. At some point, he wakes up to fetch the pill bottles and more water. Before I fall asleep again, he adjusts us both so I can lie with my head in his lap and his hand in my hair. Later, I get up to pee against my will, but he's still there when I return. I've lost all track of time.

"Stay here," he says when he finally stands again. "I'm making a late lunch. Or an early dinner."

I'm planning to ask what he's making when I close my eyes again, my body demanding the rest it's been denied for days. The white noise from the tv blurs with the clatter in the kitchen. I sleep heavily enough to be grateful when Mateo wakes me gently. His fingertips brush along the side of my neck. Then he kisses my forehead because we decided a while ago that it's something friends do.

He pulls away, and I see my late lunch or early dinner on the coffee table. "Looks delicious."

"My grandmother's tortilla soup," he says. "It's the first time I've made it since she died, but it's—I think it'll help with some of the congestion. She swore it was better than chicken noodle, and I—"

"You weren't gonna argue with her."

"Absolutely not."

As I sit up, Mateo drapes the blanket over my shoulders and ducks the next several coughs. I still feel like shit, but I'm more alert shit now. I wasn't lying about how good the soup looks.

My stomach growls. He smiles.

The bowl is hot in my hand, but the warmth feels good. I'm not shaking when I reach for the spoon. Mateo stays near me anyway, uninterested in babying me, but even less interested in keeping his distance while I take my first bite of his soup. Then a second, and a third.

"Jesus, this is really good."

"Why do you sound surprised?" he asks.

I frown because some of it's surprise, but more of it's regret—the reminder of missed opportunities. "You and I usually ordered take-out. Or hit Kai's. Or went out for Mexican with Sophie. Or drove up and down the coast on a dozen secret adventures. We didn't do any of this."

"No, I guess we didn't."

"But you loved making this soup today. I can tell."

Mateo nods, wary. "Yes, I loved making it."

"Do you cook for Logan?"

"Jamie. Don't."

"Do you love—"

"Stop."

I obey him, mostly because his fingers are against my lips, and all I can think about is the night I came with them in my mouth. Instead of wrapping my lips around them now, I move to swallow another spoonful of soup. I hate that it doesn't taste the same as it did a minute ago.

"Are you going to spend the night again?"

He'd implied as much when he was worried about living out of my suitcase, but I was weaker and quieter then. If I keep eating, he'll be able to leave without dragging a guilty conscience behind him, his work here done. We'll exchange a few texts about how I'm feeling. If

I'm lucky, I'll see him another year or two from now.

When I start to cough—the pneumonia to blame more than anything—he takes the bowl away and returns it to the coffee table. I don't know whether it's enough to undo the trouble I've just borrowed, but I help myself to water and wait for him to answer. My dramatics aside, he doesn't need to stay, and we both know it. I want him to, and we both know that, too. My chest is almost clear for now, and it makes the tv suddenly loud. I turn it off just as Mateo walks away.

He's in the kitchen before he speaks. "When are you flying back to New Jersey?"

"Not before bedtime."

It's a poor attempt at a joke, but I see the disappointment on Mateo's face when I turn to look at him. I push myself off the couch and chase him because it's all I know. He waits because he's done what I've asked for far too long. He attempts to busy himself with dirty dishes the closer I get, but I just shake my head and he gives up. I watch him rinse and dry his hands as I step around the island, and he uses the blanket I forgot was around my shoulders to pull me into him.

"You're going back soon, right?" he asks.

"I have to. It's my *job*."

"The season's over."

"Sure, for the guys on the team. You know I have more responsibilities than that."

Mateo snorts. "Yeah, I also know you need to take it easy for a while, but you're gonna push yourself past this no matter what you should do."

"I gotta say, it's nice to have something I can push past." I'm referring to my fucked up leg, but it sounds a little like I'm talking about falling in love with him, and he flinches. "No. Wait. That wasn't—"

"It's fine."

I drop my head onto his shoulder. "Why do we keep doing this? It's always so easy with us right up until it's not. We should know how to be friends by now. We still love each other. I *know* we do. Nothing has changed, so why is this still so hard?"

"Because nothing has changed," he says, too fucking tender when he reaches between us to tilt my chin upward. The tears in his eyes are almost unbearable. "It's so easy when we're alone, but we've never learned how to let the outside in. We've never really been allowed to try."

"And we can't try today."

"No," Mateo agrees. "But I'll go home and get some clothes and anything else I need, and then I'll stay here until you leave. I think it's your turn to walk away."

It's strange, the specific way those words sting. He's not putting all the blame on me, even if I think that's where most of it belongs. Mateo's acknowledging the hug on the dock and all the times he's held lines I would've crossed for the chance to love him and wreck us. He's telling me now that he'd stay even longer if it weren't for the fact that I've chosen hockey over him every time. He's also being loud about his choice to watch me go.

I won't let it happen for a while.

Most of that night is spent in the comfortable silence around my uncomfortable coughing fits. My fever is gone, and neither of us is left sweaty when we share my bed and keep bare skin against bare skin.

The next few days are filled with Mateo's home-cooked meals, comfort movie marathons, and several trips to the backyard to soak in my hot tub. We talk about a hundred different things while we avoid details that could give the wrong things away. He's brought me a stuffed penguin from a spring break everyone else has probably forgotten, and it's softer than I remember.

We're not nobody anymore, so I can tell him when Harper texts me about several interviews she's lined up for teaching positions in the L.A. area. I understand little about Simon's job, other than it being some super techy app programming thing, but I know he's been willing to move to Southern California if that's where Harper ends up. The implications of that remain clear enough—even if Simon doesn't propose, he's incredibly committed to their future. When I catch Mateo's smile, it's as genuine as mine.

To celebrate her college graduation, Harper and I are going on a romp through Europe. Telling Mateo about that earns me another grin. It's almost enough reason to invite him along with us, or at least to the graduation ceremony, but neither invitation is wholly mine to extend. Besides, I'm selfish enough to want alone time with each of them. Quieting, I press my body against Mateo's, waiting for the stories he has to share.

I get to hear a lot about his family and the time he's spent with them over the past couple of years. Everyone is happy and healthy. I'm glad the wounds from his grandfather's life and his grandmother's death have healed as well as anything like that ever does. He's more excited than I've seen him in a while when he tells me he'll be taking his nieces and nephews on a multi-week cross-country road trip during the summer.

"Will I hear from you while you're gone?" I ask.

"Should I call you when I'm standing next to America's biggest ball of twine?"

Imagining him there is enough to make me laugh and then wheeze. "Either that or from any gas station mini-mart just before you blow an obscene amount of money on snacks you could get down the street from your apartment."

Later, Mateo talks about Sophie and the nights they watched my games at the bar with Kai. I'd known about some of it, but not all. I'm weirdly glad Kai felt like he could welcome them without alerting me.

Mateo also shares a few things about his classes this year. He shares much more about soccer and the summertime clinic he's continued to hold with Harper's help. I don't think I'd realized the players were local middle-schoolers. The oldest among them would still be about four months from being able to try out for his team.

It makes me curious. "Why not run something for your current players? Why younger ones who might not end up playing for you at all?"

"I love the high school kids, obviously," he says. "But there's something about the younger group—the way they don't already know better. How much they—"

"Are nervous and eager and want your help."

"Exactly. And you know I just want to be out there, running around with them. Coaching them and celebrating their little wins."

I do know. I feel the same way, and have thought about it a lot lately, but I just nod because I don't want to talk about my job. It's nicer to bite my tongue and crawl into Mateo's lap and let him hold me. We don't kiss, either because we've learned exactly one lesson, or because I'm still sick enough for us to use that as an excuse. Still, we keep a blanket close and each other closer, and I'm only frustrated when I wonder why we're not on the bench. I hate that the connection we've remade feels too fragile for me to ask us to move with it intact.

It doesn't stop me from pushing us somewhere while my fingertip traces the collar of his t-shirt. "It's been days, and you're not just waiting for me to go. You're waiting to see what new promises we'll make before I do."

"There aren't new promises to make," Mateo says, pulling my hand away to lace our fingers together. "Let's just figure out how to keep some of the old ones."

I want that more than he probably believes, but I have hockey and he has something like a boyfriend. Even once the school year ends, I'm going to be busy with Harper for a while, and Mateo will be busy with soccer and his road trip. And whether it's right or wrong, I already know I'll be going to the lake house this year. I need to let go of the baggage I've brought along before—envy, secrecy, and submission—and introduce a few more people to me.

Jamie. Not Jameson Sinclair.

Mateo whispers my name now, and I whisper to him, too.

The night I need to go to the airport, he drives me there. It's cruel to one or both of us, but we're done fighting about it. At the last red light before we approach the departure zone, I stare out the window at the rain that had started minutes ago. I don't let myself turn to reach for him, even when I have something important to say.

"Spend Christmas with me," I murmur. "The way we used to be, when we were counting down to something and got so fucking close."

"The way we've been the past few days."

I nod, tracking the path of a raindrop on the glass. Neither of us mentions Logan, but we both know he wouldn't fit into these plans. Neither of us wants to wait until December, but we both know time's never been on our side. Neither of us asks whether this means we're counting down again, but we both know we never stopped.

"Let's keep a promise," I say.

About 30 seconds of silence follow, the car rolling forward while I try to remember what hope feels like. I see the signs for my airline as Mateo slows, and then I get my answer.

"Okay."

"You're still welcome to come over for Christmas, Sinclair. To my big house, where I have a lot of room for eating and drinking and celebrating."

I raise a tired eyebrow as I look up at Taylor. "I already told you I have plans at my house for eating and drinking and celebrating."

"Yes, your *small* house. That you don't even own. And since I assume your plans are with someone, I thought maybe that someone might appreciate actual holiday joy." He stops and smirks, and nothing about it surprises me. Not even when he goes on. "Unless this someone would prefer it if I hosted Christmas at the lake."

"Mmmm, that sounds like fun. Maybe next year."

He studies me for a few more seconds before he throws a dirty towel at me and walks away. I know he's trying to figure me out. He does it with the same slight condescension with which he does everything, and I've given him little in return. I don't think I need to, really. Especially since my mostly sober, entirely celibate stay at the lake house in August. But while there's plenty to know, there's not much I'm ready to talk about.

I'll have to eventually. And probably for a while. But not yet.

I skipped college altogether, but if last year's conversations with Harper are anything to go on, I'm as overwhelmed by conflicting emotions as students approaching their graduation. I'm excited and nervous and so close to moving on to a new chapter. I'm also terrified I won't remember any of what I've been taught.

I'm not sure I'll be able to run back to a classroom if I screw this up.

But there's still so much to do, and none of it will happen today. My priority is getting back to the small house I don't even own, and the man sleeping off a red-eye flight while buried under my duvet. I can only hope it will still smell like him tonight.

The past several months have felt so close to the relationship Mateo and I had before I was hired here. It's what we almost were before I moved away from California and fractured something we'd held together with stick tape and twine. It's what I'd wanted us to become once I got settled as a coach. Phone calls and distant honesty and hope that obstacles wouldn't be in our way forever.

Or that I'd finally stop clinging to those obstacles just because they're the only escape I've ever known.

I'm helplessly in love and helpless to make that matter more than something fickle and familiar.

The shift between us started when Mateo answered a late-night call from my daughter. It slid ungracefully past a shared shower, a bowl of tortilla soup, reclaimed intimacy, and another spring break we can't forget. After I landed back in New Jersey, I suffered a predictable setback from the clash of altitude and illness. Everything slowed for a while. Texts kept us afloat, but I needed to get back on my feet. He needed to figure out where things stood with Logan.

Well, all three of us knew where things stood, but it took some time for him to decide what to do about it.

In the end, Logan spared Mateo the trouble. I don't know the details. Given how little Mateo offered to tell me about their last night together, I don't want them. There's something fond about the way Mateo still says Logan's name that makes me fiercely jealous. I'd bring up Lena if I thought it'd do any more good than throwing a bucket of water on a wildfire.

I still haven't seen Mateo in person since he dropped me off at the airport in April. This morning I hurried out for early meetings with Taylor and left a spare key behind. But he and I had texted each other throughout May, and I sent postcards from Germany,

Italy, and France. By the end of his school year in June, we started sending regular voice notes again. Phone calls became more frequent during the summer, even while he was in gas station mini-marts and I was on a dock. When the new hockey season approached, and I got busier again, we traded some quantity for quality, and made video chats a priority. All of it has loosened bands I wrapped around myself as a child. None of it has come with a promise of more than these couple of days.

Still, I'm humming with anticipation of what comes next for us. This is the eighth Christmas since we met, but only the second we've celebrated together. On the front porch, I'm uncharacteristically clumsy when I fumble with my keys, but I get inside the house in time to catch Mateo coming from the direction of my bedroom. He's fresh out of the shower and just tugging a dark red sweater over his head.

My grin must be damning, but I don't care. "Merry Christmas Eve."

"Merry Christmas Eve," Mateo says, his smile almost shy in response. "I didn't think you'd get home so soon."

It's not quite noon, but I hang up my coat and take off my boots as quickly as possible. I don't want to waste any more time being across the room from him. Sweeping him up in a hug is too romantic and close to unnecessary, but he's the one who won't let go for a long, long time. There are no tears this time, just a giggle or two from 40something men who suddenly sound—and maybe feel—like teenagers.

"How much did you snoop?" I ask as I force myself to take a step back to look at him.

"Enough to find my old hoodie, a nice picture of a bench, and all the groceries I asked you to pick up for tomorrow."

"Nice work."

"Nice place."

"It's still not home," I say, abruptly shaking it off a moment later because we're done with that conversation. "How tired are you? And how hard would it be to drag you out of here?"

"Not hard at all, but you already know that. Where are we going?"

"New York City."

His eyes go wide. I laugh. It doesn't take us long to get bundled up. Mateo borrows one of my scarves and looks better than I ever have. On the train, I pull my beanie low, but locals usually mind their own business and most tourists would rather spot a celebrity than a hockey coach. And honestly, I don't get recognized much anymore.

I also don't miss it as often as I thought I would.

It's cold, but not quite freezing. When we arrive, there's no rain to get in the way of me watching closely as Mateo gets his first look at the city. I have to move him soon, the pace here faster that what he's used to, but the crowd means I can hold his hand and lead him through it. I'm very willing to trade my stare for the contact.

We stop for pizza because it feels like the right thing to do. I tell him stories of times I played here, including our second Cup win and some of the trouble I got into afterward. He wonders aloud about coming back when we have time to explore museums and catch a Broadway show. I agree to everything easily. Then I wonder silently about where else he'd want to go if we weren't hiding from the whole damn world.

I try to show off as many of the obvious tourist sights as I can in the afternoon we have. The Empire State Building and Grand Central and Times Square and St. Patrick's and The Plaza and Central Park. As long as he's already daydreaming of a return, I imagine bringing him back during the summer to visit Chelsea and walk the Brooklyn Bridge and spend some time on Governors Island and tuck ourselves into a corner of the New York Public Library. We barely let go of each other, and I believe in forever all over again.

Eventually, we end up at Rockefeller Center, swept up in the Christmas of it all. It's dark, and the tree is bright, and the noise is a comfort. Then I nod toward the rink where so many people are skating while my leg aches.

"Do you want to watch them or sit down?" Mateo asks softly, his gloved hand slipping past my coat to rest at my waist.

I hate that he knows, and love that he knows. I smile more than I frown. "Watch."

We wind our way past people who don't care who we are or what we're doing. They're too busy being themselves and going every-where. It's difficult to get a decent view—and will be until some of this crowd swaps out for others—but Mateo brushes his nose against mine and takes my breath away.

"I'll be right back."

It's probably unwise to let him go, now and always, but I'm counting on him to wander off and find his way back. Again. I shift my weight onto my good leg for a while and get lost in the around and around and around below me. That happy distraction fades into another when I think about tomorrow. Mateo and I will cook together. Or he'll be cooking while I drink and observe from a distance. But we're not leaving the house, and we're not ordering in, and we've agreed that we won't exchange gifts this year. It's fine with me because I can't think of a single thing I want more than him.

I won't *really* have him tomorrow. But also, I've really had him for eight years.

The nudge against my shoulder is distinct, even when I'm being bumped into from every angle. I turn to find Mateo's dark eyes and gorgeous grin and an ice cream cone. A fucking ice cream cone.

"You remembered?"

He shrugs. "There's no snowstorm today, but it's pretty damn cold."

"And that's a frozen lake if we squint."

"Maybe you should talk Taylor into having a 48-hour Christmas party next year, just so you can have the real thing."

"Upstate?" I chuckle, swiping my tongue over both scoops at once. "He actually brought that up this morning, just to give me shit."

"Give you shit about what?"

I take a breath or two. "About whatever secret plans I'd made for Christmas this year, while being pretty fucking clear he knew I'd made them with you."

"So, Taylor—"

"Knows at least as much as Harper, yeah," I finish.

"Because I once showed up at his door to see you, and we locked ourselves in your room all night, and I left you alone on his dock like I'd never been there at all?"

"Locking ourselves in the room the year before might've been his first clue, but I assume your surprise reappearance answered any lingering questions."

Mateo pushes the cone toward me. It's a reminder that I should keep eating, even if the ice cream's in no danger of melting out here. He turns his attention back to the skaters. I give him time to sort out whatever he's feeling. Nothing has changed, but the crisp air is charged. I think we both know it wouldn't take much to set fire to the bridges we've crossed before we light our way forward.

"He hasn't outed you," he says. "Probably not even on a small scale, or you would've heard rumblings by now."

"What good would outing me do? He'd gain nothing from it."

"Do you think that's the reason he hasn't? Because he has nothing to gain?"

"No."

Mateo nods and takes my ice cream, sexier than he means to be when he licks it. "He'd potentially have things to lose. After working so closely with you for years, there'd be some scrutiny."

"Agreed. It would hurt him before it would help."

"But you don't think that's why he's staying quiet either."

"No," I say with a strange little sigh. "I think he might be looking out for me."

There's more to say about that—probably a lot more—but my phone vibrates against my ass. I reach for it, half expecting it to be Taylor. It's not. It's Harper, and the call makes me nervous because she's supposed to be busy skiing with Simon. She and I aren't supposed to talk until tomorrow.

I let Mateo keep the cone while I drag him away from the crowd and swipe to answer. "Hey, pixie, is everything okay?"

"Yes, yes, sorry, are you—it's loud there. Are you outside? Is Mateo there? I didn't think you had any big plans. Am I interrupting something? I just had to call because—" Harper pauses for a breath. It helps give me just enough time to pull Mateo into the only empty space in all of New York City. "Okay, sorry again, Simon is staring at me. Is Mateo there? Can you put me on speaker, or are you, like, in a restaurant or something?"

"No, I—he's here. And it's fine." I'm not sure it is yet. I wouldn't usually put anyone on speaker in public, but chaos continues around us, and I want to know why she's calling. Mateo is already waiting impatiently, his anxiety fed by mine. "Okay, go ahead."

Harper has said a million words since I answered, but I swear she quiets now, just because she can. I want to blame her mother for the dramatic effect. Mateo's glare suggests he's prepared to blame me. Then I hear a voice mumble something just before she squeals.

"Simon and I are getting married!"

CHAPTER TWENTY: MATEO

(I WAS SURPRISED BY THE INVITATION)

Mr. Mateo Zavala.

I hold the envelope in my hand and arc my thumb over my name for the hundredth time, noting—also for the hundredth time—that it's *only* my name. The wedding invitation wasn't addressed to *Mr. Mateo Zavala and Guest.* It's almost as if Harper and Simon know there's no Logan, or anyone else like him, in my life anymore. They haven't drawn the outline of some hypothetical man I might want to bring as my date, and there's no suggestion that I should bring Sophie along, even though she'd also taught Harper many years ago. I've been invited, very cordially, but I've been invited alone, because it's the closest they can get to making me someone else's plus one.

Jamie and I got the call about Harper and Simon's engagement about eight months ago, and the time since has been full of phone calls, video chats, one quick visit, and the same hope I carried for years before it got too heavy. I'm waiting again, and I love him too much to want to stop, but I can't pretend the ache in my shoulders isn't returning under the weight of something familiar. Maybe it's time for me to break more rules. Maybe I could do it for more than the one night I once suggested. Maybe I could do it without being as angry as I was at the lake.

Maybe I could do it forever.

It's been over a year since I last saw Logan, but I think of him as I leave the empty envelope on my dresser and return to the bathroom to finish getting ready. It would've been so easy, having a real relationship with him. He was silly and sweet and smart. Everything about our time together was simple, and the sex was wonderful. My family loved him, and I could've.

But Logan and I had both known it was over by the time I put Jamie on a plane. I suppose we had both known it was over the night I walked out of his bedroom. And really, there shouldn't have been anything requiring an official goodbye when he'd been aware all along that I was using him, but he was eager to let me hurt him one more time. We'd gathered up the traces of each other left behind on too many mornings after, and we'd slept together for something like old times' sake. Strangely enough, it had been one of the best nights of my life, but now I shake my head at my reflection, wrap my tie around my neck, and forget.

Mr. Mateo Zavala, sans guest, has a wedding to attend.

The venue is probably 30 to 40 minutes away, Harper and Simon picking an oceanside hotel halfway between where they live now and where she grew up. I'd met the groom about a month ago, when they'd taken me out to lunch between wedding errands, and it had overwhelmed me to remember the ambitious 14-year-old who'd once introduced herself from the front row of my honors English class. She's 23 now, and just as ambitious, and if I'm this proud of her today, Jamie must be ecstatic.

Actually, I know he is because he hasn't stopped texting me since he landed in California yesterday morning. We haven't seen each other yet—he's been busy with father-of-the-bride duties, and I've been busy pacing Sophie's apartment—but he sent me pictures from last night's rehearsal dinner. His smile was magnificent in every one of them. I hate that he's expected back in New Jersey tomorrow when I have so many things to say.

I'm ready to go. My tie is tied and my hair is pulled into a perfect ponytail, and I will carry my suit jacket with me until I've arrived at the hotel. I have a duffel bag and a wedding gift with me too, and I set them on the back seat before I take a deep breath and prepare for a night I've been looking forward to, and maybe fearing, for months. Once I'm parked and as put together as possible, I head inside to check in, greeted first by a gorgeous flower and balloon arrangement pointing me toward the ceremony. It's all so real, and I think I say something stupid about it to the clerk who's just trying to give me a room key. I gather myself somewhere between the front desk and the elevator, and I'm mostly fine once I'm alone in my room for a few minutes. Then my phone vibrates and I have no idea how I'm doing.

Let me know when you get here and I'll meet you in the lobby

I'm already here. See you in just a minute.

I study myself in the full-length mirror and decide I look fantastic, then I grab the gift and hurry out the door. This elevator ride causes all the butterflies to return, and I remind myself that nothing has changed between us yet.

I haven't said anything important.

I haven't told him I'm willing to cross whatever lines will let me have him in secret while we wait another one or two or ten years to let the world in.

Jamie and I are still friends, but the doors open and he's there in his tux, and I just stare until I remember that I have to *move*. His nervous giggle is as beautiful as he is, and I feel it against my chest when he hugs me. When we pull away, almost dizzy over the only semi-private moment we might get tonight, he takes the gift from my hand and ushers me toward the festivities.

"How's Harper doing?" I ask.

"She hasn't stopped talking about how excited she is. I only got a break now because she's getting dressed with her crew, but once we get you seated, I'll check back in with them."

I'd heard the wedding party included her friends Lizzie and Kate, both of whom I know from their high school days, plus a roommate of hers from Washington. Danielle must be around somewhere, though I haven't seen her since the handful of soccer games she attended, and I'm not sure which one of us is more likely to recognize the other. Abruptly, I realize Jamie's parents will be here, too. I don't know why that hadn't occurred to me—or why he hadn't brought it up—but it has me grabbing for his arm.

"Your mom and dad."

"Mmmm, yeah, they're here. Had a lovely conversation with them last night. They detailed the things I could've done better as a coach this season. Getting back to the second round of the playoffs after missing them entirely the year before wasn't good enough. Obviously. Coaching was supposed to be my chance to remind everyone who I am and recapture the success I surrendered when I—"

"You didn't surrender. You—"

He peels my hand off him and interrupts me with a peaceful little grin. "I know. And it's fine. I'm fine, I promise. They're here, but so are you."

I bite back most of what I could say and only tell him I'll find a seat on my own while he drops off my gift and catches up with Harper. It's impossible to ignore how calm he is on an evening that would excuse him for being more manic. Not only is his only child getting married, but his ex is here and his parents are here and *I'm* here, and Jamie's carrying the foolish confidence reserved for the times we're alone or in the middle of New York City.

I'm the unsteady one tonight. It's been so long since I've had to keep from loving him out loud.

The ceremony is scheduled to start in 15 minutes, and when I spot Kai, most of my anxiety quiets. I'm impressed he took a Saturday night off from the bar, and say so as I take the chair next to him. We haven't seen each other since May, but even side by side, it's easy to make the same small talk we do when he supplies me with wings and beer. Eventually, there's a shift in the music, and we turn to watch as older family members are walked down the aisle. Without my having to ask, Kai whispers to me when Jamie's parents arrive among other grandparents. Once all the special guests have been seated, the music changes again, this time to a beautiful instrumental, and I watch Lizzie, Kate, and another young woman make their way toward a gazebo set up in front of the crowd.

Then we all stand. It's for Harper, of course. Our attention. And I'm happy to give it because I've always loved weddings, and she's absolutely stunning, and I've spent enough time imagining what it would be like to be the person waiting at the other end of the aisle to understand how Simon must feel at the first sight of her.

But I don't think I've ever wanted to get married as badly as I do when I see Jamie now.

His wet eyes connect with mine as he passes with his daughter on his arm, and I don't know whether his emotion has anything to do with me. Kai squeezes my shoulder and reminds me to breathe, and I'm okay after that, other than the tears that fall when I hear poetic vows that would make any English teacher proud.

The reception follows immediately, and we're treated to an open bar and hors d'oeuvres while we wait for the wedding party to join us. I have an Old Fashioned in my hand when Kai sees someone he knows and wanders off, and I'm surprised when Lizzie and Kate's parents recognize me years after we had a couple of brief conferences. Talking to them keeps me occupied until the DJ hypes everyone up to welcome the newlyweds. Jamie slips in just ahead of everyone else, but making a beeline for me would be unwise. By the time dinner is served, I still haven't been able to talk to him again.

The food is incredible, as is the music. Harper and Simon's first dance is followed by her dance with Jamie, and Simon's with his mother. They continue with more traditions, each new memory the couple makes backed by the laughter and cheers of the entire ballroom, and I hang back to soak it all in. I lose track of everyone at some point, and I'm mostly alone until I feel someone tap on my shoulder.

"How nicely do I have to ask to get you to dance with me?"

I turn toward Harper and chuckle. "You're the bride. I think you get anything you want, even if you're only slightly nice about it."

"Perfect. Let's go."

My suit jacket is on my chair, but I'm otherwise still fully put together, most of the guests louder and tipsier than I'll be all night. Harper is giddy as she leads me to the dance floor, but that's probably mostly *her* and not anything she's had to drink. I look for Jamie because I don't know how to stop wanting him close, but he's been caught up in one conversation after another, and I'm guessing he's even more sober than I am.

His blue eyes are clear every time I catch him looking for me.

"Congratulations," I say as I sweep her into my arms. "And thank you for letting me be a part of your big day."

She shakes her head and makes a silly little face. "At the very least, you're like, colleague-adjacent now? Totally different districts, and I chose to teach history instead, but it still counts for something. I definitely didn't need any other reason to invite you."

"Even if you have one."

Neither of us looks away when I say that. There's no need for us to play dumb when we're far from it, and I twirl her just because I can, bringing her back to me in time for her to remember what I'd said just a minute ago.

"I'm the bride, and I can get anything I want," she starts. "So, Mateo, tell me—what's the story with you and my dad? Were you friends, and then together, and then not together, and then friends again? You've been staring at each other all night, so it seems like you *want* to be together now, but if you *are* together now, you're keeping it a secret, even from me. Why haven't we ever talked about this? Why aren't you years into an actual relationship already? And please do *not* tell me it's because of his career."

"Ironically, it's because of mine."

Harper lets the tiniest frown come and go. "You guys became friends my senior year. I understand the ethical issues of dating the parent of a student, but come on. By the time you would've known you wanted anything else, I was about to grad—" She pauses and cocks her head. "When I was about to graduate, he got the job in New Jersey. Which means we're back to hockey and all of its bullshit."

I don't disagree with her general point—I've been in a fight with hockey for years—but she's also steeped in privilege. Her experience in locker rooms isn't the same as Jamie's. Her level of fame certainly isn't comparable. And whatever effect Danielle's apathy or Jamie's career might have had on her, I don't think she's known the pressure he's faced since he learned how to skate.

She can blame hockey's bullshit all she wants. I have. But it won't change how Jamie and I started, and how willing I was to wait as long as I knew where every line was drawn.

"He's never told you how we met?" I ask, curious how much longer this song will last.

"I was there. I introduced you. Back-to-school night, my freshman year."

When I look over Harper's shoulder, I see Jamie. He sees me. I sigh. "The Friday night before your freshman year started, I went to a dive bar to order takeout. Unbeknownst to me, the owner's best friend was there that night, too. I didn't recognize him, but we talked a little, and I couldn't look away. We got interrupted when a fight broke out, and he dragged me into the alley out back. Talking there wasn't enough. Saying goodbye didn't feel like an option. He asked me to drive him to a taco truck near the beach. We went for a walk afterward and ended up on a bench in the dark. I stayed with him until morning."

"Holy shit. That's—a narrative."

"Our connection was indescribable," I say. "I don't think I've ever believed in love at first sight, but after that one night? We both wanted it all, and I had no idea what he would've gone through to make it happen. I didn't realize what that would've meant for him, but hockey wouldn't have stopped him. Not then."

"It was me," Harper murmurs, and I hate that I can hear it over a ballroom full of her guests. It hits me then how intensely unfair we've been to her, allowing her to know something without telling her everything. We had our reasons when she was a kid, but no excuse in the years since. Someone comes up to us then, and asks her for a dance, but she makes him wait one more song and turns back to me as she squeezes my hand. "I'm sorry."

She might be referring to the interruption, but I don't think she is. "No, I'm sorry. *We're* sorry. And it was okay back then because we decided to wait for each other. We figured out how to be friends, and we spent time together when people weren't looking. By your senior year, we made the friendship more public, and we were close to being able to tell everyone. Then he got the job and moved away, and he asked me to keep waiting."

"What did you say? Because the two of you were still in touch after he left. He invited you to Taylor's one year. But then there were all those stories about him being out with different women, and you were with Logan. The two of you weren't talking for a while, and then you started talking again, and you spent Christmas together. And you love him. A lot."

"I love him, and he loves me. I've never, ever questioned that," I tell her. "But waiting for so long got complicated for both of us."

"And you don't want to wait anymore?"

I reach down to tuck a lock of hair behind her ear and smile softly. "I don't think I can."

It's late, and the official reception will wind down soon, but the dance floor is still packed, and I've overheard plans to join Harper and Simon at the hotel bar for a party that could last another couple of hours. I'll pass on the extra drinks. Eventually, I'll need to get some sleep. For now, I lean against a wall and scan the room for Jamie, because I haven't seen him since he escorted his parents toward the lobby, and I want to make sure he's okay.

I don't have to wait much longer to find out.

"You're still here," he says, leaning next to me and into me all at once, his jacket gone too, and his bowtie hanging loose beneath the collar of his shirt.

"Hasn't that always been true?"

"I hope it never stops."

I take a deep breath and continue to watch the crowd on the

dance floor. "You looked so fucking pretty tonight. Walking down the aisle."

"Yeah? You want to marry me?"

"I want everything. I've always wanted everything."

"You can have it," he says. "I'm not—we can have this. Anything. Everything. Tonight."

"Because I called you pretty?"

"Because right now, tonight is all we get."

There's a familiar tension between us, but as I roll toward Jamie, it licks at me like a flame eager to warm long before it burns. "You still have to leave tomorrow."

"Taylor called a press conference for Monday morning. There's a big announcement coming, and he needs me there."

"We're going to have to talk."

"Agreed."

"But you don't want to talk tonight," I say.

"I want loud and slow," he purrs, his pale blue gaze flickering down to my mouth and up again. "We deserve loud and slow."

As soft as his voice is, Jamie's fingers curl around my tie as if he's thinking of how to use it against me. I don't know if this is romantic desperation brought on by the spell weddings tend to cast, or whether he's figured out one more way to say goodbye, and I can't make myself care. Anyone could see us here, but I wrap my hand around his and hope nobody is watching.

"It'll change things between us again."

Jamie nods. "I hope so."

"There's a limit to how loud we can be in a crowded hotel."

"My house."

"What?"

"Grab your stuff and meet me at my house," he says.

I'm so aroused I think I'd meet him in the middle of the ocean if he asked me to, but—

"Don't you have a room here? And a flight in the morning?"

"Yes and yes. Grab your stuff and meet me at my house."

I take my hand off him, and he takes his hand off my tie, and when he rolls away from me, I leave without saying goodbye to Harper and Simon. It's not my most polite exit, but talking to them like this would be worse, and I hurry upstairs while telling myself I'll take them out for another lunch. I don't know where Jamie went, but I have an entire drive to think about how quickly I can get him undressed when I see him again. A minute into it, I lower every window and pray the fresh air will make me think of anything else.

When I pull into his driveway, I think I've beaten him here, and I barely knock before I use my key to let myself in for the first time since I was summoned by his daughter. I'm nervous, the thrum of it so different from when I stepped into Taylor's house. I kick off my dress shoes and move to the kitchen to leave the rest of my things on the island. My duffel bag is barely out of my hands when I hear the front door open, and I will myself not to shake.

Jamie's arms are around me before it matters.

I'm still facing the island, and he nuzzles the back of my neck as he pulls the hair tie free and tosses it out of my reach. I moan when he drops his hands to my waist and rocks against my ass, and I almost ask whether he's been hard since we spoke at the reception or just since the freeway exit a mile or so back. Instead, I turn to find his bowtie gone and his shirt untucked and half unbuttoned, and I move to remember what desire tastes like on his tongue.

The kiss should be messy. Needy. It should leave us breathless and bruised. It's our first one since we were mad about it three years ago, and I'm not sure why it doesn't carry any trace of that rage tonight, even to remind us we're happier now. But it doesn't need to be anything other than the tender exploration it is, so close to a second first time, and one we'll never forget.

He starts in on my buttons without pulling away, and I hold the sides of his face to make sure he doesn't change his mind about that. As soon as Jamie can get his hands on my bare skin, he does. There's time for me to finish with his shirt, but I haven't made it that far and I won't rush anything now.

"Upstairs," he breathes. "Let me take you upstairs."

It's a stunning request when I've been upstairs—when I've slept in his bed—so many times before, and I swallow hard. "Please."

Jamie takes my hand, and I'm dizzy with lust. I don't know why we've waited so long to do this, except that I know exactly why, and I hate the circumstances beyond our control and all the times we've been to blame. I need to tell him I'm done waiting for the things we can have just like this. I need to tell him we can keep this away from hockey and the press and everything we've been afraid of, because Harper already knows, and it would be okay if my family knows, too. I need to tell him we can be together sometimes because it's better than not being together at all.

I need to tell him before he hands me a pen and paper and asks me to make another list of rules because it's all he's ever known me to do.

In his room, Jamie lets go just long enough to turn on a lamp, and then he's kissing my neck as he pushes my shirt off my shoulders. "I want to see your body. All of it."

"You've seen my body."

"I want to see your body when I'm allowed to look," he says. "When I'm allowed to take my time with it."

"And I want to hear you while you take your time."

"Does that mean you won't put your fingers in my mouth again?"

I smile and finally get rid of his shirt, not shy about stroking his dick through his pants as soon as I'm done. "I'll put my fingers anywhere you want them."

He groans, long and loud. "I can't believe we're really doing this."

In search of more proof that we're really doing this, he kisses me, still far from rough about it, though there's something insistent now. Both of us are carefully possessive after years of knowing other people got to do this without restraint, but it's ours tonight. Jamie was lauded for his finesse on the ice, and he moves as deftly now, my belt and clasp and zipper no challenge, even while his tongue teases mine again. When I'm down to my boxer briefs, I can only assume he's racing toward naked, my hands chasing any warmth uncovered for me.

But I need to be naked too, so I let him go long enough to make it happen.

"Bed. Your bed."

Jamie throws the covers out of our way, and we climb onto each other as much as we climb onto the bed, me on top of him and him on top of me, slowly frantic about wanting everything at once. His body has continued to change, just as surely as mine has. I felt it when I hugged him hours ago, but the beautiful reality takes my breath away now. We're older, and he's so much further away from the years that demanded different things from him—both more and less in their own ways—and I'm as in love with this version of him as I would've been if I'd ended up beneath him during his MVP season.

I'm beneath him now, on my back after we've traded places one more time, and I make room for him between my legs and wrap my arms around him to keep him close. Kissing him is enough for a while, as if that's really all this is. Our hips never still while we rub against each other, and I'm reminded of how much he leaks when he leaves me slick and ready to beg. My fingers dig into his ass to demand more, and he whimpers in response.

"Jesus, 'Teo, I could come like this. I'm so fucking hard," he breathes. "I want us to. I want to kiss you and feel you against me and come just like this."

"Tonight? Now?" I ask, though I'm far from opposed. I'll come however he tells me to.

He pauses, and I'm ready to reach between us just to encourage a decision either way, but then he's at my neck again. "No, not now."

"So tell me. Tell me, tell me, tell me," I chant.

Another long kiss shuts me up until Jamie's ready to answer. "There's so much. But I don't think I want it all at once. I don't want to chase nine years of fantasies when I'd rather convince both of us we have time for them later."

"It's okay. We can keep this as simple as you want. Loud and slow aren't reserved for fucking."

"No, that's *all* I want," he says, slowly grinding against me as he speaks into my ear. "I want you to fuck me. That's—before that night, I'd never tried, and then you—it was so good. I was so mad at you, but it was so good."

The reminder of that extra layer of hurt—how I didn't take my time with something that should've demanded it—is devastating. I want to roll him over and do everything right, but it won't fix what I've already broken. His entire life, Jamie's needed to be reminded that he's worth more than what his body can do for people—that he can be adored apart from a trade of entertainment for attention. He's told me all along that he wanted it slow, and then I got him face down on someone else's bed and rushed him through something that was supposed to matter.

"I'm sorry," I murmur against his lips. "I'm so sorry. I loved you all wrong."

"No, don't say that. Don't forget that night. Don't wish you could take it back. Just fuck me like we waited for this one."

Before I can continue with more apologies or promises, Jamie moves down my body. I close my eyes as he takes the long way so he can memorize the reaction I have when he kisses or bites or licks or exhales over my collarbones or armpits or nipples or ribs. I think he needs to remember everything in case he's wrong about us having more time, and it's another three years before we find each other for another night like this.

It's why I'm paying such close attention.

But then he's at my hip, his teeth against my skin before he soothes the same spot with his tongue. He's asked me to give him something, but Jamie clings to his control for now, cupping my balls in one hand and lifting my dick to his mouth with the other. My foreskin has mostly retracted, but Jamie slides it over the head and back again before he drags his tongue from base to tip and moans.

When he does it again, I'm the one to moan. "Christ, you're cleaning yourself off me."

Jamie doesn't answer, taking me to the back of his throat instead. My hand is in his hair before I can piece together another coherent thought, but even this far gone, I don't push him. I just need to touch him anywhere I can.

When he's done with me, in this one way and for this one moment, he crawls back up my body to kiss me so briefly I almost miss it. I'd complain and hold on to him better if his next move wasn't to stretch across the bed for the nightstand drawer, and when he comes back with a bottle of lube and nothing else, I don't have words anyway.

He meets my hungry stare, but doesn't ask if this is okay with me. It's possible we both think I'd tell him if it weren't, especially when it feels like one more rule I'd follow or line I'd draw. Later, I'll tell him I'm too tired of both, but I'm still staring when he straddles me. I don't follow his hand as he works himself open because I'd rather watch how his eyelashes flutter in response to that touch.

Jamie doesn't take as much time as I expect him to, but then his wet hand is stroking me, and I finally drop to look because it's what I wished he'd done on prom night, all those years ago.

It's when everything was supposed to change for us. It was when a lot of things *did* change for us, if only in ways we couldn't have predicted. For a moment, I think about what might have been, and then I arch into his fist and breathe his name.

Jamie rises onto his knees, then lowers himself onto me, and we both cry out like everything is brand new.

"This is—"

He doesn't finish his sentence, and that's okay. When he doesn't move either, my hands bracket his waist and encourage him to ride me, no matter how slow he wants or needs this to be. My age and experience grant me the patience he deserves, and for now, everything is for Jamie.

"Take it. Take me. I'm all yours."

"Please," he moans, lazily falling forward until he can kiss me even more lazily than that.

Always coordinated and aware of how goddamn good he is at everything, Jamie finally realizes just how much control he has like this, and he smiles into the kiss. Then he picks up his pace and settles into a rhythm designed to test the patience I'd just sworn I've mastered. I bend my legs and thrust up into him, cautious and caring while his tongue moves against mine. Neither of us had thought to turn on the air conditioning in a house he hadn't planned to use this weekend, so we're sweating already, panting and trying so hard to make this one unforgettable night last.

It won't happen unless I remind him of the things we've said.

Practiced and perfect, I flip us.

"You're forgetting slow and loud, sweetheart," I say as I pull out, so leisurely about it that Jamie writhes beneath me in search of the pressure that's barely slipped away.

I don't make him wait long before I reverse course, mostly because I want the pressure too, but first I put a hand behind each of his knees and push them toward his chest. Sliding into him this time causes him to shake, ready to crumble when I reach for the precum smeared across his stomach and suck it off my fingertips.

"Fuck, baby. Fuck," he whines. "It's never been like this. Never. I want this forever."

"You can have this forever."

If my words sound more hopeful than honest, Jamie doesn't say. Instead, he makes enough unholy noises to compete with the sound of our bodies colliding, and both keep this from being anything like the imperative silence we shared once before. We're breathless, and he's beautiful, and while I'm still fucking into him, I curl forward for whatever messy kiss either of us can manage. Hovering just above his open mouth, I think I tell him I love him a hundred times.

Jamie pulls my hair, but he can't hold on—or he doesn't want to hurt me—that hand wrapping around my bicep when he drops the other to his cock. "No forever tonight. Too close."

I speed up and almost put some distance between us so I can watch, but staying close to him feels better and I force an arm under his body to keep myself there. It means I can feel him brush against me as he goes in search of an orgasm that's already inevitable, and I pant against his jaw.

"Can I come inside you?"

My question is all Jamie needs, and I feel him clench around my dick just before he sobs and spills between us, my chest at least as wet as his when he chokes out an answer.

"Yes. Fuck. Please."

I've been holding back for so long that it takes another several seconds before my body agrees to let go. By the time I do, his grip on my arm is bruising, and a sticky hand is in my hair, so many filthy things fall off his tongue that I have no chance of catching them all. I come harder than I have in years—probably about three of them—and then I collapse on top of him, my heart beating so close to his.

"Jamie."

"I'm here. I'm right here."

I don't know why I need to hear that, except for the number of times it hasn't been true. We'll have to move soon, but I feel a tear roll from the corner of my eye, and I hate it because I don't want him to think anything is wrong. Everything is exactly right for once, and it's why I don't have plans to start a more serious conversation either.

Jamie and I need to talk. And we will.

Tonight, I just want this.

I get what I want. After another couple of minutes, both of us soft and sated, we tumble out of bed and to a shower mostly made necessary by his unwavering need to touch my hair. It's been a long couple of days for him, and I'm not surprised when he falls asleep within a few minutes of crawling under the covers, my body pressed to his back while he relaxes into the embrace. I'm more surprised when he wakes me in the middle of the night for something quick and quiet, but maybe those things are okay when we have a choice about them.

I'm most surprised when I wake up later than usual and roll over in an otherwise empty bed, and I don't know why I didn't expect this when I've left Jamie more than once. I sit up and see that his clothes are gone and mine are draped over a chair next to my bag, and I sigh, hurt or mad or just generally frustrated by our inability to break habits I never wanted to have.

He's got a flight this morning, and it's possible he's already at the airport. Maybe he stopped by the hotel to see Harper first, though I'm not convinced *she's* awake yet. Regardless, he could've woken me for a goodbye. Last night deserved as much.

After peeing and brushing my teeth and splashing some water on my face, I get dressed in the jeans and t-shirt I'd packed for today, but add my suit jacket because it'll be cold where I'm going. Everything else gets folded and put in my bag, and then I jog downstairs to raid the kitchen for things that might be left from a shopping trip I made over a year ago. I find a protein bar and a coffee pot that's still half full, so I help myself to one of Jamie's travel mugs. Then I fetch my shoes and cross the great room to the doors leading to his backyard. They're unlocked, and the truth must hit me then, but I don't believe anything yet.

I walk toward the ocean, the coastal fog still clinging to a late-August morning.

If I looked carefully, I'd probably be able to step onto a footprint or two.

But I hurry, my heart wild when it doesn't need to be, and I'm at the bench before I can sort through all the things I'm supposed to say, and it's fine when he greets me first.

"Good morning."

"I thought you were gone," I rasp. "I thought I was too late."

Jamie shakes his head and kisses me as soon as I sit down. "I'm here. I'm right here."

Chapter Twenty-One: Jamie

(I Saw My Number in the Rafters)

"What about your flight?" Mateo asks.

"I changed it. I'll be taking the red-eye tonight. It means I'll more or less drag my ass to the press conference, but I couldn't run out of here this morning. Like you said, we need to talk."

"You're staying all day?"

I shrug. "Yes and no. Now that I'll be around, I want to spend more time with Harper and Simon, too. They don't leave for their honeymoon until tomorrow."

"But me first."

"You first. Yeah."

Mateo takes a long sip of what I assume is the coffee I left behind, and then he stares at the ocean. He always does when we're here. I guess I do, too. Something about its power reminding us that we're small. That we're more significant to each other than we are to the world itself. The waves soothe me, and my heartbeat only stutters when he speaks.

"I wanted to tell you I'm done waiting. I can't keep—"

"You don't have to—we didn't wait. We—"

"Jamie, please. Let me finish," he says, his voice steady enough to suggest he's thought about this for a while. "I'm one of the two loves of your life, but I can't keep giving up my share of you. And I can't make you choose, because I'm afraid you'll never pick me over hockey, and I don't think it's fair to expect you to. Hockey had you first. So, I want you to love us both, but it's okay if the world doesn't know. The only thing I'm asking is that we tell my family. That's it. Because Kai and Sophie know, and Harper and Simon know, and Taylor knows, and if my parents and sisters and their families know—that's everyone who matters. I'm—me. I won't be back in the closet. Nobody really cares about me that way. I'll be your friend, and I'll visit you, and we'll have more of what we had last night. Slow and loud and *private*. Once you've retired from coaching, maybe we can be *us*, but until then, we can be you and me. I'm okay with that. I'm more okay with that than I am with waiting anymore."

I reach for his free hand and pull it into my lap, our fingers entwined. "It's not true, though."

"Not exactly, no. And I know we've spent all these years saying we didn't want to lie, but—"

"No, not that," I interrupt again. "The part about never picking you over hockey. I'm picking you. I *have* picked you—or us, really. I've picked us, and it's not exactly *over* hockey, but it'll be different because it's not—" I growl because I don't think I'm as good with words when I'm not giving shit to reporters. Mateo kisses me because he knows, and I'm so completely undone by it that I take a deep breath. He returns to his coffee and lets me try again. "Tomorrow's press conference—it's not about a trade or a retirement. It's about me. I had a contract option and I—I didn't renew it. I won't be an NHL coach this season. I won't go back to being an NHL coach at all."

"But—" Mateo's mouth closes. Opens. Closes. Opens. "Training camp starts next month. Can you do this now? There's no breach?"

"There's no breach because I'm not really doing it now—we're just announcing it now. I told Taylor and the front office weeks ago, but I asked them to keep it quiet until after Harper's wedding. There was some back and forth about that, but Taylor put some pressure on them to agree as part of *his* contract extension, and we pointed out that they could still hire someone and not say anything. Generally, assistant coaches don't make headlines unless they're Jameson Sinclair."

"You love it. I know you love me, but you've loved being there. Why would you leave it behind?"

"Because I'm done waiting, too," I tell him. "I'm not okay with you being a friend who visits. I'm not okay with only being you and me, when we deserve to be *us*. I don't need the world to know—I won't hold a press conference for that—but I don't mind if they find out. I'm not going to hide."

"But you'll quit to put distance between you and the league," Mateo says. "It'll save them the trouble of having to decide how to handle the fallout later."

"Yes."

He combs his fingers through the hair he never put back into a ponytail last night. He's more restless than he usually is when we're here together. Maybe it's been different the times he's sat here alone. Or with my kid. It's been so fucking long since I've been the one sitting next to him.

"What about all the cheers?" he asks.

I smile, and I think it must look kind of sad. It feels kind of sad. "The cheers aren't for me anymore. They haven't been for a while."

"You haven't said anything about that."

"I haven't said anything about a lot of this."

"Should I be mad?"

"I hope you aren't," I say. "I didn't—there have been so many pieces of so many things that needed to be put into place—in New Jersey and here. It's not all official, but I wanted to have some answers before this conversation."

He tilts his head. "What's happening here?"

"Well, I was saying I didn't exactly pick us *over* hockey. As the crowds got quiet, it became easier to focus on things that weren't about me or how I could perform for my team. I spent a lot of time with the younger guys—or the ones who won't be MVP—and I tried to teach them what *they* could do for *their* team. I watched them develop those skills and get rewarded for them."

"So, you adjusted to not being the star, and then realized you don't need to coach the stars either."

"Yeah, and I remembered all the other things I loved about the sport." I stop and sigh, feeling my age. "There's the steady hum of anticipation when everyone's taping their sticks or lacing up their skates. The scrape of a blade against the ice or the clack of a puck against a stick. The genuine affection and pride that follow someone's first goal. The shared exhaustion, but then the shared playlists and inside jokes and embarrassing pictures, too. And those things aren't unique to professional hockey. Some of them aren't even unique to *hockey*, so I know you get it. You understand."

"I do," he says.

I think he's still afraid of something, so I hurry to explain. "Anyway, one of my old teammates works with an elite youth hockey program near here. And I've been talking to him about joining their staff. Working with kids."

"Youth hockey. God, you'd be incredible with kids, but is there a chance of fallout there? I'm around teenagers enough to know how often slurs get thrown around, and parents aren't much better."

"There's definitely a chance, yeah," I huff. "But I—other than Taylor, nobody in New Jersey knows why I'm leaving. I mean, they know I want to be closer to Harper, but that's it. I don't plan to say more than that. They're equipped to deal with whatever questions they get later. But I told this former teammate about us. I wanted him to know before I got hired. So, he knows, and someone above him knows, and we're gonna see how it goes. We'll see whether parents have a problem with their kids being coached by someone like me, and I'll leave if I have to."

Mateo frowns, the crease between his brows deepened by the suggestion that I'm not good enough. "Fine. Okay. What's the backup plan?"

"Some guy I know runs a soccer clinic for a week each summer," I smile, waiting until he smiles, too. "If coaching doesn't work out, I figure I can do something like that for hockey kids. Private, small-scale player development stuff. Year-round. Nothing requiring the support of an entire group at once. It means I'd lose out on some of the team vibes I love, but I'd still get to go to games and watch them succeed."

"So, step one is the press conference, and moving you home. Step two is you coaching youth hockey. Step—"

"Step two is asking you to move in with me. And holding your hand in public. And sex—but probably not in public. Step *three* is coaching youth hockey. And hopefully I don't need step four. Hopefully, my being Jameson Sinclair will be more important to them than anything else. Hopefully, my name still matters."

He kisses me again, furious and fond, his tongue there to sweep away all the things he doesn't want to hear me say out loud. I'm as smooth as Mateo is, and I take the coffee from his hand as I crawl into his lap, just like I have all the times we've believed in tomorrow. His arms wrap around me in response, but he breaks the kiss to demand eye contact that blurs as soon as he speaks.

"Jamie, your name will always matter."

The press conference is easy, my lack of sleep notwithstanding. Journalists push for answers about whether Taylor and I have had any sort of falling out. Or whether I'm in talks with other teams, including and especially the one I played for my entire career. Or whether I'm finally settling down with some special woman. Once there's no real gossip to be had, and every answer is a simple *no*, they get over it. When the news breaks nationwide, even quietly, I get a call from my parents. They don't get over it for a while.

Mateo probably would've helped me pack and move back to California. And it's the sort of stupidly domestic thing I'd love to do with him, but his school year is about to start, and I'm okay with hiring strangers.

As soon as I'm back, I help him move into my house because my new job doesn't start for another week.

There's been local buzz about my decision to coach at the youth level, all positive for now. It carries forward when I meet coworkers and players. I've heard from several former pros—those I've played with and against—who have made the same decision after retirement. Their encouragement has been universal. I'm grateful for the chance to connect to the hockey world in this different way.

I don't see Harper a lot at first. She's busy with the start of her school year, too. As a second-year teacher, her workload is more overwhelming than Mateo's. Plus, Southern California traffic famously sucks, and we're at least an hour away from each other. The two of us meet for one dinner, but all four of us enjoy one amazing brunch. We're all looking forward to the holidays and more time together.

"You're mumbling about Thanksgiving, and it's not even Halloween yet," Mateo says, his glasses low on his nose.

I love living with this older version of him. He's hot. It's probably why I begged for a quickie ten minutes ago. It's definitely why I begged even louder for him to keep the glasses on while I rode him. Now he's made me return to my side of the bed so he can grade papers, but it's fine. We can do it again tomorrow.

"I just can't believe we get to have a holiday like this. Harper and Simon and his brothers and your parents and your sisters and their husbands and their kids and you and me."

"You know, a lot of people go to therapy over spending a whole day with that many family members."

"That's why we're not inviting *my* parents," I point out.

I've only seen them once since moving back, and I thought maybe I had to introduce them to Mateo then. He'd kissed me senseless and reminded me that if we waited so long for us to have this, then they can wait a little while to know about it.

Time is finally on our side, in at least a couple of ways. Mateo and I have the relationship we've wanted all along, without rules or reservations. Whatever years we lost figuring this thing out, the rest of our lives are still ahead of us, and we get to share them now. Out loud. In front of everyone.

But it's been almost 15 years since I was the league's favorite hero and villain. Maybe predictably, distance has given us space. As much as I've been around—commentating, autographing, and coaching—my name has become a hotter commodity than my face or my ego. There's always been another good-looking hockey player to splash on ads. Some have had the attitudes that keep post-game interviews interesting, a handful of them taking my place over the past decade and a half. All of it means I don't get recognized by the public like I used to, and sports media simply doesn't care what I'm doing if it won't earn them a click.

Out loud and in front of everyone isn't what it would've been way back then.

Yet.

Those first few months—including a perfectly loud Thanksgiving at our house—go so smoothly that I decide to make reservations at Mateo's favorite Italian restaurant the week before Christmas, and I follow that up by extending an invitation for my parents to join us.

Mateo hums. "A public spectacle will raise the chance of someone noticing it's you—and me, with you."

I smile at him even though he can't see me. We've both had long days, me with my kids and him with his. He's bending over to put some kind of casserole in the oven so we can enjoy a hot dinner before we inevitably crash. The view is distracting, but he stands in time for me to respond.

"That's the point," I say. "They care too much about appearances to cause a scene."

Mateo nods. "So, they might be upset with you for putting your reputation on the line by having a relationship with me, but they won't call attention to your relationship with me and be the ones to put your reputation on the line."

"Exactly."

And it happens, more or less, just like that.

He and I are the hottest couple at the restaurant, but we don't advertise it. Being able to love each other openly means we often don't. I'm not sure I would've predicted that when we were so busy hiding. I think maybe he's taught me how to live without needing an audience. Or maybe I'm finally old enough to have figured out how to stop caring, all on my own. Either way, my hand is pressed to the small of Mateo's back as we follow the hostess toward our table, but I'm not touching him when the four of us listen to the specials and order a bottle of wine.

A kiss could've made our point, but I fumble through an explanation instead. A lot about how much Mateo and I love each other. Very little about how much we fucked up along the way. My dad's fist clenches around a fork he doesn't need yet when he finds out we're living together. My mom narrows her eyes when I tell them I moved back home just to make that possible. They warn me about the potential consequences—about how many people who've said they love me could hate me instead. Mateo very gently suggests they not become the first two on that list. At the end of an awkward meal, they say goodnight to me and shake the hand of my *friend*.

Spending so much time with the Zavalas before and after that dinner should hurt somehow. The comparison between our families is striking when I watch Mateo be embraced by such unconditional love. But grieving the loss of something I've never had is impossible when his family turns and welcomes me with that same unfamiliar thing. I'm adored through cookies and carols, a church I only know through its carnival and funerals, and gifts that mean more than most of what I've been given before.

I overhear Logan's name once. Somehow, I don't feel any less loved.

Then, just days after my parents first met Mateo, and after almost 36 hours straight with his family, we go to Christmas dinner at my childhood home. Harper and Simon meet us there, as does a pretty blonde woman I don't know. I really hope she's not joining us for the reason I think she is. Then it becomes pretty clear pretty quickly that hope is a foolish thing for me to have brought to my parents' house. She and I are introduced smoothly and seated next to each other. Mateo's across from me and next to my daughter. The woman's a flirt, and my mom encourages it. Simon redirects her attention whenever he can. Mateo stays quiet because he won't fight this battle for me. My dad also stays quiet, but his fork is clutched as tightly as it had been a week ago. I'm trying to get through one bite after another because it feels like the best way to survive.

Harper, however, has had enough.

"What is going on here, grandma? Grandpa?" she asks. "Why would you do this? Why would you invite a stranger—no offense—to Christmas dinner, as if you didn't already know my dad and Mateo would be here together? Did last week freak you out so much that you had to make some weird attempt at damage control for something that isn't damaged?"

I open my mouth, but Mateo subtly shakes his head. She's not a little girl anymore.

"Oh, dear, there's nothing freaking us out," my mom says. "We understand your dad has a new friend, but it would be a great idea for him to have one more. A friend who won't undo everything he worked hard for his entire life."

Harper rolls her eyes. "Nothing is being undone. Nobody's going to scratch his name off the Cup or kick him out of the Hall of Fame."

"But the press—"

"Fuck the press," Harper spits. "No offense—*again*—but dad and Mateo have been in love since I was 14, and this is our first Christmas as a family, and I *hate* that. I hate that we haven't already done this for years. But we're here now, and you're going to keep calling them friends because you're worried that—what? The hockey world will turn on him when they find out he's queer, and you'll realize you wasted decades not getting to know your own son off the goddamn ice? Because I think you could still get to know him now, but you'll need to get to know Mateo, too. He's not going anywhere."

My mom says nothing. My dad continues to say nothing. The

flirty blonde excuses herself soon after that. Harper, Simon, Mateo, and I excuse ourselves soon after *that*. The four of us end up back at our house for a little bit of hot chocolate and a lot of Bailey's before we all crash. Harper helps Mateo out with soccer practice the next afternoon. We don't see Harper and Simon again until my birthday.

Everything changes about a month after that.

Mateo and I have continued to live weightlessly. I've never completely forgotten the morning I choked down a breakfast sandwich made by my best friend, so I try hard to give myself credit for how far I've come. I try hard to celebrate the distance we've put between us and the secrets we used to keep.

We still hang out with Kai and Sophie, but we don't sneak away for dates up and down the coast. We enjoy local concerts and dinners and movies without a foot of space between us. I show up at some high school soccer games. He shows up for some youth hockey. I'm sure plenty of people assume we're a couple. Outside of my job, I'm not sure anyone's noticed I'm me, and our respective seasons come to uneventful ends.

In hindsight, it's probably why we got stupid. Or just complacent, I guess. Or, no. We're stupid.

It's fine because we've known for almost six months that a headline about us would only require one person whispering into the ear of one person who cares. Ultimately, we don't keep it anywhere near that simple, outing ourselves at the arena where my jersey number hangs from the rafters. It's the first time we've been here together since Harper's senior year. We hold hands on the walk from the parking lot without thinking twice, nobody paying much attention outside. The concession line should make us more cautious, but we stand too close to each other, our fingers resting low on each other's backs. While watching the game, we do little to draw attention, except for the times we lean in to talk to each other. Then we end up with hands on each other's thighs, thumbs brushing across denim pulled tight. At some point—I still don't remember when—I have something to tell Mateo. I don't pull away without kissing the gray in his stubble first.

It's soft and sweet, and pretty damn sexy. I know that because I've been able to see it from several slightly different angles, social media humming before more official gossip sites throw together a few sentences about it.

I hadn't been sure how loudly anyone would react. All logic and emotion collided when I could hear decades of slurs amid the absence of cheers. Jameson Sinclair comes out as bisexual? Huge news if I were still splashed across billboards to sell jockstraps and vodka. Far less interesting if I've finally become the thing I tried to use as a mantra once.

Nobody.

But then the calls, emails, texts, and DMs come in. I'm not proud of myself for considering, even for a moment, how I might be able to lie my way out of this, or at least run to that flirty blonde for help. A deep breath steadies me before I respond the first time. Every official request for information is met with the same simple statement.

His name is Mateo, he's the love of my life, and we appreciate everyone's respect for our relationship. We have no further comment at this time.

After a conversation with Mateo that I could've had back in August, I decide there are two important exceptions to make. When I hear from one of the longtime broadcasters for L.A.—a guy I sat next to for most of my guest commentator gigs—I meet his immediate support with the agreement to sit down for an on-air interview during the intermission of an upcoming home game. I only ask that he be honest with me in advance if he hears any rumblings from other members of the broadcast team who have a problem with it.

Then I reach out to a favorite sports journalist, already confident that he'll have my back. I offer him a lengthier exclusive with both Mateo and me. In turn, he mentions the name of a photographer I've adored for years, and tells me they'll work together on this. It'll almost certainly be the cover story of a magazine. My face is likely to be on display in countless supermarket checkout lines among tabloids with their candids and alleged insider information.

It's nice to bring balance to the moments of this that will hurt.

Speaking of hurt, Mateo, Harper, Simon, Kai, Sophie, Crissy, and Isa make me swear I won't read the comments left by internet trolls. Taylor calls me just long enough to say, "Fuck 'em," and then he's gone again. In interviews, he replies with a more professional, "I will not talk about what I know, nor how long I've known it. I *will* say that Jameson Sinclair has been in my life for almost 30 years, first as a foe, then as a friend. If anyone had to break my single-season records, I'm glad it was him. For what it's worth, I'm also glad the career records are still mine. I've had the pleasure of welcoming Mateo into my home, and I've enjoyed his company very much. You all know I'm not in the habit of being anything less than blunt with you, much like Sinclair himself, so believe me when I tell you I'm happy for them both."

"He really said all that," I murmur, my mouth against Mateo's. "About both of us."

"He really did. But you can't be that surprised. Not after the last few years."

"No, but I think I'm still surprised by some others, both good and bad."

There are plenty of people from my past who have stayed silent, of course. I've tried not to wonder why they aren't reaching out because it's easy to assume the worst. Among people who have been in contact, I've been hurt by the few who felt it was necessary to express disappointment or disgust, especially a teammate I'd considered a friend back then. The parents of one player pulled him from our juniors program, and I apologized to everyone else. A couple of former New Jersey players have made biting comments to the press, but I shrug those off okay. I know there are fans who have thrown my jerseys in the trash, if they're not burning them outright, but maybe having the cheers fade around me prepared me well.

Or maybe I've been so grateful for all the brand new applause, no matter how quiet some of it has been.

There are teammates and rivals who've reached out to support me. Some have had personal stories I wouldn't dare share with anyone but Mateo. So many fans have started wearing my jersey again, after having kept it in the back of their closets for years. And more parents have thanked me for the effect my honesty could have on their kids' future, and maybe that's what gets to me most of all.

Coming out like I have won't change hockey culture overnight. I'm not sure it'll change anything—notably, at least—in one year or five years or ten. But I've taken a step, and that step leads somewhere.

The league hasn't released a statement, but that doesn't mean they don't know it, too.

My thoughts fade when Mateo kisses me deeply and grabs my wrist, moving me until I can touch his dick beneath our duvet and over his boxer briefs. We've been in bed for a while, talking drowsily, mostly about things we've discussed before. I don't think we'd had any plans to fuck about it. Maybe we still won't. Both of us are soft, and the kiss isn't hurried. But then his tongue slows, and he moans when I stroke the fabric pulled tight over him.

"Do you really want to keep this conversation going?" he asks. "Or can we move to something far more incoherent instead?"

His hand is cupping me now, and I've never been less than pliant in his grip. "Incoherent is good."

We stop talking and go back to the kissing that could keep me almost as satisfied as anything else he has in mind. We're older and more tired, and we can have each other any night we want. There are no demands being made by either of us now, but our bodies respond to this familiar want. Even with both of our hands between us, we arch into the contact, seeking more pressure. It's so simple, rubbing each other's cocks while pushing up against the back of our own hands. Still, something about it feels at least as filthy as anything else we've done. It's probably because Mateo doesn't want to get closer to naked first.

The next few minutes are clumsy and desperate. I kick at the duvet because it's too warm. We're panting into each other's mouths as much as we're kissing now, but it gives us the space to say a dozen vulgar things. By the time we come, our briefs are more of a mess than our hands, and we find ourselves in a fit of laughter that lasts a while. When that dies down, and we're still breathing the same air, Mateo surprises me more than anyone has in the days since our arena video went viral.

"Should we get married?"

My eyes go wide and my jaw drops. I think I giggle like I'm eight years old. "Should I consider this an actual proposal when our hands are still sticky and you're asking like that?"

"I—I'm not sure whether I meant for it to be a proposal or just a—we've never really talked about it," he says, his sleepy smile enough to make me say yes to anything. "Everything we've said has been about forever, but I don't know what forever means."

"And you taught my daughter's English class? *Twice*?"

Mateo's tongue in my mouth means I have to shut up. Just as abruptly, he pulls away and rolls out of bed to toss his boxer briefs in the hamper and wash his hands. I follow, do the same, and grab clean clothes for both of us. Then I drag him back to bed—to sleep this time.

He tugs the duvet over us, and I press my back to his chest so he can speak into my ear. "We don't need to figure it out now. I know I get forever with you either way, but maybe we can talk about it sometime soon. Maybe we can—"

"Yes," I say, clearing my throat when it's not clear enough. "Yes, we should get married."

It happens in our backyard on a warm August evening, ten years after I brought Mateo home without him knowing. Only about 20 guests are in attendance, more than half of them family. All of them are overcome by laughter and happy tears. We'd invited my parents, but they'd declined to celebrate with us. They sent a card, fancy Hallmark script wishing us the best.

Our honeymoon is full of hammocks and Mai Tais and loud and slow.

Six months later, we take advantage of Taylor's gift to us and spend a week on a frozen lake.

In between Mateo's non-proposal and the wedding and more wishes come true, I get formally interviewed during a game. Mateo and I pose for pictures and tell our story. Public reaction remains mixed, but it feels more positive than not, and I couldn't imagine still waiting for the rest of my life to start. Hockey loved me for as long as it could. I don't think it'll ever fully let go, but I had to let something else in.

I had to remember who else I am.

"Hey, Jamie," Mateo calls out. "There's someone here to see you."

I turn to look at him and push my sunglasses to the top of my head. Another school year has just come to an end, even more of his graying hair well-earned. We're enjoying the summer morning by the pool, the ocean out of sight from where I lie on a lounge chair. He'd only left to get us something to eat and drink, so I'm surprised that we're no longer alone. For a moment, I study him where he stands calmly at the patio door. A soft smile is on his face, and damp swim trunks cling to his muscular thighs. I assume Harper must've driven down, since she's on her summer break, too. Or maybe Kai, if he's got someone else opening the bar today.

It's neither of them.

When Mateo takes a step to the side, I almost can't believe I'd missed the sheer bulk behind him. It's Sami Eriksson, one of the young guys I'd coached in New Jersey during his first two years in the league. For a strange second, I wonder if he's here to brag about their Cup win a couple of weeks ago. The thought doesn't last because I'm entirely happy for them, and he looks as nervous as he did the first time he walked into my office.

"Hey, Eriksson," I say, sitting up and swinging my legs until my feet are flat on the warm concrete. "This is a surprise."

"Yes. It's a surprise. I'm sorry, but McKeon gave me your home address so we could speak privately. It's very beautiful here."

I appreciate the quick answer to a question I hadn't asked yet, and the compliment to go with it. Then I motion for him to sit on the lounge chair I'm facing. Mateo returns with chips and dip and two open bottles of beer, but he leaves them for us and nods toward the house before slipping away again.

I meet Sami's blue eyes with mine when neither of us reaches for the food, his hands in anxious fists against his knees. "Take a deep breath, kid. I'm right here. I don't have anywhere else to be."

"But you were swimming," he says. "With your husband."

"I was," I concede, something about his tone helping me understand Mateo's soft smile from before.

"That's good. It's what I would like to talk about. I would like to know more about how to be so brave. You helped me when you were my coach, and I would like your help again."

My next inhale catches on something I'd once thought was cowardice, and I swallow hard. But that's not what he needs from me. I reach for his fists and gently uncurl his fingers until his hands rest flat in his lap.

"Of course, Sami. I'll help however I can."

Epilogue

(There Was a Rainbow)

Honestly, for as often as my husband and I go hiking, I'm getting too old to do this on my own much longer. It's just steep enough to be considered careless, the path still familiar, but unwalked for years now. I glance toward a fence I can't see from this far below, and I know Simon's waiting nervously in our backyard, just in case he needs to come to my rescue.

Our rescue, actually, because I'm not on my own today. I'm just the stronger one. Physically, anyway. Probably not emotionally. Emotionally, I'm not sure, because I've never been in a situation like this, and I'm in no rush to understand it any better than what empathy allows.

I'm in no rush to be the one saying goodbye to the man I love.

"It's been so long."

I startle when his gravelly voice cracks the quiet morning, partly because I'm too far inside my head and partly because he's spoken so little lately. That could change today, but I'm not counting on that just because we're making this climb together, nor will I push to make it happen. I'm not even going to ask him what he's referring to. It could be a lot of things.

And though it's a surprise to almost everyone who knows me, I haven't felt much like talking lately, either.

I'm mourning too, and nobody would expect less, but I think they expected me to be louder about it. I've ached for days and weeks and months. I think maybe it's been more than a year already. I've pressed my hand to my chest and I've cried, my husband holding me close when I've needed that crushing promise that every once in a while, time slows down to let love catch up.

I look up to the man I'm holding close now and remember so many lessons he's taught me about that. Time. Love. How the loss of one doesn't have to mean the loss of the other. Of course, he's been teaching me for years. And from the moment I first walked into his classroom, some five decades ago, I think I knew my life was about to change.

Moments are like that sometimes.

With my arm around Mateo's waist, I continue to guide him forward, and several seconds later, the sight of the bench is enough to make a few tears fall. Mine, at least. I'm not ready to look too closely at him. Reminders of his age are reminders of mine, and while I rarely mind getting older, it's harder when the lines around his eyes are teeming with the grief that lines my own.

"Watch that last step," I warn softly. "The ground here isn't as flat as it used to be."

He nods and moves to hold my hand as he sits, any stubborn need for independence weakened by the privacy we're given here. I look toward the house Simon and I own now, Mateo and my dad having deeded the property to us when they moved into the downstairs guest suite, steps increasingly too much for a leg pieced together so many years ago. Then I turn back to the sky. The sun shines down on us through the lingering fog, a promise of what waits on the other side of this morning, but there was nobody on the shore when we approached from below.

It's only the two of us here, laying a third to rest.

"Thank you for coming with me," he says.

Once I'm settled next to him, I use my free hand to reach for the thin gray hair he keeps shorter than he used to, but still long enough to tuck behind his ear. "I'm sorry I had to. I'm sure you would've preferred to do this part alone."

"No," Mateo argues, as tender as he's ever been. "He and I had too much time alone, away from you. More than we should have."

It's something we've talked about so many times—the secrets they tried to keep from me for too long—and even though it's been a while, we don't need to do it again. It hurt back then, but we're very far away from a grudge I barely held.

"In that case, I'm glad I'm here."

"I should've brought tomato basil soup."

"Oh my God. New Year's Day, when I caught you here." I laugh in spite of myself and shake my head. "I can't believe you remember that."

"My memories are remarkably intact," he says. "A blessing and a curse."

"Will you tell me something I don't know? About you and my dad? A memory you consider a blessing?"

Mateo squints at the misty morning and the sunlight determined to brighten our day. "He and I watched the sun rise over all five oceans."

"Intentionally?" I ask. "I mean, obviously I know you two traveled a lot, but were the sunrises always part of the plan, or just luck once you realized you could check another ocean off the list?"

"Very intentional—from a cruise ship in the Arctic and from beaches for the rest. We collected those sunrises. They were a reminder that our time together would always count."

"That's from your wedding vows—that your time together would always count."

The smile he gives me is fragile. "It's from the very beginning."

Mateo continues with another story, and then he doesn't stop—not for a while. He stares at the ocean as he talks, our hands clasped together between us, and he tells me about their long, long life together. A few anecdotes are ones I've heard, but most aren't, and my chest aches from the weight of so many small stories piled on top of one another. He and I have suffered losses that weave their way through layers of memories, and we smile and cry about them together.

His family had swept Simon and me into their arms the moment we met, and those who are gone now—Mateo's parents, one sister, and one nephew—only said goodbye when there was no other choice. My grandparents died years ago, and I couldn't begin to guess which one of us had a more complicated relationship with them. After a while, my dad didn't speak to them at all.

When we lost Kai, it cut all of us deeply, but I think Mateo was surprised by how much he hurt. He'd been so busy making sure we were okay that it took him a while to mourn the man who'd remained good to him even while he and my dad struggled to hold on to what they'd never let go. I remember my dad telling me about the day it finally hit Mateo, and how they'd spent the night with a mess of tears and greasy appetizers.

Speaking of people who'd remained good to us, I don't think any of us were prepared for the news that Taylor McKeon was killed in a car accident about five years after my dad last coached with him. Publicly, he'd never stopped supporting them with the same abrupt and vaguely condescending tone with which he addressed anything. Privately, he'd become a close friend, maybe even more so to Mateo. His death devastated the hockey community, certainly, but I watched it rip ugly holes in the hearts of two men who took a while to heal.

The day our family announced the death of Jameson Sinclair—the choice to keep *Jamie* for ourselves was all his—the ripples throughout the sports world were different. While I'd been correct that they didn't scratch his name off the Cup or kick him out of the Hall of Fame, the slurs never fell fully silent. Fortunately, neither did the gratitude. Even without having been on the ice in years, coming out like he did unlocked doors for other players.

Unlocked, not opened.

It still took time and effort for anyone else to walk through, but in the past 40 years, a handful have. All of them thanked my dad, and it never failed to overwhelm him. As often as he sought attention, being with Mateo was never about that, and I think it always surprised my dad that his greatest hockey legacy was love.

"He won a stuffed penguin at the church carnival the year you told him to stay with me, and he gave it to me at the end of the day."

I chuckle. "I think I only knew about the trio of church ladies wrapped around your finger and your disgust at his need to add heaps of toppings to his funnel cake. Oh, and that it set off a weird tradition of significant spring breaks for the two of you."

"We flirted our way through the midway games. Or I guess we flirted our way through the whole day," he amends, glancing sideways at me. "But he won, and gave the penguin to me, and it was ridiculous how happy I was."

"Not ridiculous at all," I say. "Although he used to give *me* all the stuffed animal prizes."

"I should give it to you now."

"Mateo. No."

"You know I'm right. It will be yours either way."

I do, and it will, but it's nearly impossible to swallow around that reality. "I'm more patient than he was. There's no hurry."

He shifts a little then, turning toward me and letting go of my hand to put his against my jaw. I've been grown for a long time—I was grown before I ever saw them kiss—but Mateo can still make me feel like a young girl, eager to learn from someone thoughtful and wise.

"I'm sorry you'll have to do this again so soon."

More tears fall. How could they not? "I'll be okay. I've got Simon."

"You do," Mateo smiles, his shaky thumb brushing across my cheek. "And you've been married even longer than we were."

That extra year has been a long-standing joke in our family, but my wedding night was good for all of us, so there has always been a meaningful depth to it that many wouldn't understand. I'm careful when I reach up to curl my fingers around his wrist, and even more careful when I speak.

"You don't regret any of it."

I'm not naive enough to have suggested it was a question, nor does Mateo take it as one. "Not a single moment. We did a lot wrong in those first ten years—nonsense rules and misplaced priorities and people we'd never love right—but our devotion never wavered. It was always going to be us. It's still us."

I nod. I sigh. I look at the ocean, then back at him. "Is it time?"

"I think so," he murmurs. "But I don't know how to do this. It's still us, but I've never known how to say goodbye to him."

"That's why he hated saying goodbye to you. So much." I pull away from him so I can pick up the heavy box I'd set next to me on the bench. It's held my dad's ashes for a couple of weeks now, but this was always the plan—leaving him here, where he'd spent years trying to let go of everything and shut out all the noise. When I open it, there's a small cup inside, and I nod to Mateo. "I'll hold this. You go ahead."

As I help him stand and he begins to scatter the ashes, the sky offers us a rainbow, and I quietly sing. It's the same song my dad used as a lullaby when I was little, and more like a requiem now. Its movie is well over a century old, but lemon drops and bluebirds and wishes are everlasting, and I have little doubt Mateo understands the promises the lyrics hold.

When he's done, he returns the cup to the empty box and lowers his head, taking several deep breaths as he prays. I'm silent, giving him as much space as I can here, but then our tired eyes meet, and he pulls me into a hug we both need.

"It's okay, Harper," Mateo whispers. "He'll wait for me."

More to Read

Coming Soon:

Tread Lightly (Trailhead Book Three)

Available Now:

Margins
Take It Outside (Trailhead Book One)
Second Nature (Trailhead Book Two)

ACKNOWLEDGEMENTS

First. Foremost. Still. Always. My wife, Natalie. There's not much I can write now that I haven't already acknowledged a few times over, but these books end up in your hands because of her loud, eager, unwavering support of my dreams. She's my very best friend, and I'm able to take leap after leap—and spin love story after love story—knowing she's got my back. We've recently made some positive changes in our lives, and I'm grateful for the extra time I have with her now. Especially after writing Jamie and Mateo's story, I know I'll want to enjoy that time forever.

I remain incredibly thankful for my kids and their constant encouragement. My daughter is sure this book is going to be The One, so I'd love to give her all the bragging rights when my sales skyrocket. I still have so much fun talking to my son about book plots, both mine and not, to see where our story interests overlap. And yes, I get to spend more time with them when they aren't out on their bikes with friends or staring at their phones. We have adventures planned, and I'm looking forward to more conversations, laughter, and inspiration.

My bff, Zahli, once told me she wanted to be part of everything, brainstorm to beta, and I'm careful not to check in with her about that too often because I'm terrified she might change her mind. Last I heard, she's up for another 11 books with me, which is convenient because that's the exact number I currently have planned. Our only problem may be that she never tells me *not* to write something, so 11 will become 12 and then 13 and…yeah. Zahli, I love you. Please never leave me.

Doing any of this without my betas is unimaginable. In addition to Zahli, I was also fortunate enough to have Ryan, Grace, Brittany, and Dhara to help me hurt you in all the right ways. They're amazing at telling me what I got *right* at least as often as they tell me what I got wrong, and all of that motivates me to improve a little more with every book I write. I'm not sure they always understand what they mean to me, but I'm so damn lucky to have them. And an extra thank you to Kri for helping me work out early issues with this book so I could focus on giving you the best possible version of Jamie, Mateo, and their long, long life together.

I have so much gratitude for my extended family and how effortlessly they cheer me on. My ongoing thanks to Kandi, Kari, Donna, Emily, Mark, and Nancy for listening to me babble incessantly about my characters and the plans I have for them. Your support has never gone unnoticed.

Estee, Angelina, Janice, Lisa, V, Emory, K, Teenie, Lo, RM, Jon, and Jack…I know I've said thank you before, and I wish I had a better way of expressing myself, but feelings and I are often strangers. Please know how often I revisit messages from you. They keep me going more than you'd imagine.

Evergreen thanks to my mutuals. I love hiding from the world with you.

And thanks to everyone I've forgotten to mention, before and still. If you've made it this far, I sincerely appreciate you. I'm sorry I ran out of words <3

ABOUT THE AUTHOR

After decades of dreaming of being an author, Landry Brennan published her debut novel, *Margins*, in 2024. Early in 2025, she introduced readers to her Trailhead series with *Take It Outside*, and welcomed them back to the bar in *Second Nature*. She's written her most personal story yet in *Nothing to Know*, and she's so grateful for the chance to share it with everyone.

Happily brainstorming and adding to a growing spreadsheet of titles and characters, Landry has many more love stories to tell, both within the Trailhead universe and not. Always full of heartache and healing, these romances celebrate the beautifully complicated flaws and dreams so many of us recognize in ourselves.

When she's not writing, Landry loves oversharing with online friends, watching hockey, drinking coffee, planning road trips, and spending time with her family.

Landry lives in the beautiful Pacific Northwest with her wife, Natalie; their twins, Amelia and Oliver; and the family's black lab mix, Charlie.